Craig Carter's Dilemma

Ilona Hawkins

Craig Carter

Book 4

TSL Publications

First published in Great Britain in 2023
By TSL Publications, Rickmansworth

Copyright © 2023 Ilona Hawkins

ISBN: 978-1-914245-31-2

Cover courtesy of : Jonathan Kandolo

PART ONE

1

The year was 4 000 AD, the date 20 July. Craig Carter, famous Space explorer and his wife Constance had just returned from a long and enjoyable honeymoon. They had been married for three months and were welcomed back by Commander Simms.

"Hello you two lovebirds," said Simms as he grasped Craig's hand firmly. "I can see the honeymoon has left you two still deeply in love – your eyes say it all."

"But of course!" giggled Constance happily, "Craig is wonderful and I love him dearly."

"I'm glad for both of you! Love is wonderful and I too had someone to love once," the Commander sighed. "If only my dear wife hadn't died three years ago. I have never found anyone else quite like her. Well anyway, welcome back."

"Thank you, Sir," replied Craig sincerely.

"Well I have a lot to do, so I'm going to carry on here. I realise both of you also have plenty to arrange. Get settled in at home and I'll drop by for a visit in two days."

"No problem Sir. Come for supper," invited Constance.

Simms shook his head emphatically. "Nonsense, I'll drop by afterwards."

"Please come and have dinner with us, Sir," pleaded Craig. "You know we appreciate everything you have done for us to now, and anyway, Constance is a very good cook."

Commander Simms grinned. "All right then, thank you. I accept your kind offer."

On arriving at their apartment, Craig slid the card into the door and punched in the relevant code. The door opened quietly and Craig scooped his bride into his arms. Once inside, he set her down in the lounge, then stepped outside to collect their luggage. It was late after they had unpacked and Constance made her way to the kitchen.

"I guess I had better execute my wifely duties, darling. What would you like for supper?"

Craig stole up behind his wife and put his arms around her waist, whispering tenderly into her hair. "Forget it sweetheart, we're going out tonight. I don't know about you, but I'm tired from all the travelling we've been doing. Tomorrow is good enough. Meanwhile, put on your pink evening dress. I love it and it makes you look like a queen."

Constance smiled at her husband and went to get dressed. "Craig, we mustn't be out late tonight! I need to get to bed early. We have lots to do tomorrow."

Once ready, they climbed into their helicar and came to rest on a high platform, several hundred feet up in the air. A valet came to greet them and moved their car, while they went into the restaurant to have their dinner. The place was really expensive and carpeted from wall to wall in a delightful green colour. The furnishings carried the matching colour in their design. On the walls, candles burnt in delicate holders, giving the place a romantic look. On each table stood a single lit candle, as well as a vase of sweetly smelling flowers. The band was playing soft, romantic music. The carpet was opulent and thick, and not a sound could be heard as people walked on it. A waiter showed them to a secluded table in a corner, and took their order. While they were waiting for their food, Craig held Constance's hand and squeezed it affectionately. She smiled at her husband and snuggled closer to him. Their food arrived and both began to eat. Afterwards a band began to play and the couple danced to a few of the tunes. Much later they returned to their apartment and climbed into their double bed.

The sun streaming through their window woke the couple and they blinked. Constance sighed and snuggled closer to Craig. They fell asleep once more, waking up at 9 a.m. Constance climbed out of bed and went to prepare breakfast for them both. However, when it was ready, there was no sign of Craig.

"Craig, come and eat your breakfast!" she called.

He didn't answer and she went back into the bedroom, only to find he had fallen asleep once again. She prodded him.

"Hey sleepyhead, time to wake up!"

"Uh wasamarrer?" he grunted.

"Breakfast is getting cold."

Craig yawned and stretched, pulling Constance down beside him. They kissed long and passionately and she sighed. "I guess I could warm it up again later!"

The couple made love and afterwards he reluctantly let her go. They spent the day buying groceries and enjoying one another's company.

In the evening, Constance began preparing supper for three. She took a lot of trouble over the table settings and the food and Craig sniffed appreciatively as the aromas wafted through. At the appointed time, Commander Simms rang their doorbell and Craig invited him in. He offered his boss a drink while Constance put the finishing touches to the table. While they were eating, the Carters began talking about their honeymoon.

After Constance had made them some coffee, Commander Simms said, "Craig, now you are back, are you going to continue working for the Space centre?"

"Why wouldn't he, Sir?" enquired Constance in puzzlement.

"Well I was just thinking, now you two are married, it could prove more dangerous."

Craig smiled at his boss. "Sir, I have lived with danger all my life. Even when I was going out with Constance, I faced danger. I wouldn't want it any other way and I'm sure Constance agrees with me."

"You know I do! Commander, I met Craig at the Space Control Centre. I understand how Craig feels and I certainly don't want him to change. I would still like to go out on missions for you as well."

Commander Simms smiled gratefully. "Well, at least that's something. Now I don't have to lose my best Space explorers."

"You don't need to worry about that, Sir. Even if I did decide to get another job, I'd probably still attract trouble," Craig grinned.

"Well, I'm glad we have settled that at least!" said the relieved Commander.

Although Craig was only 25 years old, he had managed to make a name for himself. He began working for the Space Control Centre in Houston, Texas soon after he had left school. He was 18 at the time. Young Carter worked behind the scenes for three years, operating the transmitters from time to time and doing maintenance and repairs on the spacecrafts. He absorbed everything he could about every aspect of Mission Control and excelled at everything he did. Simms watched Craig every step of the way and soon learnt of his incredible talent to retain all the information. He had a photographic memory and soon was trusted more and more with items that were confidential in nature. The Russians got to hear of this exceptional young man and Colonel Ivan Petrovsky was given the task of learning everything he could about the young man. When Craig took to Space exploration, Petrovsky was always around, waiting and watching for an opportunity to get him in his grasp. Craig had been captured more than once, but he always managed to get away without telling the Russians anything of value. Petrovsky was still his most cunning adversary and he never gave up the quest to capture the evasive young man. Now after working for Commander Simms for the last seven years, both on the ground and in space, Craig was his best Space explorer. He got on well with everyone and had few enemies at his place of work. Constance was also very good at her job. Most of Craig's assignments had been fraught with many dangers and he had the scars to prove it. After some time, Simms left, promising to inform the couple when anything came up.

Another six months passed, with Craig and Constance going out on a few missions. One particular night, Craig held his beautiful wife tenderly and stroked her cheek.

"My love, don't you think it's time we tried for a child. We have settled down pretty nicely and it would really be great."

Constance sighed and snuggled closer to her husband. "I think that's a wonderful idea. Our parents would love the idea of babysitting their grandchild."

He held her close and she crept deeper into his arms. His strong arms encircled her waist and she sighed with pleasure as he caressed her eager body.

Several weeks later, Constance had made an appointment with her doctor.

"Mrs Carter, welcome. What can I do for you?"

"Doctor, Craig and I want to have a baby and I wondered if you could help us. We've been trying for a few months now and nothing has happened."

The Doctor smiled encouragingly at his patient and told her lie down on the bed before he examined her. "Mrs Carter, you definitely aren't pregnant just yet. You have only been trying for a short while, so give it time."

Another few months passed and again Constance found herself at the doctor's rooms. This time Craig was with her.

"Mr and Mrs Carter, I don't know what the problem is. It might be a good idea if both of you went for fertility testing. Once I know what the problem is, then I can treat you. Shall I schedule an appointment for both of you?"

The couple nodded in unison and the next day they went to the local fertility clinic. They were subjected to a number of tests and told to go home and wait for the results which would take about two days. Constance went to the Space Control Centre to catch up with some of her reports, which had become overdue. Commander Simms would look pointedly in her direction every time he passed her desk and she smiled sheepishly, and continued typing them on her laptop. Craig had gone to a meeting on their Moon base, but he was scheduled to return the same evening.

During a break in their meeting, Craig switched on his mobile device and found a message from the doctor's receptionist. He went to stand outside on the balcony and contacted Constance. It rang and Craig's face was visible on the screen.

"Hi honey, I'm just phoning to check if you have heard from the doctor yet? I missed his call, and I wondered if you had spoken to him perhaps."

"Hi sweetheart! I got a missed call and I was just about to phone him. I'm going to take a break and then we can set up a conference call. Do you have a few minutes?"

"Sure I do. We have stopped to have lunch, so I'm free right now," Craig replied.

"Excellent! Give him a call back. I'm anxious to know what he found out."

Her husband put her on hold and she smiled when she heard their favourite tune playing through the phone. He contacted the doctor and his secretary answered. "Oh yes, good morning Mr Carter," she replied breezily. "Hold on for Dr Marques please."

Craig returned to his wife's call and both their faces showed on the screen. There was a delay of a minute or so before the doctor answered. "Good morning Dr Marques. I'm returning your call."

"Ah, Mr and Mrs Carter. Good morning to you both. I have your test results in front of me. You are fine Mr Carter. I found nothing wrong with your results. You are very fit and healthy. There seems to be a slight problem with you Mrs Carter. It's nothing serious though. You have a blockage in both your fallopian tubes. I would have to perform a small operation to unblock them and afterwards you shouldn't have any more problems."

Craig looked at his wife's image on the screen. "Well it's up to you honey. Do you want to do this?"

His wife smiled. "Yes of course I do! When can we schedule this?"

"I should be back from the Moon tonight, but I have another meeting with Commander Simms tomorrow morning. Doctor, can I bring Constance in on Thursday morning?"

"That will be fine. I'll have my secretary diarise it for me. I just want to discuss your options with the two of you first."

Both husband and wife looked expectantly at their specialist.

"You have two options of getting pregnant and I just wanted to discuss them with you briefly. If you wish to conceive in the natural way, you will just have to let nature take its course, but there is another alternative. You could use the 'tank' option. Many expectant parents prefer this, because they get to watch the baby develop out of the womb. All we require for this procedure are some eggs from you Mrs Carter, and sperm from your husband. The rest is done clinically."

The young couple looked at one another and shook their heads.

"No, Doctor, I want to conceive the natural way. I realise it's much simpler using the 'tank' method, but I prefer growing the child in my womb," replied Constance.

"Okay then, that's settled. I'm going to make arrangements for your operation now. You should only be in the operating room for a short while and a few hours later you'll be able to return home. Just make sure someone can drive you home afterwards, because you'll still be a bit drowsy."

The couple agreed and the Doctor disconnected.

A few days later, Craig took his wife to the hospital and waited nervously for her to reappear. An hour later she was awake, but still groggy from the anaesthetic. She was allowed home that afternoon and told to take it easy for the rest of the day. As they were leaving, the doctor stopped them. "Mrs Carter, if you experience any problems, please let me know, but I'm sure everything will be fine now."

A week later, they tried to conceive again. As Constance lay beside her husband, his arm resting across her body she whispered tenderly. "Oh Craig, I hope it works!"

He kissed her gently on the forehead and held her tighter. "I hope so too."

Two days later, Craig was called to the Space Centre and given an assignment. He hurried home to pack.

"Darling, an emergency has developed on one of the Meltonian planets. I have to deliver some vaccine to them immediately, to control an outbreak of disease that has hit them. I'll be gone for about a month or so."

Constance sighed and handed him a suitcase. "Oh well, work is work. I'll miss you though."

"I'll miss you too, sweetheart," he sighed.

The journey to the blue universe was uneventful and soon Craig had arrived. He handed over the medical supplies and stayed to see if it would work. A few days later, the results were positive and the inhabitants started to recover. A delighted Craig got ready to return to Earth. The leader accompanied Craig to his craft. "Thank you for bringing the medicine to us Craig. We owe you a debt of gratitude."

"Not necessary I assure you. What are friends for, if not to help one another?"

Craig waved goodbye and climbed into his craft. The steps began to lift automatically, until they were flush with the rest of the craft. He rose into the blueness of Space and soon left the planet behind. However, not long afterwards, the computer flashed a warning.

The image of a beautiful woman looked seriously back at him. Her long blonde hair was tied up with a light green hair tie and her bright green eyes were gazing at him.

"What's the problem, Janine?"

The holographic image bit her lip before replying <We have engine trouble Craig. Do you wish me to run a diagnostic check?>

"Yes, please do."

Craig hung onto the back of his chair as his craft tilted dangerously. Without waiting for the diagnosis, he turned his craft around and headed back to Melton. By the time he had landed once again, the computer had the answer.

The Meltonians were surprised to see him back again, but his face was grave as he landed.

"You have trouble, Craig?"

"Yes, one of my retro rockets has malfunctioned. The other three are fine, but I need all four of them. If I should land on a planet that has a strong gravitational pull, I'll never be able to get off and I run the risk of losing the other three rockets. Someone will have to come from Earth to replace it. Could I impose on your hospitality for about two weeks?"

"But of course. It will be our pleasure."

"Thank you. I'll just contact Commander Simms and let him know what the situation is."

Craig returned to his ship and contacted Earth.

"Commander Simms, I apologise for disturbing you, but I have a problem. One retro rocket has malfunctioned and I need you to organise a spare one for me. The Meltonians will put me up in the meantime. Please could you also let Constance know about this?"

"I'll do so as soon as I disconnect. I'll organise this immediately and you should get the part within the next two weeks."

Things began to go wrong and there were several delays. The equipment arrived a month later and proved more difficult to install than was at first realised. Eventually the retro rocket was hoisted into place and the final screw was tightened. Relieved, Craig got ready to return home. During his absence, Constance had felt unwell and returned to see her doctor. He gave her the good news that she was pregnant. She was so excited, but held back from contacting Craig, intending to tell him face to face when he returned, so they could go out and celebrate.

2

Finally, Craig arrived back. He hurried home as he had missed his wife terribly. On opening the door, however, he found no one home.

"Oh well, she probably went to visit friends," he thought.

He dialled her number on his mobile device, anxious to hear her voice once more, but it went straight to voicemail, so he left a message. Craig made himself something to drink and sat down to wait. The time dragged on and still she didn't appear. By this time Carter was frantic with worry and he contacted all the hospitals, just in case she had been in an accident, but no one knew where she was. That night he lay in their double bed and couldn't sleep. When he finally drifted off, he had disturbing dreams and woke with a start in the early hours of the morning. By the time the sun had come up, he had been awake for hours. As he went to make himself breakfast, he glanced at his mobile device's screen, on which his message icon was flashing.

Hello once again, Comrade Carter. By now you are obviously aware that your beautiful wife is missing. Don't worry about her; she is well, and safely in our custody. You know I am a man of my word, so I won't lie to you. We have nothing personal against your wife, but you are a different matter. I am presently here in America – yes you may wonder how I achieved it without being detected, but I am acutely aware your people are anxious to interview me, just as mine are anxious to meet with you. I know where you live and I'll come by tonight. Don't alert anyone, for your wife's sake.

Goodbye for the moment, Comrade.

IVAN PETROVSKY

Craig stared at the text message and his hands closed into fists. He punched the desk angrily.

"Why can't they leave me in peace! I have no wish to fight with Petrovsky, but when the Russians want something, they always resort to underhand measures. Even though Petrovsky is my enemy, he is a man of his word, so I have no choice but to believe him. I'll just have to wait until tonight to get to the bottom of this."

That evening there was a knock on the door and Craig went to open it. Petrovsky ambled inside.

"Good evening Comrade Carter. You got my message I trust?"

"Where's my wife?" he demanded angrily.

Petrovsky ignored him and sat down on one of the easy chairs, "Your wife – how strange it sounds. She is in good health, as I said before. Nice place you have here," he remarked amicably.

"Get to the point Petrovsky. What do you want from me and where's Constance?" Craig snapped.

"I don't know where your charming wife is."

"What! But you said…"

"I said she's safe, but only Andocia knows where she is," Petrovsky replied.

"Andocia! Is she in on this as well?"

"Yes, along with Tyrus. You have some powerful enemies, Comrade."

Craig sat down and ran his hands through his hair. "I don't understand…"

"You should. Both Andocia and Tyrus hate you for different reasons. Russia wants information from you."

"I see. I suppose if Constance is to continue in good health, I have to do something for all of you, is that it?"

"That's it exactly! For me of course, you are requested to part with some secret information," he purred.

Craig looked unhappily at his enemy. "What do the others want from me?"

Petrovsky shrugged. "I don't know. No doubt they will contact you soon."

"Am I expected to just wait around until someone gets in touch?" asked Craig angrily.

"It would seem so, yes. I hope you love your wife enough to do what we ask of you, Carter. If you disobey, she'll die!"

They were interrupted by a knock on the door. Petrovsky acted quickly and took a small laser gun out of his pocket. "Were you expecting anyone?"

"No. Do you want me to answer it?"

"Go ahead, but get rid of your visitor quickly. Don't mention my presence here."

Carter moved to the door and opened it. Commander Simms smiled and elbowed past him.

"Good evening Craig. I just thought I would drop by and visit for a while. I have something I would like to speak to you about."

"Uh Sir, this isn't a very convenient time. I... was getting ready for bed." Craig hedged as he moved in front of his boss.

Simms laughed and elbowed him good naturedly out of the way. "Oh don't be ridiculous! It's only 20H00."

Craig followed his boss to the lounge, where Simms stood still and gaped at Ivan Petrovsky. His gaze wandered to the gun, which now pointed at his stomach.

"Yes Carter, it's only 20H00," mocked Petrovsky. "Commander Simms, please take a seat opposite me. You join him Carter."

Commander Simms sat down and looked suspiciously at his explorer.

"Craig, I demand to know what's going on. Why is Colonel Ivan Petrovsky sitting in your living room?"

Craig shrugged. "Sir I suggest you ask him yourself. He's the one with the gun."

Commander Simms looked penetratingly at the Russian. "Well Petrovsky?"

"Ah, Craig and I were having a discussion. His wife is our guest and I was just delivering the message."

"You have Constance, why? How is she?"

"She's well, as I told Craig." Turning to the explorer, he stared at him in annoyance. "Comrade Carter, we cannot discuss the matter in question, because I am awaiting further instructions. I'll be in touch. I'm leaving now, but it would be in your best interests not to alert the authorities of this fact, otherwise Constance will die. I don't have time to tie you both up, so please, do not be foolish!"

Petrovsky backed out of the room and went to the front door, where he let himself out. Immediately Commander Simms took his phone out of his pocket, but Craig grabbed it.

"No Sir, Constance's life hangs in the balance. I can't let you do this."

"Craig, don't be an idiot! Petrovsky is wanted by our authorities and what a prize he'll be."

Carter held his employer's wrist firmly and looked beseechingly at him. "Please Sir, this is my mess and I'll clean it up."

Commander Simms returned to the chair and sat down. "Look Craig, I'm going to ask you a direct question and I'd like a direct answer. Are you working for the Russians on the sly?"

"Don't insult me Sir! Haven't I proved my loyalty to you over and over again?"

"Yes, but Constance's capture could change things somewhat."

Craig looked miserably at his employer. "Sir, Petrovsky isn't the only one involved in this. Andocia and Tyrus are in on this conspiracy as well."

Simms arched his eyebrows in amazement. "Those two are your most hated and feared adversaries. This is bad news! I suppose Petrovsky wants you to give him secret information."

Craig nodded unhappily. "It would seem so, but I want to listen to the demands of the others first."

"Do you think Andocia will come to Earth?" asked Simms nervously.

"I doubt it. She may want me to meet her in Space."

"What about Tyrus?"

"I honestly don't know. I suppose I just have to wait and see."

Simms sighed and put his hand on his employee's shoulder. "I'm really sorry about this Craig. If there's anything I can do to help, let me know. All

I can do now is wish you luck. I won't assign any missions to you for the moment."

"I appreciate that Commander, thank you. It looks like I'm going to need lots of luck to get through this trying time. I should have realised they would get at me by using Constance as bait."

"Craig, Constance can take care of herself. Don't feel guilty about this. She knew the risk involved in marrying you and did it anyway."

"Yes, we discussed it at length, but I still can't stop worrying about her."

"All right, Craig, I give you my word that I won't alert the authorities. Keep hoping – I'm sure everything will work out in the end," replied Simms reassuringly.

When his employer had gone, Craig paced the floor restlessly for a time. As it was now late, he retired to bed and slept well, despite his anguish.

The following evening, Carter was preparing supper when he was alerted by a sound. A strange shadow fell over him and he turned around, knowing already who his visitor was.

"Hello Tyrus. I wasn't expecting you to come here. I'd offer you a chair, but I don't want to spend a lot of time visiting with you. What do you want and where's Constance?"

"I left that part of the proceedings up to Andocia. She alone knows where your wife is. I know my limits and I won't mess around with the most powerful being in both universes. To answer your first question about what I want; no doubt Colonel Petrovsky has contacted you with his request. As for mine, well I just want you to give yourself up to me. We have plenty of unfinished business to discuss and obviously it will go better for your wife if you do so willingly."

Craig stared at Tyrus. "Tell me the truth, Tyrus. Is Constance really still alive?"

"Well, of course she is. What would be the point of all this rigmarole if she were dead? We all know you won't co-operate with us unless we have an ace in the hole, so to speak. What about my proposition?"

"I'll have to speak to Andocia before I make a decision," hedged Craig. "Do you perhaps know what Andocia wants from me?"

"No, she didn't discuss it with me. I brought a message from her though. She wants you to meet her in Space tomorrow."

"Had she any particular destination in mind?"

"No, but you have to take this," remarked Tyrus, holding out a circular object.

Craig stared suspiciously at it and refused to take it.

"What is it?"

"This little device is part and parcel of the deal. It's a device that sends out a signal – a homing beacon, I believe you would call it. Andocia said you must attach it to your control panel when you get on your ship. It's a form of insurance, just in case you get smart and try to disappear on us. This way, all of us will know where you are every second of the day."

Craig took the object and stared at it. "An electronic watchdog!" he exclaimed disgustedly.

"I suppose you could call it that. By the way, if you're planning to interfere with this device, it will blow you and your ship to smithereens. If that blip disappears from Andocia's screen, your wife will die immediately and you'll follow suit when she captures you. Is everything clear?"

"Like crystal," replied Craig sourly. "If you have to report back to Andocia, you can tell her I'll take a ship out tomorrow morning."

Tyrus began to disappear and soon there was no evidence of him ever having been there. Craig rescued his food, which had begun to burn and ate it thoughtfully.

"What a predicament this puts me in! The demands so far have been quite outrageous. No doubt Andocia will have something unpleasant planned for me as well. Damn it, that woman is a nuisance! She seems to think I am her personal pet – always at her beck and call!"

The following morning, Craig went to see Commander Simms.

"Sir, can I take a craft out into Space?"

"You've heard from Andocia?" he asked nervously.

"No, Tyrus brought me a message from her. I have to meet her out in Space. Sir, she wants me to put this homing device in the ship. I have to do it, but it occurred to me it could work for us as well as against us. I'd really appreciate it if you could use it to keep an eye on me – you know, just in case of emergencies."

"Of course, I understand. Let's go to the technicians and they can work out the frequency."

They went to the technical department and soon everything was sorted.

Craig was given a ship piled high with provisions and Commander Simms watched with trepidation as his best explorer blasted into Space.

3

Carter pointed his ship in the direction of the Golden Way and placed the homing device onto his console. The moment the magnetic back attached itself to the metal console, a light switched on and began to blink rapidly. A few hours later, a small trident ship docked with his and he went to join Andocia.

"Hello Carter, come and sit down," she invited.

He moved to a chair some distance from her.

"All right, I came as you requested. Where's Constance?"

"Have patience. She is in good health. I have to admit I was surprised to learn you had married her. Surely you knew she could be used as a lever, a bargaining chip?"

"We discussed the matter and she married me anyway. Look, I have no desire to indulge in small talk with you. I want to know what you have done with my wife. Petrovsky and Tyrus told me you have her."

"She is my guest!" Andocia admitted. "However, it wouldn't do you any good if I told you where she was; you can't rescue her anyway."

"I would still like to know," he replied doggedly.

"Very well; she's on Pluto."

The words were like a slap in the face to Craig and he paled. "No! They have probably killed her already!"

"She is safe and well. All beings who come into contact with me and still disobey my orders know I shall destroy their entire planet."

Craig stared unseeingly ahead of him and his mind was racing. "The Plutonians are a terribly hostile race. They have three pairs of arms and are only waist high, but they have the ability to grow to an incredible height. They hate all forms of life other than themselves, but they despise Earthlings most of all. I had a close call once while I was looking for Roland Stone. They nearly turned me into toast. I can't rescue Constance; Andocia is right as usual!"

The devilish woman interrupted his train of thought.

"You see it's impossible to get to her. I'm the only one who can free her."

"What do you want from me, Andocia?" he asked mournfully.

"I would have thought it was obvious. This concerns Tanus and her wretched pet Tarmin."

"I suppose the two of you are still fighting for dominance. Good is much more powerful than evil, I thought you knew that Andocia. How exactly does this concern me?"

"Tanus is strong, but if you recall, I had her in my power a while ago."

Craig couldn't meet his enemy's eyes and looked down at his feet. He remembered vividly what transpired.

Andocia read his mind and couldn't resist a smirk.

"Yes, you had a bad experience too, as I recall."

"It was no picnic," he admitted. "Obviously, whatever you have in mind for me concerns Tanus."

"Yes, of course, it does! I want you to visit Tanus and trick her into drinking this," said Andocia as she handed Craig a bottle. He stared at it and watched as it changed colour in a different light.

"What will this do to her?" he asked curiously.

"It should knock her out for a few days and give me enough time to recapture and imprison her once more. If Tarmin interferes, save some for her."

"I don't know what you're planning Andocia, but I don't like this at all! Tanus is the only one who can stand in your way of achieving domination of both universes. With her out of the way, what guarantee have I got that you won't make a play for Earth again?"

"Your role is to follow my orders, not question them," she snapped angrily. "My plans don't concern you right now, but one thing I know for certain and that is, if you fail to carry out my orders, Constance will be the first casualty."

Craig opened his mouth to speak, but a shape coming towards them distracted both of them. Tyrus materialised in the craft with them.

"Hello again Carter," sneered the creature.

"What do you want here Tyrus? I told you Carter will be handed over to you once he has done what Petrovsky and I have requested of him," Andocia snapped irritably.

Tyrus made a mock bow. "Forgive me, mighty one, but I was just checking up on him. I know you have a temper and I just wanted to make sure he was still in one piece."

Tyrus stared at Craig through the three eyes on his head, and smirked. "Ah, I see by his expression that you have already issued him with his instructions. It seems he doesn't like them much."

"No, but he has no choice. Of course, if he refuses, I'll issue the order to terminate his wife."

Craig glared at his enemies. "If you kill my wife, I won't honour any agreements anyway."

Tyrus looked at Andocia and his eyes were glittering with excitement. "Andocia, why don't you kill her now and you can make him watch? I can then just take him back to my planet and end this nonsense once and for all. A small electrical charge and he'll be all mine," said Tyrus as he advanced on Craig. The explorer took a few steps back and tensed to defend himself. A red beam exploded at their feet, stopping Tyrus in his tracks.

"That's enough! I have given him a job to do, so you can just wait patiently. Well Carter, what's your answer?"

The Space explorer glared at both his enemies in turn, then stared into Andocia's red eyes. "I want proof that my wife is alive. Until I know she's in good health, I won't help you. Let me see her."

Andocia shrugged and Tyrus snorted. "Huh, you are calling the shots here Andocia. Why should you accede to his request?"

The woman glared at Tyrus. "Back off, Tyrus! I didn't have to include you in this little adventure because you are just small fry compared to some of Craig's other enemies. His request is reasonable given the circumstances he finds himself in and he will help us – he has no choice. Follow me please!"

Craig walked behind Andocia with Tyrus ambling along behind him, almost as though he was afraid his prey would escape at any moment. They went into the control room of the ship and Andocia contacted Pluto.

Even though Craig had tangled with them before he couldn't suppress a shudder when a Plutonian was staring at him from the large screen. The creature's face was benign, almost angelic in appearance and Carter knew many had lost their lives because they had believed the odious creatures were friendly.

The creature saw Andocia and hissed and Craig took a step back when he heard the menace in the being's voice.

"What do you want now Andocia?" it snarled. "It's bad enough we have to babysit for you. Why is that human with you?"

Andocia smiled but the smile never reached her eyes, which narrowed into slits. "This human here is the other one's mate. I trust she is well."

The creature hissed again. "The human female is fine but my people are restless. Humans are considered one of our enemies and there is dissent among them about having the woman with us."

"I don't care about the feelings of your planet, just the welfare of your guest. Is she well?"

"The woman is in excellent health. We hate you – that's no secret, but we would not dare disobey you."

"Good! Now I wish to see her. Link me to her quarters at once."

The scenery changed to that of a comfortable room. In a large armchair sat Constance. She was staring pensively out of the window. Suddenly she stood up and her face filled the screen. It was filled with hope which faded when Andocia spoke to her. Craig was out of her line of vision so she never saw him at first.

"Andocia! What do you want now? I thought you would be tired of gloating by this time. I hate this place and I hate these awful beings!"

"All the more reason to keep you there. See you don't even need bars to keep you in check. You can go for a stroll anytime!" she smirked.

"Oh sure!" Constance snorted. "I love risking my life for fun! You know how dangerous the Plutonians are."

This time Andocia smiled genuinely. "Well cheer up, I have a surprise for you."

She beckoned to Craig and he came forward. He stared miserably at his wife.

"Hello honey," he sighed.

There was a moment's stunned silence while they stared at one another. Constance was the first to speak.

"How stupid of me! I should have guessed of course! Andocia is up to her usual tricks – using me to get back at you. I can't say I'm surprised. I did wonder why she kidnapped me, but Andocia has her own agenda," she replied angrily. Turning to Andocia she glared at her. "What must he do for you now?" she asked sarcastically. "Kill someone?"

Craig blanched at the hatred in his wife's voice, but at the same time he knew she was justified in feeling this way. Hastily he interrupted her. "Constance, listen to me! I know you are stressed right now and I cannot blame you. I wish I could trade places with you."

However, Constance wasn't looking at him. She was staring at something behind him and as he turned, he saw Tyrus had moved closer to him and had rested a hand lightly on Craig's shoulder. The explorer removed it and stepped away.

"Tyrus is in on this as well? Something very big must be about to go down," she replied quietly and the menace in her voice was evident.

Tyrus came forward again and sneered at Constance. "Ivan Petrovsky is also involved in this matter. We have plans for your husband!"

Constance was horrified. "Craig, what the hell is going on? Why are all three of them ganging up on you?"

"Constance, don't worry, I can handle this," Craig replied with a confidence he didn't feel, keeping his expression neutral. "Just tell me, are you well?"

"As well as can be expected, under the circumstances," she replied icily.

Andocia interrupted. "All right Carter, you can see she is well so say goodbye! We have much to discuss and time is moving on."

The Space explorer just managed a hurried goodbye but he never heard her reply as Andocia broke the connection. "All right, as you saw, your wife is fine. She is as fiery as ever, I notice. Well, down to business I think. It's time for you to do as I asked. Are you going to co-operate?"

Craig stared at his arch enemy and sighed heavily. "You made the situation plain, Andocia. I'll go and do your dirty work, but don't expect me to like it."

He turned on his heel and made his way back to his spacecraft. Tyrus said nothing until the two ships had separated. "Andocia, I feel I should warn you, Carter plans to go against you and confess to Tanus. I read his mind."

The devil woman slammed her fist down on the table. "Damn him, I always presume he'll do as he is told. Well I'll deal with this in my own way."

"What of his wife?"

"She is not going anywhere. I still hold the trump card because without his wife, Carter can be manipulated. Leave this matter with me and when the time comes, I'll deliver him personally into your grasp. Do not try to double-cross me, or my vengeance will be swift."

"I wouldn't betray you, mighty one. I'll wait for you to contact me."

⌁ ⌁ ⌁

The explorer hovered above Tanus's planet and his spaceship was ordered to land. Tarmin greeted him at the landing strip and pecked him affectionately on the cheek.

"Welcome, Craig. Tanus is anxious to see you. How have you been?"

He smiled distractedly and went into Tanus's lounge, where he sat down opposite her. "Tanus, I must speak with you."

"You have a problem, don't you? I can sense it."

"Yes. Andocia captured Constance, now she and others want me to do bad things to pay for her freedom. I have to do as they say, or Constance will die."

"I understand. Andocia wants you to do something to put me out of action, doesn't she? And she has no doubt has supplied the means."

"How did you guess?" he asked lamely.

"It's obvious, because I know how she operates. Are you going to do what she said you must?"

Craig shook his head and handed Tanus the bottle of liquid, which she held up to the light. "What is this supposed to do?"

"She said something about putting you to sleep for a few days so she can move in and recapture you. I was told to use it on Tarmin as well if necessary."

Tanus's expression was grim. "I don't know what this is, but I'm going to have my lab check it out. Stay awhile and let's see what that she-devil had planned for me."

Craig waited tensely and one of Tanus's assistants came and whispered in her ear. Her expression hardened and she turned to Craig. "Do you know what that vial contained?"

"No, Andocia never shared that knowledge with me."

"That bottle contained a very strong elixir which could not only put me to sleep, but keep me in that state indefinitely. If you had used it on Tarmin, death would have been instantaneous. That she-devil plays for keeps."

"I should have realized she meant to cause you serious harm! Tanus, I need your help. Once Andocia finds out I didn't do what she told me to, she'll kill Constance and come looking for me. Couldn't you just get Constance off Pluto somehow?"

Tanus looked calmly at the explorer, but her reaction surprised and confused him.

"I'm sorry Craig you have to go it alone. I can't help you every time you tangle with Andocia."

"But the odds are stacked heavily against me!" he pleaded.

"You aren't the top Space explorer at Mission Control for nothing. Before I came on the scene, you must have clashed with many strange foes. You have a good head on your shoulders, so use it. Tarmin, escort Craig back to his ship."

"Come along Craig," replied Tarmin as she nudged him gently.

When they reached his craft, he questioned Tarmin. "What have I done to offend her? She looked as though she resented my presence."

"I think you had better go," replied Tarmin, and her voice held menacing undertones.

Craig climbed into his ship and blasted off. He watched as the big bird returned to her mistress.

"I don't understand it! Tarmin always flies part of the way with me. Oh well, time to look out for number one, seeing as no one else is going to."

Craig had been confident Tanus would understand his predicament and help him, but it looked as though there was no one he could turn to anymore. Whichever way he looked at it, he had no choice but to do exactly as he was told. His brain was filled with conflicting emotions and he felt he needed to take a break from everything, just for a short while, in order that he might think more clearly. Unfortunately, being with Andocia didn't help matters at all. It only made the situation worse. When he returned to her planet, she would know he had betrayed her and he was sure she would do something awful. He hoped fervently his wife wouldn't pay the price for his treachery.

On an impulse, Craig set course for Venus and stared at the homing beacon.

"Damn it. I don't want to go back to Andocia just yet, but she'll know of my whereabouts because of this thing. There has to be a way to disarm it, or at least fool Andocia. If I land anywhere, she'll take it out on whoever tries to help me."

The explorer pondered the problem for a while and then smiled. He fetched a screwdriver from the emergency toolbox and moved to the console. Craig unscrewed the portion of the console onto which the beacon was attached and re-routed the wires to another outlet. He took the homing device, together with the loose section of the console and ejected it into

Space. Craig grinned when he saw the device was still flashing away. Satisfied, he continued on his way to Venus, but decided to contact Commander Simms and let him know what had happened so far.

Some hours later, he contacted the Venusians and they offered to put him up. On arrival, he discussed his problem with them.

"Craig, we would gladly give you sanctuary for a while. We have never met Andocia, but we have heard many stories about her. How long do you plan on staying?"

"Only two days. I can't avoid her forever, but at least I'll have time to think of something. I must find a way to get my wife safely off Pluto."

"What do you need from us?" the gentle plant like beings asked.

"I only want time to be away from all my enemies for a short while so I can think of a solution to my problems, without having my enemies looking over my shoulders."

A few of the beings sat down nearby. "Are you just going to meditate, or are you looking for advice?"

Craig smiled sadly. "I would love some advice! I'm desperate to find a solution to my problems, but there isn't one."

A number of beings circled him and placed their "hands" on his body. "On our planet, we believe in oneness. It isn't difficult to understand why this is useful in our environment because we are all plants. We Venusians share the same characteristics, yet each plant is different just as Earthlings are, but our needs are similar. Both our species need air, food and company, for we cannot exist alone. We have those who help us survive, just as your species does. We have enemies too, but they are not the same as those who oppose your people. Tell us what troubles you and we will try to help."

Craig looked at all the beautiful plants that surrounded him and he began his story.

"I've been working for NASA for several years and I always enjoyed exploring Space – until now. I have many friends, but also some powerful enemies. Now I find myself in a situation I cannot cope with. My mate has been taken prisoner against her will and I have no choice but to obey my enemies who are forcing me to do things that go against my moral standard.

"The one known as Andocia is my most dangerous enemy yet, but there are others also involved in this plot. If I wish to see my mate again, I must do illegal things to help my enemies get information they require. I was also ordered to cause harm to the one known as Tanus. I confessed to her what I had to do because I didn't want her to be compromised, thus leaving Andocia free to rule both universes. She deserted me because of this and now I'm alone in this quest. My mate is on Pluto and at the mercy of those beings who live there. They are terrified of Andocia so I don't think they would harm Constance, but she lives in constant fear of her life and I'm powerless to help her."

The plant beings looked compassionately at him and one stroked his forehead. It was hot to the touch and it could feel his sorrow.

"Craig, we admire you for what you have achieved in both universes. No one has ever come close to duplicating your deeds. Truly you are a legend, but being a legend does have its problems. The fact that your enemies are ganging up against you like this, means they admire you a great deal as well. Why else would they bother with you?"

Craig sighed. "I never thought about it like that, but I don't feel any better. How can I solve this problem?"

Another plant commented. "You have the answers in your head already, but your mind and your heart are anxious and that's why you cannot think straight. We know how much you fear Andocia and probably your other enemies as well, but you have to get over this hurdle. Andocia is going to be a part of you and your mate's lives for eternity. Probably those of your offspring as well one day. If you cannot conquer your fear, at least learn how to control it."

Carter spread out his hands in supplication. "Teach me how to achieve this!"

A few beings huddled together and nodded their heads.

"We have something to help you calm down. You have obviously also not been sleeping very well since your mate was captured."

One of the beings returned with some liquid. It handed the explorer a leaf in the shape of a cup and he drank it. It tasted like honey, infused with herbs.

"You'll sleep now and when you wake up, your mind will be calmer. While you are resting, we will stay with you."

Craig thanked them and yawned. The liquid soothed him and he was soon fast asleep on the soft grass with many plant beings surrounding him. They covered him like a blanket, leaving only his head exposed so he could breathe. The sun sank slowly and Venus was plunged into darkness.

He woke the next morning feeling refreshed and much calmer, but still didn't have the answers he needed to rescue his wife. The explorer spent another day with the plant beings. They took him to sit by a stream that seemed to sing to him. Strange little butterflies flitted around him and he was left to think about his situation. The plants were everywhere. If he needed anything, they complied.

He spent two days with the inhabitants of Venus and when he got ready to leave and return to Andocia, he felt a lot calmer. He thanked them for their help and rose vertically into Space.

As he flew away from Venus, he saw a trident ship hovering above him. He was just about to send them a message, but before he could do this a tractor beam shot out and ensnared him. His engine spluttered and died. Unable to restart his craft, he was reeled in like a fish on a hook. Once his ship had come to rest inside the belly of the bigger craft, he came out and was met by Andocia and several of her followers.

"You know Carter; you never cease to amaze me. That was really clever of you to rid yourself of that homing device, but I expected that and made alternate arrangements. What were you doing on Venus anyway?"

"I just needed some time to think and I couldn't do that while I was with you. I was about to contact you when you dragged me here."

"It doesn't matter anyway because I found you, so we don't need to waste any more time. I need you to run an errand for me."

Craig sighed. "I won't betray Tanus, no matter what! I really love my wife, but I can't sacrifice the only being who can stop you from having complete power."

The devilish woman waved her hand dismissively. "It doesn't matter, I'll find some way to use you at a later stage. Right now, your wife is in need of some clothing and she wants you to buy these for her. I shall personally accompany you back to Earth to purchase the items in question. We can go in my ship. Yours will be safe here. In any case, my ships are faster than yours."

"I don't understand! When I last spoke to her, she said nothing about needing clothing. Andocia, we have to pass Pluto on the way to Earth. Please will you let me see my wife? I need to know that everything is all right with her."

Andocia considered his request for a moment and nodded. "I suppose we can – it's on our way. Come with me to another section of this craft."

Carter followed her and she selected a ship that could hold two people, plus some luggage.

4

Soon they were on their way again and made for Pluto. On landing, the Plutonians glared angrily at Andocia and the new arrival. "What is he doing here?"

"I have brought him to see his wife. I don't want him harmed or your planet will suffer."

The beings grunted furiously and made way for them to walk. Craig stared at the Plutonians in morbid fascination as he had never seen them this close before. For the first time, he noticed they had spikes down the middle of their heads all the way down to their torsos. These stood straight up and quivered menacingly. Their legs were small but very muscular and there was a protrusion at the base of their bodies, which looked like a small tail. Their faces were kind and gentle looking. On the viewscreens, it looked as though these beings had fur. Seeing them up close like this, Craig realised these were in fact the spikes. They had very sharp tips, and when released, their unfortunate prey was impaled. Carter recalled that many people had taken them to be friendly and landed. None of them ever left Pluto alive. Of course, their viciousness was well documented now.

Andocia arrived at a building and they went inside. Craig noticed there were no bars anywhere, but he assumed Constance's fear would keep her from exploring too much anyway. Andocia stopped at another door and pushed it open, allowing Craig to enter. She watched from the doorway as the man approached his wife. Constance had her back to him and was wistfully combing her hair.

"Constance?"

On hearing her name, Constance stopped, her hand holding the brush was poised near her head, ready for the next stroke. She turned slowly and looked disbelievingly at her husband.

A smile spread across her face and she ran into his arms, happy tears glistening in her eyes. Andocia stepped outside and closed the door, allowing them some privacy.

"Oh Craig, has Andocia given you permission to take me home?"

Craig shook his head regretfully. "I wish I could, but I'm sorry, she won't allow it. I was told you needed some clothing and she's going to accompany me back to Earth. Have you made a list of the things you need?"

"Well yes I have, but most of it is maternity wear."

"Fine, I'll go home and organise some for you." He paused for a few seconds and then broke out in a disbelieving grin. "Maternity wear! Does that mean what I think it means?"

"Yes, darling, I'm pregnant! My clothes are getting a little snug now and soon it'll start showing."

"You're pregnant, at last! Oh Constance, you have no idea how happy this makes me."

He kissed his wife soundly once more, and her face clouded over.

"But Craig, I'm a prisoner here and they won't help me. I don't know what's going to happen when my time comes. I don't want to lose this baby!"

Craig grasped his wife's hand tightly. "You won't, I promise you. I'll do whatever it takes to get you off here, I swear it. You will have this baby on Earth, I guarantee it."

"I hope so. Darling, I know I was captured for a reason and I'm so sorry I had a minor meltdown when I spoke to you last time, but I wasn't feeling well and I kept throwing up. I knew the reason of course, but I didn't have time to break the news to you on Earth because you were delayed by the repairs that needed to be done on your spacecraft. When Andocia let me speak to you a few weeks ago she never gave me time to tell you I was pregnant. Andocia contacts me sometimes just to gloat, even though the excuse she gave me was that she was checking up on me. Oh Craig, can you cope? I don't like the idea of everyone ganging up on you."

"Don't worry about me. It's minor details that I can easily deal with," he lied.

He peeped outside but Andocia had left them alone. Craig took Constance's hand and sat down on the bed with her. "Tell me the truth Constance, are you really all right?"

"I'm fine, except for some morning sickness. Just hurry back to me, okay."

Craig turned away, but then thought of something. "Honey, why do you want me to go back to Earth for all the stuff you need? You can order anything you like on the universes' websites."

"I know! But I gave Andocia some story about a shop in our complex at home – you know the one I mean! We always stop there when we are doing our shopping and they have such adorable things for babies."

Her husband nodded. "I know the one you mean, but they do deliveries just like every other shop anywhere in the world."

Constance stared at her husband as though he was an idiot. "Yes, I know that! I wanted Andocia to let you go back to Earth where you could get some help from our colleagues. Perhaps Commander Simms can organise something. You know my dad would be chomping at the bit to help us. He commands a formidable force in the Army."

Craig looked miserably into his wife's sparkling eyes. "If only I could, but unfortunately it won't work. Andocia doesn't trust me. I refused to help her incapacitate Tanus and now she is clamping down on my freedom as well. That evil vixen is coming to Earth with me and there is nothing I can do about it."

Constance sighed and shook her head. "Damn her! She is such a nuisance."

"My darling, I'll think of something, just give it time. I know it's hard being here with these treacherous Plutonians, but they won't harm you. They are terrified of Andocia."

Carter took his wife's face between his hands and kissed her gently. "Just hold on and try to think happy thoughts. I'll be back with the things you need before you know it."

An hour later, Andocia came to fetch him. "Time to go, Carter. Say goodbye now."

He kissed his wife tenderly once more and followed the woman to her ship.

They touched down on the roof of the high rise building in which the Carters lived and Andocia followed him to his apartment. She made herself comfortable as Craig moved about getting some toiletries, which he put in a suitcase.

"Andocia, I have to go into the city to see about some maternity clothing for Constance. There is a baby shop in this complex, but it is very small. I can come to this one when I get back. Why don't you stay here and I'll join you later."

"No, I don't think so. I feel like a drive into the city. We can take your car."

Craig sighed heavily. "Look I understand why you want to accompany me, but this is ridiculous! Everyone on every planet knows who you are and no one likes you. Your attempt to take over Earth a few years ago still angers many people. It's not a good idea."

Andocia sighed. "Oh my, humankind can be very obstinate, can't they! Very well, I'll make a plan, but I will still come with you. I don't want to let you out of my sight. I have trust issues concerning you."

The Space explorer opened his mouth to protest, but he snapped it shut when something strange began to happen.

A red mist appeared in the apartment and began swirling around Andocia. It began at the top of her head and continued down her body until she was completely covered. For a few moments it just shimmered, then slowly began to clear. Andocia posed before Craig, smiling triumphantly. "Ta daa! What do you think?" she asked playfully.

The explorer looked dumbly at her. "What are you talking about? I saw a red mist cover you, but it just vanished!"

She ran her hands slowly down her body. "Do I pass inspection or not?"

Craig shook his head. "Did I miss something? What was supposed to happen?"

His enemy looked strangely at him. "What do you see when you look at me?"

"I see you. Was something else supposed to happen? That mist was very freaky though."

Andocia looked puzzled for a moment, but then shook her head. "It can't be"… she muttered. "Is it possible??? Oh yes, of course, now I understand! Interesting though!"

"Andocia! What's going on??" he demanded crossly.

She grabbed Craig's wrist and took him to a mirror. He looked questioningly at her and she pointed. "Take a look in the mirror."

Convinced she had lost her mind he obeyed. His eyes opened wide and for once he was speechless. He was looking at himself in the mirror, but next to him stood a statuesque brunette. The image had emerald green eyes and her shiny straight hair was cut stylishly. It hung down and embraced a swanlike neck, just touching her shoulders. The smile was warm and friendly. The image wore a beautifully cut two-piece ensemble in black. A green top offset the outfit and she wore high heeled black shoes. Some simple but stylish accessories completed the look.

Carter was speechless, but he couldn't help smiling.

"Ah, seems you like my creation. Would you like me to make any changes perhaps?"

"Uh no... that's fine. How come I only see your image and not this lovely vision?"

"It has something to do with the time when we first met."

Craig frowned. "I remember. That was when you thought I was a criminal mastermind and you blinded me when I refused to join you."

"Yes. Remember I interfered with some of your neural functions and created a pathway in your brain. That is why we can speak telepathically to one another. That connection obviously is the reason why you cannot see the image I have created. What matters though is that every other human on your planet will see what I show them. Use the name Wanda when you speak to me in public. Now we have to purchase your wife's requirements, so let's go."

Carter decided not to argue further and went down to the basement where his car was parked and Andocia climbed in next to him. He got a parking space quite close to the shop he wanted to visit and went inside. Andocia followed him and watched in fascination as he went from rack to rack choosing maternity wear for Constance. Many shop owners knew Craig and he introduced his companion as one of Constance's cousins. When he had bought all the necessary requirements, they went back to his apartment, where he packed the new items into another suitcase. He felt thirsty and asked Andocia if she wanted something to drink. Once they were settled, he turned to his captor.

"Look Andocia, until I saw Constance I wasn't prepared to help you or the others. I planned to rescue her and take her somewhere safe. We have been trying to get pregnant for quite some time, but nothing happened. Now that she is expecting, everything has changed. I know what Petrovsky wants from me, but the information is stored on the computers at work and I can't access them from here. The documents are of a very sensitive nature and I need to copy them onto a data drive. I have to put in an appearance at the Space Centre, but you can't come with me. Will you allow me to go and get the relevant information unaccompanied? I'll need about two hours to complete the task."

Andocia considered the request, but she wasn't happy. "All right, I'll allow you to do this, but if you aren't back by the time the two hours have elapsed, I will organise your wife's demise."

Craig went to the Space Control Centre and hurried to Commander Simm's office, hoping desperately that the man wasn't in a meeting. He breathed a sigh of relief when Commander Simms' secretary buzzed him through. The Commander stared quizzically at him.

"Craig, there's no record of your having returned to Earth. How did you get here?"

"It's a long story, but I rode with Andocia in one of her ships. Her craft are very sophisticated, as you know, but she landed on the roof of my building. Sir, I haven't much time, but I wanted to tell you the good news first. Constance is pregnant!"

The Commander shook his hand warmly. "That's wonderful Craig. Congratulations! Do you know where she is?"

"She's a prisoner on Pluto. Sir, you told me that if I needed any help, you would give it to me."

"You know I will do anything to help you. What do you need?"

"Colonel Petrovsky is expecting some top-secret documents from me. He didn't specify what he wanted exactly, but it obviously has to be something genuine, otherwise he'll tell Andocia, and Constance could suffer the consequences."

"Did you have something particular in mind to offer him?"

"I actually do have a plan, Sir."

"Let me hear it then," Commander Simms stated.

"Do you remember when Constance and I were on honeymoon and the Saturnians gave us the instructions for the new cloaking device, and the speed boosting device."

"Yes, I remember."

"They also told us we would have to share this technology with all the Space agencies around the world – including Russia, and, so far we have neglected to share this information."

"I normally have a good memory Craig, but somehow I have just been so busy, I must confess it slipped my mind."

"Well, I think now would be a good time to share this technology with the Russians. I won't tell them that the Saturnians gave it to us as a gift, nor will I tell them we intend to share this technology with all space-going agencies. They may not trust us if I tell them the information was free. It's much better if they think I was giving it to them illegally."

Commander Simms smiled. "That's an excellent idea Craig! You have a devious mind and I like it!"

"It's a good plan and I don't have to feel guilty about it. I know the Russians are our enemies, but everyone deserves to have protection from Andocia."

"That's true!" Simms agreed.

"I have another suggestion to make, Sir. The devices are very effective as we have already found out, but there are some things about them I don't like. For example, when our enemies use the new cloaking devices, we won't know where they are, especially if we are being pursued. It would mean they could follow any of our spacecrafts and just capture or destroy it before our astronauts can call for help."

"The Saturnians forgot to mention that part," Simms grumbled.

"I don't think it occurred to them Sir. In their own crafts, they can pinpoint the location of a strange ship. I still have access to the computers in the technical department, so if you would give me permission, I just need about half an hour to re-program the device we will be giving to Colonel Petrovsky. At least we will be able to escape from the Russians if they pursue us and they won't even know about it."

Commander Simms grinned wickedly. "Now I know why you are my top Space explorer! You have my permission to do it. Come with me and I'll give you one of the devices."

Commander Simms took him to a restricted area of the complex and stopped at a solid steel door. He looked into a device that scanned the retina of his right eye, and at the same time placed his left hand on a device located near the door.

<Welcome, Commander Simms! Access granted!> the computer replied.

The door slid open and both men entered the restricted area. The place was filled with security men and women who all nodded politely to their boss. Simms went to a room further down the passage and explained what he needed. The guard on duty nodded and went to fetch one of the devices.

He handed an electronic notebook to his Commander, who signed his signature and took possession of the device.

When they had returned to the Commander's office, he handed the device to his employee. "Okay Craig, do what you have to and then come and report back to me before you leave."

Carter switched on one of the computers and isolated the components accordingly. He spent some time typing in different codes and finally sat back, satisfied with the day's work. Once he had saved the changes, he returned to his boss.

"Have you finished reprogramming the device, Craig?" Simms enquired.

"Yes Sir, everything is fine now. They won't know the difference and this device should make them very happy."

Craig's mobile device rang suddenly and he looked at the display. He deactivated the viewing facility so his caller couldn't see his face.

"Hello Andocia."

"Where are you Carter and why have you deactivated the viewing screen?"

Craig exchanged glances with Commander Simms. "Sorry but I'm driving at the moment. It took longer than I thought and I'm stuck in traffic. I'll see you shortly."

Andocia disconnected and the man put his phone away.

"Sir, I had better go now. Thank you for all your help."

Simms placed a restraining hand on his arm. "Craig, this may clear your debt to Petrovsky, but what about Tyrus? All he wants, is to see you dead."

"I know that, but I'll cross that bridge when I come to it. I had better go now before Andocia becomes impatient and gives the order to dispose of Constance. I don't know when I'll be back."

Simms nodded in agreement and shook his explorer's hand. "Go well, Craig."

Carter returned to his apartment and picked up the suitcases of clothing and other essentials for his wife. They went back to the roof and Andocia lifted off. Soon they were in the blackness of Space and heading to Pluto. On arrival, he was escorted back to Constance, where he showed her the clothing he had bought.

"I hope this will tide you over now. I can only spend an hour with you, because Andocia wants to deliver me to Tyrus. I have to meet with Petrovsky and Tyrus in her mother ship later."

"Craig, are you sure everything is all right?"

"It will be, just as soon as I do what they ordered me to. I promise, I'll try to hurry back."

Constance clung to him and they sat in silence, just enjoying each other's company. The hour flew by and Andocia called for him. After giving Constance a hurried kiss, he went to meet her.

Before long, Pluto was far away and Craig watched silently as the planets sped by. Andocia came to join him. "I assume you have the information Petrovsky asked for?"

"Yes, I told you already."

"I sense you are worried, but I imagine that it's normal. What will happen when your commander finds out you have the information?"

"He won't, because I copied it and left the original behind," Craig lied. "I'm more concerned about what Tyrus has planned for me. All he understands is termination. Andocia, I have a wife now and a baby on the way. I want to be with my child and watch as it grows up and if it's up to Tyrus, that won't happen."

"I never found out why he hates you so much. Will you tell me about it?"

Craig shrugged. "Some years ago, he was terrorising the Saturnians and I happened to arrive quite by accident. Those poor creatures were being treated badly and forced into slave labour, because Tyrus planned to take over their planet. He killed a few of them to make a point and as you know, they are few in number. The Saturnians are our allies and also scientists, not labourers. I got involved and managed to kill one of the beings. It was an accident, but Tyrus took an instant dislike to me and he keeps trying to justify what he did. It doesn't bother him that he killed some of the Saturnians, but when he got a taste of his own medicine, he tried to kill me."

"Hmm, you do have a talent in that area, I must admit."

"What do you mean?" asked the confused explorer.

"You have a way of stopping takeovers of planets."

Craig stared into her red eyes and averted his gaze. He moved over to the observation window and stared moodily outside. His thoughts returned to the time he, Constance and many of their friends had managed to stop Andocia from taking over Earth by force. There was certainly no love lost between him and the woman he considered his most dangerous enemy.

Andocia joined him and admired the view. "There's nothing like the view out in Space, is there?"

"No, nothing compares with it. Are you meeting Tyrus at some rendezvous point, or are you taking me directly to Tyrome?"

"Tyrus and Petrovsky will meet up with us near Tyrome."

She tried to engage him in further conversation, but he ignored her and she went to speak to her pilot.

The spacecraft hovered above Tyrome and Tyrus materialised in the ship. Not long afterwards, Colonel Petrovsky docked in the landing bay and came to join them. The Russian nodded curtly to Andocia and she smiled.

"Good day, Andocia. I see you've brought our friend here."

"Just as I promised. However, I would like to speak to both you and Tyrus alone for a moment."

Tyrus looked at Craig. "When can I take him?" he asked eagerly.

"Patience Tyrus," admonished Andocia. "Colonel Petrovsky and I hatched this little scheme, so you have to wait your turn. When he gets what he wants from Carter, then it will be your turn. Be warned though, I don't want him killed, but I'll allow you to make his life uncomfortable."

Craig glared at Andocia, but kept quiet.

"I thought you were finished with him," grumbled Tyrus.

"No, not yet because he disobeyed my orders. If he wishes to honour the agreement and see his wife freed, he'll do as I ask next time. If not, maybe I'll allow you to terminate him, after he watches his wife die. I have things to do and I am on a tight schedule. I'm going to put Carter somewhere safe for now, because we need to have a discussion."

She signalled to some of her security people and they took him to one of the guest rooms and locked the door.

Hours passed with nothing happening and Craig was anxious. He knew his life was literally in Andocia's hands and was under no illusions about Tyrus. Much later, the door opened and Petrovsky and Tyrus entered. The Colonel was beaming from ear to ear.

"Ah Comrade, at last I have you just where I want you. Andocia told me your wife is expecting a baby. May I be the first to offer my congratulations." Petrovsky extended his hand. Craig stared dubiously at it, then reluctantly allowed the Russian to shake it.

"This is a very fortunate event I must admit," Petrovsky gloated. "It gives you the right motivation in this situation if you want to be reconciled with your wife and unborn baby. Andocia mentioned you would be willing to co-operate with us every step of the way. Is this correct?"

"Yes, I'll do whatever you and Tyrus want of me, but I don't have to like it," grumbled Craig.

"Excellent! I'd be a fool if I didn't derive some morbid pleasure from your capitulation. I can see you squirming like a worm on a hook and it pleases me."

Tyrus interjected. "I assure you his mind is in turmoil. It's like boiling larvae inside his head."

"Fine, have your fun, both of you, but just get on with it!" he replied through gritted teeth.

"Andocia mentioned you have some top-secret information for me. Where is it?" asked Petrovsky, licking his lips in anticipation.

"Petrovsky, can we have a little privacy? What I have for you doesn't concern Tyrus."

"Leave us alone for a while Tyrus! I'll call you when we're done here."

The silver being glared at the two men and left.

5

The explorer reached into his trouser pocket and withdrew a data drive and a small square metal box which he handed to Petrovsky. The Russian held it up to the light and examined it.

"What kind of information is stored on this?"

"It's the complete blueprint of our new cloaking device, which is currently in production. There's a speed control device inside there as well. We have done tests and our crafts are much faster than they were before. As we improve the designs of our spaceships, the speed can be increased as well. I know you, Andocia and Tyrus are friends right now, but once you've all got what you need from me, they will be your enemies again. It doesn't hurt to have an unfair advantage over them that they know nothing about, don't you agree?"

Petrovsky smiled triumphantly. "Wow, you took quite a chance getting this. It sounds very impressive! I'm sure you understand I'll have to let our technicians examine it to see if it is real. I can't just take your word for it. When my government are satisfied it's genuine, only then will your obligation to me end."

"I understand your caution. My country would do the same if something like this was given to us," Craig replied.

"Have these devices been placed on any of your ships yet?" Petrovsky asked.

"As I mentioned, it's still very new technology, but some ships have been equipped with the device and it has been very beneficial so far."

"Does your ship have the device?" he asked slyly.

"Yes."

Colonel Petrovsky rubbed his jaw pensively. "Can you tell me where it is located in your ship?"

"It's on the console, naturally."

"I believe you, but there's a problem. Once this device has been placed in our ships, we'll need to test it and someone has to show us how it works. You have obviously used it, so you will have to teach us."

Craig's mouth dropped open in astonishment. "What are you saying, Petrovsky? Do you honestly expect me to come to Russia with you?"

"It's the only way. If you are present with us, you can help us iron out any kinks. This device sounds too good to be true and I don't want to leave you here with Tyrus, just in case there isn't much left of you when I report back to Andocia. Also, if this is an elaborate plot to make us look foolish, you'll suffer the consequences."

Craig was dumbfounded. "Commander Simms will never give me permission to go with you."

"Then I suggest you don't tell him!"

"That won't work Petrovsky. If I don't tell him and he finds out, I'll be arrested for treason! You know I'm wanted in Russia, just as my country would love to capture you. What guarantee do I have that I'll ever leave Russia again?"

"You have my personal guarantee that no harm will come to you."

"I'm sorry but that isn't enough. How do I know I can trust you?"

Petrovsky shrugged his shoulders. "Think about your wife and unborn child, my friend! If you don't do as I say, they could pay for your stubbornness."

"There's another problem as well. What plausible reason can I give Commander Simms for going to Russia with you? I stole this device and if he finds out I'll definitely be arrested for contravening the Official Secrets Act. If I have to accompany you to Russia, I want my superiors to know about it. That way if something happens to me, they can take official action. I may be forced to help you, but I want my safety guaranteed."

"Let's discuss the matter with Andocia and see what she suggests. I also have to break the news to Tyrus that he has to wait a while longer before he can make your life miserable."

They went back to Andocia and Tyrus.

"Have you finished your discussion now? Can I take him with me?" asked the silver being eagerly.

"Sorry Tyrus but something's come up. I still need Mr Carter for a while. When I'm finished with him, I'll personally deliver him to you."

"When will that be?" Tyrus complained.

"It depends on a number of things. I'll keep in touch through Andocia. You can leave anytime!"

"Just remember I am a part of this deal," Tyrus reminded them. "You promised I can have him and I'm getting impatient."

Andocia glared at him. "Listen Tyrus, we didn't have to include you in this deal. If you don't like the way things are, you can just back out anytime. I'm sure Mr Carter will be relieved, but frankly we don't care about your feelings!"

Tyrus grumbled under his breath and vanished from the ship.

"Okay Petrovsky, what's the problem now?" Andocia asked him. "Aren't you happy with the device that Carter gave you?"

"I'm very happy Andocia, but I need Comrade Carter to install it on one of the ships in Russia. It seems like something we would be very anxious to have, but I don't trust him. If it does all he claims it will do, we would need to test it out. He has the expertise to correct any fault that might appear, as well as train us in the use of this device."

"How long would you need him for?"

"I would estimate about one week to eight days. He has given us a prototype, so if it works, we can copy it. However, he refuses to accompany me to Russia."

"I see his point Colonel. He would be in danger once he arrived there."

Colonel Ivan Petrovsky put his hand over his heart. "I swear to you Andocia, I'll keep him safe. I know he has still not fulfilled his obligation to you or Tyrus – not that I care much about what that idiot thinks, but I would never double cross you!"

Andocia turned to Craig. "He has given his promise and I'm happy with that. I'm prepared to let you go with him to Russia. You'll be in capable hands."

"I'm glad you're satisfied Andocia, but I still have a problem. As I mentioned to Petrovsky, I cannot go without telling my superior about this. If he finds out what I've done, I could lose my job! I love my wife and I would do almost anything for her, but this is treason. I'm prepared to help you, Petrovsky and yes – even Tyrus if I must, but it's not fair for all of you to put my job in jeopardy."

"What do you propose then?" asked Andocia.

"Let me speak to Commander Simms. I'll make him understand the importance of this trip."

"What if he refuses?" Petrovsky enquired.

"He won't. I'll convince him, somehow." Craig assured them.

Andocia looked at Colonel Petrovsky. "What do you think?"

Petrovsky shrugged his shoulders. "Well he cannot tell the good commander that he stole some top secret hardware or he'll be arrested when he returns home anyway. Let him try and convince his boss."

They went to Andocia's communications room and contacted Commander Simms. He answered immediately and scowled at Andocia.

"What do you want?" he snapped.

"Good day Commander Simms," she replied pleasantly. "I have someone who would like to talk to you."

Craig stepped forward and immediately his employer's expression softened.

"Hello Craig. I see you are still with Andocia. Are you okay?"

"I'm fine, thank you Sir."

"How is Constance? Is she well?"

"She was doing fine the last time I saw her."

"Isn't she with you on Andocia's ship?"

"No Sir, she is elsewhere. Commander Simms, I have a problem and I need to discuss it with you urgently. Colonel Petrovsky is here with us as well. I have no easy way of saying this so I'll ask you outright and hope you can keep an open mind."

Commander Simms' smile disappeared. "This sounds serious! Well, out with it, young man."

"Sir as you may remember, I told you that Andocia, Colonel Petrovsky and Tyrus have combined to ask certain things of me in exchange for Constance's well-being. Well, Colonel Petrovsky has requested I go with him to Russia for a few days."

"What? Is he out of his mind?" Simms yelled. "I cannot allow this! Request denied!"

"I understand Sir, but I have no choice. He suggested I just go secretly, but I refuse to betray your trust and that's why I asked Andocia to contact you."

"What does he need you to do in Russia? Will they interrogate you for secret information?"

"No Sir, Petrovsky needs me to help them reprogram the computers on some of their ships. They had a breach in security and caught one of the programmers, but now they don't know who to trust. I can help them to repair some of the damage."

"How long will you be staying there?"

"Approximately a week, according to Petrovsky."

"I want a word with Colonel Petrovsky. Is he there?"

The Russian came forward and saluted. "Good day Commander Simms."

Craig's boss stared witheringly at him. "I want to tell you that I find this request despicable. You are taking advantage of my employee and I don't like it! I will however give my permission, because I love Constance like my own daughter. Craig may accompany you to Russia, but I have some conditions of my own. Firstly, I want to know where he will be staying while he is in Russia, and secondly, I'll be contacting him at least once a day, at different times of the day. If he doesn't answer his phone and it goes to voicemail, I'll be sending out a search and rescue team immediately. Do you understand!"

"I hear you loud and clear, commander. Mr Carter will be staying with me in my flat while he's helping us and you have my solemn promise I'll keep him safe from harm. Your conditions are acceptable and on behalf of Russia, I thank you," replied Colonel Petrovsky. He saluted smartly once more.

But Commander Simms wasn't finished. "Andocia, I don't like you very much, but I want you to make sure that while Craig is in Russia, you take good care of Constance and the baby."

"I mean them no harm, I assure you. As long as Craig does what he's told, she will be safe. In fact, I'll also be contacting Mr Carter once a day to make sure he's in good health. I also have a vested interest in his safety."

"You do indeed, but for different reasons," Simms remarked snidely. "However, I'm glad to hear that."

He turned to Craig and smiled. "Good luck Craig. I'll be in touch."

"Yes Sir. Thank you for understanding."

The screen went dark and Petrovsky was delighted. "That went very well Carter. You think quickly on your feet. I see why you wanted Commander Simms to know your whereabouts. You still don't trust me, but I probably would do the same thing if the tables were turned. Well, time is moving on so I suggest we get ready to leave as soon as possible."

"Wait a moment Petrovsky, I want a word with Andocia – in private."

"Go ahead. I'm just going to get the ship ready for departure. I'll meet you at the hangars."

The Colonel left and Andocia sat down. "What did you want to speak to me about?"

"Please can you fetch Constance from Pluto and take her to your planet. The Plutonians hate everyone, especially humans and Constance is tense and nervous around them. She is still in the first trimester of her pregnancy and she could abort the baby if conditions aren't right. What happens if complications develop? Ideally, she should be on Earth, but you have a fully equipped hospital on your planet that can help her in any emergency. I thought Colonel Petrovsky would be happy when I delivered the device to him and I never expected him to insist I go to Russia with him. Now more time will be wasted before my debt to the three of you is paid. Each day I spend away from Constance is another day where things could go wrong."

"I'll think about it."

"Please Andocia, I would appreciate an answer before I go with Petrovsky. I can't stand not knowing what will happen."

"Okay Craig, I'll do that for you. I'll take her to my planet."

"Thank you Andocia! I had better get my things and join Petrovsky in his ship. I guess I'll be hearing from you soon."

"You can count on it. Keep your phone close to you."

"I will. I'll see you in about one week then."

Craig left Andocia and went to collect his personal effects for the journey to Russia.

Not long afterwards, the Russian spaceship exited from Andocia's mother ship and they headed for Russia. Craig sat in the co-pilot's seat alongside his enemy. Petrovsky was in a good mood and chatted to his companion.

"I hope you packed your overcoat. It's cold in Russia."

"I did include it. I honestly don't know how you can live there. It's always cold."

"It's only cold outside. The dwellings are centrally heated and quite comfortable."

"Petrovsky, something has been bothering me. I just want to know whose idea it was to kidnap my wife and force me to do things against my will?"

The Russian smiled. "I have to take credit for your situation. I devised this clever little plan. Andocia loved it and she contacted Tyrus, knowing how much you despise him."

"It was your idea? I thought Andocia planned it."

"Actually, Andocia wasn't interested in you. I persuaded her to join forces with me. At the time, we didn't know your wife was pregnant. It did present a small complication but it wasn't that important. Women get pregnant all the time. I still find it hard to believe you are married! You know as well as anyone your jobs would keep you apart for months at a time. That can put quite a strain on a marriage."

"Constance and I discussed it and we decided it could work, so we did it. What about you Petrovsky? Have you got somebody waiting for you back in Russia?"

The Russian laughed. "I have a few young ladies I look up from time to time, but no one I feel obliged to get involved with. My motto is to love and leave them and I'm happy with my life at present."

"I suppose it does make life less complicated," Craig agreed.

The Colonel was silent while he did some course corrections and spoke to his companion again. "Can I call you Craig? We will be inseparable for about a week and I feel stupid calling you by your surname. You can call me Ivan if you want to."

Craig shrugged his shoulders. "It doesn't bother me either way, just as long as you don't think it makes us friends. I'm still doing this against my better judgement."

"Thank you… Craig. I was also wondering if I can trust Commander Simms. What if he decides to go back on his word and send someone to rescue you, or your lovely wife?"

"I know my boss very well, Petrovsky… uh… Ivan. I would bet my life he won't do anything to jeopardise this mission. You heard him tell you he loves Constance like his own daughter. He has watched her grow up. General Mark Gregg is the head of the army in America and also a personal friend of his. If he does anything that might cause Constance to come to any harm, the General will make his life miserable."

"Ah, General Gregg is Constance's father, isn't he?"

"Yes. That's why I knew Commander Simms would give me permission to go with you to Russia. He probably fears the General's wrath even more than Andoica's, or yours. General Gregg is a very influential man. You won't encounter any problems while I'm your guest in Russia, unless you break your promise to Commander Simms."

"I find that very reassuring Craig."

A few days later, they arrived in Russia. Ivan landed in their Spacehanger and was greeted by many of the staff. His colleagues looked curiously at Craig and spoke in hushed whispers when the pair had passed by. Petrovsky went to greet his boss, who shook his hand energetically. He stared at the American Space explorer and shook his hand as well.

"Craig, you remember Colonel Trotsky?" Ivan asked.

"Yes I do," The explorer replied.

"It's been a while, Mr Carter. Welcome to Russia!" He turned to his employee. "Ivan, can I speak to you privately for a moment?"

"Yes, of course! I'll just take Mr Carter to the restaurant. He can wait for us there. I'll return shortly and meet you in your office."

The American explorer sat down and ordered a cup of coffee. The waitress brought it to him and he took his time drinking it. Half an hour later, Ivan returned.

"It's getting late now. I'll just take you to my place. We have to get started early tomorrow morning. There's a lot to be done."

Petrovsky walked to the parking lot and unlocked a sleek red helicar. Craig ran his hand tenderly across the smooth paintwork and sighed. "This car must have cost a fortune! I suppose you get paid a great deal of money to afford something this beautiful."

Ivan smiled enigmatically. "I can't complain. I am valued by my employer, just as you are. Also, I am not married, so I can spend much more on myself. I wine and dine pretty ladies often, so I am free to do what I wish, when I wish."

Carter nodded in agreement, climbed in and they rode to the Colonel's flat. Ivan manoeuvred the car onto a landing strip twenty floors up, then drove his car inside and parked. The pair walked down one flight of stairs where Petrovsky stopped at a door and inserted his key card in the slot.

"After you Craig."

The American walked inside and looked around. "This is very nice. A bit minimalist, but very cosy."

Petrovsky locked the door behind him. "I'm out in Space more than at home, but I have everything I need. Please make yourself comfortable."

Carter went to the lounge and sat down on a leather couch. His host handed him a drink and took one for himself. They drank the liquid from the bottle and Petrovsky lifted it in a toast. "To us working together for a while."

They clinked bottles and swallowed the cold brew. Afterwards Ivan took him on a tour of his apartment. There were two bedrooms, each with their own bathroom. The lounge/dining room was quite spacious and there was a table that could seat four people. The kitchen wasn't very big, but everything was well laid out. His freezer was filled with ready prepared meals. There was milk and a few perishables in the fridge.

"My helper comes and cleans once a week. She gets notified when I'm coming home and buys me some fresh produce. If I feel like something special, or I want to entertain a lady friend, I go to one of the nearby restaurants in this complex. I generally have lunch in the canteen at work if I'm there. Well anyway it's getting late now. I'm going to have a shower and then going to bed. Set your alarm for 6H30 tomorrow morning. Sleep well, Craig."

His host left him. Craig went to the window and looked outside. The sky was a dark grey and he could see lights twinkling in the distance. He decided to go to bed as well, so went to his room.

The next morning the two men returned to the Russian Space Control Centre and preparations to install the cloaking device got underway.

6

Meanwhile, back on the Red Planet, Andocia had arrived with Constance.

Mrs Carter was grateful and thanked her hostess.

"I'm doing this as a favour to you and the baby. I would have left you there but as Craig mentioned you could have complications and the Plutonians wouldn't be able to help you. If we had known you were expecting a baby, you would never have been imprisoned on Pluto in the first place. I expect you not to cause any trouble while you are here. Before we go any further, I want to ensure your good behaviour. Let's go to my laboratory before you get settled in your room."

They went to a room and Constance was asked to sit down. A woman entered, carrying a small device which she showed to Mrs Carter.

"This device is an electronic watchdog." Andocia explained. "It is placed around your ankle and locked in place. There's an explosive device inside. If you tamper with the lock, it will explode, killing you instantly. You can do anything you like, even swim with it on as it is waterproof. It contains a locating beacon, so I can track you wherever you go. If you try to escape and manage to steal a ship, the device will detonate the moment you leave the atmosphere. Should someone try to free you, the device will explode, killing everyone on board the rescue craft. It's safe to ride on transport vehicles on the ground. It's very light and comfortable and you won't have any discomfort at all. You have a choice not to wear the watchdog device, but then your freedom will be very limited and I'll place you in a very secure environment. If you co-operate though, you may use all the facilities available to my staff. Your room will be comfortable and have a built-in bathroom. The only non- negotiable part is that you'll be locked up at night. My staff have enough to do without spending their time worrying about you plotting all sorts of things."

"I understand and accept your terms Andocia. I'm just grateful to be away from Pluto."

The "watchdog" was placed on Constance's left ankle and Andocia stood up.

"Excellent! You'll be escorted to your room now and later when you have settled in, I would like you to go to the hospital and have a check-up. Let's see how that baby is doing!"

Later on, a guard fetched Constance. "I've been ordered to take you to the hospital now. Please come with me."

They climbed into a hovercar and fifteen minutes later Constance saw the hospital. The driver parked the vehicle in a nearby parking bay and she followed him to the doctor's rooms. He left her with the receptionist and gave instructions that he should be contacted when he had to return. Mrs Carter waited a while and was then told to go inside.

The doctor shook her hand. "Good day Mrs Carter. I am doctor Brandy Weinhouse. While you are Andocia's guest, I'll be available to help with any problems that may occur. Please get undressed and lie down on that bed over there. You will find a dressing gown on the hook by the door. I'll be with you shortly."

Constance did as she was told and Dr Weinhouse gave her a thorough examination. Afterwards she was taken to the X-ray department where a sonar was done. She returned to the doctor's consulting room.

"Everything looks fine, Mrs Carter. You are eleven weeks pregnant at the moment, so it is still early days."

The doctor questioned her about her health and jotted down notes in her electronic notebook. An hour later she was given pills to help her with nausea, and some vitamin medication to build up her system. She was instructed to return in a month's time for another examination, if she was still on Andocia's planet. Constance hoped she would be home long before then.

Her driver returned and took her back to Andocia's castle. Constance sat on a bench near a fountain and examined the device on her leg. It was black and there were no obvious seams visible that she could prise open. The lock was deeply recessed into the band which was made of toughened silicone. She decided not to tamper with it for the moment and her thoughts turned to her husband who had gone to Russia with Colonel Ivan Petrovsky. She feared for his safety, but Andocia had assured her she was in contact with him every day and he appeared to be fine.

A while later, Andocia sent for her. She joined the woman in her control centre.

"Hello Constance, I was just about to phone Craig and I wondered if you would like to talk to him. I can link up via his mobile device."

"I would love to! Thank you!"

Constance saw his device ringing in Russia and Craig picked it up after the second ring.

"Hello Andocia," he replied.

"Hello Craig. I am checking in as I promised. Is all well over there?"

"Yes, everything is fine. I'm nearly finished here, but I'll let you know when we'll be returning to your planet."

"Excellent! I have someone who is anxious to talk to you. I'll call again tomorrow."

She handed over to Constance, who smiled at her husband. "Hi honey, it's good to hear your voice."

"It's good to see you Constance. Are you well? How is the baby?"

"Everything is fine Craig. I saw a doctor here on Andocia's planet and she was happy with my pregnancy so far. I am now eleven weeks. I miss you so much!"

"I miss you too my angel. Well I had better get back to work. I'll see you soon."

He disconnected and Constance felt a lot better. She nodded to the staff and left.

Three weeks later, Craig and Petrovsky returned to the Red Planet. Constance ran into her husband's arms and kissed him. He kept his arm around his wife's waist and Colonel Petrovsky smiled at Constance. "You are looking well my dear. I just want to have a meeting with Andocia and then I must get some supplies. There is no rest for the wicked and I have a mission to complete. I'll join you for some dinner before I leave."

Craig and Constance went into a secluded part of the garden and sat down.

"I owe you an explanation Constance. You have no idea what this mission was about and I don't want you to get the wrong idea about what happened in Russia. Commander Simms knew about it and gave me his blessing, although reluctantly of course."

Her husband explained what had happened and Constance sighed in relief.

"I didn't know what to think when Andocia told me you were on your way to Russia. That was very clever of you to give them the cloaking device, which was given to us legally anyway. At least Petrovsky is happy and you never gave Russia anything that would have compromised America in any way. I suppose you had to show them how the device worked."

"Yes, that was the plan, but neither Ivan or myself have told Andocia the real reason for the visit. Even though the Colonel is our enemy, he deserves protection from Andocia as well. I still think he had a cheek asking me to go with him to Russia, because their technicians are just as efficient as ours and they would have figured out how the device worked. He just did it because he knew he had me at a disadvantage. Anyway, my debt to him has now been settled."

"Thank you for asking Andocia to bring me back here. It's not ideal of course, but I feel a lot less stressed than I was on Pluto. I may still be in captivity, but at least I can walk around and use all her facilities. I need to remain fit and healthy for our baby's sake."

Craig hugged his wife. "I promise you I'll do anything in my power to get you away from here. I need a day or so to think up a plan and then hopefully we can escape from here and go home."

Constance sighed. "I have to show you something Craig. Andocia isn't stupid. She knows you'll be making plans to escape. I thought about it as well, but I had no contact with you in Russia and we couldn't talk on the linkup because we didn't have any privacy."

His wife pulled up the leg of her jeans and showed him the device. "This is an electronic watchdog device. Andocia said that as long as I stay on the ground, I'll be safe. It has an explosive device and a locator inside. She said if I tampered with it in any way, it would explode. I also can't leave the planet, because once I'm in Space and she cannot track me, the watchdog will explode and kill everyone on board. I've been thinking of a way to disarm the device, but it's too risky. I'm sorry, but escaping isn't an option at the moment. If I hadn't been pregnant, I would still be on Pluto and she would never have brought me here."

"I guess I'll have to go to Tyrome then. I'm not looking forward to being in Tyrus's company."

"I know that, and you still have to do something for Andocia. I hope this will be over soon. I want to live peacefully with you and our baby."

One of Andocia's followers came to call them and they returned to the castle. The threesome enjoyed a sumptuous meal and Petrovsky was in high spirits. He told them he had received a promotion and he had Craig to thank for his good fortune. Carter wished he could punch the man, but he shook his hand instead and congratulated him. After supper, Petrovsky left to begin his mission.

When he had left, Andocia spoke to the couple. "Craig, you have one night to spend with your wife and tomorrow you'll be delivered to Tyrus."

That night they were locked in Constance's room and they made love with quiet intensity. Husband and wife clung to one another, each concerned about the other, but anxious to get this part of the bargain over with.

Early the next morning, Andocia came to fetch Craig. He clung to his wife and reluctantly let her go when their host became impatient. They landed on Tyrome and Craig was taken away to a cell and locked in. Andocia called Tyrus.

"I know you're anxious to begin your experiments, or whatever it is you will be doing, but just a word of warning; you may do whatever you wish to Carter, but don't kill him. I still have a use for him and I want him to be in one piece when I return. You have four days, so use them well."

7

Andocia left and Tyrus went to Craig's cell.

"So now, it's just you and me, Earthling! I must confess I'm disappointed in Andocia. I wanted to kill you so badly, but I'll make you regret the day you ever tangled with me. I've done quite a bit of investigation on your species, so I know just how much electricity to use on you, and there will still be plenty of you left over for Andocia. Do you know what the best part about this is? You have to do whatever I say. If you step out of line, I'll inform Andocia and your precious woman will die. I must admit I'm keen to begin right now, but I have things to prepare, and we'll have a few days at least to enjoy one another's company. I'll leave you alone for the rest of this day, but when the new day dawns, your punishment will begin. Sleep well!"

Craig lay on the bed and closed his eyes, strengthening himself for the ordeal he knew he would face the next day. He slept and dreamt bittersweet dreams about himself and Constance playing with their child in a garden. The child laughed and seemed to be happy, but he couldn't see its face. The images faded away and the door opening roused him.

A silver being came in and set down a tray of food, then left without a word. Carter had no appetite but forced himself to eat. After breakfast he went to the washbasin and splashed cold water on his face to chase away the sleep in his eyes.

Not long afterwards, Tyrus appeared and motioned for Craig to follow him. He took him to his laboratory.

"What devilish scheme have you got planned, Tyrus?"

"Why, are you going to object? I could of course contact Andocia if you want me to."

"I know I have to do what you ask, but surely I'm entitled to know what I'm letting myself in for."

"I suppose that's reasonable. Today I just want to run some tests. I don't often get a human subject to study and I would like to expand my knowledge of your race."

The rest of the day was spent with Craig being used as a human guinea pig. He was poked and prodded, but he put up with it. When he was returned to his room and locked in, Craig was exhausted and fell asleep almost immediately.

The next day was a different story though. Tyrus paid particular attention to his neurological functions and by the end of the day, his head was splitting from a painful headache. He was ordered to swallow some medication and hoped it wouldn't poison him.

On the third day, the explorer's pain threshold was expounded on and he began to hate Tyrus more and more with every jolt of electricity that flowed through his body. Time and time again he thought he would pass out, but he kept focused on Constance and their unborn child and managed to make it through.

By the time the fourth day had begun, he refused to participate in the experiments. Tyrus didn't seem to mind, but spent the day ridiculing him in front of the others. He was ordered to perform menial tasks and the creatures enjoyed every minute of it. Every time Tyrus goaded him, he refused to rise to the challenge. As he lay in his cell that night, he wondered what the next day would hold.

On the fifth day, Tyrus brought in his breakfast.

"Andocia has contacted me and she should be here about lunchtime. I wish I could keep you longer, but it seems she's anxious to have you back. I'm very pleased with the experiments I did on you. I have learnt a good deal more than I knew about human anatomy and I enjoyed causing you discomfort. This was quite a novel experience. My most dangerous adversary was subject to my demands. I must say that in the light of this, I'm glad you and the lovely Miss Gregg were united, for I have her to thank."

"I'm glad you had an enjoyable time," he replied sarcastically. "As far as I'm concerned, I've fulfilled my part of the bargain with you."

"I'll fetch you later, when Andocia arrives."

Tyrus closed and locked the door behind him and Craig winced in pain. He lay down on the bed again and tried to rest.

He was startled by the door opening, and when he looked at his watch, he realised that several hours had passed. He yawned and sat up. Tyrus escorted him to the landing pad and he walked towards the trident ship that waited for him, and climbed aboard. They lifted off vertically and soon Tyrome was just a speck in the distance.

They rendezvoused with Andocia's ship and he went to join her. She paid close attention to him, but couldn't see any sign of ill treatment. However, when Craig undid his shirtsleeve to rub his arm, the woman noticed it was full of purplish blotches. When Craig moved around, she also noticed he walked stiffly.

"All right, time is getting short, so let me tell you what I want from you. I've had another flask of liquid made up and this time I want you to finish the job on Tanus."

"Andocia, don't be ridiculous! Tanus won't fall for that now, not when she has been forewarned. If I show my face on the White Planet, she'll have me locked up. I won't even get close to her."

"You don't need to see her to administer the liquid. All you have to do is pour this into her water supply. I have had a much more concentrated version made up and it should put everything and everyone who drinks the water into a deep sleep. You won't be able to approach her castle directly, but I'll drop you off on the far side of her planet. You will have two days in which to complete this task. When I return to fetch you, everyone had better be asleep, or Constance will die. If you fail this time, there will be no second chances."

Craig sat down on a chair. "Andocia, your own followers could perform that task just as well as me. Couldn't you send one of them to do it? Surely you must have something else I could do for you."

"No, I want you to know you were responsible for her defeat all the rest of your days. In return, you'll have your wife back and you can bring your child up knowing I won't trouble you again. The choice is yours – your wife's life and that of your unborn child in exchange for the life of someone you hardly know. Choose now – I won't ask you again."

Craig glared at the woman he disliked so much.

"All right, you win! I have no choice in the matter. I hope you realise just how much I hate you for making me do this."

Andocia was unaffected and began making the relevant plans. The ship headed towards the blue universe. Carter was placed under heavy guard and wasn't left alone for a second.

Just before they made the jump however, the co-pilot hurried to Andocia and whispered something in her ear. The devilish woman was furious and Craig was puzzled.

"Is something wrong?" he wanted to know.

"I'll say! It seems Tanus is going to have to wait for a while, because something is wrong with this ship. I'll need to get another one, but I'm going to lose valuable time."

Despite his situation, Craig smiled and she rounded on him furiously.

"Don't think you're off the hook yet, Carter. I'll put my plan into action later and you will do the honours. I've been instructed to get off this ship and return home in one of the smaller crafts on board. It seems this ship will survive the journey back to my planet, but it has to be done with a minimal amount of people. Something is wrong with the life support system. You and I will undertake this journey together because this spaceship will have to travel slowly in order to consume the minimal amount of power. I want to get this over and done with soon. Only when Tanus is safely out of the way can I relax."

They went to another ship and the technicians on board checked it thoroughly, then Craig and Andocia boarded the craft and headed for the Red Planet. They arrived back and headed to the hangar to get another ship. While the technicians were checking the ship, Craig asked if he could see Constance. He was given permission and went to find her.

She rushed into his arms and he kissed her.

"Oh Craig, I'm glad to see you. How did it go with Tyrus?"

"It wasn't pleasant and I'm pleased it's over now."

Constance looked at him and sighed. "I suppose Andocia isn't going to let us go home anytime soon, is she?"

"No, I guess not. She has something planned for me, but her ship malfunctioned and she had to return home to get another one. I'll do what she wants me to and then we can go home and hopefully that will be the end of it."

Constance cupped her husband's chin in her hand and made him look at her. "Oh Craig, what does she want you to do?"

"Oh darling, I have to betray Tanus and make her Andocia's prisoner."

"But that's impossible surely!"

Craig shook his head and held his wife tightly. "No, it isn't! I wasn't completely honest with you the last time we spoke. Andocia has developed a formula that can place Tanus in a coma almost indefinitely. I went against Andocia and confessed this to Tanus before, because I got cold feet. Well Tanus had it examined and it's very powerful. She was understandably angry with me for having the audacity to land on the White Planet with such a dangerous item, but she destroyed it and let me go. There's a lot more to the story, but suffice it to say Andocia has redoubled her efforts and made an even more concentrated form of this liquid. When her technicians have finished checking the new ship, I'll be forced to take it and pour the liquid into the water on Tanus's planet. Darling, if I don't do as she says, she'll kill you and our baby. Right now, I have no choice and we both know it."

Constance reeled back as though she had been struck in the face. "Craig, Tanus is our friend! If you do this thing, nothing will be the same ever again. We both know Andocia's ultimate plan is domination of all the planets in both universes. Without Tanus to oppose her, she'll achieve that."

"I know," he replied miserably. "I'm hoping for some kind of miracle, but I don't think I'll get one."

While they waited for Andocia, the couple occupied themselves by going for a short walk. One of Andocia's employees came and called Craig. He took his wife in his arms and kissed her tenderly. "Take care of yourself my angel! I'll be back before you even miss me, and then we can go home."

"Goodbye Craig. Please be careful!"

He smiled sadly and waved to his wife.

8

Craig and Andocia had been travelling for about two hours, when the ship lurched suddenly.

"What was that?" Craig asked.

"I don't know! Everything seems fine and nothing has malfunctioned."

Carter looked outside, but everything seemed normal. "Did a stray meteorite hit us?"

Andocia checked the hull of the ship, but it hadn't been compromised. They continued on their journey.

Suddenly Andocia swerved violently and Craig grunted when he slammed his wrist on the armrest of the co-pilot's chair.

"Did you see that?!" she exclaimed suddenly.

He twisted in his seat and looked above the ship. "Something flew past us, but I don't know what it was."

"Nothing showed up on my screen! It just appeared out of nowhere!"

The computer beeped. <Warning, unidentified planet nearby.>

Andocia called up a map of the universes and looked at it. She shook her head in disbelief. "Look at this map Craig! I don't recognise any of these planets."

The explorer looked disbelievingly at the display. "Neither do I. Wait, give me a minute!"

He studied the map of the universe and noticed the positions of the planets. The sky around them was black, so he deduced they were in the Milky Way.

Several planets looked like the ones he recognised, but some of the names were different. He had a sinking feeling in his stomach and asked the computer to identify the planets he recognised. Most still remained the same, but he couldn't find Earth on the map at all.

"What year is this?" he asked the computer.

<4500 A.D.> The computer replied.

"Where is Earth located?"

<There is no such planet in this universe! Earth was destroyed in the year 4250.>

"Synchronise maps for 4000 A.D. onto present chart."

The maps were placed on top of one another. The blue one was dated 4000 A.D. and the red one showed the present universe. An arrow began flashing and pointed to the planet nearby.

"Andocia, look at this! The planet over there is known as Saurus, but on the other map, it is named Darr. I don't know what happened, but we have somehow travelled into the future. We are currently 500 years ahead of our own time! I know that in our time, Darr is an uninhabited planet." Carter spoke to the computer again. "Give me a report on Saurus."

<Saurus is inhabited by various life forms. The air is breathable and safe for human occupation. Humans co-exist with other species on this planet. The temperature is 26° Centigrade and it is sunny today.>

Andocia looked dazed. "How is this possible?! More importantly, how do we get back to our own universes?"

"I don't know, but let's concentrate on one thing at a time. I suggest we scan the planet Saurus and see if we can find a safe place to land. We can't just fly around aimlessly without a plan. I have no idea if there are even any Space stations here where we can get fuel and supplies. We have to conserve what we have. I don't want to be stuck here forever."

Craig took control of the ship and they glided closer to the planet known as Saurus.

"Scanners on," he ordered the computer. "Scan entire planet."

A diagram showed up on the console and they watched as it panned from side to side. Andocia read the information as it began to appear on the screen.

"There are a number of rivers on this planet. Almost all are safe to drink. I see a number of life forms, but I cannot make out what they are at this height. There is dense vegetation everywhere so this planet is flourishing. I cannot make out any buildings because of the dense growth. Must we ask for permission to land?"

Craig shook his head. "No, I don't think we should. There may be humans here but I don't know if they are friendly. If we announce our presence, we could be in trouble. I'll try to find somewhere safe to land and we'll take it from there. I don't suppose you have a laser gun handy?" he asked hopefully.

"No, why would I need something like that?"

Craig sighed. "You have powers, but I have nothing to defend myself with. Maybe I'll find something to use down there."

Carter flew closer to the planet and checked for any high buildings, but he found nothing, except high mountains. He checked the thermal imaging and found a number of hot spots where some life forms seemed to be moving around, then flew away, and settled in a less populated area, far from the figures he had seen. The planet had many trees and he coaxed the spaceship into the thick of them. The vegetation was dense and they concealed the ship with vines and branches.

"What should we do now?" Andocia asked curiously.

"We have to make our way to where the inhabitants live and try to find out if they know a way for us to return home again. I hope they are friendly!"

They began walking in the direction where the thermal images had shown life existed. As they walked, several pairs of eyes peered from the bushes and watched their progress with great interest.

The twosome walked along a dirt path and stared at the bushes and trees around them. Craig stopped from time to time and examined the ground beneath their feet. It felt soft and slightly damp to the touch. The trees were made of real wood as far as he could tell, and the leaves were soft and springy. Some of the trees contained fruit and he picked an orange orb off one of them.

"What are you going to do with that?" Andocia asked.

"I'd like to eat it, but I'm not sure if it's poisonous or not. It looks like an orange, but appearances could be deceiving." He examined it, then handed it to Andocia. "Here, maybe you should try it. If it's poisonous, you'll just get sick, but I could die."

His companion glared at him. "Really! How considerate of you," she replied sarcastically, but she took the fruit anyway. Carter looked anxiously at her as she peeled the fruit and broke segments off. The juice ran down her arm and she wiped it off on the grass. He stared mesmerised at her as she began to eat the juicy fruit.

"Does it taste okay?"

Andocia gagged and clutched at her throat. His eyes opened wide and he took a few steps back from her, when she began to laugh. "I wish you could have seen your face! I'm just joking; it tastes delicious! Here, have some."

Craig glared at her. "Very funny! I think I just aged ten years."

"You deserved it," she replied laughingly.

They shared the orange and continued their journey.

Something rustled in the bushes and Craig stood still. A cute little rabbit bounded out of the bushes and stopped in its tracks when it saw that it wasn't alone. Its tiny whiskers twitched and it began to come slowly towards them. Carter stretched out his hand towards it.

"Oh look Andocia, it seems to be tame."

Suddenly a man came out of the bushes and threw a stone at the rabbit, chasing it away.

"I wouldn't do that if I were you! That little beast would take your hand off with one bite! I haven't seen you around here before."

"Er no, we've just arrived."

The man smiled. "Oh. Welcome to Saurus. My name is Galen."

"I'm Craig, and my companion is Andocia."

The man looked curiously at Andocia, but said nothing.

"You seem to be lost. Haven't you been shown to your section?"

"We were given directions, but we got lost." Craig lied. "Perhaps if you could give us the names again, we can find where we should go."

"Hillvale is just a few kilometres down this path. Meadowbrooke is further away, past those hills in the distance. Forestown is to the left of us, about thirty minutes' walk. Pine valley is quite a distance away. It will take you a day's travel to get there, but you would need transport. The paths here are dangerous and you need a guide."

Craig looked searchingly at Andocia and spoke telepathically to her. "We have to decide where to go. Which one should we choose?"

"Let's go for Meadowbrooke then. Until we know what we are up against, we don't want to stay too close, or venture too far away."

"We have to go to Meadowbrooke! Thank you for your help," Craig replied politely.

They began to walk in the direction Galen had pointed out to them, when he came hurrying after them. "Wait a minute, please!"

They stopped and he looked searchingly at them. "You haven't been assigned to any sector, have you? If you had been interviewed, they would have told you about the perils of this place. No one knows you are here, do they?"

Craig felt Andocia tense up beside him and he put his hand warningly on her arm. He decided to take a chance.

"Galen I'm sorry for misleading you, but we landed here in secret a while ago. We have somehow become lost and we need to try and get our bearings before we can move on."

"Have you come from outer Space?" he asked excitedly.

"Yes," Craig replied.

The man looked up at the sky. "I knew it! Our minders are constantly telling us there is no such thing as Spacetravel, but I was sure there are other worlds besides ours."

"Many worlds, and at least two other universes we know of exist out there in space. If your minders are trying to convince you no other planets exist, I suggest you keep quiet and not share this knowledge with anyone until you have positive proof. Andocia and I would appreciate complete secrecy, otherwise you might be asking for trouble, and we'll also be in danger."

Galen looked around furtively. "Speaking of danger, it is getting late. If no one knows about your existence, you had better come with me to my home. You won't last a day out here without help. I live in Hillvale with my woman."

"Thank you. We appreciate your help," Andocia replied.

Their companion nodded. "Follow me please."

They had been travelling for ten minutes, when Craig heard a sound. Galen had also heard it and he pointed to the bushes. "Quickly, hide there. One of the sentries is coming!"

The pair hid behind a tree and a huge shadow fell across the path. Galen stood his ground and a large grizzly bear approached. He walked on two legs and a crossbow was slung over his shoulders. Galen bowed politely.

"Greetings Bruno."

"Galen! It's getting late. Soon it will be dark and you know you have a curfew."

"I apologise. I didn't realize what the time is."

"Carry on then!"

Galen bowed again and continued walking. Craig and Andocia stared wide-eyed at the bear's departing back.

"Was I imagining that?" Andocia asked.

"No, he really spoke. This place is weird!"

They fell into step with Galen who didn't seem at all surprised he had spoken to a bear.

Further on they saw a number of people milling about. Someone started walking up to Galen and Craig gently pushed Andocia behind a tree. He disappeared into the shadows and returned with a dress he had stolen off a line nearby.

"Here, put this on, Andocia. You'll stand out in a crowd and I don't want to be discovered. We may never leave this place alive."

She pulled the long dress over her head and tied the cord around her waist. There was a hood attached to it and she covered her head.

A woman approached Galen and clasped his hands firmly. "I was worried about you! Supper is ready and the guards seem restless tonight. We don't want to antagonise them."

"Daphne, I found some travellers in the woods. Come, let's go inside quickly and I'll explain everything to you."

He gestured for Craig and Andocia to approach and they hurried inside.

Daphne stared at the pair and wrung her hands miserably. "Where do they come from? Have they been assigned to Hillvale?"

"No, my dear, they are strangers from another place. They were lost and I found them wandering in the woods, so I brought them here. No one knows about them."

"If our minders find out about them, we'll be punished for harbouring fugitives."

"They won't find out. We must help them – it is our duty."

Craig leaned forward. "Please don't upset yourself, Daphne. My companion and I don't plan on staying here very long. I have to calculate a way to return to our homes and I just need a few days to think about this."

Galen went into another room and brought Craig a set of clothing. "Here Craig, you are about my size. Put these on. Your clothing is very strange and someone will get suspicious. I see you have found something for your companion already. You may change in our bedroom if you wish."

The explorer went into the room and closed the door. He looked around, but there wasn't much to see. There was a bed that rested on a wooden frame, and tables on either side of the bed. A small chest of drawers stood in a corner and there was a cracked mirror hanging on the wall. A wardrobe stood at the opposite end of the room and Craig couldn't resist looking inside. He saw a few brown dresses belonging to Daphne and some shirts and pants similar to the ones he was now wearing. There was no jewellery, except for a tortoiseshell clip which obviously belonged to Daphne. Two sets of brushes and combs stood on the chest of drawers.

He joined the others in the small sitting room and Daphne went to make something to drink. Andocia offered to help her and she watched as the woman put an old-fashioned kettle on the coal stove and waited for it to heat up. As she made the tea, Daphne questioned her.

"Where exactly do you come from? It is far away? There are other planets I believe, but we know nothing about them."

"It's really far away. I don't know how to explain it to you. You seem like kind, simple folk and you wouldn't understand."

"Do you come from beyond the stars?"

"Yes we do. We are Spacetravellers."

Daphne's eyes lit up in excitement. "How I wish I could go up in your ship with you! I would love to see what exists beyond Saurus."

Andocia smiled and took the tray from their hostess. "Let me carry this for you."

The foursome spoke for a while. Galen and Daphne were very curious and questioned their guests about their origins, but both Craig and Andocia told them only what they felt the couple should know. It got steadily darker and the lights came on. Daphne yawned and stood up. "Forgive me but I'm tired and it is getting late. We have a busy day tomorrow, but you are welcome to stay up later if you wish. I have made up a bed for you in this alcove. If you wish to freshen up, the bathroom is just along the passageway."

Craig and Andocia went into the alcove and saw a double bed mattress on the floor. A floral duvet and fluffy pillows looked very welcoming, but they stared uneasily at one another.

"Is something wrong?" Daphne asked.

"I'm sorry, but we are not… together," Andocia explained.

Daphne's face coloured in embarrassment. "I apologise! You travelled together, so I… we just assumed you were… uh… you know!"

"I'm sorry, we should have explained," Craig replied. "We did travel together, but we're not a couple. If you have another blanket, I would be happy to sleep on your couch, if that's okay with you."

Daphne nodded and went to fetch another blanket. Craig took one of the pillows off the bed and placed it on the couch. Galen waited until his mate had brought another blanket and they headed for their bedroom.

"Well good night. Sleep well. Just a word of warning though. Don't leave the house during the night because vicious creatures roam the area and you wouldn't be safe."

He went into his bedroom and pulled a curtain across the entrance of the room.

They waited a while until there was no sound from the bedroom and then Andocia motioned him outside. There was a small porch outside the front door. They sat down on the step and spoke quietly. The lights in the house had switched off, but the stars were bright and they could see one another clearly.

"Craig, these people seem very kind, but I'm worried. We haven't seen much of this place, but it creeps me out. How long do you think it will take you to figure out a way for us to return home?"

"I don't know, Andocia. I have to get back to the ship and figure this out, but I want to know more about this place before I attempt anything. When I'm ready to go to the ship, I'll have to do it at night. I don't want to risk someone seeing me during the day and reporting us to some higher power. We know so little about these people. They aren't savages though. The lights are solar powered and they have running water so someone has to be in charge of this place. I'm still freaked out about that bear and I'm wondering what other strange beings inhabit this place. There are no electronic devices anywhere."

"Do you really believe someone is in charge of this planet?"

"Someone has to be! A talking bear is not normal! Someone or something must have created it. Where do the humans come from? How do we know unless we try to find out more?"

Craig took his mobile device out of his pocket and switched it on. "Luckily I charged it before we landed here, so the battery should last for a week or more if I'm careful."

Andocia looked strangely at him. "There's no signal here! How are you going to get help?"

"I don't intend using it for that. No one will hear us. We must be millions of miles away from our homes. I've put it on silent mode. Some of the functions will work though. I'm particularly interested in using the camera."

He pressed the camera icon. "Smile, Andocia!"

She smiled, but it was more of a grimace and Craig took the picture. He went into his photo gallery and the picture was as clear as daylight.

"It works! I'm going to take as many pictures as I can. When we return to our homes, this can be stored for future knowledge. Maybe we can figure out how we ended up here, and prevent it happening to others."

Andocia yawned. "I think we have had enough excitement for today. I'm going to sleep."

"I'm tired too. Let's go inside."

Andocia climbed into the bed and Craig lay on the couch. He looked up at the ceiling and thought about his wife.

"I wonder how you are Constance. I miss you! I have to figure out a way to get back to our own time period. I need you so much!"

He closed his eyes and was soon fast asleep.

The next morning, he woke suddenly. He had been dreaming about being chased by Tyrus and looked around, but nothing stirred. Daphne came into the living room.

"Good morning! I see you're awake. I've made you some breakfast."

Andocia sat up and rubbed her eyes. "That smells delicious! Is it bacon and eggs?"

"Yes. Come and eat before it gets cold."

They sat down at the dining room table and Andocia ate ravenously. "I don't remember when last I ate bacon and eggs!"

Craig also scooped the food up and groaned with pleasure. "This is delicious!"

Daphne offered them seconds and they ate hungrily. Afterwards, they realised Galen wasn't around.

"He's gone to work in the fields but he might come home for lunch. I have some chores to do so please excuse me. You're welcome to look around, but be careful! Most of the other beings are tolerant towards us. Just don't antagonise them. Stay nearby and try to blend in."

Craig and Andocia went outside. They saw other humans in the distance. Some were watering the ground, while others were planting seeds. Someone else had an ox tied to a plough and they were ploughing the land.

"That's something I haven't seen in a while," Andocia commented. "Those people are farmers. Most of the things we have growing now are cultivated by special machines."

"Does it bring back memories of your childhood?" Craig asked curiously.

"Yes, it does, but that was a long time ago."

"Where should we begin exploring?" Craig asked. "I don't want to go near the spaceship just yet."

"Let's take a walk to Meadowbrooke. It doesn't seem to be far away."

They set off towards Meadowbrooke, but Craig stopped when they were in a thicket of trees. "I feel naked without a weapon! I'm going to get a stick."

He went to a tree and found a strong branch, but he tugged it and it refused to break off.

"Andocia, can I have a little help here!"

She looked around but nothing could be seen, so she extended her finger and a red beam sliced the branch off. He thanked her and they continued on their way.

When they had been walking for a while, Andocia wiped her sweaty forehead. "I'm thirsty! I hear a river just over this hill."

They knelt by the river, but Craig refused to drink. "You first Andocia. It looks clean, but I don't want to take any chances."

She cupped the water in her hands and drank deeply. "It's deliciously cold. Help yourself."

He drank his fill and they continued.

The pair hadn't gone far before they heard a sound.

"That sounds like a cat meowing. It came from that tree over there!"

Craig began walking to it, when Andocia cautioned him. "Remember what Galen said!"

He looked up and a pair of green eyes met his. The cat meowed again and started climbing down the tree. Craig backed away and the animal began to purr. Its fur shone blue in the sunlight. The cat came up to him and rubbed its head on his jeans leg and the man stood rooted to the spot and pointed wordlessly to the rear end of the animal. The front end was definitely that of a cat, but the bottom half of its body looked like a peacock, with a large and impressive tail, which opened like a fan.

"She won't harm you! That's my pet, Mia."

A young girl about ten years old, approached them and the creature jumped into her arms.

Andocia smiled at the girl. "Hello dear, and what's your name?"

"Alyssa," she replied.

She looked at the two people curiously. "Are you new here? I don't remember seeing either of you before."

"We arrived yesterday afternoon," Craig replied. "We are staying with friends in Hillvale until we get settled."

The girl tucked a lock of light brown hair behind her ear. "Oh yes, you must be the newcomers our minders are talking about."

Mia began to meow and she pawed her mistress. Alyssa smiled at her. "Yes Mia, I know you told me strangers had arrived." She giggled and turned to the two newcomers.

"I'm sorry, please excuse Mia. She's just curious!"

Craig looked at the young girl. "I'm sorry but did you just speak verbally to your pet?"

Alyssa looked strangely at the two people. "Yes, we can all communicate with one another. Our minders talk to us all the time! Mia thinks you are a strange couple. How did you get your green skin, ma'am?"

Andocia wasn't sure what to say and Craig answered. "It was a freak accident and she got covered in green paint. It soaked into her skin and wouldn't wash out."

"Are you both human?" she asked.

"That's a strange question to ask," Craig replied. "Yes, we are human. Are you?"

She seemed to find the question funny and laughed. "Well of course I am!"

Andocia was getting impatient and she smiled at the girl once again. "It was nice meeting you and your friend, Alyssa, but we have to be on our way. We are going to Meadowbrooke and we have to hurry. My friend and I need to find a job so we can settle down and we were hoping something would be available there."

Alyssa looked at Andocia in amazement. "Why would you need to do that? Usually, the minders interview the newcomers and then place them where they feel their skills could be most useful."

Craig realised they had made a mistake and he quickly covered it up. He turned to Andocia and shook his head. "See, I told you they would find us something to do, but you are always so impatient! We have only been here one day and the minders are so busy, they probably didn't have time to explain things to us."

Andocia pretended to be embarrassed. "Oh dear, I'm impetuous at the best of times. Craig is right of course. Do you think they would mind if we just visited Meadowbrooke, or do we need permission?"

Alyssa shrugged her shoulders. "I don't know! I suppose it would be okay. My family often travel to Meadowbrooke. My aunt lives there."

Craig and Andocia waved to the girl and her pet and walked away. When they were out of earshot, Andocia turned to him. "I can't believe you spun her such a ridiculous story!"

"You mean about the colour of your skin? Alyssa seems too curious for my liking and neither of us expected that question. I just said the first thing that came into my head. What should I have told her Andocia? The truth? What is the truth anyway? You and I have been enemies for a long time now and you know everything about me, but I know nothing about you, or your origins. I just know you were human once, but not anymore. Every day we stay here increases the danger for us. You heard what Alyssa said! They know we are here. I'm just wondering why no one has investigated."

In a tree high above them, a bird sat and listened to their conversation. The bird was about the size of an eagle and had white wings, but the body was that of a female human. Her feet were claws which gripped onto the tree branch and her arms were attached to the wings. She waited for the pair to move away, then spread her wings and flew silently away.

Craig and Andocia stopped for a moment and looked up at the sky.

"Craig, we had better hurry if we are going to reach Meadowbrooke before lunchtime. We have to get back to Hillvale before dark if we want to survive."

"I agree. Andocia, I have to get to the spaceship tonight and try to figure out a way to get back to our time period. Each hour that passes makes me more uneasy."

They hadn't gone much further before a growl disturbed them. Craig stopped and held his stick tightly. A dog came out of the thicket of trees and looked at them. It sat down on its haunches and didn't approach.

"This is something I recognise!" Craig whispered. "It's an Alsatian."

"Not a very friendly one," Andocia cautioned.

The dog stood up and sniffed the air, opened its mouth and growled. Craig and Andocia gasped when they saw its teeth. The animal had two sets of top and two sets of bottom teeth. They were very long and razor sharp. The fur on its back began to rise and suddenly it launched itself at the pair of them. Instinctively Andocia shrank back, but Craig ran towards the vicious animal and hit it hard across its chest. It fell to the ground and started to get up again, but Carter had wounded it and a jagged crimson line formed across the front of the beast. Despite its injury, it managed to get up and head for him again. He hit it across its muzzle and it shook its head, but kept on coming. Andocia reacted swiftly and slammed it backwards against a tree. Both of them heard bones crunching as the beast's back broke. It lay helpless on the ground and a mournful howl escaped from its throat.

"Andocia, finish it before it calls the entire neighbourhood!"

She aimed her finger at the beast's head and a perfect, round hole appeared in its forehead. It slumped down and didn't move again.

They ran from the dead animal and didn't stop until they had reached a dense part of the forest. In the distance, they could hear the shouts of beings who had discovered the body of the dog. The twosome got up and ran away, putting as much distance between themselves and the search party which had obviously been formed. Hours later they made their way back to Hillvale. It had become too late to explore further and they decided it would be safer to return to their hosts.

9

The pair arrived back at Galen's house just before suppertime. Craig examined his borrowed clothing, which was torn and dirty. He had a number of cuts and bruises on his hands and feet. Andocia's dress was torn, but she was unhurt. Daphne was alone at the house and she looked curiously at her two guests.

"What happened to you both?" she asked.

"We had an encounter with a vicious dog," Andocia explained.

Daphne raised her eyebrows in enquiry. "I heard there was some sort of disturbance in the woods today. Give me your dress Andocia and I'll wash and mend it for you. Craig, you and Andocia should get cleaned up before Galen gets home and I'll do the same for your clothes. Galen can lend you another pair of trousers and a shirt."

Galen was quiet while they were eating their dinner. Afterwards he mentioned the incident in the woods.

"I just want to know if either of you were responsible for the death of a beast in the woods today. I heard Bruno discussing it with some of the other sentries."

"I'm sorry Galen! We killed it, but it was in self-defence." Craig replied. "It attacked us first."

"I see! You don't have to explain. The sentries have been after that beast for quite some time now. It has killed a number of animals and also a child from a neighbouring village. Sometimes the higher powers mess up and create mutants. That beast was one of them."

"Higher powers? What do you mean Galen?"

Galen looked frightened. "I don't know who or what they are! I only know our minders are in awe of them. We never see them! We owe you our gratitude, but none of us are warriors, only simple folk. The injuries on the creature were caused by someone or something that has incredible fighting skills. So far we have managed to keep your presence here a secret, but I must warn you, our superiors are suspicious and will be combing the cities looking for strangers. A stick covered with the animal's blood was found at the scene and I heard the minders saying that the fingerprints will be scanned into the data base and the identity of the perpetrator will be discovered. Not only that, but strange wounds were also found on the beast and these are being investigated."

Craig and Andocia looked guiltily at one another.

"I'm sorry Galen!" Craig replied contritely. "Trouble seems to follow me wherever I go and I didn't mean to get you involved."

"No one knows that you are both staying with me. I've told no one about this, so we are not in trouble – yet." He turned to Andocia. "I may look like a foolish farmhand Andocia, but I'm not. Obviously it was Craig who injured the beast, but the hole in that animal's head was not his doing. Who or what are you exactly? You certainly aren't human."

Andocia smiled wickedly. "No, I'm not, but trust me, it's better if you don't know."

Craig intervened. "Galen, leave it alone! I don't know what 'higher power' rules here and I don't want to know. The less you know about us, the better. That way, if you are questioned, you won't be able to tell them anything. I think it would be better if we left your home. I have to figure out a way to get back to our own time period soon, so we'll go back to our ship and stay there instead. We will just wait for our clothing to dry."

Galen was concerned. "Craig, you know nothing about the beasts that roam around at night! Rather stay here tonight and leave early in the morning when it begins to get light. I wish we could help you further, but I think you are correct, you both need to leave soon. Things are starting to get complicated."

Craig looked at his companion. "What do you think, Andocia?"

"I agree with you, Craig. I feel we should leave as soon as we possibly can, but Galen is right – we don't know the woods, so we should just spend one more night here."

Their host nodded in agreement. "Well that's settled then! Daphne can make us something to drink and if you don't mind I have a few questions to ask you. I may never speak to a spaceman from another time ever again, so I want to take advantage of this moment."

Andocia sensed their host wanted to speak to Craig alone, so she offered to help Daphne make the drinks.

When they had gone into the kitchen, Galen sat close to Craig on the couch.

"Please forgive my curiosity, but something has been bothering me since the first moment I laid eyes on you and your companion."

"Well as I mentioned before, we aren't a couple. We are just travelling companions. I'm married to another woman and she's expecting our first child."

"What does 'married' mean?"

"It's a ceremony performed by a religious leader whereby a man and a woman are joined together for life. Don't your people have the same custom?"

"No. We are free to mate with whomever we wish. We can stay with one woman our entire lives, or we can mate with as many as we like. Procreation is welcomed here. You said your woman is pregnant. How wonderful for you! No wonder you are anxious to get back to your own time period. Daphne and I haven't been together very long, but I'm confident we'll have children soon enough."

"I'm sure you will."

Galen looked guiltily at the kitchen door, which was partly closed. "Please don't misunderstand me, but why are you with Andocia?" he whispered. "She seems like a strange companion."

"She is very strange companion to have, but she is powerful in our own universes. She lives in one of the universes, and I live in another. Our spaceships are very fast and I travel everywhere, because my job is exploring space. She isn't a friend of mine, but we need one another right now because she doesn't know how to program the computers on board her ship, so I'm the one who will have to get us home again. We landed here by accident and I cannot explain why we travelled through time and came to Saurus."

"But why were you travelling together in the first place?"

Craig smiled. "I'm sorry but I can't tell you that. It's very complicated."

"I understand."

In the kitchen, Daphne was questioning Andocia about the very same thing, but the immortal said very little about their situation. They carried the coffee to the men in the living room. Galen was now sitting in the chair opposite his guest. The four adults drank their beverages in silence and made polite conversation. It got late and Galen and Daphne excused themselves. When the light went out in their bedroom, Andocia stood up. "We should turn in as well. We have to get up early in the morning."

"Andocia, do you think we're safe? What if someone comes in the night to arrest us?"

She laid her hand on his arm and smiled. "I doubt it very much. If there are vicious beasts in the woods, why would anyone risk their lives to come and get us at night? Just before sunrise will be the perfect time, I'm sure of it. I estimate it'll take us about half an hour to reach our ship. As long as we're inside before sun up, we should be safe."

They went to bed, but Craig lay awake in the darkness, too tense to sleep and was glad when Galen came through to wake them. Daphne put on the kettle for something to drink and when they had washed up, she handed them a parcel of provisions, and the clothes she had washed the previous evening. Daphne hugged them both, while Galen patted them companionably on their backs.

"It was a privilege to meet you both," Galen said. "I wish you luck and hope you'll get back to your universes safely."

Craig was overwhelmed by their hospitality. "I wish there was some way to pay you back for what you have done. You took a great risk helping us, especially as we landed here unintentionally. I hope you don't get into trouble!"

The man smiled and pushed them gently. "Go on, get lost now. Safe journey to you both."

Craig and Andocia went outside and began walking quickly in the direction of their ship. It was still very dark, but the Moon was bright and lit their path enough for them to see where they were going. Each step they took, the sky lightened a bit more. Now and again, Craig doubled back a few metres to check whether anyone was following them, but nothing stirred. They reached the ship and Andocia opened the hatch. They climbed in and Craig sighed with relief when the door closed behind them. Andocia went to the tiny kitchenette and packed the food away in the refrigerator. She came back with a torch and a small gutting knife that their hosts had kindly donated as well.

Carter went to the computer and powered it up. He took out his mobile device and connected it to the machine. The battery bars began to fill up and he downloaded the photographs he had taken secretly of the beings living on Saurus. Andocia came and stood nearby. "How long do you think it will take you to figure out how to get back to our time period?"

"I don't know. I have to take a look at the flight recorder. The idea would be to reverse the process and, in that way return to our previous destination, but it isn't as easy as it sounds! Somehow, a rift developed in Spaceand we were sucked through it. I'm not sure exactly when that occurred. Nor do I know if it's still there."

"If it closed up again, we could be in serious trouble!" Andocia remarked. "We may be trapped forever in the future!"

"Don't say that! Everything and everyone I know is back on Earth. We have to get back!"

He turned his attention back to the computer and began making some notes on the electronic notepad. By lunchtime, he was no closer to solving the problem and he rubbed his tired eyes. His head throbbed from all the concentrating and he went to the medical cabinet and swallowed some tablets. Andocia brought him something to eat from the provisions Daphne had given them. After a short break, he returned to his calculations.

As the day moved on, he made some progress and was beginning to get excited.

"I think I have a good idea what we should do now! I just have to synchronise some of the components and then we should be able to leave this time period. I'm still concerned about the rift in Spacethough! Everything depends on us getting through that hole, but I'm prepared to risk it. Are you Andocia?"

"I guess we have no choice, but we need a plan B just in case. Have you any suggestions?"

"Not right now, but let's tackle one problem at a time. We can only leave at nightfall though, because we don't want to attract unnecessary attention to ourselves."

"I'll leave you to make those calculations then."

Much later, Craig called Andocia. "I've managed to synchronise everything, but I found another problem! I did a system check and found that, although we have enough oxygen to make the journey back, there is a blockage in the system somewhere. Oxygen isn't being fed into this section of the ship. I tried re-routing the oxygen away from another less crucial area, but it's not working."

He showed Andocia a part, which had burnt out.

"Do you have any spare parts on board this ship? Once this is replaced, we should be good to go."

They went down to the cargo section of the ship and Andocia unlocked the spares cabinet. "Have a look if you can find a replacement."

Carter began rummaging around amongst the parts, when suddenly he stiffened. Andocia opened her mouth to speak but he put his finger on his lips and whispered, "Did you hear that?"

She nodded and he pointed to a box. "It's coming from over there!"

The explorer crept forward stealthily with Andocia trailing behind him. He peered behind the crate and lunged for something. There was an awful shriek, as Craig grabbed the intruder by the scruff of its neck. To Andocia's astonishment, Mia wriggled helplessly in Craig's grip.

"What are you doing here?" she demanded angrily.

The peacat yowled and screeched in his grip, but stopped struggling when Craig spoke to her. "I can't understand you, Mia! Try speaking slowly!"

The blue cat spoke in a high-pitched tone. "Please, put me down and I'll explain!"

He put her down on the crate. "Okay, I understand you now. How did you get here?"

"I'm sorry, I meant no harm! I followed you both last night. I was curious about your ship. It's very big! Impressive too!"

"Why did you follow us, Mia?" Andocia asked.

"Like I just told you, I was interested to see what your ship looked like. I've never seen a spaceship up close before. I've heard our minders talking about them, but no one has ever seen one so close to the settlements."

"What do you mean? Are you saying that other spacecrafts have landed here before?" Craig enquired.

"Yes, many have landed here."

"Why didn't Galen mention this to us? When I discussed it with him, he said he had never seen a spaceship before. He was surprised to learn we had even come from space, much less another time period!"

Mia extended a claw and cleaned it with her teeth. "I know you and your companion haven't been here long, but surely you've noticed the humans do the work and the other species take care of them."

"I have noticed that, but I don't suppose you know why this is the case?"

Mia shrugged. "That is the way of things here on Saurus. The higher powers cannot do without the humans because they do all the work, but they aren't the most important beings on this planet. The animals are in charge. It's always been like this, but I don't know why. I don't really care either!"

"Alyssa said you are her pet. Is that true?"

Mia snickered. "She's actually my pet. I let her think she's in charge and it amuses me."

"So what do you actually do then?"

"I am a watcher," she replied proudly.

Craig and Andocia exchanged looks and they spoke telepathically. "I don't like the sound of this Craig! Ask her to explain, but be careful not to aggravate her."

Craig smiled and tickled the cat/bird's ear. "What is a watcher?"

The creature purred happily. "Oh yes, that's the spot! Scratch a little lower!"

He did as she asked and she continued. "A watcher has a very important job! We do exactly that! We watch for newcomers and report them to the higher powers so they can be interviewed and assessed."

"That sounds very interesting Mia. What happens to them when they have been interviewed?"

The cat/bird looked up into his eyes. "I don't know what happens afterwards, but a lot of them must like it here because they never want to go home ever again. The higher powers find them jobs in the various towns."

"That sounds very nice!" Craig replied. "Tell us Mia, have you told the higher powers about us yet?"

Mia purred again. "No, not yet, but they know about you. Other watchers have reported your presence, but you keep moving around and they can't find you."

Andocia knelt down by the cat and scratched her chin. "How long have you been hiding in our ship?"

"Most of the day actually. There are so many interesting things to look at. I can get into very small spaces."

Craig looked warningly at Andocia, having anticipated what she was about to do. 'Don't kill her! She can be useful to us. Anyway, their leaders know we're here so killing her won't solve anything. Let's just look for that part I need and then we can get the hell out of here!"

Andocia stood up and spoke to the creature. "Mia, you can look around some more if you want to, just promise me you won't touch anything. Me and Craig have some work to do."

The animal jumped onto a shelf and then climbed even higher. "See you later!"

They waved to her until she was out of sight.

"I'll help you find that part now. I'm starting to get very uneasy about this situation. Our luck won't hold out forever!"

Andocia and Craig looked everywhere for the part, but couldn't find it anywhere. They unpacked all the parts in the storeroom. Craig went back and consulted the stores directory. He typed in the name of the part and the computer responded. "Oxygen regenerator out of stock!"

Craig slammed his hand on the console. "Damn it Andocia! Without that part, we aren't going anywhere! Whoever is in charge of your supplies on the Red Planet haven't been doing their jobs properly."

"I'll be sure to chastise them when I return home again!" Andocia replied sarcastically.

Craig shook his head and wordlessly went to sit on his bed. He knew both he and Andocia were upset, but it didn't help to fight about it.

Carter heard a sound and Mia jumped down from an air vent just above his head, and landed on his bed.

"You certainly get around don't you Mia. What is it now?"

"I'm sorry, I didn't mean to eavesdrop on you and your friend's conversation, but I was exploring the air vents and I heard everything. Your ship is broken and you can't leave Saurus."

"It's not broken exactly, but I need to replace a part and we don't have a spare one."

"Does every spaceship have one of these parts you need?"

"Yes, they do. It's a very common part."

Mia looked smug. "Maybe I can help you! I know where they keep the other spaceships! If I take you there, can you find the part you need?"

"I certainly can!"

"The only problem is that it's quite far away. They store them in 'The Forbidden Valley'. I have friends who could help us, but I must speak to them first. It's a very dangerous journey and you have no weapons to defend yourself with. My friends are sentries who are well trained and you would be in good company. Do you want me to get them, or must you consult with your companion first?"

"No, that won't be necessary. I'll tell her when you have left."

The peacat got up to leave and Craig stopped her. "Just a minute Mia! Make arrangements for us to meet them somewhere else! I don't want anyone seeing where our ship is hidden."

"I understand. I'll get back to you shortly."

"Just one more thing Mia. Why are you helping us? What will you get out of this?"

The blue cat looked hurt. "I like you, Craig. You are completely different to the humans here on Saurus. I just want to help you and I expect nothing in return. I'll see you later."

When the cat had left, Craig told Andocia what she had said.

"I don't like it Craig, but we have no alternative. It just means we'll be exposing ourselves to even more beings, but as long as we get that part it'll be worth it."

"I'm happy to go along with Mia's friends, but while we're there, I want to try and find some weapons. I'm at a disadvantage without protection. It still bothers me no one has found us yet. Mia said the higher powers – whoever or whatever they are, know we're here, so why haven't they come for us?"

Andocia shrugged her shoulders. "I don't care either way! As long as they stay away, we stand a good chance of getting off this planet and going home."

10

Meanwhile on the Red Planet, Constance was worried. She went to the mirror in her room and brushed her hair nervously.

"I am getting very worried about Craig. It has been nearly three weeks since he and Andocia vanished. The guards are very nervous as well. They look away when I ask them where Craig and Andocia are. I get the feeling something is very wrong, but no one is telling me anything!"

Constance moved to an armchair and sat down to read her electronic device, but she couldn't concentrate and threw it on her bed. Her baby seemed restless as well but she knew it was her fault because she was so anxious. She stroked her tiny bulge affectionately. "Oh my sweet little angel, don't fret so! We will be home soon, I promise!"

Constance pulled up the leg of her jeans and glared at the little black box in hate. "I have to think of a way to escape from here! I must make every effort to disarm this thing."

She stared at it for a while, wracking her brain to find a solution.

The woman knew she was due for an exercise session soon, as the doctors had suggested she get as much fresh air as possible, especially now she was pregnant. An hour later, two guards came to fetch her and accompanied her to the grounds. Constance dutifully went for a walk, her guards trailing behind just far enough to give her some space. After a while the woman sat down on a bench and stretched her arms out, enjoying the breeze that caressed her body. She had taken her electronic book with her, but while she appeared to be reading, her eyes were darting from side to side as she memorised the closest route to the spaceships. In her head Constance was also mentally calculating how much time she would need to reach the hangars. Although the route to the ships was relatively flat, there was very little cover. A plan started forming in her mind, but first she had to remove the explosive device from her leg. The woman knew she had been booked for a pre-natal check-up and scan the following day, so she would be taken to the hospital, which suited her perfectly. When her guards came to take her back inside her room, she got up immediately and went with them. There she closed the blinds and bedroom door, saying she was going to have a nap. Instead of sleeping though, Constance began making final plans for her escape.

The next day she was escorted from her room by two guards. She was helped into a land vehicle, not the usual hovercraft and she looked questioningly at her captors. One of the guards smiled at her. "It's nothing to worry about. I know you are bored here, so I thought I would give you a change of scenery. It takes a little longer to get to the hospital, but some of the scenery is very pretty on the way."

Constance nodded and returned the guard's smile.

They drove for fifteen minutes when the scenery changed. It became very lush, with high trees and bushes everywhere.

"This area is lovely! It looks like paradise."

Her guard nodded her head. "It is beautiful, but also very deadly. The ground is fenced in for a reason. There are many dangerous animals living in this place. Nothing here is tame or friendly."

"Why does Andocia leave them there? What will happen if some of them escape?"

"It's impossible. The fence is electrified and will fry anything that comes into contact with it. The beasts inside know this and they keep their distance. When Andocia found this planet, she separated the creatures by fencing them in. This planet is surrounded by the beings and forms an effective barrier against anyone who tries to land here. This is a large planet and it is difficult to monitor all Spacetraffic. Anyone who is unfortunate to land behind these barriers will not live very long."

Constance nodded. "I see. Well thank you for taking me on this tour. It was very interesting."

They drove for a while longer and finally reached the hospital. Constance looked at her watch and realised the journey had taken fifteen minutes longer. She was accompanied into the doctor's rooms and when his assistant called her inside, the guards left, reminding the assistant to call them once they had finished checking the patient.

The doctor called her in and proceeded to examine her carefully, asking various questions about her health. Mrs Carter answered his questions and asked a few of her own. At the end of the examination, her doctor smiled and told her everything was well. She thanked him and returned to the assistant's office.

"How is everything?" the lady asked brightly.

Constance smiled and told her everything was fine. The lady reached for her phone to contact the security staff, but Constance gently put a hand on her arm.

"Please don't call them yet! I need to go to the bathroom."

"Okay, sure hon. I know what it's like being pregnant. You know where the restrooms are."

Constance smiled and walked out of the room. She looked up and down the corridor, but it was empty. When she reached the lifts, she got in and went down into the basement area, where repairs to all hospital equipment were done. A door was closed, but not locked so she walked in without knocking. A man was bent over a workbench, soldering some wires onto an operating lamp. He never heard her approach. Constance quietly locked the door and picked up a slightly bent scalpel, hiding it behind her back. She touched him gently on the shoulder and he dropped the lamp.

"What are you doing here young lady? No one is allowed entry to this area!"

"I need some help please," she replied pleasantly.

The man put down the soldering iron and crossed his arms over his chest. "I'm sure you must be in the wrong department. What do you want?"

Constance put her leg up on a chair and lifted her jeans leg, revealing the ankle bracelet. The man looked at her in horror. "Lady, I can't help you!" He reached for a button on the desk, but Constance grabbed him around the neck, pressing the scalpel against his flesh. He pushed away from the desk and tried to pry her arm loose, but her grip was too tight and he began to gag.

"Mister, you will do this or I'll kill you and do it myself!"

The man struggled ineffectually for a while, but Constance simply pressed harder until he felt dizzy. He held his hands up and stopped struggling and the pressure on his neck loosened. He took a few deep breaths and gasped. "Okay, okay I'll help you!"

She released him and he selected some tools and began removing the device. In a few minutes he put down his tools.

"Okay, it's done," he grumbled.

Constance gave him her sweetest smile, then swung her fist, catching him squarely on his jaw. He landed hard but felt nothing as he hit the floor, unconscious. Constance looked around for some wire which she used to tie his hands behind his back. The woman found some duct tape nearby and taped the man's mouth shut. She gently placed the black box under the table, hiding it from view.

Sighing with relief, she unlocked the door and peered out. No one was around. After locking the heavy door securely, she headed for the stairs and ran up them, returning to the Doctor's rooms. The assistant was relieved to see her. "Are you okay? It took you a while to get back."

Constance smiled sheepishly. "I know! The toilet was out of order and I had to find another one. There was a queue."

The woman nodded and called her minders. Constance went with them as though nothing had happened and informed the guards her tests were all good.

On their way back to Andocia's castle, a sudden storm lashed the land vehicle, causing the startled driver to turn sharply as a branch was sheared from a nearby tree, almost colliding with them. Constance was thrown into her minder's lap and in that instant, her hand came into contact with the escort's gun, which she pocketed hurriedly. Her guard grabbed her by the shoulders and steadied her. "Oh my stars; are you okay?"

"Whew that was close!" Constance exclaimed. "How are you? I hit into you pretty hard."

"No, I'm fine, thank you." She placed her hand on the driver. "Well done, Dana. Your split-second actions saved us all!"

Constance also thanked her and the rest of the journey passed without further incident. They arrived safely and Constance went to her room.

She was so excited and sat on her bed, grinning from ear to ear. "What a stroke of luck! I had planned to get the guard's gun anyway, but fate intervened and gave me a better opportunity. It's time to go home!"

For a moment she stared at nothing as unwelcome thoughts entered her head. "I have to go! I don't know what has happened to Craig and Andocia. It won't be long before Andocia's followers also get bored having me here and terminate me. I hope Craig isn't dead, but I have a responsibility to our child. We must go home!"

She stroked her tiny bulge tenderly. "You will love Earth, precious one! You have some very eager grandparents who are just dying to meet you."

Constance was excited as she thought about returning to Earth. She tried to settle down, but instead spent time going over her escape plan.

After supper the explorer decided to take a shower. Afterwards she began packing all her belongings, as well as the baby's things Craig had brought her. Her bottom lip trembled when she held the baby's soft garments and she wiped the tears from her eyes with her fists. Taking a huge calming breath, she put everything safely into one large suitcase. Once she was certain nothing of hers had been left behind, she pressed a button on the suitcase. Immediately it began to shrink until it was the size of a small tote bag. When she was done, the explorer took one last look at the room she had been imprisoned in for several months and her spirits soared.

It was very dark by now. Constance unlocked the door, grinning wryly when she knew she could have escaped anytime, but the time just wasn't right. She closed the door softly and it locked behind her. Keeping to the shadows, she doubled over, trying to look as inconspicuous as possible. When she came across some guards, she crouched down and melted into the shadows. When she was nearing the hangars, there were no more shadows and she bolted for the crafts.

A shout rang out and Constance swore under her breath. She drew the gun she had stolen and prepared to engage her enemies, determined not to be recaptured. Instead of firing wildly, she took a calming breath and crouched down on one knee. One by one the soldiers fell, each shot finding a victim. More were pouring out of their barracks and Constance knew her laser gun would stop working, leaving her defenceless if this onslaught went on for too long.

She turned and ran into the hangar, shooting at the few soldiers guarding the facility. They came rushing at her like an angry river, but she sped up and found Craig's ship. Her enemies were far away but still coming on relentlessly. The woman found the keypad beneath the door and pressed the required digits. A scary moment passed when the ship asked for her identification, but she kept her cool and typed this on the keypad. It seemed like ages before the door opened, but only seconds had passed. Rushing up the ramp, she headed for the cockpit and pressed the emergency switch. This activated the force field around the ship which would stop any armour penetrating devices from breaching the ship. She watched as many soldiers jumped all over the ship, trying to smash their way in, but they were wasting their time. Constance entered her code into the computer and it switched on. A hologram of a beautiful woman appeared. <Good evening Constance! You have activated Craig's profile, but he is not here.>

"I know Janine, but switch to emergency protocol. I will be flying his craft."

The female holograph smiled, revealing dazzling white teeth. <As you command Constance. There are many beings trying to gain access to the ship. What are your orders?>

"Begin flight sequence immediately. Destination N.A.S.A. Mission Control, Earth."

<Beginning flight sequence at your command.>

The engines came online and the spaceship began to rise slowly. The panicked soldiers jumped off and ran away from the rockets pulsing fire as it began to lift off. There was terrified screaming as some soldiers could not get off in time and were hurled to the ground where they lay in a crumpled heap. Rockets were fired at the escaping craft, but the barrier repelled everything. There was a final blink of light before the spaceship disappeared.

The soldiers on the Red Planet groaned. "Well, there goes Andocia's hostage. What happens now Captain?"

Their Captain threw her weapon down in disgust. "I don't know, nor do I care! Andocia and Craig Carter are probably dead by now. Besides I was sick and tired of having to babysit that woman. If it had been up to me, I would have killed her long ago!"

11

About two hours later, Mia returned.

"I have good news! My friends have offered to help you. They said they would meet with you under the big tree in one hour. I'll take you to them. We have to meet under cover of darkness so no one sees us. I know it's dangerous, but I'll keep a lookout for any nasty creatures and warn you in advance."

The threesome left as soon as the sun went down and Mia led them deeper and deeper into the forest of trees. Craig patted the gutting knife in the pocket of his suit, grateful for some sort of protection at least. Andocia held the torch Galen had kindly given them, but on the advice of the peacat, she only switched it on for brief periods when they passed through very dark places where the moonlight didn't reach. Mia told them proudly she could see perfectly in the darkness. Fortunately, it was still early so they didn't encounter any vicious creatures.

They reached a certain spot and the cat told them to wait. She returned with what looked like a very tall human female, followed by an equally tall male, but when they got closer, Craig's mouth hung open in astonishment, for only the front of the creature was human. As they moved into a patch of moonlight, he saw they were attached to bodies of horses.

He shook his head in amazement and stared at the mythological creatures in disbelief. "Centaurs! You are both centaurs! This place never ceases to amaze me."

The woman nodded politely. "My name is Sabrina and my friend here is Rusty. Mia tells us you need our help to get to The Forbidden Valley."

"Uh, yes we do. Mia tells us there are spaceships there and we need to find a part for our ship."

Sabrina looked him up and down. "What you are asking us to do is very dangerous! No human has ever set foot near The Forbidden Valley. They are content to hide behind their walls and tend their fields. What makes you any different?"

Mia jumped onto Sabrina's back. "He isn't like the others! He killed the mutant wolf beast."

She stared at him in amazement. "That was you? We heard it had been killed, but no one mentioned a human did it. If you are a warrior, where are your weapons?"

"They are attached to our ship. We don't need weapons when we explore space."

Andocia had remained silent and was obviously in awe of the large centaurs. They stared at her and Rusty came closer. "Are you the one who has magical powers?"

She was puzzled. "Magical powers? Well yes, I suppose I do," she responded.

Rusty nodded his head sagely. "Ah, so you are a witch then?"

Craig looked at the ground and hid the smile on his face. He recovered and spoke to the centaurs once more. "We'll have plenty of time to discuss our powers on the journey. Just tell us if you want to help or not. Every day we stay here increases the danger!"

Sabrina put out her hand and Craig shook it. "We have a deal then! I'll give you a list of things you'll need to bring with on the journey. We will bring two more friends to help us on this quest when we return. Meet us back here in two hours. Mia will be joining us on this journey. She can enlist the help of other watchers on the way. We can use their eyes and ears for it is a perilous journey. It will take us four days to reach our destination, because we can only travel at night."

The two centaurs moved a little distance away and began writing out their list.

Craig was very impressed by the beasts. Sabrina had dark brown, almond shaped eyes and short black hair cut in a pixie style. Her figure could rival any human model's and she was curvy in all the right places. She wore a blue tank top. The rear part of her body was black and white, but her tail was pure white. Sabrina had a quiver of arrows slung across her body, and a bow nestled inside it as well.

Rusty had light brown hair and blue eyes. His body was light brown and white and his tail was a mixture of brown and white. He had a mace nestling in a cylindrical container slung over his back. Rusty's torso was very muscular and he looked like a model. He wore a sleeveless checked shirt buttoned down the front, but several buttons remained open, revealing a sculpted chest. Craig saw Andocia ogling him and grinned. He was very handsome.

The centaurs handed their list to Craig. "Here, bring these things with you and don't be late! We need to leave as soon as possible. What is your choice of weapon, Craig? We had better bring you something, seeing as you have none."

He wanted to say a laser gun, but he doubted they had any. "A couple of knives would be very helpful, thank you."

They nodded and left. Mia joined them again. "Okay let's hurry back to your ship and get these things."

12

One hour later, they both came out of the spaceship, carrying knapsacks loaded with provisions for their journey. Andocia sealed the ship and they followed Mia into the woods. The lights in the settlements were all switched off and Craig thought about Galen and Daphne sleeping in their bed in Hillvale.

The threesome met up with Sabrina and her companions. Craig saw that the two newcomers were also centaurs. Rusty introduced them to one another, then took Andocia by the hand. "You can ride with me. It is a long and arduous journey and we can travel faster this way. Hold onto my waist."

He took Andocia's knapsack from her and gave it to the other female centaur to carry.

Sabrina held out her hand to Craig. "Do you wish to ride with me?"

He thanked her and climbed onto her back. The other female centaur took charge of his knapsack. The second male carried all the articles they would need to set up camp. Mia jumped on the other female centaur's back and they began their journey. Sabrina had given Craig two knives, which were now belted around his waist.

The group set off at a trot and were soon lost in the jungle of trees. It became pitch dark and the humans couldn't see where they were going, but the centaurs and Mia had no trouble finding their way. Occasionally they would stop for a short break and Mia would jump off and go ahead of them. Once or twice, she would return and whisper in one of the centaur's ears and it would go and investigate. Lori, the other female, carried a blowpipe and some darts coated with poison, while Sandy, the second male, carried a sword in a scabbard, belted around his waist. The centaurs took it in turns to hunt and every time they went out, Craig and Andocia heard the screams of something dying. The centaurs didn't elaborate about what they had killed and their passengers didn't ask.

It began to get light and Sabrina explained what they would be doing.

"We'll be coming to a cave soon where you can both rest. We cannot travel during the day because there are watchers everywhere and we could be discovered. Not all the watchers are friends of Mia's."

The group reached the cave and their passengers climbed stiffly off their mounts and sagged down thankfully on the grass. Andocia rubbed her nether regions and groaned. "Owww, I think I have blisters. Even my blisters have blisters on them."

Craig lay on his stomach and sighed. "Ouch! I wish I had a trained masseuse to massage out all these kinks."

The centaurs and Mia didn't complain at all. Lori took out some cooking utensils and lit a fire just inside the cave. It wasn't long before the smell of the food drew the two travellers and they ate hungrily.

When their stomachs were full, Lori pointed inside the cave. "There's a river further along this passageway. It's cold, but refreshing. The two of you can freshen up."

Andocia got to her feet and went inside. The river was indeed cool and inviting and when she splashed her face and drank some of the cool water, she felt much better. She took off the long brown dress and splashed her body with the cold water. When she came out of the cave Craig went in and washed up.

They sat down to rest again and the Craig got his first real look at the other two centaurs. Lori had long blonde hair that she tied in a ponytail. She had green eyes and was light brown all over, except for her tail, which was a mixture of white and brown. Her figure was just as stunning as Sabrina's. She wore a green top which matched her eyes perfectly.

Sandy was slightly smaller than Rusty. His eyes were a golden colour and his hair was ash blond. His body was a tan colour, but his tail was elegant and black. He wore a sleeveless vest fastened with wooden buttons in front. The horse part of him was more muscular than Rusty's and his legs were thicker. His muscles rippled every time he moved and he also looked like a male model.

Craig wondered what the higher beings looked like. He decided they must be either very clever or totally mad to have created mythological creatures and given them life.

He was curious about the creatures and wanted to question them about their origins, but he wasn't sure if they even knew how they came to exist. Carter looked across at Andocia, who had fallen asleep just inside the cave. She looked so peaceful as she slept and as much as he hated and feared her, she looked vulnerable and beautiful. He realised her past was as much a mystery to him as that of the centaurs and the strange blue cat that watched over them. Finally, his eyes closed and he too fell asleep.

The two travellers woke to the smell of something cooking and stared up at the sky. The light was already beginning to fade. They had slept almost the entire day. Rusty trotted over to them and smiled. "Good afternoon sleepyheads! You looked so peaceful, we didn't want to wake you. After supper we must continue our journey. The first part of the trip was the easiest. It gets more treacherous from here on."

Craig yawned and stretched. He excused himself and went behind a tall tree to urinate. Andocia did the same a short while later. They both went into the cave and splashed cold water on their faces.

After their meal, Lori washed and packed the dishes away, while Sandy took all the canteens and filled them with water. The sun sank below the horizon and instantly it became dark. The absolute blackness disorientated Craig and Andocia, who were used to seeing some form of light.

"It has become cloudy suddenly," Sandy explained. "That's why the Moon is not visible. We will be getting some rain later tonight, or early tomorrow morning. We had better continue quickly and try to make as much progress as we can before the storm breaks."

They changed mounts. Andocia rode with Sandy, while Craig got on Lori's back. Sabrina carried the cooking implements and Rusty took charge of the provisions. Mia climbed on Craig's lap and snuggled against his chest. Occasionally the centaurs switched on torches to light their way as the sky grew steadily darker.

They began their journey at a steady trot, but after they had been travelling for a few hours, their pace slowed as the terrain became more uneven and rocky. The path dropped downwards and Craig saw they were descending a steep hill. It wasn't very wide and they travelled in single file. They slowed down even further and the party heard the ominous peals of thunder, and lightning crisscrossed the sky in a blaze of purple flashes. Sandy, who was leading the procession, stopped and looked around. "We have to get to the bottom of this mountain before the rain comes, or we'll be washed away. There are some small caves there and we'll have to wait out the storm."

He began trotting faster and his companions followed his lead. They had just reached the bottom of the mountain when the heavens opened and the rain poured down. Within minutes, everyone was soaked to the skin. Sandy pointed to a spot a short distance away. "The caves are over there!" Sandy ran past the first couple of caves and ploughed into the bushes. Wet branches slapped at their hands and feet and pulled at their skin and clothing. He took out his sword and made scything motions in the foliage. Leaves and branches sailed upwards and fell to the wet Earth.

Suddenly the bushes parted and Craig saw a cave which they ran towards. By the time all four centaurs had gone inside, it was very cramped. Andocia and Craig slid off their wet mounts and huddled in a tiny corner, their bodies touching in the small space. Outside the rain had increased and a solid curtain of water hid the outside world from view.

Mia shook the water from her body. "Ugh, I hate rain!" she grumbled.

Rusty and Sabrina had removed their bundles from their backs and managed to find a small space to sit. Everyone barely had space to move. Rusty rummaged in one of the bundles and brought out some food for everyone to snack on.

"Will it rain for a while?" Andocia asked curiously.

"No, it usually rains for a short time, but it rains heavily," Lori replied. "If you look outside, you'll see what I mean."

Craig stood up and edged past her. He looked out of the cave entranced and whistled. The mountain they had just descended was transformed into a giant waterfall.

"We cannot go any further tonight. Even if the rain stops soon, the path will be too slippery to travel on. We have to wait for the water to soak into the ground before we can proceed any further," Sandy explained. "That's also why I didn't seek shelter in the caves closer to the hillside. They will be flooded with water now. We might as well all get comfortable. It's going to be a long night."

The travellers all lay down where they stood. Craig resumed his position by Andocia's side and he could feel the heat of her wet body against his own. He leaned against the wall and closed his eyes, while outside the storm raged. Mia slipped in between Craig and Andocia and got comfortable.

The next morning, the sky was blue once more and all traces of the storm had passed. Carter had not slept very well and had kept on having bad dreams. Andocia was also tired and didn't say much. Craig left the cave and looked around. The rain had left the ground smelling fresh and renewed and he realised it had been a very long time since he had smelt wet soil.

Everywhere on Earth was densely populated and only a few parks remained for people to walk around. Rusty came up and looked about.

"We can't stay here for the rest of the day because we have lost too much time already. It's risky, but in order for us to reach our destination on time, we'll have to travel in daylight, as well as night. Are you prepared to risk it Craig?"

"We have no choice! Every day that passes makes me more anxious. My wife doesn't know what has happened to me and by now she probably thinks I'm dead."

"Your wife? What is that?"

Craig smiled. "Sorry, sometimes I forget to explain. My mate is waiting."

"You have a mate? Oh, I understand now! Andocia is not your mate?"

"No, definitely not! We are companions."

Rusty nodded. "It makes sense, of course. You don't behave like a couple, but your choice of words is very interesting. You say 'companion', not 'friend'."

"Exactly. My mate is carrying our first child and I miss her. I would like to get back to her as soon as I can, so I'm prepared to take the risk. I'm sure Andocia would like to get back to her planet as soon as possible too."

"Her planet is not the same as yours then?" the centaur replied thoughtfully.

"No, we live in different universes."

The centaur looked strangely at him, then changed the subject. "I'm going to check on the others. We must leave soon."

The centaurs came out of the cave and proceeded along the pathway. Rusty was now in the lead. They had kept the same order as the previous night and Andocia rode on Sandy's back, while he partnered with Lori once more. The lead centaur carried the backpacks as before, while Sabrina was in charge of the cooking utensils again. The ground was level, but rocky, and they had to tread slowly to avoid falling.

Craig looked up at the sky and saw many birds flying around. Mia was travelling with him again. "Mia, what kind of birds are those? Are they birds of prey, or just harmless feathered ones?"

Mia looked strangely at him. "Why do you ask such a strange question?"

"I'm human! We are naturally curious. I was just wondering if we have anything to worry about, or if we can proceed safely. We are out in the open and at the mercy of anything that wants to cause us harm."

Mia looked upwards. "Uh, they are too high for me to know for sure. Some of the avian species are vicious, but they usually only attack if they sense something is ill or weak. We are safe for the moment. They are just watching us."

Carter was suspicious and his sixth sense was tingling. He felt uneasy and kept glancing into the sky. He tapped Lori on her shoulder and pointed upwards. She stared at the birds.

"Are they going to be a problem?" he asked her.

"No, Mia is correct. They are just watching us. I do see a few predatory birds, and several watchers too. Most of them are just curious, I think. Not many beings travel so far from the settlements. We'll keep checking to see if their numbers increase, but I'll warn you if we are going to have trouble."

The human man looked at Mia again. "I wonder why there are several watcher birds here. Are they your friends Mia?"

The blue cat shook her tail feathers. "I don't know any of them, but they too are just being curious. If they had wanted to report you to the higher authorities, they would be here by now."

Craig was worried. He wondered why the spies hadn't reported them and he concluded that perhaps the higher authorities were just interested in the party and wanted to see what they were doing.

They continued for a while longer, then stopped to take a break. A makeshift shelter was erected and they drank some cold water and ate some fruit. When they got ready to leave, the centaurs changed riders again. Craig now rode on Rusty's back, while Andocia rode with Sabrina. Mia climbed on Andocia's lap and settled down. Sandy took charge of the cooking utensils and Lori took the backpacks and camping equipment. The birds had lost interest and flown away.

The travellers continued their journey. Every eight hours they stopped for a break and changed over. In this way they travelled both day and night, but their longest rest periods took place during the day, when they found suitable places to shelter from the hot sun. Finally, the centaurs reached the top of a hill and stopped for a break. By now Craig and Andocia were no longer stiff and sore because they had got used to travelling on the creatures' backs. Rusty called them over and pointed down the hill.

Craig and Andocia parted the bushes and stared in amazement at the sight of many spaceships parked haphazardly in a large clearing. There were too many to count, but they ranged from some very outdated ships to some of the most modern ones. Craig took out a set of binoculars and trained them on the ships. He could make out the names of some spaceships and was amazed. There were ships from America, Russia, South Africa, England and China, and many more, but some names were hidden from view.

Rusty came over and looked at the two travellers. "Do you think you can find the part you need for your ship from any of these?"

"Oh yes, definitely! How long will it take us to get down there?"

"Approximately half a day. The mountain is steep and slippery. We should set up camp here and eat something before we go."

Craig was excited. "I'm not hungry. Let's get down there first and we can eat later."

Andocia nodded. "I agree! There will be time for refreshments later. I'll just have some water to drink and then we should make our way down there."

Rusty didn't move and Craig questioned him. "What's wrong? Why are you reluctant to continue?"

The centaur shook his head. "I don't know but something's not right. Last time I came here, there was a high electric fence around this place."

Andocia stared at the ships. "I suppose they took it down. This place is so remote, I doubt anyone would come here without a very good reason."

"Maybe," he conceded. "Well, let's go down the mountain, but there are many loose rocks so you two will have to travel on foot. Take a canteen of water and your weapons with you. We are going to lighten the loads by taking only the bare necessities with us."

They started down the perilous mountain, walking slowly and carefully to avoid being injured. Carter was impatient to get the part for their ship and it seemed to take an eternity, but finally they reached level ground and began walking to the spaceships.

Carter looked up at the sky but nothing moved. There was an eerie silence, but he was focusing on reaching the ships and didn't dwell on it. Suddenly the bushes began to move and the centaurs reared up on their hind legs. Craig and Andocia watched fascinated as several small animals appeared from the long grass and headed purposefully towards them. They had the sweetest expressions on their faces and the rabbits bounded eagerly up to the pair.

"Look out!" Sandy screamed. "Those are rabids! One bite and they will kill you!"

Craig unsheathed his knife and swung at the first creature that leapt for him. He slashed it across its throat and it died at his feet. The others seemed to make a humming noise and increased their pace. Andocia released bolt after bolt of power and the red beams claimed many victims. The four centaurs also did their part and the vicious creatures died. A few still staggered around when the sky suddenly filled with birdlike creatures who swooped down and grabbed the dead and dying rabids. Chaos reigned and the fighters were desperately trying to get out of the way of the winged predators. Andocia and Craig stared at some of the birds. They were all different. Some had hooked beaks, but human faces, while others looked like vultures. Others were more human than birdlike, but the bloodthirsty beings all had the same purpose in mind and that was to eat the dead rabids. They glared at the strange party, but didn't harm them.

Suddenly a huge shadow loomed over Craig and Andocia screamed. "Look out, Craig!!"

He ducked as the creature flew over him and landed a short distance away. It turned around and came running back and his mind just had time to register it was a tiger, but it had a collar of spikes around its neck. Andocia slit its throat and it fell at his feet and growled, showing very large teeth. It shuddered and died and he stepped back.

"Thank you!" he replied gratefully.

Andocia smiled, but it turned into a grimace and Craig watched in morbid fascination as an even bigger tiger lept up behind Andocia and swatted her like a fly. She flew through the air and landed with a sickening thump a short distance away and lay still.

The tiger growled and headed for the unconscious woman. A volley of arrows pierced its skin, but the beast didn't slow down. Craig got up and saw some steel bars lying nearby. He picked up two of them and smashed them together, making a noise. The beast stopped and turned around. It stared at the new target and growled so loudly that the ground shook.

"That's it ugly! Come here!" he taunted it. Then got to his feet and ran away from the rest of the party.

The beast was undecided and looked at Andocia, then back at Craig. Then, deciding the man seemed to be a much tastier option, loped after him. Carter zigzagged across the grass and the beast swiped at him, narrowly missing him every time. Craig had reached a hill and he scrambled up as fast as he could, until he was level with the oncoming beast's head. The tiger stopped at the foot of the hill and growled again, then leapt into the air. At the same time, Craig jumped to meet it, plunging his knife into the animal's eye until it was embedded to the hilt in the socket. Both man and beast tumbled to the ground, and he jumped clear, doing a somersault as he landed. Behind him the giant tiger fell to the ground and didn't move again. A gigantic cheer broke out and the four centaurs applauded him.

"That was incredible!" Sandy shouted.

The man ignored them and ran over to Andocia. Her skin was pale green and she was unconscious. He felt her pulse and was relieved to find she was still breathing. Sabrina galloped up to him. "Craig, you're bleeding!"

He looked down at his arm and saw there was a deep cut, stretching from his wrist to just below his elbow. Blood welled from the wound and pooled on the ground. He sat down while Lori found a bandage and some water to clean his wound. She looked at his injury and gasped. "That's going to need stitches; it's very deep."

Mia ran up to the pair and looked nervously around. "Is it over now? Are they gone?"

The centaur stared at her. "Yes, it would appear so."

The blue cat sniffed Andocia. "Oh… oh my, that doesn't look good. Is she dead?"

"No, just unconscious," Craig replied.

When Lori had finished bandaging his wound, he went back to Andocia, who still hadn't moved. He turned her over gently and gasped when he saw blood oozing from her stomach and head. He probed her body carefully and sighed. "This is bad! She has sustained serious injuries. I can see some bones are broken."

"Will she die?" the cat asked tremulously.

"No, but she needs urgent medical attention."

He sat with his head in his hands for a few moments, and made a decision. "Mia, are some of your watcher friends around?"

The peacat nodded her head and pointed to a nearby tree. Two birds sat in the branches, watching them. They both had human torsos, but instead of mouths, they had beaks. The male had brown wings, while the female had white ones. Their feet were shaped like claws.

"How long would it take them to report this incident to the higher powers if they left now?"

"About an hour and a half."

"How long will it take for your creators to reach us afterwards?"

"I would estimate about 30 minutes."

Carter thought about it. "Tell them to do it!"

Mia was surprised. "Does this mean you are surrendering? Why, after all you have been through, are you giving up?"

"I'm not giving up! I'm just making a logical decision. Andocia is in no condition to travel all the way back, and nor am I. Anyway, you know as well as I do that time was not on our side. Your creators have been watching us from the beginning. I'm sure they have had their reasons for not apprehending us before, but this has gone on long enough."

He pointed to his arm where the blood was seeping through the bandages again. "I might make it, but I risk getting an infection in my arm."

"Why don't you just leave your companion here for the higher powers to find? You could escape from her clutches forever and go back to your time period."

Craig smiled. "That sounds very tempting, but I can't. I came here to get that part for my spaceship and I'm going to get it, otherwise all this has been for nothing."

The centaurs came closer and Rusty sighed. "I guess this is the end of the road for you and your companion. Will we ever see you again?"

"Probably not, so thank you for everything you have done for us. Can I just ask you to wait and look after Andocia for me? Once I have got this part for my spaceship, you can go. I don't want you to get into trouble for helping us."

The centaurs watched as the man hurried to the nearest spaceship and climbed inside. Mia went to the tree and spoke to the two watchers, who flew away a few minutes later.

Craig had chosen an American spaceship that had been manufactured about ten years earlier than the ones he currently flew in. He powered up the computer and left it to warm up. Because of his technical background, he knew the exact layout of the ship and went immediately to the storage area where he selected two brand new oxygen regenerators, which he sealed into strong plastic bags. He made his way to the arsenal and broke the seal with a crowbar. Several laser guns were stored on a shelf and he chose two at random, checking they were fully charged. Then he returned to the flight deck and checked to see when the ship had last been flown on a mission. The computer informed him its final mission was two years ago, but there was no indication of any damage to the ship, nor the fate of the astronaut who had been in charge. Carter checked the time on his mobile device and saw he only had fifteen minutes before the higher beings would be coming for him. He powered down the computer and climbed out of the ship.

Mia ran to him. "Did you find what you were looking for?"

He nodded and went back to the centaurs and Andocia, but there had been no change. She was still unconscious. Carter checked her pulse again and found it was slow and steady. He left Mia with her and shook each centaur's hand. "You had better go now! They'll be here soon."

The centaurs looked at him, but they were reluctant to leave.

"We would rather stay here and wait with you. Some more rabids or other nasty beings could come back and attack you. You'll need our protection."

Craig was quiet while they waited and the centaurs stood guard until Mia pointed up at the sky. "They have arrived!"

13

A large black object came and landed near them. It looked like a S.U.V. but without wheels. It had arrived quietly and landed without a bump. Idly Craig wondered how it was powered. Several humans climbed out of the transport and came towards them. Some held strange devices in their hands and the explorer assumed they were weapons. Behind the guards, two other humans came forward. One went to Andocia and knelt beside her. She held a scanner in her hand and ran it up and down the woman's prone body. The doctor looked at the display and consulted with another human, who went back to the vehicle and brought out a bed. They lifted her gently and placed the bed underneath her. Another male came to Craig and wordlessly examined his arm. The bandage was saturated with blood and the doctor wrapped something resembling clingwrap on his arm. It shrunk onto his arm, but when he looked at the dressing, it was covered with tiny holes. The doctor took out a syringe and filled it with some liquid. "This injection which I am going to inject into your arm will help to stop the bleeding." He rolled up Craig's sleeve and plunged the needle into his upper arm.

One of the guards pointed at Craig. "Come with me."

Craig watched as Andocia was lifted into the vehicle, then followed her. He waved to the centaurs and they walked away. The vehicle had ten seats and the staff folded down some of them to make a level surface for Andocia's bed. He was waved to a seat further along and told to put his seatbelt on. The man went outside and called to Mia. "You! Come with us. You will be required to give your report to your superiors."

The transport ship lifted upwards very quietly and sped off to its destination. Mia looked miserably at her friend. "I'm so sorry it had to end like this! I've never met anyone like you and I was truly hoping you would make it back to your universe."

The explorer stroked her gently on her head. "Don't blame yourself. It was my decision and mine alone! You have nothing to feel guilty about. Have you ever met your creators?"

"No, but I have been inside the building where they are taking you. This isn't the first time I have delivered a report, but I never get to meet the creators, just some of their helpers."

The ship flew to a high building that looked as if it was made from glass. A panel slid open and the transport ship flew inside. It landed on a platform and the rear door opened. Andocia and Craig were split up. She was taken through a door on the left, while he and Mia were directed to another door on the right. Someone came up to Carter and he followed the man. Mia was told to go to the debriefing chamber and she looked miserably at her friend. "Goodbye Craig! May it go well with you!"

He waved to the peacat and the door closed.

The man took him to a glass chamber.

"You have to be decontaminated," he explained, pointing to the explorer's torn and dirty clothing. "Go inside and remove all your clothing. You will see an alcove to the left of you. Place all your belongings inside and return to the middle of the chamber, where there's a line indicated in red. Stand on it and wait for the decontamination process to be completed. When the light turns green, you may walk through to the other side."

The astronaut did as he was told and the door sealed behind him. He undressed and placed everything in the allotted space, except his mobile device, which he concealed in his hand. Jets of warm water cascaded over him, followed by a soapy substance, which coated his body. More water ran down his body and the dirt pooled at his feet and disappeared down a drain in the floor. Afterwards, warm air was blown on him and he was dry almost immediately. A green light blinked and he walked to the door on the opposite side, where he was handed a loose-fitting top and pair of drawstring bottoms. He put his hand in one of the pockets and dropped his mobile device into it.

Carter was taken to a room containing only a bed and two chairs.

"You are in the hospital wing. Take a seat and wait here. A doctor will be in to see you shortly."

Not long afterwards, a man came in. He smiled and nodded at his patient. "What is your name?"

"Craig," he replied.

"Well Craig, I am Dr Mullins. Do you mind if I examine your arm? My colleague mentioned your injury is quite serious."

The explorer offered his arm and the doctor ran a scanning device over it and examined the wound carefully. Then he cut off the plastic sleeve. Immediately the blood began to seep slowly through the bandage. The doctor placed his patient's forearm in a basin of water that smelt strongly of antiseptic and the bleeding stopped. He examined it carefully.

"Craig that beast cut you open to the bone. If you had been any slower, your arm would have been amputated, causing you to die from shock and major blood loss. There is a distinct line running across both the radius and the ulna bones, where something scraped you, but the good news is they are still intact. However, you are going to need surgery to close the wound. You must have a general anaesthetic and the operation is very delicate. I'm going to schedule the operation for an hour's time. It looks as though some dirt has already got into the wound and I don't want it to turn septic. That's why time is of the essence."

"I understand, doctor. Just before we do this though, how is my friend?"

"The lady who came in with you is still unconscious. She's being operated on as we speak. When you have recovered from your surgery, I'll update you on her condition. In the meantime, let's get you settled in a ward and I'll send someone to record your particulars."

Craig was admitted to a private ward. He was given a set of theatre clothes and told to put them on in the meantime. A nurse took down his details and he was given an injection. He hid his mobile device in the drawer beside his bed and wrapped it in the clothes he had been given after being decontaminated. The orderly came to fetch him half an hour later. He was pleasantly drowsy from the injection and the last thing he remembered was Dr Mullins greeting him in the operating theatre.

He woke suddenly and found he was back in his bed in the private ward. His arm was wrapped in a sling and he examined it. It was very tender and pain shot through it. Dr Mullins peeped in the door and smiled.

"Ah, I see you are awake at last! You must have been very tired. Are you in pain?"

Craig nodded. "It hurts when I move it. How long was I asleep for?"

"About fifteen hours at least. I'm going to give you an injection for the pain, then I'll explain what I did when I operated on you."

Dr Mullins returned with a syringe and injected him in his leg. "This should take care of the pain. When you are discharged, I'll give you some tablets to take away with you."

The doctor threw the empty syringe away and sat down beside his patient.

"The operation went well and I'm happy with the results. It took four hours to complete the surgery because it was very delicate. I had to repair your muscles and tendons. I grafted a special skin over the wound and it will bond with your DNA and grow back quicker. The wound will take about one month to heal properly so you are to wear the sling at all times. Your hand might still be a bit stiff for a while after it has healed. If you have trouble using it, or you experience any pain, you must see a doctor. When you shower, you may take the sling off, but put it back as soon as possible. The dressing can get wet as the bandage is waterproof, but it's designed to let air in when dry, to speed up the healing process. Your dressing must be changed every second day for eight days. Afterwards, it can be changed once a week until it is healed."

"How long must I stay in hospital?"

"Two more days should be sufficient. I just want to make sure nothing goes wrong. If you see any discharge oozing through the bandage, come and see me immediately."

"Thank you, doctor. I'll do that."

"It's a lovely day outside. If you want, you may sit outside in the gardens. You can find them at the end of this passage. Lunch will be served soon so perhaps you could do that afterwards. I'll check on you tomorrow."

The doctor got up to leave but his patient stopped him. "How is my friend doing? Has she woken up yet?"

"She drifts in and out of consciousness and is in a lot of pain. Several bones were broken and those that could be mended, were attended to. Others will just have to heal by themselves, but she will improve daily. My colleague is hopeful she'll recover eventually.'

"Can I see her?"

"I'll speak to Dr Porter. He was the one who patched up your friend. When he has a free moment, I'll tell him to come and see you."

The doctor left and Craig looked out of the window. He saw nothing but grass and a high steel fence. Sighing, he sat down and waited for his lunch to arrive.

After he had eaten, Craig decided to go and look for the gardens and walked down the passageway. He looked curiously into the other wards as he passed by, but the curtains were drawn around all the occupied beds. Carter found the garden and sat on a bench in the sunshine. There was a small pond and he peered inside, not sure what to expect. To his surprise, he saw what looked like normal koi fish swimming around.

He had been outside only a short while, when a pretty nurse came out and sat on a bench. She held a disposable cup in her hand and was blowing on the hot liquid. It smelt like coffee. She smiled at him. "Hello! You must be the new patient everyone is talking about."

He grinned at her. "Hi there! You are a sight for sore eyes! Everyone else seems to be ignoring me. I've only spoken with two other people since I arrived here."

"I know, they aren't a very chatty bunch are they! You'd think their creators would have programmed some kind of emotion into them."

Craig looked curiously at her. "Excuse me? What do you mean?"

She laughed at the expression on his face. "Haven't you noticed! Most of the beings here are androids. The doctors and a few nurses are human, but the majority of the others are just robots."

"Well, under the circumstances, I hadn't really noticed! I was brought here, by androids obviously, now I think about it, but I was rushed into hospital and operated on before I could register that fact. I've been asleep for most of today, recovering from the anaesthetic and my ordeal. Thanks for telling me though. At least I understand why they seem so distant."

"I'm glad I could help. Are you going to be staying here long?"

"Dr Mullins says I must spend at least another two days here, just in case of complications with my arm. I'm also waiting for Dr Porter to come and see me. I'm concerned about my friend and I want to know when she'll be able to leave the hospital so we can go home."

"Which settlement do you come from?"

"Settlement? Oh, you mean Hillvale and the others. No, I don't come from any of them. My friend and I are from – another place."

"I'm sorry, it's rude of me to question you like this." She stood up and threw her cup into a dustbin and began to leave.

"Wait a minute! I don't even know your name. I'm Craig, and you are?"

She smiled and shook his hand. "My name is Erin. I'll probably be seeing you around then."

"I hope so. Goodbye Erin, it was a pleasure to meet you."

When she had gone and he was alone again, Craig decided to walk around the garden. It wasn't very big and he stared at the high fence surrounding the building. On closer examination, he could see the electrical connections, and the fence hummed with power. He walked around the corner of the building and found a locked gate leading to another section of the building. In the distance, he could see another locked gate. When he changed direction, and walked to the other side, he found the same thing. Idly he wondered if the fence was there to keep things in, or out.

Dr Porter found him on the covered porch when he arrived. He was older than Dr Mullins and had greying hair. He had the air of a man who knew what he was doing and Craig got the impression he was probably an orthopaedic specialist. They shook hands and sat down on some comfortable chairs.

"Young man, I'm going to get straight to the point! Your friend sustained many broken bones and contusions, including a severe concussion. She had a stomach injury and one kidney was also damaged, but no one has told me what happened. I've discussed your case with Dr Mullins and obviously the two incidents are related. I would like to know what happened in The Forbidden Valley. Why did you even go there in the first place?"

"I'm surprised no one informed you. Surely the 'higher powers' recorded the whole incident?" Craig remarked carefully.

Dr Porter snorted. "Hah! That bunch of supercilious people think they know what's good for everyone. They probably have documented the entire thing, but they don't feel the doctors need to know everything, that's why I'm asking you."

The explorer decided to tell him what happened, but he left out some of the parts, including the fact that Galen and Daphne had helped them. When he had finished, Dr Porter pondered on what he had been told.

"I knew there were other universes and I've met many who have travelled from your planet. Every traveller is brought to the hospital so that the 'higher powers' as you call them, can see what they are dealing with. We were ordered to conduct certain tests on our subjects and submit them to our leaders. Both you and your friend were tested while under sedation."

"What sort of tests are you talking about?" the explorer asked suspiciously.

"Oh, nothing that could harm you! Our tests determined you are a human male, aged 25 Earth years. You are in peak physical condition and have a very high IQ. Your companion however is a completely different matter entirely. What does a human male have in common with an immortal being?"

"Uh… how do you know she's immortal?"

"That's a foolish question! Her DNA is different to yours. Also, it's very uncommon for an immortal to have such serious injuries. They have – skills to protect themselves from injury. You have enlightened me as to the reason for the injuries, but I'm still confused as to how she managed to sustain these. I can only conclude the beast was too fast and too powerful and therefore took her by surprise."

"I would have to agree with you, doctor."

The doctor looked piercingly at Craig. "I can see why our superiors are interested in you! I have never heard of anyone escaping alive from The Forbidden Valley. You fought and killed a vicious beast almost three times your size. You must have incredible survival instincts!"

"Do you know what they have planned for me when I'm discharged from the hospital?"

"No, they have said nothing regarding your fate. I think our leaders are waiting for your friend to recover sufficiently before they send for you both. I assume you'll be taken to the guest quarters when you leave the hospital. I do as I'm told and I don't interfere with their policies. Our jobs here are just to take care of the sick and injured. The rest is out of our hands. I haven't even met these so called 'higher powers'. I just talk to them through the share link."

He pointed to his ear and Craig saw the tiny earpieces nestled in the doctor's ears.

"When will I be able to see my friend?" he asked.

"I want to watch her for another day. She's still very weak and sleeps most of the time. Immortals have a natural immune system and many of the smaller bones are now cracked, not broken as they were before. Her body is starting to fight the injuries. I've given her some very strong antibiotics and these will also help."

"Thank you, doctor. I can see she is in good hands. I'll speak to you tomorrow then?"

The doctor nodded and shook his hand again. "You take care, young man!"

Craig went back to his room. He took out his mobile device and switched it on. The date and time showed up on the screen and he pressed an icon. His electronic notebook opened and he jotted down some of the things he had heard. The battery was still three quarters full and he was glad he had charged it on the spaceship when he had gone looking for the oxygen regenerators. He switched it off again and hid it in the drawer.

There was a button near the headboard of his bed and he pressed it. A cupboard in the wall opposite him opened and a screen was revealed. A holographic controller popped up beside the bed and he pressed it. The screen lit up with information about different channels. It gave him information when the next meal would be served and what food they would be eating. Craig could also choose different menu options if he wanted something else. There was even a lounge where he could go and play games, or visit with the other patients. He could also call for a nurse if he needed one. While surfing through the channels, he found some interesting things to look at, including a movie channel which played very old movies.

When the nurse brought his supper, he watched her carefully. She smiled at him and told him to enjoy his meal. When he looked closer, he could see she was an android, because she never blinked her eyes once. Humans blink their eyes every few seconds and he mentally thanked Erin for bringing this to his attention. When his food was taken away, he noticed that a robot removed the tray. The androids fascinated him, but they weren't really a novelty, as androids and robots already existed on Earth. The only difference he could really make out was the fact that the androids of the future looked much more human than their earlier counterparts. That night he watched some more television and then settled.

Just before lunchtime, Dr Porter sent for him. He went to the doctor's office.

"Ah yes Craig, come in please."

He did so and sat down on a chair.

"I sent for you because your friend is feeling much better today. She's definitely more alert than she has been the last few days, but she is still experiencing severe pain. Under the circumstances, it's normal and every day should show a marked improvement in her condition. She's struggling to walk and can only manage a few steps at a time, so we have put her in a wheelchair. Your friend has asked to see you. Go and visit her for a while, but I don't want you to tire her out so limit your visit to an hour at the most. Follow me and I'll take you to her."

Carter got up and followed the doctor. He was taken to another private room several doors down from his ward.

Dr Porter went ahead of him and spoke to his patient. "Good day my dear! How are you feeling now? That painkilling injection should have taken effect. Look, I brought you a visitor!"

Craig and Andocia's eyes met for a second and she smiled wanly. "Hello Craig! It's good to see a friendly face. I was getting bored just lying here."

The doctor went to the door and looked back at his patient. "I can see you're improving. I'll leave the two of you alone so you can have a chat. Remember Craig, one hour only!"

When the doctor had left, Andocia's smile vanished. "Where have you been? I heard you were also a patient here, but they wouldn't allow any visitors."

Craig stared at the woman. "Andocia, you scared me when that beast nearly killed you! I wanted to visit, but Dr Porter forbade it. You have been delirious or unconscious most of the time."

She cocked her head at him. "Did I hear you correctly? You were worried about me? How sweet of you."

"Andocia, this hasn't been easy on me either! I've never seen you injured before. Why didn't you summon that barrier to form around you?"

"Everything happened so quickly, I didn't have time to react! One minute I was saving your butt and the next I was flying through the air! The rest is hazy and I don't remember much. What happened?"

Craig explained what had occurred and she was quiet for a minute.

"So, you returned the favour! I guess we're even then. What happened to your arm?"

"After you killed the first tiger, I saw the second one lunge for you. Its mate obviously saw you kill the female and it attacked you. I managed to distract it, and it followed me away from you. I stabbed it in one of its eyes, but before it died, it clawed me down to the bones in my forearm. I had to have an operation too, because I almost lost an arm."

"I see! Well thank you for saving my life. I'm sorry if I snapped at you, but I'm in a lot of pain. The medicine only helps for a few hours, then I need to have some more."

"I understand – and thanks for saving my life too."

Andocia nodded. "Other than being incarcerated in hospital, has anything else happened that I should know about?"

"No, nothing. Our hosts are being very mysterious. The leaders of this planet haven't introduced themselves to me as yet. Your doctor seems to think they are waiting for you to get better before we're summoned into their presence. I don't want to rush you or anything, but time is moving on and every day that passes is another day where I'm away from my wife and my job. By now your people and my friends probably think we are dead. I'm losing track of how many days have passed by since we got here. When do you think you'll be well enough to travel?"

Andocia shrugged her shoulders, then whimpered. "Ow! I still hurt everywhere! I have no idea, when I'll recover. It hurts just to walk! I guess we just have to wait and see."

Craig looked at his watch and stood up. "I have to go! Your doctor told me to only visit for an hour and time's up. I must go and get my dressing changed now. I'm going to be discharged from hospital tomorrow, but I'm sure I'll be able to visit you. Apparently the 'higher powers' or whoever they are, have guest rooms for extended stays. I'm probably going to be taken there. I'll talk to you tomorrow."

He left Andocia's room and went to his doctor's consulting room, where a nurse changed his dressing. When the old one had been removed, Craig looked miserably at his arm. It was red and very tender when he touched it. The wound looked sore and inflamed. When he tried to move his hand, his fingers felt as though they were twice their normal size and he could only bend them a little. Carter went back to his room and took some painkillers.

14

The next day he was discharged from hospital. Two androids escorted him through a door, which led to the main entrance where he had first come in a few days earlier. He noticed a set of very ornate double doors, inlaid with brass. Two androids stood guard at either side. Instinctively Craig knew this was what the inhabitants of Saurus had called "the inner sanctum". He was escorted past these and taken into another section of the building. It looked like the lobby of a hotel and he was taken down the passage. One of his escorts swiped a key card through the slot and the door slid open. He was in a small but comfortable room with an adjoining bathroom. A small lounge led off to one side and a window let in some sunlight, giving the room a rosy glow. There was a tiny kitchenette containing a small microwave and kettle, as well as some tea, coffee, hot chocolate and sugar in various containers. One of the androids handed him the key card.

"You are free to look around, but the main entrance is out of bounds. If you continue down this passageway and turn left, you will find a dining room where you can have your meals. The times will be displayed on this screen above the console here. If you arrive late in the dining room, you won't be served so please be on time. Check this screen regularly as any information you require is available here. Personal messages will also be displayed. You are to read them and obey quickly. This icon is for your entertainment unit. The screen is also for viewing the different programs. If you go right at the end of the passage, it will take you to an entertainment area, where all the facilities are at your disposal. When you are requested to go back to the hospital, a message will be displayed on the screen above the console. If you wish to visit your friend and you haven't been summoned, press this icon and a member of staff will escort you to the hospital, provided the doctors give their permission. Lastly, you are not allowed to wander around the complex alone after supper. All areas will be on lockdown. There are scanning devices hidden in the walls, and alarms will sound. The security staff have orders to incarcerate offenders in the cells if they disobey these orders. Do you have any questions?"

"No, I understand."

"Excellent. Please remain in your room for a while as one of the housekeeping staff will be bringing you a few sets of clothing. You will be given a bag to place your dirty clothing in. Put this outside your door and someone will collect it."

The androids left and Craig locked the door. Not long afterwards, a woman rang his doorbell and he let her in. She handed him three sets of clothing, some underwear and socks, as well as a pair of sneakers. He was also given a comb, toothbrush and some shaving essentials and toiletries. He stacked the shaving and toiletry items in the bathroom cabinet and put the rest of the things in a cupboard that stood near his bed. He had hidden his mobile device in his sling when they had moved him and concealed it under his pillow when the servant left. He had been paying attention and could tell the androids apart from the humans. They never blinked, and seemed to be staring right through him, but he knew they could see him. Most of the staff were androids. They obviously did the menial work, while the humans were given more responsible positions.

Much later he decided to explore the entertainment area. The passage led to another grassy section, also sectioned off with electric fencing. Tall trees grew all around and easy chairs stood under them. There was a small swimming pool that looked cool and inviting. When he had sat down, a waiter appeared and asked him what he would like to drink. He asked for a cold drink. The waiter brought him something cold and refreshing, but he wasn't sure what it was and he didn't want to question them. He had noticed though that every being in this complex wore what doctor Porter had called the "share link", in their ears.

That evening he went to the dining room and sat down at a table. Others also came in to eat and he waved at them. They waved back, but didn't speak to him and he wondered why, but he left them alone. The waiters were polite, but also said very little. When he had eaten his dinner, he went back to his room. He had taken his mobile device with him as he was afraid someone would search his room. The complex looked well run, but he was uneasy and suspicious of everyone. He put the device back under his pillow and the screen above the console beeped, signalling a message. Carter pressed the messages icon and the letters flashed in blue. <The time is 19H00 exactly. Please do not leave your room. Enjoy your evening and remember breakfast will be served precisely at 07H00.>

Craig waited for another hour and then decided to try something. He switched on his mobile device and pressed the "computer" icon. Immediately a holographic computer and keyboard appeared. He had noticed the built-in cable for his charger matched one of the ports on the information console and decided to do a bit of cyber snooping. The man plugged his cable into the console, hoping there wasn't some kind of security code that he would have to type in to gain access to their memory banks. The console lit up and displayed a menu, but the icons made no sense to him. The same screen was displayed on his computer. He studied them for a while and found one that looked like a tiny fire. When he pressed it, another box opened and he clicked on it. Immediately the layout of the complex was visible. He typed in a command and all the guest rooms were revealed. He clicked on them all in turn and several names popped up, including his. Craig noticed they didn't use surnames and wondered why, but remembered he hadn't given his surname.

Carter decided to take a chance and typed in "restricted areas". The computer obliged and brought up a map of the entire complex. He wasn't surprised to learn that most of the restricted areas were located behind the "inner sanctuary". The explorer knew it was only a matter of time before he was taken to the leaders and he didn't relish the prospect. Judging by the behaviour of Galen and Daphne, and also the other strange beings he had met, everyone was afraid of them, yet another part of him was curious to meet these leaders. Even the doctors had not seen the higher beings and that also made him wonder. He closed the file, after saving the map of the complex on his mobile device. Then he tried a few other files, but there were literally hundreds of them on the computer and he found nothing he could use. Craig switched off his mobile device and was pleased to see that while he had been working on the computer, it had charged his device fully. He looked at his watch and found it was late, so he got ready for bed. He stepped in the shower and immediately the water came out of the shower head at just the right temperature. When he washed his hands, the tap would run, without him touching anything. The same thing happened when he used the toilet. When he had finished and walked away from the unit, it flushed just the right amount of water to clear it. Even the lights worked automatically. They switched on when he entered a room and switched off when he exited. He was tired, so climbed into bed, and fell asleep almost immediately.

The console chimed and wished him good morning at 6H30, and told him to get ready for breakfast. He arrived ten minutes before the time and waited. A few people arrived and once again they stared at him but didn't approach. He had been shown the breakfast menu and chosen what he wanted to eat. A male android brought his order which he then ate.

Later he was informed Andocia wanted to see him and was instructed to wait for someone to escort him to the hospital. One of the androids fetched him, but this time they didn't go through the main entrance. Instead they took him to another entrance. The android took out a key card similar to the one he had, and swiped it in the slot. While they were walking through, he saw a full length glass partition separating the passage from another large room. This one was full of people/androids, working on computers. Carter paused to brush some imaginary dust off his shoe. While he was doing this, Craig checked the passageway. Several red lights blinked in the walls and cameras panned from side to side. He noticed a large glass door further down and when he and his escort had passed it, he glanced idly upwards. More lights blinked above the door and a camera took pictures of them. He looked at the rows of computers and noticed each one had a different icon displayed on its screen. Craig remembered seeing these icons on the console in his room. They weren't files, but represented different computers! He glanced quickly at the computers and memorised some of the icons. They carried on walking down the passageway until they reached the other end.

The android swiped his card in the slot and they passed through into another section of the hospital.

Craig knew immediately where to go and the robot left him. He went into Andocia's private ward and found her sitting on a chair, reading from an electronic device. Her colour looked much better. She put down the device and smiled at him. "How are you feeling now Craig?"

"Okay I guess. My arm's still stiff and sore though, but I'm more interested in how you are."

"Each day is better than the previous one, so it's good news I suppose. I've still got a long way to go before I'm mobile again. I tried to walk today and managed about six steps before my legs gave way. I can operate my own wheelchair though so I've been exploring the area. It's boring just sitting here in the ward. At least if I want to go anywhere, I can stand up and get into the wheelchair without constantly asking for help. What's the weather like outside?"

"It looks like another fine day."

"It's nearly teatime and I think the medicine makes me hungry. Let's go to the communal area outside and get something to eat and drink."

Andocia stood up and Craig held the wheelchair for her to climb in.

"Your chariot awaits madam. May I have the honour of escorting you to the patio?"

She laughed. "Why thank you, kind sir! You have my permission!"

He grinned and followed closely. Unexpectedly she reached up and stroked his hand. "You know Craig, I often wonder what it would have been like if we were friends and not enemies."

A thoughtful expression crossed his face and he sighed. "Life would have been a lot less complicated, that's for sure."

"Do you think that day will ever come?"

He shrugged his shoulders. "That would be wonderful, but I doubt it! You and I are so different. It's a pity really!"

"Yeah, I guess so," she conceded.

They went to the patio and were served something to eat and drink. Andocia ate hungrily, but her companion nibbled at his food. When she saw he hadn't finished his sandwich she looked at it. "Do you mind if I have that?"

He pushed it over to her and she ate it.

"Andocia, can I ask you a question?"

"Sure, what is it?"

"When do you think you'll be well enough to leave here?"

She shrugged her shoulders. "I don't really know. As I mentioned I'm getting better every day."

"That's wonderful, but aren't you getting homesick at all? I'm sure your followers will be glad to pamper you. It's not as if you even have to fly the ship. I can do it for you while you rest. The hospital on your planet is quite capable of taking care of you."

"I can't answer that question Craig. I suppose it will be up to Dr Porter."

Carter sighed and looked around. "Well I'm certainly feeling homesick. I would like to get back to our time period before my child is born. I can only imagine what Constance must be thinking and the stress isn't good for her."

Andocia wasn't very concerned. "You forget just how strong your wife is! I'm sure she's just fine. I have to be honest though; I'm a long way from being able to take care of myself. My body is healing, but that beast caused a lot of damage. I guess we'll just have to wait and see."

Craig stayed with Andocia for a while longer and then offered to wheel her back to her ward but Andocia declined. He spoke to one of the androids who offered to call his escort.

The same android that had brought him to the hospital wing, returned him to his room. They went past the computer room as before and Craig studied the security measures once again. When they had arrived back in the lobby where the guest rooms were, the android closed the door. Craig tripped on a loose piece of carpet and stumbled into the android.

"Oh sorry, pardon me! I didn't see that piece sticking out."

"I'm fine; don't worry about it. You know where your room is so I'll just leave. Call me if you need anything."

"I will, thank you."

The robot turned a corner and a smile played around the edges of Craig's mouth as he hid the robot's key card inside his sling and walked nonchalantly back to his room. He had work to do!

He amused himself by watching movies in his room, but he couldn't wait for night to fall. After supper, he locked his room door and waited for the place to quieten down. He took out his mobile device and plugged it into the console in his room once more. He brought up the menu bar on the complex's computer and paired the two devices. He clicked on one of the icons he had remembered seeing in the computer room and a new screen appeared. He scrolled through the menu, looking especially for the personnel files, but found nothing of interest. Then did the same thing with another of the icons. This computer had different files loaded onto it, but again he couldn't find what he was looking for. After searching through the menus of seven different computers, he was about to give up, when he finally got lucky. The eighth computer had a personnel file on its database.

Craig clicked on the file and saw many names in alphabetical order, but he was only interested in two of them. By now it was the early hours of the morning, but still he decided to continue with his snooping. He typed in the name "Galen" and waited. A picture of the man who had helped them, appeared at the beginning of the file.

<Galen Semenov: Age 36. Taken from planet Earth in the year 2964. Place of birth: Russia; City: St Petersburg. Occupation: Nuclear Physicist. Considered an expert in his field. Re-located to Hillvale. New occupation: farmer.>

The file contained lots more information but he didn't have time to read it and saved the file to his mobile device. He typed in "Daphne". The computer did nothing for a few moments and then her file appeared.

<Daphne Hamilton. Age 33: Taken from planet Earth in the year 2050: Place of birth: England: City: Sheffield; Occupation: A famous neurologist who won an award for her work. Re-located to Hillvale and is currently the mate of Galen the farmer.>

The file had a copy of her photograph and her life history both before and after she had been brought to Saurus, just as Galen's had. He copied this to his mobile device as well and shut down the computers.

He lay down on his bed but sleep eluded him. There was so much information that could be found in the files, but he didn't have time to search through everything that interested him. He wondered why two intelligent people were listed as farmers. They had obviously been kidnapped because of their skills, but what had happened afterwards? Something bothered him but he couldn't put his finger on it. Another thing concerned Craig and he wondered why these files were not encrypted, or protected by some kind of security, because he was able to access their files so easily! There were no passwords on any of the computers. He made sure he deleted his activity from the console in his room and also the other computers he had hacked. Carter had one more task to complete but this would be the most dangerous. He had to get into the computer room and steal an electronic reading device and download the information he had gathered.

Craig's intercom chimed, warning him that breakfast was being served in half an hour and he swore loudly. He had fallen asleep fully clothed and his head was pounding from lack of sleep. He was tempted to just skip breakfast, but thought better of it. Someone could come and check up on him and he didn't want to attract any attention to himself. Hurriedly the explorer changed out of his clothes and put fresh ones on. Carter brushed his teeth and combed his hair in the compact bathroom. Just before he left his quarters, he took two prescribed painkillers out of the medicine cabinet above the basin, swallowing them with some water. When he got to the dining room no other patients were seated. Craig was glad to be alone. When he had eaten, he went back to his room and showered. The man hoped Andocia wouldn't bother him and decided that if she did ask for him, he would tell her he had a headache. Craig spent most of the day planning how he could get into the computer room once everyone had gone home for the evening. It was very risky but he was confident he could do it.

Later that evening, he slipped out of his room. He had worked out the angle of the camera and stood just out of its line of vision. Switching on his mobile device, he took a picture of the corridor outside his door. He enabled the holographic mode and the picture was superimposed over the real one. The cameras only picked up on the image of the empty corridor and he passed through undetected. When he got to the door which led to the computer room, he swiped the stolen card in the slot and the door opened. Once again he took a picture of the corridor and used the holograph to fool the security cameras. Carter wasn't sure about the angle of the cameras in this room, so he stood at the doorway and quickly took a video of the room. He breathed a sigh of relief when the alarm didn't go off. He aimed his mobile device at the camera and the video image played constantly.

Craig knew what the electronic reading devices looked like, so he ran from one computer to another and opened the drawers of the desks searching for them but found nothing useful inside. A cupboard stood in a corner and he rummaged around and found a few on the top shelf. He grabbed one and put it in his waistband, under his shirt. He picked up his mobile device and went out. The door locked behind him and he used the hologram to move undetected down the passageway. When he got to the door that led back to the guest section, he glanced up. A red button was flashing and his throat went dry. He had obviously triggered a silent alarm and could hear shouting and footsteps in the distance. Carter peeped around the corner, but the security staff were not in that corridor yet. The man used the holographic image to run down the passage and he shut his door at the same instant another door further along was flung open. He sprinted to the bathroom and pulled off his clothes, hurriedly stepping into a pair of sleeping shorts. Carter could hear the footsteps coming closer and he climbed up on the toilet and hid the incriminating evidence in an air vent. Lastly he mussed his hair to make it look as though he had been sleeping, then dived into bed.

Seconds later, someone banged on his door and ordered him to open up immediately.

He opened the door and looked blearily at the people standing outside and pretended to rub the sleep from his eyes.

"Uh… what's wrong?" he asked sleepily.

"Someone broke into our computer room earlier tonight! Have you seen or heard anything?"

"No, you woke me up when you banged on my door. I was asleep."

The security guard came inside. "We have to search your room! Step aside!"

Carter did so and three men came inside and began opening and closing drawers. They pulled his bed apart and looked under the mattress and inside the pillowslip. They even checked behind the toilet, but they never examined the air vent. The guards also opened the window and looked outside and Craig was glad he hadn't thrown the evidence out of the window, although he had been tempted to do so.

When they were satisfied, they left without apologising and he locked the door again. For a long time, he heard them searching the passageways and other rooms. By the time things had quieted down again, he found he couldn't sleep at all.

When morning came, he went to eat breakfast and heard the waiters discussing the previous evening's incident. He went for a walk later and threw the access card, which he had cut into tiny pieces, into a dustbin overflowing with trash. He now wanted to transfer the data he had taken from the computer onto the reading device and went back to his room.

The console chimed and he looked into the face of Dr Porter.

"Ah Craig, can you come to the hospital please? I need to talk to you and so does your friend. I've already sent someone to fetch you. I'll see you shortly."

The screen went dead and not long afterwards, a knock sounded on his door. He opened it and a different android greeted him.

"Please come with me. You are expected at the hospital."

The explorer followed him and this time they went past the main entrance. He wasn't sure if it was just his overactive imagination, but everyone they passed seemed to look curiously at him and he wondered briefly if they had somehow found out he was the burglar.

They went to Dr Porter's consulting room and the man stood up and shook his hand. "Good to see you again, young man. I have news for you! Your friend has been doing some extensive physiotherapy and is much better now. She still needs a lot of attention but I'm discharging her from hospital today. Andrew here has been instructed to take her things to the guest rooms and get her settled in. While he does that, I'll be taking you and Andocia to meet our superiors. Come let's not waste any time. You are both expected."

Andocia was sitting in her wheelchair and she smiled at Craig. "Did Dr Porter give you the good news? Finally, we get to meet the secretive leaders!"

Craig smiled but said nothing. Dr Porter pushed the wheelchair and the explorer followed him.

They arrived at the ornate doors which led to the inner sanctum. Everyone looked curiously at them and Craig wondered what lay beyond this point. The doors slid open and Dr Porter smiled brightly at them. "This is as far as I go! It has been a pleasure knowing you. Goodbye and good luck!"

15

Andocia operated her chair and went inside, with Craig following behind. The doors closed again and two female androids joined them. "Follow us please!"

He walked beside Andocia and looked curiously around. This place was a complete contrast to the outside world, where everything was simply functional. The furniture was opulent and the carpets were so soft and shaggy that he couldn't hear his own footsteps. Works of art decorated the walls and although he wasn't an expert, Craig was sure these were the real thing and not copies. The light fittings shone like gold. Everywhere they walked, he could see outside, for the walls were made of glass. Beautiful flowers bloomed beyond the walls and he could see some water features dotted around. The figurines over which the water cascaded, looked as though they were made from pure gold.

They arrived at another set of doors and they slid open quietly. The two androids stood on either side of a red carpet and waved them forward. The chamber they entered was so bright and for a moment they were blinded, but as their eyes adjusted, the image became clearer. The twosome stopped at the end of the red carpet and looked up at their host. In that second, Craig's mouth hung open in astonishment and Andocia gasped audibly. She grabbed her companion by his good arm and hissed. "Craig, kneel down!"

He obeyed and fell to his knees. Andocia tried to stand up, but the woman spoke.

"Andocia! It is so good to see you, my sister! No, no, please stay seated. I am aware of your injuries and I shall not take offence."

Andocia murmured something and bent her head in supplication. "Mighty Valdena! It has been many years since I last laid eyes on you. I thought you were dead!"

"I too thought the end had come, but fate was kind to me and I survived. I have been eager to speak with you and your companion since your arrival a few days ago, but Dr Porter informed me of your injuries and suggested I wait until you were feeling better. Do you still have much pain?"

"No, 'learned one'; there is pain but I am much better now."

"Excellent! We have a great deal to talk about. Please dear sister, call me Valdena. My title only applied when I was on Darkos."

While Valdena was talking to Andocia, Craig had got over his initial shock. He studied the woman before him curiously. She was tall and he estimated she stood a head taller than him in her bare feet. She was incredibly beautiful, with long wavy black hair that hung halfway down her back. Her skin was green and her eyes were red, just like Andocia's. She wore a purple brushed velvet dress with a low V neck that showed her assets to perfection, and clung to her body like a second skin. It flared from the waist and pooled on the floor around her. Her elegant ankles showed under the fabric, and she was wearing very high heeled sandals in the same shade as her dress. For an instant, her eyes met Craig's and she smiled and spoke to him. "Patience Craig Carter – yes I know who you are! You have many questions, but I will endeavour to answer them for you later. You may stand up now."

In that instant, Craig knew she too was telepathic and he tried to stop his mind from wandering and concentrated only on the conversation taking place between her and Andocia. He got carefully to his feet and stood beside Andocia. The two women spoke for a while about things Craig knew nothing about, but he was determined to get Andocia to explain everything in great detail later.

Valdena stared piercingly at Craig, but spoke to Andocia. "My dear, I'm curious! What is an immortal doing hanging around with a mortal? You two arrived here together, but you aren't friends, are you?"

"Not really, no," she replied hesitantly.

Valdena looked at Craig and he answered honestly. "We are enemies in our time period. Andocia has been a thorn in my side ever since I met her. We were travelling together when we ended up here in the future. I still don't understand what happened."

The immortal smirked. "There is an anomaly out in Spacethat occurs every couple of years. A rift develops and objects travelling through Spaceget sucked through. It isn't just a gateway to the future though; if one knows how to navigate it, one can revisit the past as well. This rift is a time travel portal!"

"Is there some sort of pattern to this portal opening?" Carter asked.

"No, it is very unstable and can occur anytime. The only thing that can prevent anyone going through it by accident is if your technical people could invent a warning device that pinpoints it. Then your spaceships could avoid it. I have invented a device that opens the portal anytime I wish to go through it, so I can travel anywhere I like, whenever I want to. I can obviously also close it when I have passed through."

Craig looked at Andocia and she nodded her head. "Valdena was a scientist on Darkos. I believe her."

Suddenly everything made sense! Craig began to understand just how the planet Saurus came to be populated, but now he had even more questions than before. Valdena interrupted his train of thought.

"Okay, enough of me and my history. I want to know all about the two of you. I see we have a lot to get through, so I suggest we go somewhere more comfortable where we can discuss everything at length. I have a private sitting room where we won't be disturbed."

She got up and walked to another door and opened it. A man bowed his head as the three beings walked through.

"Vincent I am taking my guests to my parlour where I don't wish to be disturbed for the rest of the day. Bring us some refreshments."

The man bowed. "I'll bring something right away."

They followed their host to another door which opened into a spacious lounge. Many comfortable chairs and couches stood on a plush carpet and Valdena moved to an overstuffed chair.

"Andocia, you will be much more comfortable sitting here. We have a great deal to discuss."

She held the wheelchair still while Andocia settled herself into the chair and stretched her legs. Valdena pointed to a couch. "Craig, you can take a seat over there."

He sat down on the couch and it seemed to mould around his body. The couch was much lower down than the two chairs in which the women sat. Drinks and snacks were brought in and placed on a table near their hostess. She busied herself for a few minutes by making them some beverages and offering around the plate of snacks. When everyone had taken what they wanted, she sat down on her chair.

Valdena looked at both her guests in turn and smiled.

"I must say your landing here has caused quite a stir amongst myself and my staff. As you may have noticed, most of my employees in this particular complex are human, like yourself, Craig. May I call you Craig? We don't use surnames here because I feel everyone is equal and it's also more informal. Most of my security staff are androids, but there are a few humans in charge of them. Outside this particular complex, most of the staff are androids, again with just a few exceptions. All those who live in the cities are human."

"I noticed that," Craig replied. "However, I'm curious about the other beings that live in and around the cities. Talking animals! Really! Why?"

"Craig, I find humans very interesting, but they have one very bad flaw!

Human beings know only how to fight to get what they want and they kill for greed, amongst other things. Animals however kill only what is necessary, for example, they kill to sustain themselves, not because of any ulterior motives. It is for this very reason that the Earth you know was destroyed a few centuries ago. The animals are the peacemakers in the settlements."

"That still doesn't explain why they have the ability to talk. Also why have you created mythological creatures? They have never existed, except in fairy tales that children read."

Valdena chuckled. "Yes, I know, but I have the ability to create these creatures, so I did, just to see how they would turn out. You were quite taken with the female centaurs, so I've been told."

Andocia interrupted. "Forgive him, learned one! Sometimes he doesn't know when he should stop asking questions."

Craig glared at her, but Valdena shook her head. "Nonsense, he can ask me anything he likes. This young man is quite exceptional and I see why you are so interested in him. We have no secrets here on Saurus. The reason why the animals can talk is because they have been created, using some human DNA. As you probably saw, some of the animals looked more human than others. Human beings have more logic than animals and sometimes I exploit that. An animal has to know the difference between a human who is blatantly aggressive, or extremely passive! I don't want the animals killing the humans for the wrong reasons. Fortunately, most of the humans here know their place and they respect the fact that the animals are actually in charge, nor do they question this."

Craig looked at Andocia and she shrugged her shoulders.

"Valdena, I was wondering where all the humans come from. Were they here when you decided to make this planet your home?" Andocia asked curiously.

"I was wandering around looking for a place to settle down and I found this planet. It has a similar atmosphere to Earth in the very early days of creation. The ground was fertile and everything grew well. After Darkos had been destroyed, I had nowhere to go, so I decided to live here. The rift I mentioned earlier was already in existence, but it wasn't as frequent as it is now. Every chance I got, I visited planets and brought back plants and equipment and slowly I built this place. I've had years to accomplish this and it's good to be busy. Even now I'm constantly experimenting with different things, so I'm never bored."

Craig went to get some more snacks and helped himself to something else to drink. He passed the plate around and both women filled their plates again. When he had sat down, he questioned Valdena further.

"How did the humans get here? I suppose you 'imported' them as well."

"Yes of course I did! Because I had the knowledge to travel from the past to the present and also to the future, I brought them along with me and created my own inhabited planet. I was very choosy however and I only chose the smartest, most intelligent people. I gave them homes in the various cities and they multiplied, increasing the population. Any man and woman here are free to choose their own partners to breed with. They may breed with multiple partners if they wish. I don't mind, just as long as they increase. This gives me an unlimited supply of human DNA which helps me to create more creatures. As you can see, everyone is content."

Craig shook his head. "I still don't understand! The people I saw when we arrived did seem content, but surely those you kidnapped had family and friends got left behind. Why would they suddenly be happy to do menial jobs and breed with women they don't even know?"

"Craig, you are forgetting who you're talking to. You are going too far!" Andocia warned him.

Valdena's smile disappeared, but she looked challengingly at the man. "I suppose I can tell you. It won't really matter later anyway. Everyone who comes through those double doors you entered today, is questioned about their lives and their work. As you have no doubt guessed, humans, being the undisciplined creatures they are, don't always embrace change, so I help them to see the error of their ways."

Craig was silent, pondering what this woman did to unsuspecting humans and cursing his stupidity.

She smiled cat-like at him. "You really are very nosy, aren't you?! I'm going to answer your question even though it's none of your business. I have invented a device that clears their minds of every memory they have ever had, and replaces the information with whatever I want them to know. For example, if I want someone to be a farmer, I give that person the knowledge to do the job and they become experts at it. I don't destroy their minds. They can still do the normal things that humans do, but their previous life is obliterated and they become what I want them to be. They do whatever they have been told, without question! Are you satisfied now?"

Craig nodded and looked down at his hands.

Valdena pressed a button and someone came and took the snacks away. She looked over at Andocia and ignored Craig. "My dear, I have so much that I wish to speak to you about, but I think we'll do that another day, without your companion being present. Seeing as he is so curious about us, I want to question him at length about his own life. I sense you are getting stiff and sore again, so I'll have you escorted to your room where you can rest. One of my androids will explain how everything works. Your things have been placed in the guest quarters and your room is located a few doors down from Craig's. We can have some breakfast together tomorrow morning. I'll expect you then."

"Thank you, Valdena. I could do with a rest. See you tomorrow."

One of the androids came in and helped Andocia into her chair. Then she wheeled the woman out and closed the door behind them.

16

Valdena's expression hardened and she stared down at Craig. "All right, I want to know everything about you. I have encountered many humans who had the same qualities as you, but every one of them obeys me now. I know what you are capable of and I must admit it was very impressive. I have been watching your every move almost from the time you landed here. In the beginning though we lost track of you, because you just happened to land near Hillvale. The trees grow high and close together so the watchers couldn't find you. You obviously didn't crash land, like some of the inhabitants, so your ship was well hidden and you gained some time. It was much later on when I learnt you had killed a mutant dog. Andocia left her mark on the animal as well, so I knew you were travelling with an immortal and we stepped up the surveillance of the settlements. I know of only a few immortals, so I didn't know which one you were travelling with, until one of the watchers found the two of you and furnished me with a description. Once my people located you, they followed you secretly. Everywhere you went, you were never alone."

Craig nodded. "I knew we had to have been discovered, but Andocia believed we had not. I'm a Space explorer by profession and we are naturally curious. I guess I'm a lot like you in that respect. You also travel from place to place, but for different reasons obviously. I'm sorry if I offended you earlier, but Andocia's right – I don't know when to keep my mouth shut. I meant no disrespect."

"I accept your apology. However, you still want to know why I didn't have you brought here earlier."

Craig sighed. "How did you…? Oh, never mind – I keep forgetting you are also telepathic."

She raised her eyebrows briefly. "So, you are familiar with telepaths! That's interesting!"

Craig stayed silent and she nodded her head. "Well anyway, the reason I never had you brought here earlier was also out of curiosity. The watchers all carried miniature cameras that filmed you and Andoica. The footage they sent to me was very exciting. I can see just by looking at it that you are a born leader. Even the animals I have created, looked to you for guidance. You have an… essence that inspires leadership. I just want to know where you hid for the first few days before we discovered you and Andocia, because you just seemed to appear out of nowhere. If any of the inhabitants living in the cities see a stranger they must, by law, reveal this to us so we can investigate and interview them, yet no one came forward with that information."

"We stayed in our spaceship and only came out to explore the surroundings." Craig lied smoothly.

"I see! That was very clever of you both. It certainly makes sense."

Valdena was quiet for a while, then spoke to him again. "You have already mentioned your profession is to explore space, but it seems your fighting skills are quite unbelievable. You killed my tiger beast when it attacked Andocia. No one has ever defeated one of those mutants before! Why did you go to The Forbidden Valley anyway? Surely the centaurs warned you about that place?"

"They did, but I had no choice. I needed a part for our spaceship. It was a very common part that could be found on any spaceship and I heard there were other spaceships in The Forbidden Valley and that's why we went there. The centaurs offered to show us where it was."

"Who told you about the other spaceships?"

Craig stared levelly at his hostess. "I don't remember!"

Valdena got up from her chair and looked outside for a moment. "You have morals too I see! Obviously, you don't want to get anyone into trouble! I'm going to ask Andocia the same question and she'll probably give me the answer."

"Does it really matter? Look what happened when we entered The Forbidden Valley. Both Andocia and I got injured. Even the centaurs didn't make it through unscathed."

"Did you find the part you needed?"

He looked at the ground and nodded. "Yes."

"It was confiscated when you were brought here, wasn't it?"

Craig nodded again.

Valdena crossed her arms and paced back and forth in front of him. "So, even if by some miracle you managed to escape from my sanctuary, you cannot leave without replacing this part!"

"Unfortunately not."

Valdena thought about this and looked penetratingly at him.

"Every time I think I'm beginning to understand your logic, you confuse me further. I have already ascertained you and Andocia aren't friends, yet you stayed on Saurus when she became injured. You have already admitted you knew we were aware of your presence here. Why didn't you go back with the centaurs and leave Andocia for us to find? You could have replaced the part that you needed and escaped – unless you don't know how to return to your own time."

Craig smiled despite the circumstances. "I have figured out how to return to my planet and time period and believe me, I was tempted to do just that, but I felt sorry for Andocia and I didn't want to leave her here. Anyway, when she had recovered, she would have come looking for me, and most probably killed me for betraying her. Unfortunately, my arm wouldn't stop bleeding either and I knew I needed medical help. It would have done me no good to escape and then bleed to death out in space, so I told Mia to let her friends know and report to you, which they did. The rest you know."

Valdena looked aghast at her guest. "So, you surrendered in order to get the help both you and Andocia needed. Words fail me, they truly do!" she replied, admiration evident in her voice. "It's no surprise why Andocia holds you in such high esteem! You two may be enemies, but she admires you a great deal."

"Until she has her next temper tantrum and takes it out on me!" he grumbled. "You wanted to know why she and I were travelling together when we landed up here, well, I'll tell you! She has kidnapped my wife and threatened to kill her and our unborn baby, unless I help her to destroy Tanus! We were on our way to the White Planet when the ship got pulled through the rift in Spaceand we landed here on Saurus."

Valdena's face twisted into an evil sneer. "Tanus! That bitch! So, she is still causing trouble! I had hoped she was out of the picture, but obviously she still presents a problem."

"I'm actually on Tanus's side! If it wasn't for her intervention, I would probably have been killed long ago," Craig remarked.

Valdena glared witheringly at him. "You are a brave person, admitting to me that you are friends with Tanus. I should just kill you and forget you were ever here. You, Craig Carter, are a legend, trusted by many and hated by some very powerful people for your endeavours. I, too, have heard about your exploits and adventures!"

Craig forced himself to look into her flashing red eyes and he saw hatred, envy and anger there. He looked out of a large window and saw some beautiful fountains and chairs surrounding a magnificent lake. Staff members were enjoying lunch breaks and chatting amicably to one another.

Valdena interrupted his thoughts.

"So, what was your plan going to be when you got to Tanus's planet?"

He shrugged his shoulders. "I honestly don't know! I was just going with the flow and hoping for a miracle, I suppose."

"So, what you're telling me is you were Andocia's captive when you got sucked through the rift in space."

"No, not her captive – her unwilling participant!"

Valdena picked up a remote-control device. "You know, the longer I listen to you, the more complex I realise you actually are. It's lucky there are two reasons why you cannot escape from this planet. Number one, is the fact that you need to replace a part on your ship before you can leave here, and, number two, is the fact that we have found where you hid your spacecraft."

Craig looked disbelievingly at her.

"I thought you wouldn't believe me, but it's true," she said as she pointed the remote-control device at a picture, which rolled upwards, revealing a screen. She pressed another button and a video began to play.

He watched miserably as the camera panned over their ship and paused on the logo, identifying it as belonging to Andocia. The ship was surrounded by heavily armed guards. Several frightened people were walking around and obviously being questioned by the security forces, but Carter didn't recognise any of them.

"See, I told you we found it."

"I guess it was inevitable, but I still wish it hadn't been discovered. So Valdena, what happens now? You hold all the cards."

"I assume you mean that I win and you lose!"

"Something like that, I suppose," he grumbled.

"Craig, don't feel bad! You had already lost the moment you stepped into the inner sanctum anyway." She replied triumphantly. "Your fate now rests in the hands of myself and Andocia. Tomorrow I'll be discussing a number of things with her. I have so many ideas, I'm actually looking forward to our meeting."

Craig stood up slowly. "May I be excused, or is there more information you need from me?"

She waved her hand dismissively. "You have my permission to return to your room. I'll get someone to come and escort you back. Just one more thing!"

The man stood silently and looked at her.

"I'm warning you, don't try to escape. If you have some crazy plan in mind, just forget it! My staff have orders to shoot and kill anyone who disobeys me."

Craig looked miserably at her. "You don't need to threaten me; you've won. Where could I go anyway?"

Two androids accompanied him back to his room. They went a different way and Craig wondered just how many routes led to and from the inner sanctum. When he was safely in his room and had locked the door, he sat down on his bed and punched the pillow furiously.

"Supercilious bitch! What is it with these immortals! They think they own everyone and everything! I should have been an actor! She fell for my little charade! Tomorrow I'll be on my best behaviour and once Andocia has spoken with her, I'll decide what course of action to take. I have work to do tonight. No matter what my future holds, I will leave a lasting impression with some of the inhabitants on this planet. Things need to change drastically around here!"

Craig went to the bathroom and checked the air vent. His mobile device and the data reader were still there and he took them to the bedroom and switched both on. He was tempted to hack into the computers and find more information on other residents of Saurus, but he decided it was too risky now Valdena and her cohorts knew someone had broken into the computer room. Carter paired the two devices and began downloading the information he had found on Galen and Daphne, into the data reader. He left the two devices on and went to make himself something to drink. Afterwards he watched some television. Much later, he checked on the devices and found the information had been copied successfully. He then deleted the file from his electronic device. Using the keyboard on the reading device, he added everything he could think of that would help Galen and Daphne. He explained what had happened when he finally went to see Valdena, and gave them possible suggestions on the way forward for them. Deciding there was nothing more to add, he went to have a shower and got ready for bed.

He lay awake for a while, wondering what tomorrow held in store for him, but finally fell asleep. That night he had a dream in which Constance came to him. She had a glow about her and she smiled at her husband. Her stomach was much bigger than he remembered and she placed her hands lovingly on the bump. "Don't give up, my angel! You are a very enterprising man and that's why I love you so much! Everything is going to be okay, you'll see. Do whatever it takes to come back to us. Never give up! Just remember 'winners never quit, and quitters never win'."

Craig woke with a start and realised that the alarm reminding him about breakfast was going off. He cancelled it and stood up. He looked around the room, almost expecting to see Constance there. The dream had seemed so real! The young man got dressed and locked the door behind him.

As he made his way down the passage, Andocia came out of her room, accompanied by an android who was pushing her in her wheelchair. They passed one another in the passageway and he greeted her. She returned the greeting, then went in the opposite direction, obviously to meet with Valdena. When Craig sat down at the table, he saw two heavily armed androids, who nodded at him. He waved back and began eating his food. His waitress was a human and her hands were shaking as she placed the tray down on the table and scuttled away. After breakfast he returned to his room and the two androids took up positions on opposite sides of the passageway. Obviously Valdena was worried he would try to escape and he was secretly pleased she thought of him as a threat.

Shortly afterwards, he came out of his room and the androids stood straighter and their hands hovered near their guns. He ignored them and went outside to the small swimming pool. Although his arm now felt much better, it was still stiff and he decided to risk exercising it a bit to strengthen the muscles. He discarded the sling and climbed into the heated water. The androids had come outside and sat down some distance away from him, but he ignored them completely and swam around and around the pool. By the time he climbed out of the water, he was actually feeling tired and he decided he needed to do some more exercise to regain his strength. Drinks were brought for him and he spent an hour on the patio. The androids stayed put the entire time.

A woman came up to him in the early afternoon and told him he was expected at the hospital, where his dressing would be changed again. He went back to his room and put on some clothes and when he came out, the androids were waiting for him.

"I know my way to the hospital, thank you." He remarked when they came closer.

"We have orders not to let you out of our sight, Sir. We shall be accompanying you to the doctor."

The Space explorer shrugged his shoulders and began walking. The androids fell into step on each side of him and the procession went to the hospital.

Once they had gone inside, the staff looked nervously at them, but Craig was unruffled.

One of the nurses smiled nervously. "Dr Mullins is expecting you. Please follow me."

Carter walked next to her and the androids began to follow them. The nurse turned around. "Only patients are allowed into the consulting rooms," she stated bravely.

The androids ignored her and continued walking. Craig put a cautionary hand on her arm and whispered to the frightened nurse.

"They have their orders miss. It would be better if you just let them be."

Dr Mullins's eyes went wide for a few moments when he saw them, but he smiled bravely and tried to ignore them. They went to a corner of the consulting room and waited.

The doctor took his patient's arm and studied it. "How are you feeling Craig? Do you still experience pain?"

"Only sometimes thanks. I feel much better."

"That's good! I need to do an X-ray to see how those muscles and tendons are doing. Your fingertips are a healthy pink colour so your circulation is excellent."

Dr Mullins spoke to the androids. "I have to take him for an X-ray now and you cannot accompany us. The machinery will interfere with your circuitry. Wait here."

The androids looked menacingly at the doctor. "If you help him to escape, you will be shot."

The doctor stared witheringly at them and put his arm around his patient's shoulder. "Come along Craig."

They went to another section of the hospital and Dr Mullins stared curiously at his patient. "This is new! Why suddenly do you have an armed escort?"

Carter smiled mirthlessly. "Doctor, have you ever been inside the inner sanctum before?"

"Once, long ago."

"Do you know what happens behind those doors?"

"Not really. They seem reluctant to allow humans inside. Only the androids are allowed to enter."

"Have you met your superiors at all?"

"Now you mention it, no, I actually haven't. They are this planet's most well-kept secret."

"There's a good reason for that. Do you know what an immortal is?"

"I have heard of such people, but your friend Andocia is one of them, so I've been told. You won't report me for disclosing this, will you?" he asked nervously. "Dr Porter was amazed and he shared this information with me."

"Relax, I'm on your side. I promise this conversation never happened. Andocia was never my friend, but the details aren't really important. Your superior is a woman who is also an immortal. They know one another and it came as a surprise to me as well. Even Andocia was taken aback. Anyway, I wanted to warn you to be careful. The other immortal is unscrupulous and dangerous, but unfortunately also very clever. She uses humans as guinea pigs, by getting hold of their DNA and then uses it to make her animals. If you have ever lived out in the settlements, you would know what I mean."

"All the doctors and nurses have homes in this complex. We don't mix with those in the cities."

Craig nodded. "It makes sense. Look we don't have much time, but all the humans who inhabit the cities have been kidnapped from different time periods and brought here, where she does something to their brains. They are made to forget their pasts and she creates a new life for them. Everyone works for free to benefit this planet. For all you know, even the doctors, including you, may have been brought here and brainwashed as well, for want of a better word. At the moment this woman and Andocia are discussing my fate. By tomorrow I may be joining the humans out there, with no recollection of my life, my wife and my unborn child. That's why I have an armed escort. That woman doesn't want me trying to escape and reveal this to anyone. You can't do anything to help me and I don't want you to try! Just remember this conversation and if you can, do something about it, not for my sake but that of humanity. Oh, and one more thing: be careful around that woman. She is telepathic and very powerful. Let's do this X-ray quickly before the androids come looking for us, I haven't mentioned her name, because if she talks to you and reads your mind, she'll know we spoke and your life could also be in danger."

Dr Mullins was speechless for a moment. "Thank you for sharing that information with me. At the appropriate time I'll tell my colleagues about this conversation, but I also want to see what happens to you first before I pre-empt anything. You are truly a brave man and I salute your courage."

They went to the X-ray room and Dr Mullins took the colour photographs back to his consulting room where the androids waited.

"Craig, the X-rays are looking good. Every muscle, tendon and nerve has been reattached and I'm very happy with the results. Your skin is still raw and I'm going to put anther dressing on so it can heal completely. I suggest you still wear the sling for a while, but I'm going to give you some exercises to do so you can begin strengthening your arm and hand. I'm going to write out my report and suggest you also undergo some physiotherapy once the bandage has been removed. Do you need any more painkillers?"

"No thanks, I'm fine."

Dr Mullins shook his good hand. "Then may I take this opportunity to wish you well. Take care, Craig."

"Thank you, doctor. I appreciate all you have done for me."

He left the consulting room with the androids trailing behind.

That night he went to eat his supper and again the androids sat at a nearby table and watched him. When he was returned to his room, he saw Andocia going into hers. She looked up at him and he could see she was tired.

"Craig, I wanted to discuss some things with you, but I had hoped to return earlier. Right now, I just want to rest. I know you are anxious to hear what happened today, but it will have to wait until tomorrow morning. I have instructed the kitchen staff to serve us breakfast in my room. Come at about 07H00."

"Okay Andocia. I'll see you then."

Craig swallowed his disappointment and went to his room. He switched on the electronic data reader and began typing some more information onto it. When he was satisfied he had covered everything of importance, he opened the door a crack and peered out. The androids were still patiently standing at either side of the passageway. The explorer closed the door quietly and went to watch something on the television, but he found it hard to concentrate. While he lay in bed, he knew one thing was certain. Tomorrow would be a turning point in his life, one way or another. He would just have to wait and see.

17

The next morning, the alarm woke Craig at 6H30 and he got ready to meet Andocia. When he stepped out of his room, the androids were nowhere in sight. Craig knocked on the door and Andocia let him in, then locked the door behind him. She was walking unaided and looked much better. Valdena had obviously lent her a dress and Craig's eyes roamed over her body. The figure hugging dress clung to her curves as though it was made for her. She looked self-consciously at him. "I know! I look like a tart! This is Valdena's style, not mine."

"No, it looks good on you," he complimented her.

She smiled and indicated to a small table with two chairs. "The meal will be here shortly. I think we should eat and then we can discuss yesterday's meeting."

As if on cue, there was a knock on the door and Andocia opened it. The food was brought to the table and set down in front of the two guests. Carter wasn't feeling very hungry, but when Andocia opened the cover on the serving dish, his mouth watered. A veritable feast lay before them and he helped himself to some of the delicious fare. When they had finished eating, Andocia pressed a button on the entertainment console and one of the androids came and took the plates away.

Craig sat back and looked at Andocia. "Okay, the suspense is killing me! What does the future hold for me? I'm sure your friend has made sure you'll be taken care of."

"She's not my friend!" Andocia snapped irritably. "I don't even like her!"

Craig's mouth dropped open in astonishment. "What? But you and her are alike!"

"Only in appearance I assure you."

"But she called you sister!"

"It's just a term of endearment, that's all. I'm not related to her in any way, thank the stars. She was one of the leaders of Darkos before the planet disintegrated."

"Well I know nothing about your life or why you became who you are and I think it's about time you told me your story! You know everything about me and I think we should even the score, but first I would like to know my fate. What have you and Valdena decided should happen to me?"

Andocia smiled. "You can relax Craig! We are both free to return home. Once I have explained everything to you, we are going to have to go and see Valdena again and make arrangements for our departure."

Craig smiled happily. "Really! We are free to go? I'm not going to be brainwashed and forced to stay here?"

"No."

The explorer was overwhelmed and he took both Andocia's hands in his. "Thank you!" he replied gratefully. "I owe you, my life!"

She looked down at their intertwined hands and guiltily the man released hers.

"What happened when you met with Valdena?" Craig enquired.

"As I have mentioned, I don't like her very much, but that woman has a brilliant mind! She was a scientist on Darkos and is very clever. The reason I took so long to get back after our meeting was because she showed me around the whole complex. She showed me how the animals were created and the process was mind boggling, but very cruel. Valdena wanted me to watch how she 'brainwashed' someone but I declined. I may not be a good person myself, but I don't agree with her methods. I understand why she feels she has to wipe out their previous lives and create fictional ones for the humans she kidnaps though, because if she left them with their original memories intact, she would constantly have trouble with them. Humans are naturally violent beings and there I do agree with her. However, what about the families they leave behind? They suffer too when their loved ones disappear without a trace. Using her method of course, human beings lose the inclination to fight and they become her willing slaves by looking after this planet for her. Did you know the animals she creates have no reproductive systems, so they can't have any offspring?"

"What happens to them when they get old?"

"I don't know how long their lifespan is, but when she is tired of them, they simply cease to exist. She just makes more as needed. By injecting the unfortunate beasts with human DNA, they can think. I wonder what they would say if they knew this?"

"They would certainly be angry." Craig answered.

"I have to be honest with you Craig. Valdena wanted to keep you here and wipe your mind of everything you ever knew or loved. She was very impressed with you and felt your DNA could have been used to make exceptional children, or animals if she liked."

"Speaking of human DNA, how does she keep a constant supply handy?"

"That's the easiest part! All the inhabitants in all the cities are required to come in for a medical examination once a month. When they go to the hospital, the doctors extract whatever Valdena requests. It could just be blood, or anything she wants really. There is no shortage of human beings to help her continue with her experiments. Some people never return from hospital because Valdena may want that particular person's heart, for example, to use on someone more important, and their partners are just given a replacement. Their partners don't even question why their loved one hasn't returned."

"Diabolical, and they don't even know they are being used for ulterior motives."

"Precisely."

Carter shuddered. "Ugh, I'm glad we are getting out of here soon. Do you think she might change her mind about letting us go?"

Andocia shrugged her shoulders. "I wouldn't put it past her, but she and I are evenly matched, so if it came to a fight, I would happily take her on."

"Hold it a minute! You look much better but you can't be completely well yet. She's stronger than you right now. When I got the oxygen regenerators out of that spaceship, I also took two laser guns. I'm hoping she doesn't recognise them as weapons. I did notice the weapons her androids carry are more advanced than ours. They also look completely different to the ones we carry. Do you think you could somehow persuade whoever is looking after our stuff to return it to us?"

"I could do that. I'll speak to the person concerned. She did introduce me to the man so I know who to ask. He's a human male, so I shouldn't have any trouble."

"Andocia, I still don't know how you persuaded Valdena to let me go."

"I explained what our relationship is and told her the reason why we were out in Spacein the first place. She was delighted to hear my plan about getting rid of Tanus and encouraged me to continue with it when we got back. I explained I needed you to do this for me and she gave me her blessing."

"Did she say anything else of interest?"

"Well, she did question me at length about your life, so I told her only what I thought she should hear. There was no point in telling her everything about you."

"Okay, now you owe me an explanation about your life. I don't understand why both you and Tanus were so cagey about letting me have details. Seeing as you know everything about me, I'd like to learn about yours and Tanus's origins."

Andocia paced up and down. "You know, if Valdena hadn't come into the picture, I wouldn't share these details with you, but I suppose it can't do any harm. I guess I owe you that much at least."

The woman sat down and crossed her legs.

"It all began many years ago on Earth. I'll never forget the date. It was 12th September 2050. I was alone at home because my parents had gone into town to sell their produce at the local market. We lived on a large farm and were quite wealthy. I was feeding the chickens at the time, when the spaceship landed nearby. I remember that for some reason I wasn't afraid, only curious. A strange woman approached me. She had green skin and red eyes, but her hair was dark brown. Her beauty was mesmerising and when she smiled, I felt as though my legs were going to give way under me. The chickens however weren't impressed and they ran away, leaving us alone. She came to me and called me by name. I was flabbergasted, but delighted she knew me.

"The woman took my hand and told me how glad she was to meet me. She explained to me she needed my help. I was twenty-five years old, the same age as you are now. Life was boring on the farm and I always wondered if there was something better out there for me to do. I was always a rebel, constantly questioning my parents about the world outside of farming. I got into trouble often and faced my parents' wrath. I cannot remember how many times they grounded me for disobeying them. I was born telepathic and had a very high IQ. I was also telekinetic and could move objects with my mind. It freaked my parents out, but I thought it was wonderful. Anyway, this lovely creature looked into my eyes and explained she came from a distant planet named Darkos and it was dying. All the inhabitants were perishing from one or other 'natural disaster,' homes were being flooded and buildings collapsed during Earthquakes. She said their species would become extinct and only I could help them. Her name was Alyssa and she explained she was a healer – or doctor if you prefer, and she was the leader of the planet. I was intrigued and very flattered, so I agreed.

"Without my knowledge, Alyssa had written a note to my parents, in my own handwriting explaining to them I was going to visit my cousin in South Africa, and I would be gone for a few months. My parents were so used to me just taking off whenever I felt like it that they accepted this, without even checking with my cousin. I went with them and when we arrived on Darkos, the place was chaotic. Earthquakes and floods were prevalent everywhere. Alyssa took me to meet the other two rulers of Darkos. Valdena was the scientist and a man named Sebastian was a brilliant architect. The three of them interviewed me and at the time I wasn't aware that there were others who were also being considered.

"The three leaders all had the same powers as me, only theirs were more efficient and deadly. They all explained to me what would happen if I accepted their offer. They were going to channel their combined powers into me, thus giving me the entire knowledge of their origins and a way to rebuild the planet elsewhere. They explained that my skin would turn green and asked me if it was acceptable. I was young and restless as I said before, and the thought of becoming an immortal and living forever excited me, so I accepted. Alyssa and Sebastian were impressed by me, but Valdena was against this merger. They interviewed others, but in the end, they chose me. Valdena told me she thought I wasn't the right person to have all this knowledge and power, but she was outvoted by two to one, so I was accepted.

"I won't bore you with all the details, but I spent the next few days being bombarded with incredible knowledge no one knew about. My head wanted to split from all the information, but I persevered. My powers grew exponentially and the leaders taught me how to use them to the best of my ability. When they had taught me everything they could, they put me into a spaceship and returned me to the farm. I had been taught how to apply make-up to hide my green skin and I was always careful to lock the door when I got dressed or undressed. I wore contact lenses to hide the colour of my eyes.

"As I left the planet, it imploded and vanished from the universe forever, killing everyone still left alive on Darkos. Obviously, I was wrong though, because Valdena survived. I stayed on the farm until my parents died in a car crash a few years later, then I sold everything and returned to Spacein the ship I had arrived in. I did some exploring in Spaceand discovered the Red Planet, and the rest you know."

"Wow, that's quite a story! Did anyone discover your green skin when you lived on Earth?"

"No, when I left the farm, my neighbours thought I had just gone to live elsewhere on Earth. No one suspected I had been transformed."

"I hate to bring up the obvious, but Darkos was obviously a planet that preyed on other beings. Wasn't it possible that one of those planets caused the destruction of Darkos out of revenge?"

"I don't really know. It's possible, I suppose. Why did you say it was an evil place?"

Craig looked strangely at his companion. "Really! No offence, but look how you turned out! You don't exactly give off happiness and light! The last time I checked, you have spent your life ruining others'. I'm usually in the firing line as well."

Andocia glared at him. "I could change my mind and let Valdena have you, Carter."

"No, you won't, because you need me."

"Do I really? Why is that?"

"You need me to get us back to our own time period."

Andocia smiled triumphantly. "I don't actually! Valdena knows how to travel both backwards and forwards in time. That's how she finds her subjects. She offered to give me one of the devices, so I can return to my planet."

"Okay, I concede she has the knowledge to do that, but how do you know she won't trick you and send you on a wild goose chase? In any case, although you are feeling much better, I'm willing to bet you're still a bit weak. You'll need to have lots of rest periods in space, and if you have to pilot that ship by yourself, you could encounter difficulties. The computer could short out, making you pilot it manually. What if something else goes wrong with your ship? I can repair most problems, but can you? I haven't had the privilege to see Valdena's spaceships, but I'm willing to bet they are magnificent. In this time period, your ship is obsolete, so does she even have any technicians who'll be able to fit the oxygen regenerator on your ship? I doubt it!"

Andocia stared at her companion and grumbled. "I hate it when you make perfect sense! Okay, I guess I do need you. You can stop gloating now and we'll call a truce."

They shook hands.

"Well, we are friends, for now." Andocia muttered. "Time has flown and it's lunchtime already. I'm not very hungry, so I'm going to get our possessions back for us and once you have what you need, hide them in a safe place. You won't be able to take a gun into Valdena's chambers because she'll know about it. When I return, I'll ask if Valdena can see us. I would like to leave now, but there's still too much to arrange. We should be on our way tomorrow sometime."

As an afterthought, she turned back to Craig. "I was just wondering; what would you have done if I told you that you were staying here with Valdena?"

Carter smiled secretively. "I would have found a way to escape anyway. I have an idea for a plan B, and C as well if that didn't work. I had no intention of becoming some mindless slave to that woman."

Andocia nodded. "I believe you! In all my life I've never met anyone as sneaky as you. I guess that's why I keep you around. You're always full of surprises! I'll see you later then."

Craig got up and went back to his room to wait for Andocia's return.

Not long afterwards, Andocia came back with the two laser guns and the oxygen regenerators. She left soon afterwards and went to speak to Valdena. Craig hid the guns and parts for the ship inside the air vent. When Andocia knocked on his door again, she motioned him out.

"She's made time for us to come and speak to her now. We can discuss the arrangements prior to our departure tomorrow morning."

The travellers went back to Valdena's chambers and she smiled at them.

"Well Craig, did Andocia give you the news?"

"Yes, she did," he replied. "I wanted to thank you for your lenience. I'm grateful you are letting us go."

The woman looked penetratingly at him. "As I understand it, your life isn't going to be very different when you get back to your universe anyway. Andocia told me she has a job for you to do. I just wondered how you felt, knowing your fate is in her hands."

Craig shrugged his shoulders. "Valdena, I already know that! We were on our way to Tanus's planet when we went through the rift in the universe. I'll do what I have to do!"

"I remember you telling me that Tanus is your friend, so why would you betray her? I think you are lying!"

Carter looked pleadingly at Andocia and spoke telepathically. "Andocia, a little help here please! Can't you see she's trying to trap you into leaving me here. She's already regretting her decision. Remember our discussion earlier!"

His companion spoke up. "Valdena, this matter has already been decided I told you he'll do what I say! I still have his wife imprisoned on my planet. I appreciate your concern, but I can take care of everything. I've managed fine in all the years I've been the ambassador for Darkos. Carter here knows the penalty for disobedience. I want to get back to my universe before my followers think I have left forever. We have a lot to do before we leave tomorrow."

"Oh of course! Forgive me! I just want you to be careful of your companion here. He has a devious mind. I could still alter him – just a little, so he obeys you without question."

"Like I said, we're fine thank you. I also have the means to punish him if he disobeys and he won't! He wants to see his wife again. Is there anything else you wanted to discuss with us? If not, may we please be excused?"

Valdena waved her hand dismissively. "I think we have covered everything in our previous meeting. I'll come and see you off in the morning."

Craig spoke up. "Valdena, we have to depart early tomorrow, but it's going to take about two hours before we can lift off your planet. I need to double check my calculations and replace the broken part on the ship. When we are ready to lift off, your guards will have to clear the area. I drifted in under the trees, but I'll need to ignite the rockets to ascend into space. I'll need to just take a quick look around in the morning and see if I can find a clearing, otherwise we'll damage some of the trees. Instead of your employees guarding our ship, may I suggest they warn the neighbouring villagers and animals to stay away from the area, or they will be burnt alive."

The leader of Saurus nodded. "Thank you for the warning. I'll see that everything goes as planned."

"Thank you for your help, Valdena," Andocia replied. "We'll try to cause as little damage as possible."

The twosome left Valdena and went their separate ways.

Early the next morning, Andocia and Craig were wearing borrowed clothes. Valdena presented them with some supplies to take on their journey, as well as a few gifts to remind them of her planet. Both were carrying small knapsacks containing their personal belongings. Valdena met them at the entrance to the main building, inside the ornate gates. She hugged Andocia, and held her hand out to Craig, who kissed it.

"It was a pleasant surprise meeting up with you Andocia, and also meeting your companion. Go well and may the universes be kind to you."

Andocia bent forward reverently. "It was our pleasure, I assure you. Goodbye Valdena."

They waved to one another and one of the security guards led them to a transporter, where they climbed in. One hour later, the craft settled down on the grass near their ship. The security detail guarding the ship, saluted smartly.

Craig and Andocia climbed aboard their ship before Craig turned to Andocia. "I'm going to have a quick look around for somewhere safe to move the ship. I'll fit that part and do my calculations when I get back. You stay here and see that no one tries to stop us from leaving. I'll only feel completely safe when we have left this place. I want to go and see Galen quickly though, so don't worry about me. He's not far from here."

"Why do you want to see him?" she asked curiously.

"I want to thank him for his help and tell him the good news. Don't mention anything to anyone though, okay."

"I won't. Hurry back!"

Craig climbed out of the ship and was delighted to see a friendly being waiting for him. Sabrina stood nearby and smiled when she saw him. "It's good to see you again Craig! I heard you wanted to scout around for a safe place to return to space, so I thought it would go quicker if you didn't have to go on foot. May I offer you a ride?"

"Thank you, Sabrina. I appreciate your help."

The centaur smiled. "It's my pleasure, I assure you."

He got on her back and held her around the waist. They galloped into the bushes and disappeared from sight. When they were a safe distance away, Craig squeezed her shoulder. "Sabrina, will you do me a favour please? Can you take me into Hillvale? I need to speak to Galen the farmer urgently."

"I know where he lives. We should be there in a few minutes. Hold on tight!"

Sabrina galloped faster and soon Galen's home came into view. It was still early and Craig could see lights burning in his house and the outlines of two people moving around. He dismounted and knocked on the door. Galen answered and his mouth opened in amazement. He shook his friend's hand vigorously and pulled him inside, shutting the door behind them. Daphne dried her hands on her apron and hugged him.

"What are you doing here Craig? The guards told us you had been taken to the inner sanctum. No one expected to see you again."

"It's a long story and I don't have time to explain, but I have something to give you."

He took the data reading device out of his sling and switched it on. "You were both so kind to Andocia and myself and I didn't know how to repay you, but I've found a way! No one knows you were sheltering us, so you are safe. I stole this device from the inner sanctuary and when you read it, many things will become clear. I hope it helps both of you."

He pressed an icon and Galen's picture appeared. "I've copied these files from the records stored on the computers in that building. When you have time, maybe tonight, read this file. There's one with your name on it too, Daphne. I've also included other pertinent information for your eyes only. Switch it off when you aren't using it to conserve the battery power. I saw an outlet in your bedroom where you can recharge this device. It just looks like two holes in the wall, but it has a purpose. Hide this device in a safe place!"

Craig spent a few minutes explaining to them how to navigate through the various icons, then handed the device to them.

"I have to go now. If it wasn't for Andocia, I wouldn't be leaving as a free man today. We have a tenuous relationship, but she does have her uses. Go well Galen and Daphne and thank you for your help. I doubt I'll ever see you again, but I don't know what the future holds. Please study the information on this device carefully and commit it to memory."

He shook Galen's hand and hugged Daphne, before hurrying out of the door and jumping on Sabrina's back. She galloped away and soon they were far from Hillvale.

Sabrina stopped to get her breath and then pointed into the distance. "Craig, I know this terrain better than anyone and that area over there is your best option to return to space."

She walked into the trees and he saw the area was indeed very wide and shaped like a bowl. The centaur walked through the centre of the clearing and they ended up back at the ship. He dismounted and squeezed Sabrina's hand. A tear escaped from her eye and ran down her face. She wiped it away quickly. "I'm going to miss you, Craig! When you are safely back on your planet, think of me from time to time, as I will be thinking about you."

"I'll do better than that," Craig promised. "I've taken pictures of all the inhabitants living on Saurus. I'll always be able to see what you look like."

Sabrina waved and trotted away. The security detail moved away from the ship and began warning the residents of Saurus to vacate the area.

Craig climbed into the ship and went to the console. He powered up the ship's computer and went to replace the oxygen regenerator. On returning to the console he opened the file containing their flight recorder. He called up their previous flight and the computer showed them a re-enactment of their journey. Craig studied it for a while, then took out an electronic notebook and began writing codes on it. Andocia didn't want to disturb him and watched as he scribbled. Finally, he rubbed his eyes and turned to his companion. "I've finished my calculations and we are good to go. I had better warn the Saurians of our intention to depart."

Carter opened a channel and his voice was projected outside the ship. The security staff waved a flag and made a thumbs-up sign. He pushed the control stick slowly forward and the ship began to move sideways slowly. They reached the clearing and saw many humans and animals waving to them, and they waved back. The ship hovered in the clearing for a moment, then began moving upwards, until they were above Saurus. Andocia watched spellbound as the codes constantly changed. A holographic image in front of them showed the progress of the ship as it followed the flight path laid out for it. Craig's hands lay in his lap as the ship continued on automatic pilot. The explorer watched the screen constantly and then pointed to something. "Look there Andocia! We are passing through the rift in Spacethat brought us to Saurus in the first place."

She peered out of the window in wonder. "It looks almost like a lace curtain being pulled apart! I can't believe we never noticed this when we went through the first time."

"We weren't expecting it, that's why we never saw it. I programmed the computer to take us back to your planet, because I'm still not sure if we can go anywhere else without being sucked back into the time travel vortex. Estimated time of arrival on your planet is two days!"

She watched speechless as a digital clock that had begun rapidly counting down the years, now stopped at the correct year. Andocia clapped her hands and cheered. "You did it! You really did it! You truly are an amazing man!"

Craig grinned happily. "I guess I did! Whew, that was a tense moment! I never want to do that again!"

Andocia got up and went to fetch him some coffee. She brought it to him and sat down in the co-pilot's seat once more. "Craig, why did you go and see Galen? You took a risk doing that."

Craig smiled secretively. "I was just planting a seed!"

Andocia looked out of the observation window and sighed. "It's strange, but now I'm almost home, this journey feels surreal, as though we never went forward in time at all."

Craig picked up something lying beneath one of the seats and held it up. "We really did go forward in time. It wasn't a dream."

She nodded when she saw the peacock feather in his hand.

Carter removed a memory device from her console and showed it to her. "I also downloaded all the pictures I took on Saurus. We'll have quite a story to tell!"

18

A few days later, they were hovering above Andocia's planet. She contacted her control centre and identified herself. The person on the other end answered suspiciously. "What is the code? Failure to supply us with this will mean immediate destruction of your ship."

"Code is Alpha, Beta, Charlie 666999."

"Permission is granted. You may proceed to landing bay 4."

Carter put the ship down exactly in the centre of the landing bay, but didn't open the door. "You show yourself first Andocia. I don't want to get shot."

He pressed the relevant key and the ship's door slid open. Immediately a contingent of troops surrounded the ship. Andocia climbed down and the head of her security forces gasped. "It is you mistress! Where have you been? You were gone for nearly two months! What is that strange garment you are wearing?"

Craig appeared at the top of the stairs and immediately several guns were trained on him. He put up his good arm in surrender. "Don't shoot!"

The security forces lowered their weapons and stared at him as though he was a ghost, but he was allowed to pass unharmed. Andocia's people surrounded them, all asking questions at the same time. She raised her hands. "I can't hear myself talk with this din! I'll explain everything soon. I just want to freshen up first."

Carter interrupted her. "I want to see Constance! Is she okay?"

The leader of the security forces looked sheepish and Andocia glared at her. "Well don't just stand there! Craig has every right to see his wife!"

"I'm sorry, but she isn't here! She escaped five weeks ago! When you disappeared, we tried to contact you, mistress, but your ship had disappeared without a trace. She managed to get the monitoring device off her ankle and fled in Mr Carter's ship!"

"You damn idiots! Didn't you pursue her?"

"I apologise mistress, but you were gone and we didn't see the point in trying to recapture her. We thought your ship had exploded and that both of you were dead."

Andocia raised her hand and pointed her finger at her employee, but Craig grabbed her wrist and twisted it away. "Andocia, it's not her fault! Constance is gone and probably back on Earth by now. What will you achieve by killing your employee?"

The woman tried to break his grip, but her arm was still weak. She glared at him and hissed. "Release me!"

He obeyed and her anger subsided.

"Andocia, we are both tired and I don't know about you, but I need a break. We can discuss everything tomorrow."

She nodded. "I'm sorry Wanda! He's right. I'm still in pain and I could use a rest. The journey back here was long and arduous. We can explain everything when we have had a good sleep. Take Mr Carter to one of the guest rooms. I'm going to my suite. Ask the kitchen staff to make us something light to eat."

The two travellers separated and were taken to their rooms. Craig stripped off his clothes and climbed under the shower. He had a headache and was so tired he battled to keep his eyes open. When he had finished, he found a set of nightclothes and some clothing for the next day. Soon after he had changed into the pyjamas, someone knocked on his door. He took the toasted sandwich and sat on his bed. When he had finished his food, he put the tray outside his door and brushed his teeth. He climbed between the sheets and fell into a deep sleep.

The next day he woke feeling well rested and went to find Andocia. She was having breakfast outside, under a wooden shelter and he joined her. She passed the platter over to him and he ate hungrily. When they had finished, he wiped his mouth on a serviette. "I have to contact Commander Simms and tell him that I'm alive. I'm anxious to speak to Constance as well. Can we go to your control room and contact them please? I can't wait to return to Earth and I want to do that as soon as possible!"

Andocia looked levelly at him. "How do you think you are going to get home? Constance took your ship."

"I was hoping you would lend me a ship. I'm sure Commander Simms will return it to you afterwards."

Andocia folded her arms across her chest. "Really? Aren't you forgetting something? You still owe me a favour. We were interrupted when we ended up travelling to the future."

"Are you serious Andocia? You still want me to put Tanus and her people into a coma! I saved your life on Saurus. We are even!"

"No, we're not! You saved my life and I returned the favour – actually I saved your life first and then you helped me."

"So? We are even, as I said before."

"What about my intervention with Valdena? She wanted to keep you on her planet and I refused to let her do so. You still owe me one."

Carter leaned over the table and glared at Andocia. "That's not fair and you know it! I should have left you on Saurus when you got injured. Sabrina asked me why I didn't just go and like the idiot I was, I felt sorry for you!"

The raised voices alerted Andocia's head of security and she came to see what the problem was. The two enemies were so engrossed in their heated discussion that they didn't see her. She stood silently for a while and just waited for an opportunity to speak.

"If you had done that, Carter, you would have regretted it for the rest of your life! I would have come back and killed you!"

"I don't care! At least I would've been home with my wife. She is much more important than any stupid vendetta that's going on between us."

"Oh, you think so, do you? Well let me remind you that this arrangement was made long before we knew what would happen on the way to Tanus's planet! We had an agreement and I want you to fulfil your part of the bargain, then you can go home to your wife."

"The whole idea is ridiculous! You haven't recovered from your injuries yet, but you still want to go through with this plan! You know what! Maybe we should do this. I might get lucky and Tanus can imprison you, then I'll be free of you and everything you stand for!" he replied sarcastically.

Both rivals glared at one another and Wanda interrupted. "There is no one on Tanus's planet! It's deserted!"

Both of their heads snapped around and they looked at the head of security.

"WHAT!!?" they asked simultaneously.

"It's true! There's no one living on the White Planet."

"Why didn't you tell me before?" Andocia shouted.

The woman rolled her eyes in disbelief. "I wanted to tell you yesterday, but you were so tired I didn't want to bother you."

Andocia recovered her composure and stood with her hands on her hips. "How do you know this?"

"When your ship disappeared, I had a probe sent to the White Planet. I was actually looking for the wreckage of your ship, but instead I found no one was there. I left the probe on the planet and programmed it to search every twelve hours. It sent me a report early this morning and it's still deserted."

Carter interrupted them. "Andocia, it's over! You have no reason to keep me here any longer. If you won't lend me one of your ships, then at least let me contact Commander Simms. There's bound to be someone in the area who can come and fetch me. The American Space Station will definitely have some spaceships on board. I just want to go home!"

The woman glared at him. "I suppose I'll have to let you go! I hate it when you're right, but this isn't over. If I get another chance to use you, I'll be in touch, so be warned!"

Craig nodded. "As usual I suppose. Well, I expect nothing less, so you could try. May I contact my boss now?"

"Yes, you may."

"Thank you, Andocia," he replied gratefully.

"Come, let's go and talk to your commander."

Craig followed Andocia to the control room where they contacted Earth. Commander Simms looked tired and worried, but brightened when he saw his explorer's face. "Craig, you're still alive! I haven't heard from you in over two months. Constance escaped from Andocia's planet and arrived safely home, but she said both you and Andocia had vanished and no one could find you. Where have you been all this time?"

"It's a long story, Sir, but I'll fill you in on the details when I return to Earth."

"Where are you at the moment?"

"I'm back on Andocia's planet, but there's a problem! Constance took my ship when she escaped and I don't have any transport to return home. I did ask Andocia to lend me a ship, but she doesn't seem keen to let me use one of hers. Can you organise something for me please? I'm anxious to see Constance again. How is she?"

"She's just fine Craig. Both her and the baby are well and the pregnancy is progressing nicely. She isn't here right now, but I'll tell her to contact you urgently. Give me a few minutes and I'll see what I can arrange regarding transport."

The NASA logo appeared and music played. A few minutes later, Commander Simms came back online.

"Craig, a military transport ship is near that sector right now. They could reach Andocia's planet in twenty-four hours, Earth time. I can instruct them to take you to the nearest American Space Station where you can get a ship. I'll organise clearance for you when we've finished making arrangements."

Andocia nodded and Craig turned back to the screen.

"That's just wonderful, Sir. I'm very grateful."

"Okay good. I'm looking forward to seeing you again! I'm glad you're alive! See you soon."

The screen went blank and Andocia turned her attention back to Craig.

"So, a military escort, is coming to pick you up."

"It would seem so."

"Well, you have to stay here another twenty-four hours so may I make a suggestion? It has been a while since we were examined by a doctor, so I think we should go to the hospital where you can have your last check up before returning home."

"I think that it's a good idea, thank you."

"We can go now, while I still have some time. I've been away so long that my workload has increased tremendously. I'm sure you can entertain yourself afterwards."

One of Andocia's people came to fetch them and took the pair to the hospital. Both of them were examined carefully and X-rays were taken. The wound on Craig's arm had healed completely and the bandage was removed. He no longer needed to wear the sling either. Carter looked at his arm and only a fine line showed where the damage had been done, but his arm was weak and he was advised to go for physiotherapy when he returned home.

Andocia had also made a good recovery and apart from feeling a bit weak still, she was back to her normal self.

When they got back to Andocia's castle, Constance contacted her husband on his mobile device. He spent an hour talking to her in his room, grateful to hear her voice again. She told him she was now 6½ months pregnant. By the time he returned to Earth, it would almost be time for the baby to be born. Craig spent the rest of the day making use of Andocia's swimming pool and gym.

The next day the troop carrier landed on the Red Planet. Craig carried his meagre possessions in his knapsack and got into the ship. Andocia was too busy to see him off, but he didn't care. He was glad to finally be going home! They dropped him off at the American Space Station and he went to speak to the person in charge, who confirmed Commander Simms had instructed them to give him a spaceship. The man told him it would be ready in an hour, so he took advantage of the time and went to buy himself some personal items and clothing. When he returned to fetch the ship, he was told it had already been stocked with the necessary provisions, and soon afterwards, Craig was on his way to Earth.

Another two months passed before he landed safely at Mission Control. He was instructed to go immediately to Commander Simms' office. When he arrived there, his boss shook his hand vigorously. "Craig, it's so good to have you back home again. When we didn't hear from you for so long, we thought you were dead!"

"It was a trying time for me Sir, but thank the universes, I'm back alive and well. I have so much to tell you!"

Constance knocked on the door and on Simms' invitation, she came into the room. Her eyes filled with happy tears and she ran to her husband and embraced him.

"Oh Craig, I've missed you so much! What happened to you?"

"Oh, you are a sight for sore eyes, darling. I have so much to tell you, but I think it would be better if I showed you instead!"

He looked lovingly at his wife and put his hand on her distended stomach. "How have you been? How's our baby?"

"Our baby is just fine. The way it kicks, I think it's anxious to be born. The gynaecologist asked me if I wanted to know the sex of our baby, but I said I wanted it to be a surprise. Is that okay?"

"Of course! As long as it's healthy, I don't care what sex it is," her husband replied.

"I can't wait to see our child and I'm so glad you are back here with me," his wife replied.

"Constance, when is the baby due? It must be soon, surely?"

She giggled delightedly. "Yes, it's due sometime next week. You made it just in time!"

"Honey, I'm so sorry I couldn't be here to support you throughout this pregnancy! I never expected things to go wrong the way they did."

"It doesn't matter! You're here now."

Simms smiled at his employees. "I'm glad the two of you have been reunited, but I'm curious to see what you have for us."

Craig grinned. "Yes, of course! It was amazing and unbelievable too."

Carter took the memory device out of his pocket and placed it in Commander Simm's computer terminal. There was a lot of static and they waited... and waited, but the screen remained stubbornly blank. Craig took it out and re-inserted it, but again nothing happened.

"I don't understand! I took so many photographs of the planet and its inhabitants, but there is nothing on the device!"

"Maybe the memory chip is faulty?" Simms asked.

"No, it's working fine. Maybe the computers on Saurus were more advanced than I thought. They might have had some sort of security system that prevented transferral of the data. I never thought to check them – I just downloaded what I thought I had received."

Craig paced up and down. "I wonder if that's what Valdena meant! She gave me confidential information and then told me it didn't matter! I thought she was talking about something else, but she must have known I took photos, but I wouldn't be able to take them with me. It makes sense actually, now I think about it! We travelled to the future, so when we came back to the past, obviously the information didn't exist, because in our time period, it hadn't happened yet."

Simms interrupted his employee. "Craig, listen to yourself! The future! Who is Valdena anyway?"

"Sir, I know it sounds crazy, but it isn't! When Andocia and I were going to Tanus's planet, we went through a time vortex in Spaceand landed on a planet named Saurus. If you look at the maps of our universe now, that planet is known as Darr and it's uninhabited at present, but in the future, it's called Saurus. We travelled to the year 4500 A.D."

Commander Simms and Constance looked at Craig pityingly. He knew they thought he had lost his mind and he didn't know how to convince them, now that he couldn't prove anything. Suddenly he got an idea and took the peacock feather out of his bag and showed it to them. "I don't know if this will help at all, but I found it in Andocia's ship. Thank goodness this has survived!"

Constance took it and examined it carefully. "It's just a tail feather from a peacock!"

"Yes, but that was attached to an animal whose body was a cat, with a peacock's tail."

"Who is Valdena?" Constance asked curiously.

"She's one of the leaders of Darkos. That was the planet where beings like Andocia came from. It was destroyed and they gave Andocia her powers. She was just as surprised to meet up with Valdena. Andocia thought they had all died when the planet imploded."

Simms still wasn't convinced. "It sounds as though you had some kind of nervous breakdown in space. Maybe the strain of being forced to do things against your will, sent you over the edge."

"Sir, I know it sounds too fantastic to be true, but even I don't have such an active imagination. Everything I saw there was the truth! I didn't imagine any of it! Unfortunately, the only one who can validate this is Andocia, and you're welcome to contact her if you want. I don't know if she would co-operate with you, seeing as she got badly injured on Saurus. It would make her seem weak and she doesn't like to admit things don't always go her way. I got injured too," he explained, showing Simms his forearm. There was a faint line showing, otherwise the arm had healed completely.

Both Constance and their commander still weren't convinced and he tried one last thing.

"Sir, why don't you have a laboratory examine this feather? Maybe you'll find some answers there."

Commander Simms took the feather from him. "All right, I'll have it analysed. Meanwhile I think you should go home with your wife and take it easy for a few days. We can talk again, once I get the results."

Craig nodded. "Sir, may I respectfully ask you not to make any decisions about my sanity until you get those results, please? I assure you, I'm not crazy."

"All right, I give you my word," he promised.

Two days later, the Carters got a call from their boss asking them to come into the office for a meeting. They arrived and Commander Simms closed the door behind them.

"I want to apologise to you, Craig. When the test results on that feather came back, I couldn't believe what they found, so I asked them to do the test a second time, but the results were the same."

Constance was curious. "What were the results, sir?"

"It's so hard to believe, but the DNA found on the feather belonged to both the Felis catus (domestic cat) as well as the avian species. There was also human DNA in the mix, but the strangest thing is that the human DNA sample was both male and female. I wonder why?"

"I'm sure Valdena had her reasons. Maybe it made the animals easier to control, but I'm just guessing," Craig replied. "Mia's body was that of a domestic cat, except for her blue fur. Her tail was that of a peacock's and not a peahen's. The human DNA probably also had something to do with the fact that she could communicate with us. She spoke English."

Commander Simms shook his head. "It seems so unbelievable, yet it's obviously true. Were there other animals that could talk?"

"All of them we dealt with, had the power of speech."

"Craig, if I brought a graphic designer in, could you maybe recreate these animals from memory?"

"Yes, I could certainly do that. Most of them were very memorable, and some were very brave!" he replied, thinking about the centaurs who had helped him and Andocia.

"Excellent, I'll organise it for you. Afterwards you can fill me in on your adventures. Again, I'm sorry for having doubted you."

Carter shrugged his shoulders. "I don't blame you! What I'll be telling you sounds like something out of a fantasy world, except for the fact that these creatures really existed."

Constance kissed her husband on the top of his head. "While you're busy with the artist, I'm going to leave you here. I have to do some shopping before the baby comes. I'll see you later."

Craig hugged his wife. "Okay, see you soon."

Craig spent the rest of the day with the graphic artist and was happy with the results. By the time they had captured the images of all the animals and people on the computer, including a very lifelike picture of Valdena, he felt it was a reasonable copy of the original report he had lost. He saved it to his computer, then took the data drive to Commander Simms, and began explaining about his incredible adventure.

It was late when he returned home to his wife and he sat down on the couch and yawned. "I'm so glad everything has been sorted out. Now all I want to do is relax for a while because I have a feeling we won't get much rest when our baby arrives. Tomorrow I would like to take you out for lunch, just to celebrate!"

"I'd like that! We have so much to celebrate!"

Craig kissed his wife. "Yes, we certainly do!"

19

A few days later, they were watching television, when Constance went into labour, and Craig took her to the hospital. He hung around anxiously, but they told him it would be hours before something happened. The young man spent the time with his wife, discussing how their life would change with the arrival of their first-born child. Finally, the big moment arrived and Craig watched fascinated as Constance gave birth. The wrinkled bundle was lifted out and cried lustily.

"Congratulations Mr and Mrs Carter, you have a son," said the gynae-cologist as he placed the warm, wet bundle in the mother's arms. Craig hugged his wife and son and then the baby was taken away for examination. Tired but happy, Constance was wheeled away to a private ward. Her husband stayed awhile but left when he saw how exhausted she was.

Constance was discharged two days later and they returned to their apartment. Little Glenn was placed in his new cradle and his parents gazed fondly down at their precious son.

A few days passed and Constance and Glenn were fast asleep. Craig was working on some documents on his computer, when he became aware someone else was in the room with him.

"Who's there?" he demanded.

"Craig, it's me!" replied Tanus. "I'm going to appear for a short moment, but I'm just passing through. I came to congratulate you on the birth of your son. He's a strong healthy boy and I'm sure he'll grow up as handsome and clever as you."

"Thank you, Tanus."

"You see Craig, you managed quite nicely without my help a few months ago. I'm sure you understand now why you weren't welcome the last time you visited me."

"Yes I do. Andocia has been combing both universes looking for you. Please stay out of her clutches!"

"That's my intention. She can't be allowed to reign over both universes. I wanted to spend a little more time with you to catch up on things, but even as we speak, Andocia is on her way here, obviously with some evil intent. Take me to Constance and Glenn quickly. The least I can do right now is give them both some form of protection that will last an hour."

The man led the way into his bedroom and Tanus stared lovingly at the two sleeping figures on the bed. Constance had Glenn in her arms and his head was resting on her shoulder. Both were fast asleep. The woman in white hurried to them both and stroked the baby's forehead tenderly, muttering something Craig couldn't catch. She stroked Constance's hair and muttered more words. Back in the lounge, she squeezed Craig's arm encouragingly. "I must go now. Tarmin and I are safe right now and I doubt Andocia will find us in a hurry. I'm sorry I can't stay and spy on Andocia."

"I understand and thank you for what you did for my family. Go well and I hope to see you again soon."

↓ ↓ ↓

Ten minutes later, Andocia materialised in the lounge.

"We meet again Carter. I know it's late, but I wanted to pay my respects to your family."

"They are sleeping actually and I plan to join them soon. What do you want?" he asked suspiciously.

"This won't take long. I'd like to see your baby son."

"Leave him alone. He's just an innocent child and unable to protect himself."

Andocia smiled "Oh relax, I mean him no harm. I don't attack innocent babies. The only time you need fear for his life would be if he joins you in Spaceexploration and comes against me. Then he'll receive the same treatment you do. I wish to see him alone."

"Constance is with him and they are both sleeping."

"No matter, I'll go in anyway."

Andocia went into the bedroom and stared down at the two sleeping forms. She stared at Craig's offspring in hate. "I hate Carter and therefore I hate you too. How simple it would be for me to kill you, but I have other plans for you. Glenn, when you are older, I'll be visiting you. You are going to work for me against your own father and mother. I'm going to plant the seed of evil in your little mind now. It'll germinate and fertilise, as you grow older. I'll be seeing you, little one."

She called Craig in. "See your precious son is still alive. I have no fight with him. Like I said, I only wanted to see him. Goodbye Carter."

She turned to leave and he called her back. "Andocia, wait! I want you to leave us alone. I'm tired of always having to fight with you and I'd like to live a normal life without interference from you. Will you promise me this?"

"I promise nothing, but I'll leave you alone for a while. I have more important things on my mind right now anyway. I'll still be keeping up to date with your career and life though. Don't give me cause to harm you or your family and you can have peace. Farewell, Craig Carter."

She disappeared and he suddenly felt very tired, so he packed up his work and climbed into bed.

$$\text{⚓ ⚓ ⚓}$$

The years sped by and the young couple were blissfully happy. Three years later, a daughter was born to them. Craig visited his wife in the hospital and hugged his new daughter protectively.

"Oh darling, thank you for this beautiful child. Glenn will be delighted with his new playmate."

"I hope so. Craig, can we call her April? I really like that name."

"Why not, it suits her," replied the proud father as he kissed his daughter on her forehead.

"Craig, how's Glenn?"

"He's just fine, don't worry. The young girl from next door is baby-sitting for us. You just relax and enjoy the cosseting for now."

Constance sighed and settled back on the cushions.

"Oh believe me I intend to!"

Two days later, Constance was discharged and the happy couple returned home. Glenn ran to his father.

"Hello big boy. Look, Mommy brought a sister for you."

Craig held his son and Constance opened the blanket, revealing a tiny pink face, which crumpled up and began to cry. While Constance saw to April's bottle, Glenn spoke to his father. "Daddy, she's so small!"

"So were you when you were born. Come on let's make Mommy a cup of tea."

Glenn went obediently to the kitchen where he began to take out the necessary items for his father. That night, Craig was watching television while the rest of the family slept. Suddenly he remembered Andocia, who had now left him alone for three whole years. Would she come and see this baby too? Craig was concerned, but kept his feelings to himself.

That night, Andocia didn't come, but someone else did. It was Tanus and Tarmin. The man beamed happily at them. "It's good to see you again! Too much time has elapsed, but I understand you must be really busy. Have you come to see our new daughter?"

"Yes we have. Where is she?"

"We have moved her into the bedroom with us. Glenn's room is now further down the passage."

They went into the bedroom and looked at the little girl lying in her crib, then returned to the lounge.

"Oh Craig, she's beautiful. I can see her breaking many hearts when she grows up. Glenn inherited your blond hair, but I see April takes after her mother, with her dark hair."

The friends spoke amicably for a while, then Tanus put a damper on things. "Craig, Andocia hasn't bothered you for three whole years, but during that time she and I have been pitting our wits against one another. I heard from an informed source that Andocia has expressed interest in April, so be warned. She likes girls, as you know and I'm a little concerned about her. Tarmin has offered to stay here with you all, just as a precaution. If Andocia does try something underhand, Tarmin will come and warn me."

"I'm very grateful, but I don't want to inconvenience you. Don't you need Tarmin to help you when you clash with Andocia again?"

"Not this time. Craig, I have to journey far away. I must find a way to defeat Andocia once and for all. As much as I love Tarmin, she would be safer here with your family and I'll have peace of mind. Tarmin and I discussed this and she wants to do it."

"Then she's welcome of course, but in her present form she'll be very conspicuous."

"I know that, but she has the ability to change into the shape of any Earth bird, so she'll take the shape of a parrot. I suggest you buy a perch and put it somewhere. Tarmin must be allowed freedom so she can leave at a moment's notice, just in case there's an emergency."

Craig nodded. "I'll take care of it first thing tomorrow morning. Thank you; thank you both."

Tanus hugged Craig and Tarmin, then left. Tarmin changed into a brightly coloured parrot and blinked one beady eye. "How do I look?" she asked her host.

"You look just fine Tarmin! In that shape you even look intelligent."

"Careful or I may just be tempted to peck you!" admonished the bird playfully.

Craig laughed. "I'm only kidding! Tomorrow morning I'll buy you that perch. Tell me, what should we call you?"

"How does Polly sound?" she asked Craig.

He turned his lips down in a playful scowl. "That's way too common! Why not use something more exotic," he suggested.

"Why should I? I like the name," pouted Tarmin.

"All right then, Polly it is. Would you mind if I turned in now? It's getting late."

Tarmin fluffed out her feathers. "I don't mind at all. I'll find somewhere to sleep, don't worry. Goodnight."

The Space explorer fell asleep immediately and didn't hear the cries of little April, who demanded to be fed, but Constance did and tended to the needs of her baby.

The next morning, she brought Craig breakfast in bed. "Good morning sleepyhead. Craig, did you know we have a bird in the house?"

"Hmmm, a bird? Oh you mean Polly, I guess!" he mumbled sleepily.

Constance put her hands on her hips and stared at her husband. "Craig what's going on?"

Carter kissed his wife on her forehead. "Oh yes, explanations are in order I think."

However, before he could utter another word, Tarmin flew in and sat on Constance's shoulder, then pecked her affectionately. "Good morning Constance," she chirped brightly.

"Honey, this is Tarmin," he explained.

"Tarmin, how come you look so different?" Constance asked curiously.

"Let me explain, honey. Tanus paid us a visit last night and told me she has to go away for a while, so she left Tarmin here to guard us. She seems to be under the impression that Andocia will be visiting us soon. Remember, she came to see us when Glenn was born as well. If Andocia starts her nonsense and interferes with us, Tarmin has been instructed to inform Tanus. Tarmin has the ability to change shape and become any bird she chooses to be.

Constance put out her finger and the bird stepped onto it. "Of course! I remember you telling me that when I was on Tanus's planet several years ago."

"Just call me Polly."

"All right," she agreed. "Well Polly, here's a good morning kiss from me!"

Tarmin stretched her head and Constance kissed her on top of it.

"Would you like a kiss from me too Tarmin?" asked Craig mischievously.

"Well er... I, well..." Tarmin bowed her head shyly.

Craig laughed and Tarmin flew towards him and teased him by flying around and around his head.

"Constance, how can you put up with him when he's in one of these crazy moods!" asked the bird laughingly.

"Oh he's quite harmless really! I think we are going to enjoy having you here."

"Hey Polly, what kind of food do you like?" interjected Craig.

"I'll settle for whatever you're having, thanks."

"Hey Constance, this bird is going to prove very expensive," teased Craig

"No she won't! She'll need a perch though," remarked Constance thoughtfully.

"I'm going to get her one after breakfast," he promised.

Time passed pleasantly for the group and for a further year, nothing happened. Despite their fears, Andocia never came to see April at all.

⊥ ⊥ ⊥

One day, Craig decided to visit a friend who lived nearby. The road that he travelled on was very quiet and deserted.

He was unaware of the figure that materialised in his back seat and rode part of the way with him. When he had reached a stop street, a hand stretched out and tapped him on the shoulder. The explorer spun around in the seat and saw Andocia sitting there.

"You don't seem pleased to see me."

"Should I be? We are enemies, not friends. I asked you to leave us alone! Why haven't you?"

"Oh but I have — for four years in fact. Belated congratulations on the birth of your daughter. It's her birthday tomorrow, isn't it?"

"Yes, but you aren't invited to her party. You'll scare all the guests away."

Andocia smiled and Craig became uneasy. "What do you want? You never drop in just to be sociable."

"I came to give you some news. I wouldn't expect any help from Tanus if I were you. I've finally defeated her."

Craig gasped. "No, it's not possible!"

"Oh but it is. Remember that liquid I was going to force you to administer? I see you do. Well I tricked Tanus and she drank it. Now she'll 'die' for one hundred years. I haven't been able to find Tarmin yet, but when I do, she'll be executed. I just thought I would let you know. I have to go and find a way to control the whole of both universes and no one will be able to stop me. When everything has been put into place, I'll be returning for you. You have two years left to live, so enjoy them."

She disappeared, leaving a crestfallen Craig to stare at the empty seat. He visited his friend, but he was unhappy about the news, so he cut the visit short.

The explorer arrived home, not sure how to break the news to Tarmin. He went to see Constance and Tarmin and his wife took one look at his expression and stood up quickly. "Craig, what's wrong?"

"Bad news I'm afraid. Andocia paid me a visit earlier. Tarmin, I'm so sorry, but she said she has defeated Tanus once and for all."

"No, you're lying!" sobbed the bird.

Craig embraced her and she pulled away.

"If what you say is true, then you have no further use for me here. I need to see for myself."

Craig reached out a hand to the bird and stroked her wing. "Wait before you plunge headlong into danger! She may have been lying. Let me at least check if she was telling the truth!"

The bird pulled away from her friend. "No, I must go now! By the time you go to Mission Control and check the satellite feed, Tanus could be in terrible danger."

Carter sighed, "Go if you must, Tarmin but be careful. Andocia also mentioned she's looking for you. Don't fly blindly into a trap."

"I'm not stupid, you know! Thank you for your hospitality over the last few years. I have enjoyed being with you. I'll see you around I guess. Goodbye for now," sniffed the bird.

They waved but she didn't look back. Constance put her arm around her husband's waist.

"Oh Craig, do you think she's telling the truth?"

"I believe she is. What would she gain by lying to us? We'll obviously investigate."

"But good is stronger than evil!" she protested.

"Yes," he agreed, "but evil still wins from time to time."

Constance searched his face and stroked it tenderly. "Craig, there's more, isn't there?"

"I'm afraid so! Andocia gave me an ultimatum as well. I'm under sentence of death too. She has given me two years to live."

"Damn that bitch! Why can't she just leave us alone?! I'm so tired of her theatrics!" Constance exclaimed furiously.

"I'm not concerned my love. A lot can happen in two years. Everything will turn out for the best, I'm sure," he replied comfortingly.

Glenn came into the kitchen to get a glass of water and he stared wide-eyed at his mother. "Mommy, are you sick?"

"No Glenn, just angry about something. You go outside and play now. I hear April calling you."

When Glenn was out of earshot, Constance rounded on her husband.

"Craig, how can you be so flippant? If Tanus was still around to protect us, I wouldn't be concerned at all, but she isn't. Do you realise just how much power this will give Andocia now?"

"I know only too well. Honey, would you mind if I went out into Spaceand checked this out myself? I have to see Tanus with my own eyes otherwise I won't believe it. I want to try and find Tarmin too. I'd feel a lot safer if she was under my protection."

Constance sighed. "I don't want you to go, but I understand why you want to do it. Go then, but hurry back to us."

"I will, but if Tanus is truly in a sort of coma, I would like to pay my last respects to her. Andocia said the potion would last for 100 years. When she wakes up again, we'll both be dead anyway. I just want to get a few things together. Save me some of April's birthday cake, will you?"

"Oh Craig!" she sniffed.

"It can't be helped my darling. Tomorrow could be too late."

Carter hugged his son. "Look after yourself, your sister and mommy, Son. I have to go away for a while."

The explorer climbed into his car and headed for the Space Control Centre. He went into Commander Simms' office for a moment and told him what he wanted to do. The commander gave him permission to take a ship into space.

Craig entered the Golden Way. Every planet he scanned was in mourning, except Andocia's. Her people were having a feast to celebrate the "demise" of Tanus. The young man headed for the outskirts of the Golden Way, into uncharted territory. He didn't want to risk being drawn back through the time vortex, which was still unstable. Thanks to Craig it had been identified, but no one knew when it would be open, or closed so he had taken the long way around Tanus's planet.

Suddenly, a greenish blue beam shot out and ensnared his ship and he tried his best to detach himself from it, but to no avail. His vidscreen beeped and he pressed a key on the computer's console. An alien he had never laid eyes on before spoke to him in perfect English.

"Who goes there? State your business, Earthling. We have locked on to your ship and are controlling it."

"My name is Craig Carter and I'm on my way to Tanus's planet. Who are you and what do you want?"

"We are known as the Sofagins. Why have you taken such a circuitous route to visit her?"

"There is an anomaly in Spacenear the other side of her planet, so I took the long way around. I would like to proceed, but you are preventing me from doing so."

"Earthling, we are curious about your race and we would like to introduce ourselves properly. We have heard a great deal about the planet Earth, but have never met any of its inhabitants. May we be permitted to come over to your ship for a moment? We mean you no harm."

"You have my permission," he replied guardedly. Just in case of trouble, he placed his laser gun in a nearby drawer.

The computers interfaced and the doors sprung open. Three of the strange beings entered and the hatch slid shut once again, however the ship was still under their control. Craig indicated to some chairs and they sat down.

One of them seemed to be in charge and he leant forward. "Craig Carter, as I have already mentioned, we are the Sofagins. Only Tanus and Andocia know of our existence, for not many craft come this far into the Golden Way. We have been watching your progress ever since you arrived in our universe. We would be happy to answer any questions you may wish to raise with us."

"I've often come to Tanus's planet, but I have never seen your ships. Where is your planet?"

"It is far away from here. We are very private beings who just want to co-exist in peace here in the Golden Way. The only reason why we have appeared to you is because of the route you have taken. It is very unusual, but you have explained the reason for this. I assume you will be taking this route to the White Planet in the future, because of the anomaly, so we are most likely to meet up with you again. We have seen you often on Andocia's planet too. How did you get involved with someone like her?"

"It's a long story and when I have more time, maybe I'll tell you about it."

"As you wish. Nothing much escapes us, Earthling. We knew long before you arrived here, you have come to see Tanus. Don't waste your time; she is truly in Andocia's power."

"Thank you for your concern, but I wish to pay my last respects to her then. She has been invaluable to my family and me over the years I have known her and I need to say goodbye properly. The Earthling life span is much too short for me to wait until she awakens from her long sleep. Has Andocia harmed Tanus's people?"

"They too have been struck down. Andocia was very thorough."

As the creatures spoke, Craig studied them. All three were wearing long, flowing robes of different colours. Their hair was a glossy white and looked like mist. Their eyes were blue, a sharp contrast to their pale green skins. They also had two arms and two legs, but their skulls were bigger than a human's. Their brains could be seen through their light green skin. They had very large foreheads as well. Although Andocia's skin was green, the Sofagins' had a bluish tinge to it and theirs was lighter in colour. Their skins were unlined and unblemished. Each being wore gold sandals, which shone brilliantly. He couldn't make out the shape of their bodies, for their robes were worn loosely.

"Craig Carter, we know very little about your species, but what we have seen intrigues us. Tanus seldom shows favouritism to anyone, yet she seems interested in you. Andocia, too, is a mystery. She has no compassion, yet you have found yourself in her clutches on more than one occasion. How come has she kept you alive?"

"I've just been lucky I guess," he replied guardedly.

"As I said before, we are curious. Most of the time we keep to ourselves up here, but you strike us as an intelligent race. Your craft are antiquated, and you have plenty of catching up to do. We are the most intelligent race in this universe – even more so than your friends the Saturnians. We have the answer for every strange occurrence."

"If this is really true, why didn't you stop Andocia from harming Tanus? You know the woman is planning to take over both universes, don't you?"

"We are aware of this, but we are scientists, not warriors. We prefer to keep to ourselves and don't interfere in the goings on of other planets. If we wanted to, we could defeat Andocia."

"If you are all seeing and all-knowing as you profess, do you know what Tanus looks like under her veil?"

The Sofagins looked at one another in horror. "No one has seen her face, not even her friend Tarmin."

"All right, I'm still curious though. When I mentioned the rift in space, you weren't surprised, so you obviously knew about it."

"We have known about it for years Mr Carter – long before anyone else even became aware of it."

"Okay, so if you know so much, where does this vortex lead to?"

"It leads to the future, or the past, Carter. It depends on where you wish to go. Spaceships disappear through it quite regularly, but they never return."

Craig smiled at them. "That's not strictly true! Several years ago, I accidentally got sucked through that vortex, but I made it back to Earth later."

The Sofagins looked at one another in disbelief.

"Really? Truly you must be an amazing man, for even we hesitate to go through that vortex and investigate. Where did you go?"

"To a planet named Saurus, many years into the future. On our maps of the universes, the planet is known as Darr."

The Sofagins whispered amongst themselves. Then stood up and bowed to their host. "Craig Carter, it has been a pleasure to meet you. Perhaps now we are acquainted, we might meet again in the near future."

The Sofagins bowed politely and left his ship. The Sofagin craft gave control back to Craig and he continued to the White Planet.

20

Craig headed for Tanus's planet and found it still and eerie. He landed near the palace and made his way inside. Every room he passed contained the sleeping forms of Tanus's people and he continued until he reached her bedroom. He moved closer to the prostrate form on the bed and stared down at the woman he had come to respect. Carter took her pulse and it was regular. The explorer shook her gently and whispered her name, but Tanus didn't stir. Craig studied the sleeping figure for a while, hoping for some kind of reaction, but his friend remained asleep. He turned to leave the bedroom and came face to face with Tarmin, obviously on the same quest.

"Hello Craig. Is it true; has my mistress really been defeated?" she enquired.

Craig turned troubled eyes up to Tarmin and nodded. "Yes, I'm afraid so. Oh Tarmin, I'm so sorry!"

The bird stared miserably at him. "Can… can I go and see for myself?"

"Of course, dear friend," said the explorer sympathetically. "But do so quickly, because I heard Andocia knows you were headed here and she'll come looking for you."

Tarmin went inside and wept tears of misery for her mistress. "Oh Tanus, I would wait for you forever if I just could, but my lifespan is only 100 years. I'm not immortal like you. Oh, what am I to do?"

She sought comfort from Craig, who held her shaking body gently.

"Oh Craig, I love her dearly! Why has she been taken from me?"

"Because Andocia is greedy and won't settle for half measures. I'm going to do everything I can to get back at Andocia for this, in the time left to me."

The white bird blinked back her tears and stepped back from her friend. "What do you mean… the time left to you?"

The explorer bit his lip in frustration. He had not meant to let Tarmin know that there was more bad news. Gently he stroked the unhappy bird's wing. "I'm sorry, I didn't want to spread bad news, but I suppose it's better you hear it from me. When Andocia came to tell me she had defeated Tanus, she put me under sentence of death. You fled the moment you heard about your mistress, so you missed her big moment," declared Craig snidely. "Andocia has given me two more years to live, before she executes me."

Tarmin stared wide-eyed at her friend and the tears gushed out anew.

"She can't do that!" cried the bird aghast. "I don't want to lose you as well."

The bird sobbed unhappily and Craig held her tightly, lost for words.

"What a touching scene! Tanus deserved what she got!"

Both turned in horror as Andocia stood before them. They were taken completely by surprise and hadn't heard her approach. A wind sprung up and Andocia's hair blew wildly, making her look even more fearsome. The red eyes glinted with the prospect of the death of another enemy and Tarmin let out a wail of fear and horror.

"That won't help you, meddlesome creature. You are going to die now Tarmin, only your state will be more permanent."

Craig put himself between Andocia and the bird, but he was tiny compared to Tarmin.

"Andocia, haven't you done enough damage? Leave Tarmin alone! She can't oppose you, not alone. Be satisfied with your present victory and try to be more understanding."

"Get out of the way Carter. I have been generous enough to grant you two more years of life, but that can change in an instant. You could join her if you like. Be grateful that she will die instantly, because your death will be a lingering one."

Craig stubbornly refused to move, but Tarmin stepped away from him.

"Craig, thank you for what you are trying to do, but it won't help. It doesn't matter anymore; Tanus was my whole life and with her out of the way, I have nothing left to live for. Let Andocia do what she must."

Craig obeyed reluctantly and moved out of the way. His face contorted in misery as he watched Andocia raise one deadly finger and point it at the large bird. Tarmin crumpled to the ground and lay still. Craig rounded angrily on his enemy. "How can you be so... callous?" he snapped angrily.

"It's easy because I have no time for sentiment. Anyway Tarmin isn't dead, I just stunned her."

"I don't understand! You said you were going to kill her."

"I was, but it occurred to me she could prove very useful. She and Tanus have been together for a long time and she may know some secrets I wasn't aware of. I could use that knowledge to put Tanus to sleep forever. Once I have that information, I'll kill her."

"One of these days you'll go too far Andocia and then someone will defeat you," Craig snarled angrily.

"That will happen only in your dreams Carter. You may leave now. Be thankful for the two years left to you. If you make me angry I may reduce it as I said before."

Craig decided to leave before she changed her mind, so with a final glance at the unconscious Tarmin, he returned to his ship and blasted off once again.

He arrived back on Earth a few days later and returned home. Constance greeted him affectionately and asked the inevitable question. "Craig, has Tanus really been defeated?"

"I'm afraid so, darling. She got Tarmin too. I tried to intervene, but she took her along as a prisoner. She wants to get information about Tanus from that poor bird and I don't have to tell you what that means."

"Oh Craig, she'll give Tarmin such a hard time, won't she?"

"Yes she will. I feel so helpless!" complained the explorer unhappily.

"Did Andocia mention anything about your impending death?"

"Oh yes, she took great pains to remind me of the fact. Constance, this is going to be a bad time for all the planets. Andocia has free reign and there is no one who can oppose her."

On hearing voices, Glenn stuck his head inside the door. He was delighted to see his father and rushed into his arms. Craig picked him up and hugged him. "Hey young man, have you been a good boy while I was gone?"

"Oh yes, I took care of Mommy and April, just like you said I should."

"How's April?" Craig asked his wife.

"Oh she's fine now, but she had a slight fever this morning. She's been restless most of the day, but she's asleep now."

"That's great news. Would it be all right if we got your parents to baby-sit for us? It's been a harrowing few days and I would like to relax with you for a time. How about going out to dinner?"

"That would be wonderful! My parents love their grandchildren and are always looking for an excuse to have them over."

That night they had a wonderful evening. Constance relaxed more, knowing that the responsibility of running the household could be put on hold for one night at least. Life continued pretty much as normal, with Craig going out on various missions. In this way another five months passed by.

One night when the couple were relaxing in their lounge, Andocia appeared. "Hello there. I just thought I would pay you a visit."

"What do you want, Andocia?" demanded Constance angrily. "Our home is private and we don't like people barging in without even knocking."

Andocia pouted and sighed. "Oh dear, and I did want to be sociable! Don't worry, I'm not going to stay long. I only came to give you a message. I'm taking advantage of the present situation to make plans."

"Are you planning to take over Earth again?" enquired Craig.

"Well the prospect does intrigue me, but no, not at the moment. Actually my plans concern Saturn really."

"What devilish plan is forming in your mind now, she devil?" demanded Constance furiously.

"Watch your tongue around me, Constance. I know you are a mother now, but that won't stop me from hurting you if you cause any trouble. The Saturnians are an intelligent race and I would like their help on certain matters. They fear me and would not dream of opposing me. They are just a bunch of clever scientists, with not a single warrior amongst them."

"Andocia, don't hurt them," pleaded Craig. It isn't fair to terrorise such a peaceful race."

"Bah, what do I care, so long as I achieve my goals? I'm going to enlist the help of Tyrus and his friends on this one. They fear him, but if they dare to go against me, I'll destroy them all."

"Be reasonable! They are so few in number. Tyrus nearly destroyed them all once before and they could become extinct if you aren't careful."

"So, I don't care for any life, other than my own of course."

Constance was furious and spoke out. "Oh leave her alone, Craig. Andocia hasn't one shred of kindness. You can't plead with someone who has no soul, no heart. What do you expect from a disciple of the devil?"

"Constance, stop it!" pleaded Craig.

"Yes, watch your tongue!" Andocia interjected.

"What if I don't?" she challenged.

Andocia's eyes flashed dangerously. She pointed her finger at the woman, who stood her ground.

† † †

Suddenly a little voice interrupted.

"Daddy, I wanted a drink of water. I called and called but you didn't hear me. Is something wrong, Daddy?"

Glenn stopped suddenly when he realised his parents weren't alone. He stared curiously at Andocia and she studied him. Glenn turned his attention back to his father and hurried to him. Craig picked his son up and held him protectively. Glenn seemed mesmerised by the strange woman.

"Is she a friend, Daddy?" he asked curiously.

Before he could answer, Andocia interrupted. "Yes I am a friend, but this is a grownups discussion. You had better go back to bed, Glenn."

"I want my drink of water first!" he protested.

"Come along Glenn and I'll give you some," said Craig as he hastily hustled his son out of the room. Andocia watched them until they were out of earshot and then glared at Constance. "You were very lucky that time dear. You can thank your son, for he may have saved your life."

Craig gave his son some water to drink, and carried him back to bed. As he tucked him in, the boy questioned him. Glenn was only four years of age, but he was intelligent enough to know when all was not well. "Daddy, that woman isn't really your friend, is she?"

"Go to sleep, son."

"But I want to know!" he insisted.

"We don't like her very much, but I don't want you to ask any more questions. Go to sleep now," Craig hedged.

Despite his obvious curiosity, Glenn yawned and within moments he had fallen asleep. Craig returned to the lounge, where both women were glaring at one another.

"Andocia, I'd like you to leave now," demanded Constance.

"I'm going anyway. See you around," Andocia smirked.

Andocia left and Craig jumped up. "Constance, I have to warn the Saturnians. That woman will just spring this on them without prior warning."

"But Craig, you can't go to Saturn now – you'll never make it in time."

"I don't intend travelling there. I'm going to contact them by radio."

"But the only transmitter strong enough is at the Space Centre!"

"I know that, and that's where I'm heading. I won't be long."

The explorer ran to his helicar and took off immediately, landing at the Control Centre a few minutes later. He showed his security card to the guard on duty and the doors were opened for him. He dashed to the technicians who greeted him in amazement. "Craig, what are you doing here so late at night?

"I must contact the Saturnians immediately. It is a matter of life and death – their deaths."

He contacted his friends, and a sleepy voice answered. "This is the planet Saturn. What's going on?"

"Karnd, it's Craig."

"Yes I see, but why are you calling so late?"

"Listen to me," he remarked desperately. "Andocia is on her way to your planet and she's bringing Tyrus and his bunch with her. They are going to force you to help them do something awful, but I don't know what. For heaven's sake, get the hell off there. Go and hide on one of the uninhabited planets until the danger passes."

"Oh my," said Karnd, panic evident in his voice. "When will they arrive?"

"I don't know, probably… Aaaagh."

The sentence was cut short by Craig's agonised scream as a deadly beam hit his hand, paralysing the entire arm. It began to swell immediately. A green hand reached out and switched off the transmitter, severing the link to Saturn. Craig nursed his hand and Andocia smiled cruelly. "Wasn't it fortunate for me I decided to hang around a little longer? I thought you might warn the Saturnians, but it was a futile effort, as one of my ships will be landing on Saturn shortly. They have nowhere to go. Go home and stop trying to save the world."

Carter glared malevolently at his enemy. "As long as you are in this world, I'll do whatever I can to help those weaker than you. I guess I should have known you would be suspicious, but it doesn't matter because at least the Saturnians know about the unwelcome company they'll be receiving."

Andocia's red eyes flashed a warning. "This is your last chance! Go now or you will die right here, right now."

Craig went back home and Constance stared at his hand. He had put a bandage over it, but the blood was seeping through.

"Oh Craig, what happened to you?"

"Andocia was waiting for me. She anticipated my next move. What did she expect me to do? Was I supposed to just stand back and let my friends suffer?"

"I don't know. If you ask me, she's just trying to gloat about how clever she is and how powerless you are to stop her."

"Well it won't work. I have to try and help them, but maybe the answer lies in the Golden Way. They are more advanced than us, so perhaps they'll have some kind of a solution for me. I'm going back to the Control Centre and taking a ship out now. Wish me luck."

"Oh Craig, please be careful!"

"I'll be fine, I promise. I don't know how long I'll be, but hopefully what I have planned won't take long."

Craig hurriedly threw a few things together and headed for the door, but before he could leave, his mobile device rang. He answered it and his mother's sobbing voice stopped him in his tracks.

"Craig, oh thank heavens I caught you! Your father had an accident and he's been taken to hospital! Please can you come immediately!"

Carter looked at his wife miserably. "My dad's had an accident! I have to go and see him! I don't know what to do!"

"You have to go to him, of course! I'll phone my parents and get them to come and fetch the children. I'll go to Saturn in your place. We'll talk later."

He kissed his wife hurriedly. "Thank you honey! Be careful please!"

Her husband hurried out of the door and Constance contacted her parents, who didn't live very far away. Her father arrived in minutes and bundled up the children. When they had left, Constance climbed into her helicar and sped to the Spacecentre. Not long afterwards, she was urging all the power she could muster out of the spaceship. While she travelled, she contacted various planets to see if they could help.

She contacted the Meltonians and put the problem to them, but they had no solution to offer. Then Constance remembered the Sonambrians in her own universe and hoped they could perhaps help.

"Sonambro, I'm really sorry to intrude, but this is important."

"I take it this isn't a social call then?"

"No, unfortunately it's not. The Saturnians are in trouble though. Remember that incident when Roland Stone landed on your planet and nearly killed Cragus. It turned out to be Tyrus in disguise."

"Yes I remember. Is he involved in this scheme?"

"Yes, he and Andocia are in cahoots."

Sonambro shuddered. "Oh my, I feel really sorry for those poor Saturnians."

"Well so do I. Have you anything I could use to stop Tyrus?"

"No, whatever weaponry we use is electrically charged. If you used any of them on the silver creatures, it would probably enhance their powers, making things even worse for your friends. They would absorb all the electricity and use it against those beings."

"Oh how stupid of me. Of course you're right. I have to help my friends though, for I owe them a great deal."

"Constance, I don't understand you. Haven't you had enough taste of Andocia's powers? You have children to think about now."

"I know but they are in good hands and I really want to help my friends."

"That is very noble of you. I have heard rumours that Andocia has defeated Tanus. Are they true?" asked the Sonambrian curiously.

"Yes," she replied dejectedly.

"What of her pet?"

"She is Andocia's prisoner. Sonambro, I don't wish to appear rude, but I would like to continue with my journey now. I have to find the solution."

"I hope you do. Go well, Earthling."

Constance was unsure who next to ask for help, but Craig had mentioned the Sofagins in the Golden Way and she decided to approach them. She flew through the jump vortex, which led back to the Golden Way, and decided to take a chance, so she cruised in the uncharted section. Her computer went into override mode, just as Craig had explained to her, and the Sofagins' tractor beam locked on to the ship. The hatch opened of its own accord and the same Sofagins as Craig had met before, confronted her.

"Who are you and why are you here? Are you here by accident or on purpose?"

"I came here deliberately. I don't know what frequency your transmitters operate on, so I couldn't contact you unless I came in person. I was hoping you would rendezvous with me. I am Constance Carter. Craig Carter, who you have already met, is my husband and he told me about you. I know you mentioned the fact you aren't that anxious to help out all the time, but this is an emergency."

"What has happened?" they enquired curiously.

"Andocia is threatening my friends the Saturnians and I dearly want to help them. With Tanus gone, they have no chance against that woman and Tyrus. You bragged about your superiority in Spaceso I'm just giving you a chance to prove it to me."

"Mrs Carter, we have no wish to show our hand to Andocia at this time. I suggest you find someone else to help you with this foolish quest. You seem to be an intelligent being, yet you wish to cross swords with Andocia time and time again. One of these days she is going to get tired of you and just eliminate you."

"Our planet has had dealings with Andocia before and we know what she's capable of, but the Saturnians are not warriors. They are scientists. I want to help my friends, so if you are going to help me, then please make a decision. If not, I'll just be on my way."

The Sofagins stared at her with renewed interest and huddled together while she waited patiently.

"Mrs Carter, if we help you, you have to swear not to tell Andocia whose technology you were using. We have something that could help you out, but we don't want to show our hand just yet. Do you agree?"

"That's fine with me! I see no point in explaining this to Andocia. I promise that whatever you give me to use, I'll return it to you. Andocia didn't tell me why she wanted to visit the Saturnians, but I heard a rumour she wants them to build a super weapon for her. She'll use that to terrify other planets, no doubt."

The Sofagins nodded. "Yes, we are aware of the weapon in question. In fact we have seen the plans for it. We have the technology to build her weapon, but she doesn't know that and won't hear it from us."

"I won't tell her either," promised Constance.

"Very well, Earthling. We have to go and fetch the device. Unfortunately we can't take you along, as your ship will slow us down. Make your way to Tanus's planet and we will rendezvous with you there."

They separated from her ship and were gone in an instant. The explorer set course for Tanus's planet and was soon hovering above it. On an impulse she switched on the scanners and did a sweep of the White Planet, but the situation was unchanged. She focused on the palace and saw the figure of Tanus; still motionless in her artificially induced sleep. Constance switched off the screen and was thoughtful.

"Funny, the Sofagins say they are even more powerful than Andocia and I find that very hard to believe. I don't know what to make of them; they appear to be friendly, yet for some reason I just don't trust them. Are they helping me out just to prove they are powerful, or are they genuine?"

The Sofagins returned with an odd contraption. It was the size of her own laser gun and when she gripped the weapon, it seemed to mould to her hand. Although shaped like a gun, it had different colours running through it, which swirled and mixed at various places. It looked almost like a painting that a child had done and messed while still wet. The woman stared at it in bewilderment. "What does this do?" she asked curiously.

"It is known as a Candy gun. That part over there is the trigger but please keep your finger away from it unless you want to use it. It is dangerous and could take out half the side of your craft. You must use it only on your intended target, otherwise you'll cause maximum damage."

"Will this hurt Andocia?"

"When you fire it at her, she will become violently ill for a few days but it must be a direct hit in order to have the utmost effect."

"What about Tyrus and his bunch?"

"The same, only those you hit will be sick for longer."

"I see, thank you," the explorer replied gratefully. She studied the strange weapon and saw many buttons along the sides. "What do these do?" she asked curiously.

A Sofagin hastily put his hand over the rest of the buttons. "Don't press any of these!" he cautioned. "Just depress the button I showed you, all right."

Constance moved her hand away from the rest of the buttons and nodded at the Sofagin. "Okay I understand. Thank you once again for your help."

"Mrs Carter, when you have done the necessary, please return the weapon. We will meet you here, once again."

"I will, you have my word – and thank you."

21

Constance set off for Saturn and put the ship on autopilot while she planned her strategy. The Candy gun was hidden in a safe place. When she was nearing Saturn, the asteroid belt loomed up and she put her craft into time lapse. She sailed unharmed through the meteor shower, but never disengaged the time lapse function. Instead she travelled until she was hovering above Saturn, just in case Andocia was expecting trouble. Constance landed undetected and hid her ship behind some dense bushes. Then, holding the Candy gun firmly, she made her way stealthily towards the group.

Tyrus and his people were rounding up the Saturnians and grouping them like cattle. They were made to stand in a line and Andocia paced leisurely up and down. She singled out one or two of the inhabitants and killed them without ceremony. A few took flight and attempted to fly away. The evil woman pointed her finger at the airborne group and sliced their wings off without batting an eyelid. Constance clenched her fists in anger, for she knew that without their wings, they would never fly again. Having scanned the surface before landing, Constance knew that four Saturnians were dead and six were grounded for life. The remaining 200 or so were untouched. Lara was singled out and told to stand in a certain area with some of her group. One of the silver creatures stood guard over them. The explorer took out the Candy gun and blasted the being nearest to her. It screamed and lay still, but she could see it was still breathing. The others were all taken by surprise and at first didn't know where the shot had been fired from. Lara and her friends took advantage of the diversion and flew away, coming to rest near the woman. Andocia acted immediately and the remaining Saturnians were imprisoned in a bubble. Constance spoke urgently to her friends.

"Lara, listen to me! I want you and your friends to climb into my ship. Put it into time lapse and get off here, but hover nearby. Use the scanners and when you see everything is all right, land again. I'm going to settle the score with Andocia once and for all."

"Constance, are you insane! You won't survive against her; it's futile. They have killed four of us already!" wailed Lara.

"I know, but just trust me, okay. Now get going!!!!"

As the Saturnians took off in her ship, Constance climbed rapidly up a tree. She fired several bursts with the Candy gun and several of Tyrus' friends lay paralysed on the ground. The explorer had recently been given a portable rocket booster as part of standard equipment, but she had never had any cause to use it. Now however it was strapped to her back and she pressed a button on her belt buckle. There was a short hiss and she launched herself from the tree and propelled herself to the centre of the clearing, firing indiscriminately at her enemies. Many of Andocia's followers also dropped to the ground. When she was a safe distance from the angry group, Constance landed, for her battery had threatened to cut out.

"Constance! I wasn't expecting you! When will you Carters ever learn not to antagonise me?" growled Andocia furiously.

"As long as we live, we'll always bother you," she promised. "Especially when you are terrorizing my friends who are helpless to fight back!"

"Tyrus, get her!" Andocia shouted angrily.

The silver creature teleported himself close to Constance and another of his friends did likewise. The woman ducked as Tyrus hurled a bolt of electricity at her. It missed the explorer and hit another silver being, who fell to the ground. The explorer dropped to one knee and fired more bursts with the Candy gun. Dazed and humiliated, Tyrus and his friends grabbed their incapacitated friends and teleported away from Saturn.

"Now it's just you and me, Andocia!"

"That suits me fine! You fool do you think that weapon will harm me?"

"I'm counting on it actually," stated Constance matter-of-factly.

Andocia screamed and launched herself at her enemy, slamming her into the ground and pinning both her arms securely. Constance twisted desperately and managed to dislodge her enemy, then sprang to her feet and fired at point blank range. The devilish woman's eyes opened wide in shock as the beam caught her squarely between the eyes. Her mouth opened but no sound came out, so she assumed a horizontal position and lay still. Her eyes were glazed, but she was conscious.

"Never would I have believed this possible. You defeated me!"

Constance stared at the powerful woman on the ground and her mouth opened in shock. In reality she had her doubts but still hoped the Candy gun was everything the Sofagins had said it would be. Now to her surprise it had actually worked. Constance looked at the prone woman and stood over her. "That's for interfering in our lives! I'm so tired of wondering when you'll come after my family and inconvenience us. It's payback time!"

Mrs Carter stepped aside as Andocia's followers ran to help their mistress and half carried, half dragged her to the waiting trident ship. It lifted off and was gone within seconds. Constance aimed the Candy gun at the bubble surrounding the Saturnians and fired above their heads. In an instant, the bubble had burst and her friends were free. She placed the Candy gun in its holster as they swarmed around her.

"Once again your people have saved us. We are in your debt! How did you do it?"

"With a little help," she murmured quietly. Aloud she remarked. "I'm glad it worked."

Karnd shook his head in disbelief. "I have never seen anything quite so remarkable in my life. Even with all our knowledge, we have nothing that could defeat Andocia. What manner of weapon is that?"

Constance smiled. "I'm afraid I can't tell you anything, suffice it to say my planet didn't invent it. Everything seems to be in order now, so I'll be on my way."

"But Constance…"

"Sorry, I can't tell you more," she replied regretfully.

Constance's ship landed and the Saturnians got out. Lara threw her arms around her friend and held her tightly. "Oh we saw everything! You were magnificent, just magnificent!"

The explorer disengaged herself, went to her ship, and then waved. "I'm glad I could help. Take care!"

She returned to the Golden Way where some Sofagins joined her. "We told you it would work, didn't we!"

"Yes you did and I'm really sorry I doubted you. I was so surprised when she just keeled over."

"We know; we were observing and saw the look on your face. You were very fortunate to have shot her though, for when she had pinned you to the ground, we thought you would be killed."

"It was a tense moment, I admit." Constance replied. "Here's your Candy gun, and thank you once again."

"Mrs Carter, knowing Andocia, she will be coming to question you when she has recovered. Say nothing about this device or where you got it from."

"I won't," she promised.

"Oh and another thing…"

"Yes?"

"Don't seek our help often."

"I don't plan to anyway," she remarked.

They left and Constance returned to Earth.

Craig was waiting at the Space Centre to greet her. They kissed happily and after exchanging some words with Commander Simms, they returned home.

"Craig, how is your father now? I'm sorry I had to leave you alone, but one of us had to help the Saturnians."

"He's going to be okay, thank the stars! He was trying to paint the roof of their house when he fell off the ladder. Luckily the only damage was a broken leg. It could have been much worse."

"I'm glad it wasn't serious. Now he has an excuse to rest and your mom can fuss over him."

Craig grinned. "Trust me, he's already taking advantage of the situation. How did it go on Saturn?"

"The Sofagins gave me a weapon and it was amazing. It definitely incapacitated Andocia. She had to be carried to her spaceship and they left in a big hurry. I have to tell you though, I don't trust the Sofagins at all. They kept on bragging about how clever they were and how foolish everyone else is. They swore me to secrecy regarding the weapon they lent me, but I know Andocia and I can guarantee as soon as she's well enough, she's going to come and visit us."

⊥　⊥　⊥

A week later, Constance had got up to check on April, who had been niggly the whole day. She heard a movement and went to the door of the room, cursing softly as her gun lay in the drawer beside her bed in the main bedroom. The sound had come from their lounge and she had to go through that room to fetch her weapon. Suddenly her arms were grabbed and pinned behind her. Something clicked into place around her wrists and a gag was forced into her mouth. Constance's struggles ceased when she saw a weapon being pointed at her by one of Andocia's female warriors. The group manhandled her out of their apartment and forced her into a trident ship that was waiting, engine running, on the roof of their apartment building. The craft lifted off and rendezvoused with the mother ship and she was marched into a room where Andocia was waiting.

"So we meet again, through my own choice. You know why I have brought you here of course."

"Yes I do. You could at least have allowed me to put on something more presentable," said Constance, who was clad only in her pyjamas.

"I had no time for niceties," she stormed. She snapped her fingers and a woman approached. "Get her something suitable to wear, Zeen!"

"Yes mistress!" she bowed and went to find something, returning later with a tracksuit.

Andocia freed Constance's arms and she pulled the tracksuit on over her pyjamas.

"Right, now I want some questions answered, I know Earth didn't make that formidable weapon. Where did it come from? Tell me who gave it to you!"

"Lent it to me actually…"

"It is the same thing!"

"Not really, you see…"

"Shut up!!!"

"I was only trying to explain…"

"Well don't. I'm in no mood for flippancy on your part. Your position is serious, so don't mess with me," she threatened.

"I'm not stupid Andocia, but I can't tell you anything," Constance replied patiently.

"I could force it out of you."

"I know that, but I made a promise. I dare not tell you anything. I'm pretty certain these beings will be able to hurt me even more than you could."

The Sofagins were monitoring the conversation and they nodded in agreement to this statement.

"It must be some race I know of, for nothing escapes me," she replied pensively.

"Oh you know them all right. Andocia, leave it be," sighed Constance.

"No, I'll force the truth from your lips," Andocia exclaimed angrily.

Andocia hit her across the face, causing her lip to split, but she refused to answer. The evil being used her powers to cause minor but painful injuries on Constance's body. She was tempted to tell Andocia, but the knowledge that some race existed, who could at least match Andocia, kept her focussed. Even though she didn't like the Sofagins, she refused to name them.

"Mistress, maybe you should leave her to think about it for a while. Perhaps tomorrow things will be different," reasoned her follower.

Andocia considered the advice for a moment, then indicated to her followers, who helped Constance to her feet and took her to a room. They flung her onto the ground and she walked stiffly to a nearby bed, where she lay down. The room was dark and she couldn't see very well, so she waited until her eyes had adjusted to the semi darkness.

⚊ ⚊ ⚊

Something white caught her eye and she studied it. The form took shape and she realised she was looking at Tarmin. Constance hurried to the bird and ran her hands gently over the soft body.

"Tarmin, are you alive?" she asked nervously.

The bird groaned and moved. "Yes. Oh Constance, why are you here?"

She groped around and found a light switch, then went to the bird.

"Oh my goodness, Andocia gave you quite a beating didn't she. What have you done to make her so angry?" the bird asked unhappily.

"It doesn't matter," Constance replied. "You haven't been treated very well either. You have several wounds on your body."

"I know! I hurt everywhere, but I'll live."

"Did you tell her anything regarding Tanus?"

"No. Tanus may be asleep for 100 years, but my loyalty will remain until the day I depart this mortal body for ever."

Constance cuddled up next to the bird and rested her head in the bird's soft feathers. "I admire you Tarmin. If Tanus could hear you, I know she would be so proud of you. Look, I don't want to hang around here too long. Do you think we can escape from this room?"

"I've tried, but I'm too weak to attempt anything. Even if we managed to escape from here, I wouldn't make it to the Golden Way."

"But Earth is closer. You could take refuge there."

"It's worth a shot, but Constance you still haven't answered my question. Why has Andocia brought you here? She has been walking around like a thundercloud. Everyone is afraid of her at the moment, even her own people. I heard a rumour she has been sick the last few days. How can an immortal get sick? Constance, why do I get the impression you caused it?"

Mrs Carter sighed in exasperation. "All right, I was the cause of her sickness – indirectly of course, but don't question me about it, for I can't give you an answer. Even if Andocia doesn't get me, there are others who will. Can we drop the subject now?"

Tarmin didn't answer and her friend moved over to the door and tried to unjam the lock. She managed to screw the access plate off the door, but the moment she tried to cut some wires, a jolt of electricity went through her and she jerked her hand away. Above her, a panel slid open and she found herself looking at Andocia through a closed circuit television.

"Having a problem, my dear?"

"You've been eavesdropping on our conversation haven't you? Did you think I might confide in Tarmin?"

"I did think so, but I guess I was wrong. Well it doesn't really matter, because Tarmin has outlived her usefulness and you can also die with your precious little secret intact. Both of you die in the morning."

"Why don't you go to hell?!" she exclaimed angrily.

"You've always been cheeky, but it doesn't matter anymore! This is your last day alive! It serves you right for trying to be a heroine."

The screen switched off and Constance went to Tarmin who was sitting quietly, and hugged her.

"I guess this is the end for us!" the bird replied sadly.

"It certainly looks that way, but don't give up hope yet! We still have some time left, so I'm going to try and find another way out of here. Will you help me?"

The bird closed its eyes and shook its head. "Oh what's the point? I told you before I can't live without Tanus. My life is over."

She watched as two large tears glistened in the bird's eyes and plopped softly on the floor. Her friend began to press everywhere in the hope of finding another exit, but the place was sealed tightly. Morosely she went and sat a short distance away from the bird.

Suddenly Tarmin squawked and stared at a porthole.

"Constance, there's a shimmering green glow outside. What is it! We are being invaded!!"

The woman jumped up and put a hand on Tarmin's beak to still her anxious cries.

"Stop it Tarmin! Keep quiet!" she admonished.

The glow intensified in brilliance and a beam hit the mechanism that operated the door. The lock disintegrated and the door opened soundlessly. Constance grabbed the startled bird and tugged. "Tarmin, let's get out of here, quickly!"

"Who… what…?" she asked confused.

"We have to hurry. Can you carry me on your back when you go to Earth?"

"Yes, but…"

"Come on, the exit is this way," she prompted.

The green light seemed to fill the entire spaceship; giving it an eerie glow and all the personnel on board were shielding their eyes against the bright light. Constance jumped onto Tarmin's back as she launched herself out of the hatch.

The pair reached the Control Centre while Craig was talking to the security police.

"Oh Constance, I was so worried when you disappeared so suddenly. Commander Simms was going to send out a detachment to look for you. Was it Andocia?"

"Yes, but Tarmin and I escaped so you don't have to worry."

The men saluted smartly and left the building. Tarmin was still in shock.

"Constance, what manner of being freed us?"

"I don't know," she lied. "Anyway, they were obviously friendly."

"But no one alive can equal the power of Andocia, except Tanus and anyway her beam is white."

"Don't concern yourself Tarmin. Just be grateful for your freedom," said Constance secretively.

While Craig had someone treat their wounds, his wife was thoughtful.

"Why did they free me? They made it clear they were not going to get involved with my life and problems."

As time passed, they heard nothing more from Andocia. Tarmin had reverted to her role as Polly the parrot. All was well for a time, but Constance soon detected a change in her husband. Craig had taken to going out on mysterious missions, staying away for a day at a time, sometimes more. However no mission lasted longer than four days. When either Constance or Tarmin tried to question him, he evaded their probing and said the missions were important. After this had been going on for a while, Constance decided to act and she confided in the bird.

"Tarmin, Craig is up to something. I wish I knew where he goes. Do you think you could perhaps follow him?"

"Yes of course. I must admit he has me really worried as well. I'll give him an hour and then will follow him."

Tarmin waited, then set off after her friend. She located his ship easily enough, but hung far back so he wouldn't get wise to her. However, her white body gave her away and Craig spotted her.

He smiled knowingly. "Sorry Tarmin, I know you mean well, but I can't allow you to find out what I'm up to. It will spoil everything."

He pressed a button and his ship went into time lapse and disappeared from sight. The bird looked in dismay as he disappeared.

"Now, why did he have to go and do that? I'll have to tell Constance I failed."

When Craig returned, he greeted everyone affectionately.

"Tarmin, I'm sorry I had to do that, but I couldn't afford to have you following me. What I'm doing doesn't concern either of you. Rest assured I'm not doing anything illegal, I promise. Be content for a while and soon everything will be revealed."

"Craig, it isn't like you to be so secretive. We have been married for seven years and during that time we have never had any secrets," Constance challenged.

"Times change and so do people, my darling. Please be patient a little while longer."

Another year went by, during which Craig completed missions for Commander Simms. Constance too went out into Space for their Commander. During this time though, Craig still disappeared mysteriously for a few days at a time. Their marriage appeared to be over, and they fought constantly about the mysterious trips, but Craig said nothing, merely denied his wife's accusations.

22

A new year began. Six weeks before Andocia was due to carry out her original threat to end his life, the explorer vanished without a trace. He had told Constance he would be away for a week, but he contacted Mission Control, saying he would be gone for a month. During this time, all efforts to contact him were futile. Constance began to fear the worst. Exactly one month to the day, Craig landed in the Control Centre. He avoided his colleagues and their inevitable questions and drove home. Both Constance and Tarmin bombarded him with questions, but he said nothing. His wife was sure he was up to no good and refused to talk to him.

Two weeks later, Craig went to his wife. "Darling, please forgive me for all the hurt I've obviously caused you. It was never my intention to do so, but it was important. I have wanted to explain these trips to you, but I couldn't."

Constance turned her back on the man she loved more than anything and he turned her gently around to face him.

"Oh Constance, am I to go to my death knowing you no longer love me?"

"Death?" she asked stupidly.

"Have you forgotten what day it is? I've had two years my love," Craig reminded his wife.

"What do you mean, two years… oh no! When… when is she coming?" asked Constance, dread in her voice.

"Andocia will arrive tomorrow my sweet. She warned me yesterday. Forgive me please. You'll learn the secret of the mysterious trips, I promise you."

"Oh Craig, no, it's too soon!" she exclaimed, and flung herself into his arms. "I'm such an idiot! I know you love me and we have wasted precious time fighting. I should've believed you."

"It doesn't matter now. I'm glad you aren't angry with me any longer. I'm so grateful we've had eight blissful years together. I've never stopped loving you."

The following evening, Andocia arrived with four of her followers. They were all dressed in black, the execution robes.

"It is time. Come along Carter," ordered Andocia.

"I'm ready," replied Craig bravely. "Goodbye Constance!"

The group waited impatiently while he kissed his wife and children goodbye. As they walked towards the door, Glenn spoke tremulously. "Will you be coming back Daddy?"

"I don't think so Glenn, not this time."

"We'll miss you Daddy," said April tearfully.

Craig took one final look at his family and Tarmin and saw they were crying. Absently, he brushed a tear away from his eyes as well.

As Craig had expected, Andocia had informed all the planets of the impending execution. The explorer was taken to an uninhabited planet and bound firmly to a pole. His enemies and friends alike were glued to their vid screens. Andocia began talking about all the things he had done to anger her, but she never mentioned any of the times she had come off second best. At the end of her tirade, she turned to Craig. "Well, do you have anything to say?"

"Like what?" he asked sardonically.

"Like you apologise," she smirked.

The explorer laughed cynically. "Why would I apologise? I'm not sorry for anything I may have done to anger you – in fact I'm downright proud of everything I've done! Why should you always have things your own way! In fact, killing me won't solve your problems, for every single astronaut is highly trained and there will be a hundred more to take my place. Speaking of having things your own way, Andocia why didn't you mention to our friends and enemies out there in both universes that Constance defeated you with a special weapon. Are you too ashamed perhaps? If I have anything to be sorry for, it's the fact my wife got to humiliate you, and I didn't!"

Her hand swung in a vicious arc and she dealt him a stunning blow across his face. Craig smiled triumphantly. He had revealed to the universes that Andocia had actually been defeated, thus showing her up in front of everyone.

All the planets that knew of Craig and his deeds watched with bated breath as Andocia raised her finger and pointed it at the bound explorer. At the Space Control Centre, Constance watched tearfully. Commander Simms was holding one of her hands gently and Tarmin had a wing around her shoulders. The red beam left Andocia's finger and headed for Craig and soon he was enveloped in a red mist. When it cleared however, the man was unhurt and grinning from ear to ear. With a muttered exclamation, the devilish woman repeated the process time and time again, but still he was unhurt.

"What's happening? Why hasn't he been killed?" gasped Constance nervously.

"I don't know!" replied Simms in awe, "but this is surely a miracle!"

"Carter, why aren't you dead?" asked Andocia in disbelief.

"You are a fool Andocia. I knew this was going to happen."

Suddenly the sky was bathed in a white glow. In the foreground came... Tanus, followed by many of her followers in warships, which formed a guard of honour.

"No! How...?" gulped an amazed Andocia.

Craig was enjoying himself. "It seems you were not thorough enough. You lose again Andocia."

The devilish woman tried to make a break for it, but was knocked senseless as she received the full force of the blow aimed at her.

On Earth, Tarmin jumped up and down in excitement. "Tanus, Tanus, my beloved mistress is alive!!!!"

"Craig is fine too. Oh, I'm so glad!" remarked Constance excitedly as she brushed happy tears away from her face. The entire Control Centre let out a victory cheer. All eyes were on Craig as Tanus freed him and took his hand. She embraced the explorer, then turned her attention to the prone figure lying on the ground. In full view of everyone, she placed shackles on the woman and levitated her to her ship. The woman was taken away and Tanus gave her full attention to Craig. Tarmin couldn't wait any longer and she took off at an incredible speed. She joined her beloved mistress and overwhelmed her with kisses. Slowly the picture faded from the screen and Mission Control waited on tenterhooks to hear the incredible story.

When Craig returned, he was mobbed by well-wishers. Tanus and Tarmin stood respectfully aside and allowed his colleagues to congratulate their friend. Constance hurried forward and Craig held her lovingly.

"My darling, I'm sorry for the uncertainty I've caused you, but I had to do it. Come, let's go home. Commander Simms, we'll be expecting you to come for dinner tomorrow night and then I'll explain everything to you."

"It's a date, Son," replied the Commander gladly.

Craig, Constance, Tanus and Tarmin travelled together. At their flat, the children greeted their father happily. "Daddy, was that forever?"

"What do you mean, April?"

"Well you said you were going away forever."

Craig laughed at his daughter's honesty. "Oh yes, I guess that it was, but I'm back now and I'll never leave you again."

Glenn tugged at his father's sleeve. "Daddy, I thought you were never coming back."

"I know, but I had to say that, Glenn. Take your sister and go and play in your room for now. Mommy and I have things to discuss."

Both stared curiously at Tanus, but they didn't approach her. However they smiled at her before leaving.

The explorer took his wife's hand and they sat down on the couch.

"Constance, this is what all those mysterious missions were about. As you know, I've been very privileged to see Tanus without her 'veil'. No one else has. You see I went to the White Planet because I wanted to make sure she really had been defeated. When I looked at her, I didn't recognise the woman's face. Tanus told me later one of her followers had bravely offered to take her place. Tanus contacted me soon afterwards and told me to confirm she had really been defeated, so Andocia would no longer concern herself with the problem. When Andocia emptied that liquid on the planet, Tanus was far away, and hiding in our universe. Andocia was so convinced her clever scheme had worked that she never even bothered to check the unconscious woman was really Tanus. Anyway, while I was hovering above Tanus's planet, after I found out the woman was an impostor, Tanus contacted me. She asked me to come and see her so we could make plans to defeat Andocia. You see my darling, not everyone on the White Planet was put to sleep, because Tanus needed her advisors to help her think of a solution. She hand-picked those who could help the most, as well as some of her security forces and best scientists. In that way she could plan without fear of discovery. Her scientists have come up with the antidote to the sleeping potion and when every one of her followers has been revived, life can continue as usual. Now Andocia is out of the way, things should work out well for everyone concerned. It hurt me to have to lie, but it was necessary. I had to keep up the pretence, because Tarmin here gets excited quickly and might have let something slip."

Tarmin bent her head in shame.

Tanus hugged her friend. "Please don't feel bad. I love your spontaneity, but in this instance it could have caused a problem."

"Tanus said I must offer no resistance when Andocia came for me," continued Craig.

I confided in Tanus during our meetings and she told me she would protect me and show Andocia up in front of both universes, just as that woman had intended to do with me. That time when I disappeared for a month, we were making the final plans to end Andocia's reign of terror once and for all. I deliberately disconnected the transmitter so no one could contact me. I switched off my mobile device for the same reason."

"Oh Craig, I feel so ashamed! I should have known I could trust you! I'm so sorry for all those horrid things I said to you," sobbed Constance.

"Oh don't worry, I've already forgotten them," he replied magnanimously.

Constance turned to Tanus. "Tanus, thank you too, for making the universes a better place to live in. Many people will be able to breathe easier now that Andocia has been taken care of."

"Yes, but I can't hold her forever. I'll do what I can, of course, but I'm sure you don't have to worry about her anytime soon. Now I must leave. I have to go and revive my followers. Keep up the good work! I'll be in touch with you from time to time. Come Tarmin, we have plenty to do."

The couple watched as Tanus climbed onto her friend's back and soon they had disappeared from view. Life returned to normal once again for the young couple.

PART TWO

23

SON OF CRAIG CARTER

The next seven years were reasonably uneventful. Andocia was still in exile. The children were growing up quickly. Glenn, now a boy of thirteen, was attending high school and his grades were excellent. April was ten and looked like her mother, with her dark hair and blue eyes. Glenn took after his father with the same blond hair and blue eyes. The school he attended was a co-ed.

At mid-term, another girl was introduced to the class. She was twelve and had shiny red hair, which reached down to her waist. She was a fast developer with a stunning figure, despite her young age. For Glenn, this was love at first sight! When the teacher waved her to a seat, Glenn indicated the one next to him. At recess that same day, she sat forlornly eating her sandwich. Glenn smiled and went to sit near her. "Hi, my name is Glenn, what's yours?"

"I'm Deliah," she smiled, extending her hand.

"Pleased to meet you," he replied politely. "Would you like me to give you a tour of the school?"

"I'd love that, thanks. No one else seems to be offering."

Glenn showed her where all the classrooms were. He also pointed out some hiding places where he and his friends sometimes went. She listened eagerly and he felt very important. From that time on, they often sat together at break and shared their lunches. As time moved on, she made more friends, but never forgot to give him a friendly nod or wave when she saw him.

One particular day, Glenn sat daydreaming in front of his plate of food. His mother nudged him. "Glenn, did you hear me?"

"What... oh, sorry Mom, I was just thinking about something."

"I noticed. Does the something have a name?"

Glenn grinned self-consciously. "Well actually I was thinking about Deliah."

"Deliah – oh that's the young girl you mentioned a while ago. I would guess by your woebegone expression, you are missing her."

"Yes, I guess so. Mom, I like her a lot. We seem to have so much in common. I know I see her every day at school, but I miss her when school comes out. I think that I'm in love!"

Constance smiled secretively and thought, "How sweet! This looks like a severe case of puppy love. Craig will be tickled when he returns from his latest mission."

Two days later, Craig returned home and kissed his wife. "Hi sweetheart – miss me?"

"I always do, you know that," she smiled.

"Did anything exciting happen while I was away?"

"Yes. Wait for it! Our son is in love, so he says," she replied.

"Ha ha, oh that's nice. This has to be puppy love of course," he chuckled.

"I have no doubt about it! She probably has freckles and wears her hair in long pigtails."

"I'll bet Glenn pulls them."

"Maybe she wears glasses as well!" Constance giggled.

The couple chortled mischievously.

"Darling, did you wear pigtails when you were younger?" he asked his wife.

"I don't remember, why?"

"I guess I'm imagining you as a scrawny kid with long, long legs."

"I wasn't thin!" objected Constance.

"I don't know…" he mused.

"Craig Carter, you didn't know me when I was Glenn's age, so you can't judge. I wasn't bad looking."

"Hmmm, modest too," he teased.

Constance threw a sock at him and he ducked, grabbing her outstretched hand in the process. They fell on the bed and he kissed her soundly. The washing flew in all directions.

A few days passed and then Glenn entered nervously.

"Yes Glenn?" asked his father curiously.

"I… I er… ahem!"

"You failed your exam?"

"No Dad, I passed with flying colours. I… I've brought someone to meet you."

"Your little girlfriend no doubt," remarked his mother.

Glenn flushed and took the girl's hand. "Mom, Dad, I want you to meet Deliah."

Their first reaction was one of shock, for they had expected a little girl with freckles and pigtails. Instead they were introduced to a real beauty. Her eyes were large and green and her hair hung down to her waist. She had a perfect figure and long, shapely legs.

"Hello," she replied shyly.

"Hello Deliah. We are very glad to finally meet you. Glenn talks about you all the time," explained Constance.

She smiled shyly, "Thank you."

The Carters found Deliah could hold a conversation. She was very intelligent for her age. They discussed a number of things with her and her opinions were very well thought out.

� � �

When Glenn finished school, he lost touch with the beautiful Deliah. He dated other girls, but never quite got over her. The separation lasted only one year though and they met again, quite by chance. The whole cycle then began again. She came for dinner often and was always welcomed enthusiastically. Craig however began to get uneasy about Deliah, as Glenn seemed besotted with her. Every once in a while, Craig would glance over and look at Deliah and her unguarded expression would change. Even during a normal conversation, she sometimes seemed to glare at Glenn even though he had never said anything derogatory about her. Craig knew his son well enough to know he wasn't ready to settle down just yet. Every other girlfriend Glenn had ever dated never affected his son in the same way. On his next assignment, he went to visit Tanus.

"Tanus, I know this sounds really crazy. If I confide in anyone else, they'll just laugh at me. I consider myself a good judge of character and it has helped me many times in the past. I have been at close quarters with Andocia many times, but fortunately since you put her into exile eleven years ago, there has been peace. I think trouble is brewing, but it's only a hunch."

Tanus looked enquiringly at the explorer. "Explain what you mean, Craig."

"Tanus look at this picture and tell me what you think," he stated, showing her a picture of Deliah he had on his mobile device.

"She's very beautiful!"

"Yes she is and Glenn is dating her. Examine this picture closely and tell me if I'm imagining things, but to me she looks a lot like Andocia."

Tanus and Tarmin looked carefully at the picture.

"You know, now that you mention it, she does. Of course there are differences. Her hair is the same colour, but it is curlier than Andocia's. The face is slightly different too though, but there definitely is a resemblance."

Tarmin stared at the picture and nodded.

"Tanus, I know this is presumptuous of me, but both you and Andocia are immortal, right."

"Yes, but you know that."

"I need to know something very personal. Can immortals have… er… sexual relations with members of the opposite sex?"

Tanus gawked at him. "Well of course they can. I haven't really thought about it as being odd in any way."

"Can either you or Andocia conceive children from such a union?"

"No Craig, immortals are barren. Children can be born under the right conditions, as long as the tank method[1] is used. Children born in such a way, while normal in every respect, would be mortal. Immortality is not an option. All you need is a willing subject and voila, one baby!"

"So what you're saying is that it's a possibility?"

"If someone wanted to go that route, yes. Craig, don't jump to unnecessary conclusions though. Ask April to help, but don't mention our conversation to Glenn at all. If he's besotted with this girl, he could turn against you if he thinks you are trying to separate them. Keep tabs on the situation and let me know if something develops. Tell Constance of your suspicions though."

"Oh Tanus, I sincerely hope I'm wrong. One Andocia is enough; we don't need a successor. I mentioned Valdena to you some time ago, but I don't see her as a threat. She's undoubtedly still happy playing creator on her planet."

"I agree with you," she assented. "The best advice I can give you is to

[1] TANK METHOD: Technique used in cases of infertility for whatever reason. The "parents" donate sperm and eggs, which are artificially fertilised and placed in a special solution, resembling amniotic fluid. The fertilised product is placed in a glass tank where conception takes place. The foetus is fed artificially until the due date, whereupon it is taken out and given to the parents. The parents-to-be are encouraged to visit their unborn baby in order to bond with it. In this way, either a boy or girl could be ordered, if required.

check this out very thoroughly. It might just be a coincidence though and Deliah may simply be an ordinary girl."

"I hear what you are saying Tanus. I'll tell April to keep her eyes open and see if Deliah is someone we have to be concerned about."

Craig returned home and confided in his wife.

"Darling, is it possible?"

"It is, but I sincerely hope we are wrong."

Constance had an idea and the next time Deliah visited, she chatted to her for a while. "You know Deliah; you have such a wonderful skin. It's so smooth."

Deliah giggled. "Yes, I'm very lucky. I have good genes."

Constance stroked the girl's face, then purposely scratched her.

"Ouch!"

Constance gasped in shock and reached out to the young girl. "Oh I'm terribly sorry dear. Here let me put something on that – it's beginning to bleed."

"No, it's okay, thank you. I'm sure it will stop soon," remarked Deliah as she wiped the blood with a tissue.

The girl turned her head, but the skin showing through wasn't green.

Constance fussed around her. "Oh I feel so stupid. Are you sure you wouldn't like me to put disinfectant on it?"

"No, it's fine thanks," she reassured her.

They spoke for a while longer and Constance continued her subtle probing.

"Deliah you have been dating Glenn for ages, but I don't even know your surname."

"Oh it's Grace, Deliah Grace."

Glenn who came to claim his girlfriend interrupted them and they went out.

While they were dancing, Glenn happened to glance at his partner. He blinked and looked again. In the club's lighting, she looked green. "Deliah?"

"Yes, Glenn?" As she turned to him, her eyes seemed to flash reddish.

"I... I could have sworn your skin had a green tinge to it and that your eyes changed colour..."

Deliah reacted strangely. "Don't be ridiculous!" she snapped. "If that's your way of making fun of me, I think you had better take me home!"

"I'm sorry Deliah, really I am. Of course your skin isn't really green – it's just the strange lighting in this club. Just forget it okay. You didn't have to get so uptight!"

"I'm sorry. It's just I'm very proud of my skin."

"I apologise. Let's forget it now and come sit with me."

Deliah smiled and they sat down in a dark corner, where they kissed and all doubt was dispelled from Glenn's mind.

Constance confided in her daughter and told her what they suspected. She asked April if she would try and find out more and the girl agreed readily. April became very friendly with Deliah and sometimes went to her house. She met Deliah's parents, who seemed like very nice people.

⚊ ⚊ ⚊

One day there was a strange twist of fate. While April was at Deliah's home, her mother slipped and fell, grazing her hand. The skin was damaged and the colour green showed through very clearly. Of course the woman covered it up immediately, but one glance had been enough for the shaken April. She pretended not to have noticed though and visited with Deliah.

A few days later, April visited Deliah again. The girl excused herself and went to shower, while April waited for her. Deliah's parents had gone out so the two of them were alone in the house. April took advantage of the distraction and headed to Deliah's room, looking for clues. She pulled out each drawer in turn and shuffled carefully through the contents of each, until finally, she hit the jackpot. Under several layers of underwear, she found a photograph of Andocia, as well as a diary. She glanced nervously down the passage, but the splashing indicated there was still time, so with trembling fingers, April began paging through the diary entries. The book opened on a particular place and the girl read the contents.

"Mother, I shall find a way to free you from Tanus's power. I'm going out with Craig Carter's son, and I will learn of the family's weaknesses. When the time comes, I'll destroy them. They don't suspect me as yet, because my skin is fair like the Earth beings, so it will be easy. You told me how you came to be intimate with an Earthling, who is now dead. We will rule the universes together, I promise."

April gasped in shock. "So it's true! I must tell Dad about this. Thank goodness he became suspicious."

"Yes it's true, miss nosey parker. Your family are cleverer than I gave them credit for."

"Deliah!" gasped April in surprise.

She had been so absorbed in snooping around she hadn't heard Deliah come into the room and watch her as she read the diary entry. Guiltily she closed the book but she had been caught in the act.

"I knew your family were getting suspicious and I heard you scratching around in my room. I'm going to have to kill you now. I can't let a slip of a girl spoil my plans," snapped Deliah angrily.

"I hardly know your mother, but if she is anything like you, I don't want to," April remarked.

Deliah advanced menacingly and April backed away.

"Ask your father what my mother did to him in the past. He'll have some hair raising stories to tell you."

April backed further away and Deliah ran behind her at incredible speed, blocking her only avenue of escape. April knew it wouldn't do to panic, so she forced herself to think rationally. Deliah lunged at her, but she ducked and avoided the blow aimed at her face. She rolled on the floor and tripped Deliah. With a startled exclamation, the girl slipped and fell. Within seconds, April had jumped on top of her. They were near Deliah's dressing table and her hand scrabbled desperately, closing on a heavy object. April slammed the ornament into the side of Deliah's face and the girl lay stunned on the floor.

"Whew, thank goodness Daddy taught us some judo tricks. Deliah won't trouble me for a while, but I have to get out of here and warn him!"

Panic seized her and she rushed headlong down the stairs, straight into Deliah's "parents".

"Hey careful April – you nearly knocked us over."

She forced herself to smile. "I'm really sorry, but I didn't realise what the time was! I have to get going; I'm late for an appointment."

"What was the meaning of that?" they asked one another.

The woman shrugged and Deliah appeared at the top of the stairs, holding a cloth to her bleeding head.

"Stop her! She knows about us!"

They began pursuing her immediately, but April had a head start and was soon far away, so they couldn't catch her.

A breathless April arrived home. She hurried to her mother. "Mom, where's Daddy?"

"You just missed him honey. He's going on another mission now. Your dad left about an hour ago, so he's probably already in space."

"Mommy, we have a big problem! Deliah is Andocia's daughter. We must get hold of Dad. Mom, she threatened to kill me when she caught me snooping. I knocked her out and just ran. Dad must warn that other woman – what's-her-name."

"Tanus. Yes he must. Oh no, Glenn is on his way to see Deliah."

"We have to stop him Mom. Did he take his auto cycle?"

"I think so, yes."

"Then we should overtake him. Mom, we must prevent him from visiting her. She could harm him!"

Constance ignored the speed limits and roared after her son. They caught up with him when he was but one block away from Deliah's apartment. Constance landed across the road, blocking his path.

"Hey Mom, what's the idea? I was just on my way to see Deliah. We have an important date."

"Forget about your precious date! Something serious has happened."

"Is it Dad?" gasped Glenn.

"No," interrupted his sister, "this concerns your precious Deliah. She isn't who she pretends to be."

"What do you mean?" he asked dumbfounded.

"Never mind, I'll explain it when we're airborne again. Fold your auto cycle up and put it in my boot, hurry!"

Glenn was bemused and did as he was told. When the car had lifted off again, he questioned the two women. "All right, what about Deliah?"

"Tell him, April."

"Glenn, your girlfriend is Andocia's daughter. You know, that woman with the green skin who terrorised Dad before she was captured by Tanus."

"No, it's not possible!" he exclaimed in disbelief.

"I'm telling you the truth. She tried to kill me because I found out. We have to warn Dad, but he's just gone off on another mission." Suddenly April noticed they weren't heading home and she questioned her mother. "Mom, where are we going? Home is the other way."

"We're going to the Space Centre and boarding a craft. If we remain in our flat, Deliah and the others will come looking for us."

"But Mom, we aren't used to space," protested Glenn unhappily. "We've only been up with Dad a few times."

"I'm not leaving you two here, not with that girl on the loose."

They burst into the Space Centre. Simms was now very old and had white hair. He was in his last year before retirement.

"What are you three doing here? Craig has left already."

"I know Commander, but this is an emergency. We have to find Craig and warn him. I'll explain once we have left Earth. Please could we have a ship?"

"Very well, I'll organise one for you. I'll call ahead and tell the technicians get one ready for you."

The threesome blasted off within two hours of April's discovery. When they were safely out in space, Constance began to relax more.

"We should be safe now. I'll just contact Dad."

Constance contacted her husband and he was surprised to hear from them. He gave his co-ordinates and instructed his wife to join him. Soon the ship could be seen with the naked eye and the children watched goggle-eyed as they two ships aligned themselves and both hatches opened. They stepped through and hugged their father.

"Craig, I'm sorry to have interrupted your mission, but Commander Simms said another few hour's delay wouldn't make that much difference. I'll be brief though. As I mentioned to you earlier, Deliah is Andocia's daughter. She admitted it to April, and tried to kill her. You must warn Tanus and tell her to expect trouble. I don't know what that girl's capabilities are, but if she is even half as powerful as her mother, we are all in trouble."

"I'll do that of course. Constance, I want you to take Glenn and April to our Space Station near Pluto. Stay put there until I tell you otherwise."

"But Craig, the children aren't used to such a long journey."

"It can't be helped. Now is as good a time as any for them to get used to being in space."

"I don't have enough supplies to last the whole journey either. We left in such a hurry."

"Take some of mine. I'll get more at Tanus's place," he said as he dumped various parcels into his wife and children's hands. They returned to their ship and when safely aboard, the ships separated and Craig went another way.

"Mom, why didn't Dad tell us to go to the Moon? It was nearer."

"He's just being careful, Glenn. The Moon is too close to Earth and I suppose he thinks they could come after us there."

Constance put the spacecraft into time-lapse mode so they could travel faster. They landed at the Space Station and the children were given a guided tour.

24

Craig in the meantime was heading for the White Planet. He put the power on full thrust and streaked towards his destination. Carter announced his intention to land and was told where to go. Even before he had touched down, Tarmin was waiting anxiously for him. "Hello Craig, you sounded very worried when you contacted us. What's wrong?"

"There's trouble Tarmin, big trouble. Where's Tanus?"

"She's having a meeting with someone from another planet. I don't think she'll be long though. Can you wait?"

"I'll have to."

The explorer walked moodily around Tanus's garden, trying to kill some time. An hour later, Tanus appeared and he followed her to the room she had been in earlier.

"All right, Tarmin says you have an urgent message for me."

"Yes I do and it isn't good. Deliah is Andoica's daughter."

"How did you find out?" asked Tanus curiously.

"Well April did some snooping, but she was discovered. She got away safely though, but Deliah and her adopted parents know about it now. April hit Deliah with a blunt instrument, so she says. It seems obvious this girl's powers are either non-existent, or maybe she still has to develop them. April never came in contact with a barrier, but Deliah can fight."

"Or possibly that power was well developed and Deliah just didn't erect the barrier, thinking that April was easy prey."

"Well whatever the scope of her powers is, she's going to try and free her mother one of these days. If she manages to succeed, both you and I know who their main target will be."

"Yes, both of us, but mainly me. I don't really know what to expect of her, but I'll double the guards at Andocia's place of confinement. This may sound like stupid advice, Craig, but I think Constance and the children should return home. I haven't met the young lady as you know, but what would be the point of capturing Constance or the children. Even though they know, whom can they tell? The police can't help. I think she'll concentrate her efforts on trying to free her mother first, then she'll come after the rest of you. If Andocia does get free, you can panic. Rest assured though, I won't let that happen. She probably attacked April in anger, without really thinking it through. The best advice I can give you is to let Glenn continue dating her. He can explain he is in love with her and doesn't care who her mother is. It's true after a fashion, because Glenn has no real first-hand knowledge of Andocia. I know it's a long shot, but maybe she'll believe it."

"All right, if you say so. Tanus, I'll keep you informed of what's happening on Earth, but let me know if your situation changes for whatever reason."

"I will. Meanwhile, I have meetings set up all morning and you have a mission to complete. Goodbye Craig and take care of yourself and that wonderful family of yours."

Craig waved goodbye and left the White Planet. As was her usual custom, Tarmin flew part of the way with him, then returned to her mistress. Craig set his course for the planet he was expected on, then contacted his wife and told her what Tanus had suggested.

"But Craig, are you sure it's safe to return home?"

"It is, but Glenn will have to play it cool. Tanus doesn't think Deliah is all that interested in our family right now."

"Very well, we'll do as you say. Hurry up and finish your mission my darling; I'm missing you already."

"I'll try. Take care, all three of you."

Constance and her children returned to Earth and Glenn decided he had better pay Deliah a visit. He had no idea of Andocia's power, so decided it would be all right. He knocked nervously on the door and Deliah's foster mother opened it.

"Hello, is Deliah here?"

"Yes she is, but I think she is in the shower at the moment. Would you like to come in and wait?"

Glenn obeyed and sat down in the lounge. The woman went up to Deliah's room and knocked on the door. She went in and closed it behind her.

"Deliah, Glenn Carter is here."

"Glenn! But didn't his sister tell him anything?"

"I'm sure she must have. I don't know why he's here, but maybe you had better go and see him."

Deliah went downstairs and sat next to Glenn, while her foster mother made a discreet exit.

"Glenn, why are you here? April must have told you about me. Surely under the circumstances I would be the last person on Earth you wanted to be involved with."

"Yes, she did tell me. Look, I understand the situation is tense, but I still like you. I'm sure it could work out for us. Just because Andocia gave my father such a hard time, doesn't mean we can't be friends, does it?"

Deliah didn't answer. Instead she took Glenn's hand and led him up the stairs. Once in her bedroom, she took out the picture of Andocia and looked thoughtfully at it. She passed it to Glenn who studied it intently.

"Have you ever met my mother?" asked Deliah curiously.

"Yes, when I was very young. She was visiting my parents for some or other reason. Deliah, I'll be honest with you if you afford me the same courtesy. I don't know what has transpired over the years between my father and your mother, but every time my parents talk about her, it's with a sort of loathing. I'm prepared to keep an open mind, because as I said, I never really knew your mother. Everyone I speak to, quakes when your mother's name is mentioned, including my father. I don't know why that is, but you don't affect me in that way. Maybe you're different."

"My powers haven't been fully developed yet. I'm told that practice makes perfect. My foster parents tell me the woman Tanus is the one to fear most of all. You may not have heard much about your father's exploits with Andocia, but I have. She seems to be under the impression your father is also never to be trusted."

"He's very good at his job," replied Glenn proudly.

"Glenn, let's put all our cards on the table, okay. I'll admit I like you a lot. You have more brains than most of the guys I've dated and I've enjoyed your company up until now, but this won't work. I'm going to find a way to rescue my mother from Tanus's clutches and then we'll rule the universes together. If your father gets in our way, he'll die a very violent death. If you have plans to follow in his footsteps, then we'll be enemies as well and you'll be treated just the same as anyone else who tries to stop us. Under the circumstances, I really can't go out with you again."

Glenn sighed. "If that's what you want, I suppose I'll have to accept it. I guess I'll see you around sometime."

"Until I leave to rescue my mother I suppose. Bye Glenn."

The young man walked down the stairs and out the front door. He didn't look back. He returned home and sat mournfully in a chair.

"What's happened Glenn? You look as though the sky fell in on you."

"Mom, it's over between Deliah and me. She admitted everything! She's determined to go and rescue her mother from Tanus's clutches. Deliah told me that if Dad got in her way, she would take care of him too. She also said that if I decide to explore Space, she would consider me her enemy as well. Mom, I think it's about time you told me what to expect – if Andocia should get free I mean. Why does Andocia hate Dad so much?"

"Glenn, your father has managed to live so long because he never underestimates his enemies. You saw Andocia a few times when you were younger, but you have no real recollection of her, so you don't know the meaning of the word 'fear'. You think that your father's fears are unfounded, but you couldn't be more wrong."

"But Mom, you don't fear her as Dad does."

"Oh yes I do, but I just don't show it. Son, get comfortable and let me tell you what I went through when your father was Andocia's prisoner – and he was quite often. Let me tell you about the time she took over Earth, and the time she blinded your father; and the time your father suffered when he tried to help Tanus, when the tables were turned. Andocia really made an example of him. Glenn, there's much to be told!"

"Then tell me. I want to know everything."

Glenn sat and listened intently to her incredible tales. At the end of the narrative, Glenn was well aware who his father's friends were, as well as his enemies. "Mom, this is quite unbelievable!"

"Yes and every word of it is true," she assented.

"I guess Dad really has cause to fear Andocia. Deliah is another matter though. I don't think that she's so powerful. She's just a silly sixteen year old."

"That might well be the case right now because she hasn't seen much of her mother. If Andocia was freed, she would teach Deliah everything she knows and they will be invincible as a team."

Glenn was thoughtful, for he had plenty to think about. "Thanks for telling me Mom. At least I understand what the entire furore is about. I'll be in my room if you want me."

Glenn went to his room and sat down on his bed. He looked at a photograph he had of Deliah.

"It still sounds too fantastic for words. Andocia must be some witch to have everyone so worried. I don't think Deliah will be much of a threat. She has petty ideals though. I don't see Tanus letting her succeed in getting her mother freed. I've given this matter a lot of thought and no matter what my parents say I want to make Space exploration my career. My father is a legend in his own right and I would like to be one too someday. Tomorrow I'm quitting my job and taking to Space – and adventure!"

Glenn began to daydream and visualised medals being pinned on him. He didn't realise Space travel contained many hazards, as well as triumphs.

When his father returned from his mission, Glenn called him aside. "Dad, I want to become a Space explorer. Will you take me out into Space and teach me everything I need to know about Space exploration?"

Craig was shocked. "Glenn, do you realise what you have just said?"

"Of course I do. I want to explore Space."

Craig looked earnestly at his son and shook his head emphatically. "Glenn, I have many years' experience behind me and there are many hazards. You could get killed. If I had my life to live all over again, I would never have gone out into Space. Don't be foolish; rather keep working at your present job."

"Please Dad, I really want to do this," he pleaded.

"Glenn, give it another year and if you still feel the same way at that time, then we can talk about it. The applicant's course is a very gruelling one. Hundreds try out to be astronauts, but very few make it."

"I don't care. Another year won't make me change my mind. I don't mind the course."

Craig yawned. "Can we change the subject for the moment? I'm tired and I want to go to bed early. We can discuss this in the morning if you like."

Craig went to his bedroom to change. On an impulse, Glenn decided to visit Deliah and tell her he was going to explore Space. On arriving at her apartment though, he found new tenants occupying the place.

"Oh I thought the Graces lived here."

"They did, until a week ago. We are living here now."

Glenn thanked them and went back to his auto cycle.

"Hmmm, so they have left. I wonder if they just moved to another city, or maybe they are going to try and rescue Andocia. Oh well, Deliah and I are history, so no point worrying."

The young man returned home, but never said anything to his parents.

Two days later, Craig was told there was another mission for him, which involved every planet. This was just what Glenn had been waiting for. He approached his father and begged to go along with him, but Craig refused. Glenn was determined to go along anyway, so followed his father to the Space Control Centre. While he was being de-briefed, Glenn made discreet inquiries about the ship his father would be travelling in. He located it in the hangar and stowed away. His father boarded the ship and soon they were in Space. When they had passed the Moon, Glenn showed himself.

"Glenn! What are you doing here?" asked his father angrily.

"I want to explore Space. I have given this a lot of thought, but I still want to do it. You know you can't take me back now because it'll mess up your schedule."

Craig was angry his son had disobeyed and gave him a good talking to, but Glenn put up with the tirade. Finally his father's anger was spent.

"Well seeing as you are here now, I'll just have to put up with you. I'm going to have to stop at one of the Space Stations though, for I'll need more provisions. I wasn't expecting company."

"Where are we going?"

"I have to go to Venus. I suppose I had better introduce you to my friends, since you are here. I really think you should reconsider though."

"My mind is made up. This is how I want to spend the rest of my life. Please let me do it, please?"

"Oh very well then; if you feel that strongly then you must follow your heart. When we return to Earth, I'll arrange for you to be booked into the next astronaut's camp. Now I'll have to contact your mother before she panics."

He contacted his wife via his mobile device and turned his attention back to his son. "Now Glenn, I'm going to teach you how to fly this ship. It's quite easy once you get the hang of it."

He put the ship on autopilot and showed Glenn around. His son absorbed every detail, no matter how insignificant it seemed. Venus appeared on screen and Craig radioed in, then took the ship down.

"Right, I'll go and see them first, then I'll introduce you. Be careful, the soil is marshy. You must know where to walk. Follow me exactly."

Glenn dutifully placed his footprints in the ones his father left and in this manner they made it to solid ground. Craig greeted the Venusians.

"Hello. I brought the things you asked for."

The Venusian called his friends and they began to unload the supplies. Once they were neatly stacked on the floor, Craig introduced Glenn to them. They greeted him in a friendly manner and he shyly shook the outstretched leaf that was the creature's hand. "Pleased to meet you," he declared solemnly.

"Welcome young man. I hope one day you will be as famous as your father."

The little group conversed for a while and then left. Glenn was intrigued by the plant-like beings. "They are so amazing! When we landed I thought we had to go through the gardens to meet them, but they are part of the garden. The Venusians look like walking plants!"

"That's what they are essentially. This planet is very useful because they help us with a number of herbs we grow for medicinal purposes. Each plant serves a different function, but all are connected to one another and responsible for one another's well-being. We could learn a lot about their 'oneness' as they call it. Here on Venus, the plants co-exist in peace; not like us humans who always want to fight and think we are superior to others. Well anyway, let's continue with our journey."

"Where are we going now, Dad?"

"Next stop, Jupiter. We pass over Mars. Glenn, never land on that planet if you can help it. It has a strong gravitational pull and it's difficult to get off again. It doesn't support life."

"According to this chart of the universe, we really bypass Mars."

"Yes we do, but I wanted to show you every planet so you get to recognise them all."

"Thanks Dad, I really appreciate this," replied his son gratefully.

"How are you feeling? Are you queasy at all? Sometimes when humans are in Space for long periods, they feel a bit dizzy, but it gets better with time."

"I'm okay thanks; I'm much too excited to feel ill."

The duo passed Mars and Craig pointed out things of interest, then moved on.

"What's the next stop, Dad?" asked Glenn excitedly.

"Now, we go to Jupiter."

"Tell me more about Jupiter," Glenn suggested curiously.

"The beings there are not as advanced as us. They haven't evolved quite as far as us yet. Their planet is very similar to Earth, but they are several centuries behind us. It is the biggest planet in our universe. A few years ago, all they knew was sign language, but they are learning our language quickly now, although sign language remains the most popular means of communication. Seeing as you haven't learnt any yet, leave everything to me."

Craig showed his son how to go into time-lapse mode and explained this would enable them to travel faster.

They reached Jupiter and the people hurried forward when they recognised Craig's ship. He greeted them in sign language and after several gestures from both sides, Craig pointed towards his ship and Glenn smiled tentatively. They slapped him on his back a number of times.

"Ouch! Dad do they always do this?"

"Always; it's a gesture of friendship. Slap them back."

Glenn complied and after his father had spoken to them for a while, they left the planet.

"Right, now we go to Saturn. The Saturnians are a very clever race and also friends of Earth's. They have helped me out on a number of occasions when I was having difficulties, and I have helped them with their problems, in return."

Saturn came into view.

"Now Glenn, we go back into time lapse or else we won't make it through Saturn's rings. Here, you operate the mechanism."

Glenn did so eagerly. When he wasn't sure he asked his father for confirmation. The computer announced the time-lapse sequence had been successful and Glenn beamed proudly.

Father and son emerged from the spacecraft and Jorrel greeted them.

"Hello Craig. This is obviously your son. He looks a lot like you."

Craig nodded and the two beings shook hands. "Jorrel, I'd like you to meet my son Glenn."

"I'm delighted to make your acquaintance!" he replied politely. "How old are you, young man?"

"I'm seventeen," he replied.

"Ah, still young I see. Are you planning to follow in your father's footsteps, or is this just a social visit?"

"I want to become a Space explorer, like my Dad. He's just showing me around."

"I see, well I wish you luck. I suppose being an astronaut is never dull. Your father has put up with plenty of strange beings in his time. We can chat later. Please join us for something to eat – it is lunchtime."

The two men joined their hosts and afterwards, Glenn was taken on a tour of Saturn, while Craig spoke to Karnd, Lara and the other scientists.

"Craig, you have a fine young son. I hope he does well in Space, but it's so full of danger. Why is he doing this?"

"I don't know, Karnd. I tried to dissuade him about this choice, but he wouldn't listen. Do you know he stowed away on my ship because I refused to take him on a tour of Space?"

Karnd laughed heartily. "Ah, the youth of today are so forward! He looks like a sensible lad though. He has a good head on his shoulders and shouldn't panic quickly."

"Yes, he is sensible," concurred Craig "I won't stand in his way if he really wants to explore Space, but I'm not happy about it all the same."

"I'm sure he'll do very well my friend. Do you have some news for me? You sounded very secretive on the linkup."

"Yes, I have some disturbing news. Glenn was going out with a young lady not long ago and they were becoming quite serious. Karnd, we found out Deliah is Andocia's daughter."

"What! If this is a joke…"

"It isn't, I assure you. My daughter April found out about it. Later Deliah admitted to Glenn she was Andocia's daughter."

Karnd wrung his hands in despair. "This is very serious."

"I know, but she doesn't seem to have the power her mother has, but Tanus thinks these are still developing."

"That is possible, of course. Everything does improve with practice." Karnd replied seriously.

"I know. She plans to free her mother from Tanus's clutches."

"Do you think she can do it? Andocia has been trapped for eleven years and never managed to escape," Lara asked worriedly.

"I don't know, but I hope not," replied Craig fervently. "If she manages it, all of us will be in serious trouble."

"Well we had better hope it doesn't happen," replied the Saturnians.

Glenn returned from his tour and spoke excitedly about all the advanced equipment. They spent a few more hours on Saturn, then left.

Next, they went to Uranus where Craig loaded some Uranium onto his craft.

"This planet is full of Uranium. We often come here to get more minerals for the weapons we manufacture. It does not support any life."

"Do we go to Pluto now?"

"Take a closer look at the map, son."

"Oh, we have to go to Neptune!" he smiled excitedly.

"That's correct. We're going to do some underwater swimming."

"Sounds like fun," replied Glenn excitedly. "They live in the sea, don't they?"

"Yes. I'm looking forward to seeing Lolita again."

On Neptune, Craig contacted the Neptunians and they replied they would send someone up to escort the pair down to the palace. Not long afterwards, Lolita appeared. She was as beautiful as ever. On seeing Craig, she climbed out of the water and hurried to him. He grabbed her and lifted her effortlessly up into his arms. When he set her down once more, she kissed him on his forehead. "Oh it's so good to see you again, Craig. It has been a long time!"

Then she noticed Glenn. "Oh hello, you're Glenn aren't you? I see the family resemblance."

Glenn was speechless and nodded. He stared, transfixed by her incredible beauty. Lolita didn't seem to mind and handed him the gills.

"Craig, you know how these work, so I'll just help Glenn to put them in."

Once they were in place, the young man felt uncomfortable, but he was reminded his father and mother had also been in the same situation and it wouldn't be long before they became second nature to him. When all the gills were in place, Lolita dived into the water, followed by the two men. Lolita swam ahead, while Craig spoke to his son. "Glenn, your eyes are nearly bulging out of your head. Do you have to stare quite so hard?"

"I don't mean to, but gosh, she's beautiful!"

"I know. She had the same effect on me when I first met her and her people. They age much slower than we do. By Earth calculations, she should be about thirty, but she looks a lot younger."

"Is she a queen?"

"She's a princess actually. Her mother is the Queen of Neptune."

When they reached the palace, Glenn could only stare in bewilderment at the sheer beauty and magnificence of the place. Lolita offered to show him around the underwater city, while Craig discussed business with the King. When their time was up, Glenn was sorry to leave Neptune behind him.

Once back in Space, Craig and Glenn studied the map.

"Right, now we pass over Pluto."

"Pass over?"

"Yes. The Plutonians are a deadly little bunch."

Carter hovered over the planet and switched on the scanner. Glenn observed the inhabitants.

"But Dad, they look so sweet! They have such kind expressions on their faces."

"Huh, don't let appearances fool you. It fooled others and they paid for it with their lives."

Glenn shuddered. "I won't forget that ever! Where are we going to now?"

"We have a long journey ahead of us. Mercury is our next stop, but it's at the other end of the universe. It's time to have a nap, so put the ship on automatic pilot."

"Hold on a moment Dad. I'm sure we don't have enough supplies to get there. Hadn't you better check it?"

Craig called for the information and the computer confirmed Glenn's suspicions. "Oh, well done Glenn. I forgot I had another passenger who eats like a horse."

Glenn grinned self-consciously. "Well, I'm a growing boy."

"Of course you are!" his father grinned. "Well, we have to stop at the American Space Station on the way. I'll introduce you to the technicians there."

They docked in the Space station and got supplies, before continuing on their way. Glenn performed the necessary course calculations and other duties his father asked him to and they settled down for a nap. They woke when the ship was approaching Mercury and Craig switched on the heat shield.

"All right, Mercury is uninhabited. It is very hot there, so we need to put our heat shield on, otherwise the metal melts. There isn't much to see here, so we'll move on to Sonambra. This is the home of the sun creatures. They are radioactive beings, but Sonambro will organise it so we don't suffer from radiation burns. You can steer and do the necessary course corrections while I watch you. Go ahead; she's all yours!"

Glenn accepted eagerly and steered effortlessly. Just before they reached Sonambra, Craig took over the controls, for the downward thrust was very strong. They landed and Sonambro greeted them eagerly. He immediately gave them immunity against the radiation, and then Craig introduced his son. They talked for a while and again someone offered to show Glenn around the planet. As he was very curious, he went gladly. After a few hours, they were once again in Space.

Father and son went through the jump vortex to the Golden Way, where they intended to visit with Tanus. However, Tarmin spoke to them and informed them that Tanus was very busy. Craig decided his son would have to see her another time and they headed back towards Earth.

Three months later, they were home again. Constance was waiting for them and gave her son a good talking to. However, he had made up his mind that Space travel was the right job for him. Although Constance had reservations about his decision, she gave him her blessing. Craig also decided Glenn must explore Space, if that was what he wanted.

Glenn Carter signed on for the next survival-cum-training course for budding Space explorers and emerged top of his class. His family watched proudly as he was sworn into NASA as one of the new recruits. Proudly, Glenn Carter undertook minor missions for his boss, Commander Perry. Commander Simms visited the Space centre from time to time, but he had officially retired.

Another year passed. Glenn was eighteen and April had just turned fifteen. Things had been relatively quiet.

25

The day began as usual, with the Carter family having breakfast. Suddenly Tanus, who was in a state of agitation, interrupted their meal.

"Craig, Craig, come quickly! Andocia has been freed! Her daughter managed to rescue her. We have to act immediately!"

"I'm coming! Constance, be on your guard and look after the children."

Glenn stood up. "I'm coming with you."

"No Glenn. I appreciate the offer, but I would prefer if you stay behind. You've been trained in weaponry and self-defence and you may need to use those skills to defend yourself. Andocia or her wretched daughter may come for revenge and I don't want your mother and sister left alone. Andocia can't be killed, but her daughter probably can. I'm not suggesting you kill anyone, but if you have no choice, then do it. Goodbye all of you! Wish me luck! With a final kiss, which he planted on Constance's forehead, Craig and Tanus vanished from sight.

Constance wrung her hands nervously. "Why did this have to happen, why?"

"Mom, isn't there anything we can do?" asked Glenn unhappily.

"No, but I'm going to the Space centre to sound the alert. You stay here and look after your sister. April can also use a gun, but I would rest much easier if you were here. I won't be long."

Constance got into her helicar and flew to Mission Control, where she contacted all the planets in both universes. She returned home feeling slightly better.

"I alerted everyone I could think of. Now it is up to Tanus, but I wonder why she needed Craig?"

Meanwhile, Craig and Tanus were racing against time. They both knew Andocia had to be recaptured. Deliah had to be dealt with as well.

"Tanus, do you think we'll make it in time?"

"We must! They should have landed on Andocia's planet by now. This vial must be dispersed in the atmosphere over the Red Planet so all of them can be put to sleep. Deliah couldn't have done this alone; Andocia's followers must've helped her."

The ship containing Tanus and Craig hovered over Andocia's planet. However the screen revealed a startling sight.

"Tanus, they have outwitted us. There's no one on this planet. The whole lot of them have disappeared."

"Oh no, but where could they have gone? There were plenty of them; they can't just vanish."

Both Craig and Tanus were confused and disturbed by the sight.

Craig gasped, "Tanus I think I can guess what they have done. Andocia has probably transferred her people back in time. They are either somewhere in the past or future. I did it by accident when I landed on Saurus, so why can't she do it on purpose? There can be no other explanation."

"It makes sense in a bizarre way. If that's the case though, we are powerless to stop them. They can reappear at any time and take us by surprise," Tanus mused unhappily.

"We can't waste our valuable time looking for them either. What do you suggest?"

"Craig, we are going to have to be constantly on our guard." Tanus warned.

"I realise that, but I have to sleep sometime. The question is, who will Andocia seek out first, you or me?"

"I don't have the answer to that question. Craig, I can't give you immortality, but I'll do what I can to even the odds a bit. You may remember that when you bravely came to my rescue when I was Andocia's prisoner, one of my followers gave you a ring."

"I remember, but Andocia destroyed it."

"Yes she did, but I have another one," said she, handing it to the explorer. He slipped it on his finger.

"You remember how it works, don't you."

"I do. Thank you Tanus; it'll be a great help."

"There's an added feature in this one though. If you need to summon me in a hurry, speak slowly and clearly into the ring. It has a small data capture chip and will record a short message. Then prise the stone loose and it will find its way to me. I'll come to your assistance if I can."

"Thank you Tanus," replied the explorer gratefully. "What happens now?"

"I suppose I had better return you to Earth. You can do more good if you are with your family."

"I suppose so, but what happens if she gets to you first?"

"If that happens, I'll send Tarmin to warn you."

Tanus dropped Craig off at Mission Control and then ascended into Space again.

The explorer returned home and Constance ran into his arms. "Oh Craig, you're back, thank goodness. What happened?"

"That wretched woman outwitted us. She and the rest of her devilish lot have completely vanished. It is our belief they are hiding either in the past or the future."

"Is that possible?" she asked incredulously.

"Yes it is. There is no other explanation for the sudden disappearance of a whole planet full of people. It would be futile to search for them, because we have no idea where they could be hiding."

"So what do we do now?"

"We have no choice but to be constantly on our guard. Tanus has given me a duplicate of the ring which Andocia destroyed once before, but that isn't enough to make me feel secure. It might work against Deliah, but her mother is another matter. I'm sure Deliah will have some kind of protection as well."

As the days went by, the atmosphere in the Carter household became distinctly tense. Both April and Glenn had gone out, leaving Craig and Constance alone in their apartment. The Space explorer paced the floor like a caged lion.

"Darling, please try to relax a bit. This isn't getting you anywhere," sighed Constance.

"I can't help it. Any moment now, Andocia could come. As the days wear on, I become more uneasy."

"Craig, don't you think this is just what Andocia wants? She's waiting and playing with you like a cat plays with a mouse."

The days lengthened into weeks and still nothing happened. When Andocia eventually struck, it wasn't directly at Craig or Tanus, but was connected to them. She attacked them simultaneously.

Tarmin was flying about, searching for possible signs of Andocia and her group. She saw something red in the distance and made for it. Behind her, a trident ship appeared out of time lapse and followed silently. As Tarmin swooped on the red figure, it vanished. The bird realised she had flown into a trap and spun about, coming face to face with the trident ship. She gasped and turned tail once again, but the inhabitants were ready for her and a red beam ensnared the giant bird, hauling her kicking and screeching into the ship. Once she had been safely deposited inside, Deliah appeared and Tarmin got her first look at the girl. The beam still held her prisoner, but she didn't seem to notice.

"So, you're Deliah," she spat angrily. "I see the resemblance. If I don't return home soon, Tanus will know something has happened. She knows all about you, thanks to Craig Carter. You won't find it easy to capture my mistress this time."

Deliah folded her arms and smirked. "I'm not after your precious mistress! You were the intended target."

Tarmin lunged at Deliah, but the beam held her in place and the girl laughed.

"You wait until Craig hears about this! He'll rescue me, you see if he doesn't!"

Deliah was enjoying herself. "Oh really; I wouldn't expect any help from him either. Before long he's going to be very preoccupied," she gloated.

"What do you mean?" she asked suspiciously.

"Oh, why spoil the surprise? You'll find out soon enough. Now Tarmin, I want you to shrink to waist size," she ordered.

Tarmin stared blankly at her, not understanding. "What? Why?"

"Just do it!" she snapped.

The white bird did as she was told and watched wide-eyed as Deliah pulled out a gun.

"Hey, what are you going to do with that?" she twittered nervously.

"Oh relax, if I wanted you dead, I would have done it long ago. I need to put you away somewhere secure, where you can't cause any problems. I'm going to stun you, so stand still."

Tarmin stood still and closed her eyes, shivering nervously. The blast slammed her backwards and darkness enfolded her. The inhabitants of the ship carried the limp form away to a re-enforced cell. Deliah smiled triumphantly. "Right, phase one is complete, now for phase two. I hope my mother is just as successful, but then again, why shouldn't she be?"

$$\downarrow \quad \downarrow \quad \downarrow$$

Andocia was on her way to Earth. "Now whom should I go for? Craig

Carter? No, I don't think so. I could capture Constance maybe? Ah, tempting, but no, I have the perfect person in mind."

Andocia landed in a dark and deserted area and made her way to a house. All the lights were on and a party was in progress. The woman hid behind a nearby tree and scanned the area, looking for her prey. She smiled evilly when she spotted her target. April Carter was sitting apart from her friends talking to a boy. They were deep in conversation and never heard the woman approach. Instinctively April looked up and stared straight at Andocia. "Oh!" she gasped, startled.

"Hello, is this a private party or can anyone attend?" asked Andocia pleasantly.

"Who are you?" asked April, puzzled.

"Oh come on April, I'm disappointed! You should know who I am."

April searched her memory but it was blank. "No I don't think we have ever met," she replied in puzzlement. She scratched her head and an uneasy feeling surfaced. "Wait a minute! You must be Andocia!"

"Friend of yours April?" asked her date curiously.

April glared at the woman and turned to her companion. "She is most definitely not my friend!"

Andocia looked menacingly at the young man and he cringed. "I suggest you get out of here now and go back to the party. Your girlfriend and I have to get acquainted. Go on, scram!"

The boy jumped up and scuttled off hurriedly. "Uh… see you around April."

"Don't count on it," Andocia smirked.

April stared curiously at the woman standing in front of her. She took in the spectacular figure and compelling red eyes. Andocia had the longest legs she had ever seen on anyone and the girl was aware of this woman's incredible beauty. Yet even as she stared at the woman she could sense the evil radiating from her and in that moment realised why her father behaved the way he did when his enemy was around.

Reluctantly she tore her eyes away from the woman and noticed several people had come out of the house and were staring at the two of them. Andocia met their curious stares evenly, then smiled cruelly at them. An instant later she raised her hand and a tree near the house exploded into flames. The teenagers screamed and ran away. Andocia laughed loudly.

April took advantage of the small diversion and ran for the nearby grove of trees, hoping to lose herself amongst them. Andocia watched her go with great interest. She allowed the girl to get within striking distance of the trees and then loosed a bolt of pure energy. The tree in front of April was sheared off halfway and fell across her path. The girl stopped and climbed over the trunk of the tree. She scratched her leg, but still managed to continue. She looked back but Andocia was nowhere in sight. Puzzled, April wasted valuable seconds looking for her, when suddenly her arm was grabbed and forced painfully up her back. She gasped in pain and surprise as Andocia's other hand encircled her body, pinning the other arm effectively to her side.

"Scream and I'll break your arm," she threatened.

"What do you want with me? Let me go!" April demanded.

"No, I can't do that. Right now you are very important to me. I'm going to hold you hostage, as a lever against your father. All the time when I was imprisoned by that scheming Tanus, I have savoured this moment."

"Where are you taking me?" asked the girl nervously.

"You are going to be privileged to see the inside of my ship."

"So that's your plan! How did your daughter do it?"

"Free me? Oh that needn't concern you. Come along, my dear!"

April blinked and when she opened her eyes, she was inside a huge ship. Andocia released her and instantly several of her followers pointed laser guns at the girl.

"Welcome to my mother ship, April."

The girl stared in amazement at the incredible technology. Her fear vanished when she saw the huge, opulent ship. Instantly she forgot about the soldiers pointing their weapons at her, Andocia and why she had been kidnapped. She put her hands on her chest and gasped. "Ohhh my word!!! This ship is fantastic! It looks like a huge city!"

For a while April was enthralled and began hurrying towards what looked like a huge shop. Andocia motioned her surprised guards to lower their weapons and all eyes followed the young girl. They watched as she ran from place to place, gawking at everything she saw. She opened and closed doors, peeking inside and shaking her head in disbelief. All work came to a standstill as everyone watched in amusement. While April ran around and expressed surprise at the technology, she was also committing the layout of the enemy ship to memory. April saw she was coming to a part of the ship that was off limits to passengers. She bit her lip and extended her hand to open a door in front of her, hoping to get a glimpse of what lay beyond.

Suddenly she felt a firm hand gripping her by the wrist.

"Come along my dear, you aren't allowed to go inside. This section is for staff only."

April put her hands up to her face and blushed. "Ohhh, I'm sorry! I just got carried away, I guess. I love the way your ship has been designed."

"Are you impressed?" Andocia queried.

"Oh yes I am! It's not as I imagined it would be though. It's much more complex."

April's face changed to concern, as if only now realising the predicament she was in. "Why did you kidnap me? I don't even know you. Your fight is with my father, not me."

"You are going to be my guest for a while. I'm going to let a few days pass so that your parents can worry about you, then I'll contact your father. I'll have some demands for him."

"What if he doesn't comply with whatever devilish schemes you have planned?" asked the girl.

"Then I'm afraid your life will come to a very sudden end. Would you like to meet some more of my friends?"

April followed Andocia through to a recreation room where several more of Andocia's followers were seated. The girl recognised Deliah. They stared at April and she could feel the hostility emanating from them. One girl laughed snidely and turned to Deliah. "So this is the famous Craig Carter's daughter! She doesn't look so tough to me."

April glared back at her. "I don't care what you think whoever you are, but I don't like you either. As for you Deliah…"

"That's quite enough!" interrupted Andocia. "I want all of you to calm down! April, you're going to be here for quite some time, so behave yourself. You may be the legendary Craig Carter's daughter, but you have absolutely no experience in the field. Even the least experienced of my warriors can chew you up and spit you out. You're going to be a model prisoner; otherwise things could get really tough for you. Come along and I'll take you to your quarters. You won't have time to be lonely though, for you'll have a companion to talk to."

April was taken to a cell and Andocia opened the door. The girl went inside and it was sealed again. She stared at the white figure huddled miserably in a corner.

"Tarmin, is that you?" she asked nervously.

The bird opened her eyes and stared at April, then she gasped. The girl ran to the bird, who embraced her almost without thinking. "Oh April, they got you too!" exclaimed the bird unhappily.

"Yes, Andocia kidnapped me. How did you land up here?"

"I have Deliah to thank for that. She tricked me and I fell in her trap. She's horrible!"

"Like her mother," agreed April. "They were extremely clever this time. My dad was expecting one of them to try and capture him or Tanus, not strike out at both of them simultaneously."

Tarmin got up and looked longingly at the door. "Yes, we weren't expecting this."

"What do you think they plan to do with us?" asked April nervously.

"Well, when the moment is ripe, they'll inform the people we love and put their demands forward. It's obvious why you have been captured."

"It is?"

"Yes. They are going to contact Craig and make him turn against Tanus. When Andocia has accomplished what she intends to do, she'll kill us. Andocia is greedy and longs to rule both universes."

"Yes, only now she has her daughter to help her," complained the girl mournfully. She moved to the steel door and shook it furiously.

Tarmin sighed unhappily. "Oh don't bother wasting your energy April. Andocia's power will ensure the door stays locked, no matter what. Even if by some miracle you managed to free yourself, where would you go? You can't fly a spacecraft and you have very little hand-to-hand combat experience. They'll capture you again without even raising a sweat."

"Thanks for the pep talk Tarmin," said April sarcastically. "I've never been in this situation before, so this is a new and unwelcome experience for me. I'm fifteen years old! That doesn't amount to much experience anyway."

Despite her anger, April brushed away a tear and Tarmin relented. "Oh April, I'm so sorry! I should learn to keep my big mouth shut. I didn't mean it in a derogatory way. Oh come here."

April went to the bird and snuggled in her feathers. She sobbed quietly and after a while she blew her nose.

"Are you feeling better now, April?" asked the bird gently.

The girl nodded. "Yes thanks."

She sat up straight and stared determinedly at the bird. "I'm a Carter after all. I had a momentary slip there, but it won't happen again. I won't allow those scheming witches to see how upset I really am."

"Good for you! Don't apologise for being human though, April. It's a very endearing quality. Right now, I'm pretty curious actually. Deliah seems to hate you more than anyone else in your family. Is there a reason for this?"

"Yes. As you no doubt know, Deliah was sent to go out with my brother Glenn. It must have been a part of the original plan. My dad got suspicious and asked me to do some snooping, so I did. I befriended Deliah and found out her real identity. When she caught me red handed with the evidence, she attacked me. I guess I was lucky, because I managed to hit her with an ornament. Actually she should be more angry with my dad – he suspected something first. You know what makes me really fed up?"

"No, what would that be?" Tarmin asked.

"I mean Deliah is so pretty. I don't know, maybe it's just jealousy on my part, because I'm not nearly as gorgeous as her, but it just seems the bad guys should be ugly and have warts – if you know what I mean."

Tarmin chuckled merrily. "Oh dear me, I see what you mean, but life isn't always fair. Don't get yourself too upset though because you are also very pretty."

"Thank you for that, Tarmin."

The bird inclined her head and she sat down on the floor again. "Tanus and Andocia have been fighting for centuries now. I fear their feud will never end. I could tell you plenty, as I have fought by my mistress' side for a number of years. Would you like to hear some of my stories?"

The girl nodded eagerly and sat down cross-legged on the floor near the bird. April listened enthralled to the triumphs and sadness that Tarmin and Tanus had both experienced.

26

A few days passed before Andocia came to fetch April. She escorted her to the technical heart of the ship. Although the girl's heart was hammering, she kept her face impassive.

"April, I'm going to contact your father now and I want you to speak to him. You may answer any questions he puts to you, except the whereabouts of my ship. I think he has stewed long enough."

The devilish woman switched on the transmitter and April watched as the familiar logo appeared on screen. Andocia waited for the technician to answer, but instead Craig himself faced her.

"Ah, it's Craig Carter in the flesh! Just the man I wanted to talk to," she remarked triumphantly.

"What have you done with my daughter?" he demanded, without preamble.

"She is alive and well, I assure you. I've been taking good care of her. Here, you may speak to her yourself," said Andocia, as she urged the girl forward. April smiled at her father. He looked tired and there were circles under his eyes. In that instant, April realised just how diabolical the plan had been and she hated Andocia all the more for it.

"Dad I'm fine. They have been treating me well."

Her father brightened when he saw she was unhurt. "Oh April, I'm glad you haven't been harmed."

"I'm happy to see you too. How are Mom and Glenn?"

"Both are holding up well. We suspected Andocia had captured you, but we weren't sure. You just seemed to disappear on us."

"I know, but I wasn't given a choice. I'm sorry about that, but I'm fine. Dad, I think I should tell you Deliah is here with her mother. Look, I know Andocia has captured me for a purpose. She wants to use me as a lever against you. Dad I love you and I know you love me too, but I must ask you not to give in to her demands, no matter what. The fate of the universes is much more important than the life of one individual."

Andocia intervened and April watched unhappily.

"Now hear my demands, Carter. I want you to come here to my ship. You have to make a choice; a life for a life – yours in exchange for your daughter's. I'll give you two days in which to make up your mind. If at that time you agree to come to me, I'll give you my co-ordinates. If not, take a last look at your daughter, for I'll kill her – I mean it!"

"Dad, don't do it!" cried April desperately, but Andocia had signed off. She was taken back to her cell and Tarmin watched unhappily as the girl fought to control her emotions.

Deliah watched the pair and couldn't resist a dig at April. "You know what April, I actually find myself hoping your father won't come here to rescue you. If that happens, I'll be glad to perform the execution ceremony personally."

"I don't doubt it for a second, but don't expect me to stand around and wait to die. If you want to kill me, I won't make it easy for you. I may not be very experienced, but neither are you. You're only sixteen and also mortal. Even if your mother can live for ever, you'll die one day."

"Perhaps so, but before I die, I'll make a name for myself, I promise you. Even as the universes fear my mother, so will they fear me."

April glared at the girl and turned her back. "Oh get out of here Deliah. My ears hurt from all your boasting."

⚔ ⚔ ⚔

Back on Earth, Craig's mind was in turmoil. He returned home to break the news to the rest of his family.

"Darling, we suspected Andocia had April; well that has now been confirmed. If we want her back, I must go to Andocia and take her place."

"Oh Craig, what are we going to do? You can't go up there, because Andocia will kill you."

"Constance, I have always been in control of a situation, but now I feel like I'm up the creek without a paddle. I'm supposed to protect everyone and I failed. I need to speak to Tanus and ask her advice. Anyway, I promised to tell her if Andocia struck out at us."

Craig was just about to summon Tanus, when she appeared.

"Hello Craig."

"Tanus, I was just about to contact you. I have bad news. Andocia has kidnapped April and issued me with an ultimatum – my life in exchange for my daughter's. Tanus, I don't know what to do."

"Oh no!" cried Tanus in dismay.

"But we expected something like this, so why the cry of dismay?"

"It's not that Craig. This time that wretched woman has outwitted us!" exclaimed Tanus miserably.

"What do you mean?"

"I mean she has kidnapped Tarmin, so she not only has your daughter up there, but my pet as well. We expected her to come after one of us, but not both of us at the same time. It must have been Deliah who caught Tarmin."

"Oh no, what now?" asked Craig unhappily.

"I don't know. I'm very fond of Tarmin, but I don't think I would give myself up to her, even if she threatened to kill Tarmin. You do understand why, don't you Craig?"

"Of course, but what am I to do?" he asked miserably.

Tanus put a comforting hand on his shoulder. "Craig, this may be very difficult for you, but I must ask you not to go to Andocia. I need you here with me."

"But April..." he cried in dismay.

"I'm sorry, Craig. I know I sound heartless, but on no account must you give in. Please Craig listen to me," Tanus urged.

"You know, April told me not to come. My daughter is brave!"

"Of course she is! Craig, I want you to come with me to my planet. We must make final plans to end the tyranny of Andocia and her daughter."

"Very well," he sighed unhappily.

"We may be away for quite some time though. Is that okay?"

"It will have to be."

Neither of them saw Glenn enter. He stopped when he heard the names of April and Andocia being mentioned. The young man interrupted the pair.

"So, it's true! Andocia does have April."

Craig turned unhappily to his son. "Yes, I'm afraid so, but she was sneaky and took Tarmin too."

"Then we have to go and rescue them," said Glenn decisively.

Craig placed a hand on his son's shoulder. "It doesn't work quite like that, son. Andocia's ship is well guarded. Not even a mouse can get in there without being detected. I'm going with Tanus to her planet and there we can discuss our strategy."

"What about me? Can I come too please? April is my sister and I want to help!"

Tanus shook her head. "No Glenn. You're still too inexperienced to take on that devilish woman. Besides, when Andocia realises your father isn't going to give himself up to her, she may come and take revenge on your mother. It's not advisable to leave her alone at this time."

"But Mom can take care of herself," he argued.

Tanus shook her head more emphatically. "I know your mother is a very capable woman with many skills, but if she gets caught, we'll need someone to report that fact to us."

Glenn wasn't happy, but he realised the sense of the argument. "Oh all right then, I'll stay here, but I don't have to like it."

Glenn watched as his mother and father embraced tenderly, then Craig went off with Tanus.

They were gone only fifteen minutes when Glenn's mobile device rang and he took the call. Commander Perry had a mission for him and he was ordered to report for duty.

"Oh drat, now what Mom?"

"Well you have a job to do, so go and do it. I'll be fine, I promise you. I'll wear my laser gun all the time, just in case of some nasty surprises, but I don't believe she'll go to all that trouble."

Glenn reported to his commander and was given his assignment. It wasn't a very difficult one, but he would have to go to the Golden Way to complete it. The young man grinned happily. "Oh well, I'm not disobeying orders anyway. I've been told to go to the Golden Way and that's exactly what I'm going to do. It can't hurt if I poke around a little up there," he told himself reasonably. "Who knows, I could get lucky."

The young explorer completed his mission in record time, then started scouring around for possible clues. Although he had been warned on a number of occasions that Andocia was not someone he should willingly come to grips with, Glenn was still convinced he could somehow outwit the woman. Long before he spotted the trident ship, his prey was observing Glenn.

"Well, well, what do we have here? I see your former boyfriend Glenn Carter is coming towards us! Should we invite him in for a little chat, eh Deliah?"

"We might as well I suppose! I daresay he's a fool to wander around our territory so brazenly. Should I go there personally?"

"Yes, grace the ship with your presence."

Deliah left and emerged inside Glenn's craft. His first emotion was one of shock, but he soon recovered. "What have you and your wretched mother done with my sister?" he demanded.

"Your precious sister is alive and well. Did you come to rescue her?"

"Yes, and what's more, I'm going to succeed," he replied determinedly.

Deliah laughed scornfully. "Oh, you are such an idiot! You'll never succeed."

"Oh yes I will. Neither you nor your mother scare me."

"Oh how brave of you!" she snorted derisively. "Well how do you plan to get inside? The ship is heavily guarded."

"I'll find a way," he promised.

"Oh well you might as well save yourself the trouble. Andocia requests the pleasure of your company. Our guest suite is very comfortable."

The obvious menace in her voice disturbed Glenn.

"No thanks, I'll find my own way inside."

"Oh, but that won't do! My mother issued a personal invitation. It would be better if you came willingly." Deliah replied sweetly. "Besides, it's considered rude to refuse someone like my mother. Even your father wouldn't dare to disobey."

"He's not coming," Glenn declared. "Your mother is wasting her time waiting for him. So I must also decline your generous offer – but hey, thanks anyway. Tell your mom maybe next time – when hell freezes over!"

Deliah looked reproachfully at her former boyfriend and sighed. "I don't think you understand. This isn't a request, it's a demand."

Their eyes met and Glenn found himself wondering why he had ever found Deliah attractive in the first place. She was beautiful, he couldn't deny that, but her eyes were as cold as ice. Their eyes locked and Glenn felt an unusual sensation pass through his body, almost like pins and needles. When he tried to move his hands though, he found it was impossible.

"Hey, what the…? What's going on?"

"That was just a little sample of my powers. Andocia has been teaching me well. I've paralysed you, now you won't give me any trouble."

Deliah went over to the controls and prepared his craft for landing. Glenn could only watch helplessly as his ship entered the trident craft and settled in a landing bay. He watched as his door opened and the steps clattered into place. Immediately several heavily armed guards took up positions on either side of the entrance. Glenn found he had control over his body again and he stood up slowly.

"Get out now," she ordered.

The young explorer did so and stared around the ship curiously.

"Right, now follow me and I'll introduce you to my mother."

He obeyed and was soon face to face with Andocia. She looked him up and down, making him uneasy. "So, at last I meet the wretched son of the legendary Craig Carter. First I captured the daughter and now I have the son. I think I can truthfully say I have the upper hand. Your father will have no choice but to surrender to me, otherwise both you and your sister will die."

"I don't know who you think you are, but if you ask me, your powers have been over exaggerated," he replied cheekily.

"You think so? I see you haven't been well informed, or else you didn't listen to what your father told you. You would have been wise to heed his warnings. Come, I'll take you to your sister and Tarmin."

"If you have harmed her..." he remarked threateningly.

"She's in good health, I assure you." Andocia replied.

Glenn followed Andocia through to another room and she opened the door. He stepped inside and saw April, but her back was towards him. Tarmin appeared to be asleep.

"Go away and leave me alone," grumbled April.

"Hello April."

On hearing the familiar voice, she turned around suddenly and her greeting was anything but friendly. "You idiot, what are you doing here? How did they get you?"

"I like that! I try to rescue you and this is the thanks I get!"

He heard Andocia snigger, then close the door and lock it. April felt ashamed about her outburst and hugged her brother. "I'm sorry, I was just angry. Did you really think you could free me?"

"Of course I did. Commander Perry sent me on a mission though, so while I was in the neighbourhood, so to speak, I decided to look for you. The ship wasn't hard to find."

"I'll bet it wasn't. They probably saw you long before you saw them."

Before Glenn could answer, Tarmin stirred and opened her eyes. She stared at Glenn and squawked in dismay, then she rubbed her eyes with her wing and groaned. "Oh no, I thought I was dreaming for a minute. Glenn, what are you doing here?"

"He came looking for me, Tarmin. Isn't he brave?" smiled April.

Tarmin glared at him. "Stupid is more like it! All he's done is give Andocia another bargaining tool to use. I wouldn't be surprised if she isn't on the linkup, telling your father about her latest acquisition. Even if your father wasn't going to come here before, he'll be forced to do so now. Where is he anyway?"

"He went with Tanus just before I was called away to go on my mission," replied Glenn.

Tarmin began to pace the floor restlessly. "No doubt they are going to plan some strategic way to rescue us, but the tide could turn when they find out about your capture Glenn. I know this isn't the right time to yell at you, but one of the first golden rules of engagement is, never underestimate your opponents, and you have already done that."

Glenn opened his mouth to issue a sharp retort, when the door opening interrupted them and Deliah came inside. All three friends glared at her. "What do you want, Deliah?" snapped Tarmin irritably.

"Andocia has been trying to get hold of your father, but the Space Control Centre is remaining tight-lipped about it. Do any of you know where he is?"

All three exchanged glances and kept quiet.

"It's none of your business, Deliah," replied Glenn angrily. "If your mother wants to gloat about my capture, I won't give her the satisfaction of upsetting my father. He won't come here, so forget it!"

Deliah turned her cold green eyes onto him. "Ah, so you know where he is! Excellent! Well if it makes you happy then keep that little snippet of information to yourself. We'll get the answer out of you when it's time."

"Deliah, say what you want, then get out of here. We're all sick of the sight of you!" stormed Tarmin. "You're interrupting our conversation."

"It sounded more like an argument actually."

Tarmin lost her temper and began walking deliberately towards Deliah, intending to do her some grievous bodily harm. The Carter children watched with their mouths agape, for the bird had always struck them as kind and gentle. Deliah took a few paces back and extended her finger. Tarmin screamed as a cut opened in her side and began to bleed. April was stunned and Glenn ran to help the bird. In that instant, April forgot to be afraid and her instinct for survival took over. She launched herself at her enemy and slammed her to the ground. Deliah was taken completely by surprise and the wind knocked out of her. April grabbed a handful of hair and tugged viciously, slamming her opponent's head onto the carpet. Deliah recovered slightly and latched on to her hair as well. Both girls rolled in an undignified heap on the floor.

Suddenly the door burst open and the two girls were separated. April was grabbed roughly and her hands were pinned to her sides. Some guards aimed their weapons at Glenn and Tarmin, who sat unmoving on the floor. Deliah was helped to her feet and April smiled when she saw the girl had a small cut on the side of her head, which was bleeding slightly. Alerted by the scuffle, Andocia came to see what the problem was. She took in the situation in an instant.

"Deliah, what's the meaning of this?"

"April attacked me without provocation!" whined Deliah.

The girl shook herself free and glared at the two women. "She's lying! She hurt Tarmin, so I hit her."

"Well, Tarmin started it!" complained Deliah.

They all began to speak at once and Andocia covered her ears.

"Enough! One at a time! Glenn, I want to know who was responsible for this ridiculous behaviour."

"I guess Tarmin and Deliah were both to blame. Deliah came in here bragging about how clever you both were and Tarmin got mad. Then Deliah hurt Tarmin."

Glenn moved hastily aside when Andocia strode purposefully over to the bird and examined her. Then she moved away.

"Aren't you going to help her?" asked April plaintively. "She's bleeding!"

"It's only a scratch; she'll live," she remarked dispassionately. Then she turned her wrath onto Deliah. "Listen here, your powers are improving daily and I'm glad, but try to do something about your temper. If you had aimed any higher, you could have killed Tarmin."

Deliah stared sullenly at her mother. "Oh but that's the final objective anyway, so what's the difference?"

"There is a time and a place for everything and it isn't now. Craig Carter still has a day left. When we find him and tell him about his son, he'll come here, then we can kill this wretched bird."

"Hey, you said we'll be freed if my father comes here," remarked April unhappily.

"Correction dear, I said you would be freed. I never mentioned Tarmin at all. I'm still not sure what should be done about your brother though."

Deliah grinned triumphantly. "Oh don't hurt him yet mother; he knows where his father went, but he refused to tell me."

Andocia smiled. "Oh does he! Seems you and I need to have a chat then, Glenn."

Tarmin groaned unhappily and put her head under her wing.

"Deliah, go and wash your face, then meet me in the interrogation room. I'll bring our guest along shortly."

"All right mother."

Deliah glared at April and left the room. Andocia smiled at Glenn. "So Glenn, I believe you have taken up Space exploration like your father before you. How long have you been employed by Mission Control?"

"I guess about a year now."

"Has your father ever spoken to you about me?"

"Yes, often. He told me how you two came to meet."

"Glenn, do you believe all the things he has told you?"

"I guess so; why would he lie?"

"He wouldn't," she stated. "Glenn, I don't pretend to be your friend and I doubt I ever will be. Deliah says you know where your father is. Do you?"

The young man nodded. "Yes, but I won't tell you, no matter what you do to me," he replied bravely.

Tarmin whimpered. "Andocia, he's just a child! Why can't you leave him alone? Craig is your enemy, not his children."

"Anyone related to Craig Carter is my enemy, you know that. I hate you because Tanus loves you so much. As long as there's a member of the Carter family alive, I'll fight them. Besides, Craig wasn't much older than his son here when we met and you know the hassles he caused me. If you really love these children, persuade Glenn to tell me where he is. I'm leaving now, but I'll return in fifteen minutes. This is your last chance!"

The devilish woman turned on her heel and Tarmin rocked back and forth miserably.

"Tarmin is your side very painful?" asked April kindly.

"No not really — it just stings a little."

April got up and fished in her pocket. She pulled out a scarf and took it to the washbasin that stood in one corner. She let the cool water run over it and took it back to Tarmin.

"Here, let me at least clean that up a bit. It's going to sting, but that can't be helped."

The bird allowed her to swab the wound and clean the blood off. Once it had been cleaned, it looked much better. The large bird looked at the two children she loved and then asked them to sit.

"Glenn, you have to co-operate with Andocia. If you don't, she'll make your life miserable. She has no heart and things will go badly for you. Your father fears her and it's justified. I suppose you both know Andocia is telepathic don't you."

The children nodded.

"Well she could just probe your mind and find the answer there, but instead she plans to hurt you. Why suffer unduly?"

Glenn stood up and paced the floor. "I understand what you're saying Tarmin, and I really appreciate your wisdom, but what will really be achieved by my giving her the information? If I tell her willingly, then my dad will come here and die in our place. Even if for some reason he survives, they are still going to kill you. If Andocia is really as mean as you say, then what happens the next time she has a bad day? She might decide to hunt us down and kill us anyway. No, I have a better plan."

"I'm all ears," remarked Tarmin.

"We have to think of some way to escape. There has to be a solution to this somewhere. I'll hold out as long as possible, giving you both time to think of a plan. I guess I won't be killed anyway – not until my dad comes, so I'll just hope for the best." Glenn decided.

Tarmin began to cry. "It isn't fair! You both deserve your freedom."

"Then try and think of a plan! Here comes Andocia."

She entered with a group of sentries. "Well, are you going to tell me what I want to know?"

Bravely, Glenn shook his head. "No, I won't!"

The guards indicated with their guns and he stepped outside the room. Andocia locked it again and they moved off.

27

He was marched to a comfortably furnished room and was immediately suspicious.

"This doesn't look like an interrogation room!"

"Why what were you expecting; chains and whips?"

He smiled sheepishly. "I guess so."

"Relax, sit down and let's wait for Deliah. She should be here any moment. Would you like something to drink?"

Glenn shook his head nervously. Deliah entered and sat down on another chair.

"All right Glenn, fun time is over. This is where we get serious. Tell me where your father is!"

"No, I won't!"

Mother and daughter exchanged looks and Andocia moved closer to Glenn. She stared intently at him and he averted his eyes. Her voice seemed to take on a strange quality and his eyes swam out of focus and then back again.

"Look at me Glenn Carter, I order you to!"

He tried to fight her influence, but her eyes locked onto his. She stared at him in the way Craig had come to know and fear. Her eyes seemed to intensify in size and swallow him.

"Glenn, you cannot fight me! Submit to me and end this agony."

A loud buzzing sounded in his ears and he cried out in protest. His brain felt as though it would explode and he found it difficult to breathe. He fell to his knees on the floor, holding his head. The voice came again, more insistent.

"Glenn, if you fight me any longer, you'll go blind. I did it to your father, but I'll see it never gets reversed in your case. Where is Craig Carter?"

"Stop it, please stop it!" begged the young man desperately.

"Where is your father?" Andocia demanded.

Glenn screamed in agony. "All right, I'll tell you, just make it stop!"

"After you tell me," she replied dispassionately.

"He… he's with Tanus on the White Planet."

Instantly the noise subsided, but Glenn's eyes wouldn't focus. He put a shaking hand to his cheek and found to his surprise it was wet with tears. He was helped back to the chair where he sank back against the cushions, totally exhausted. His heart was beating dangerously fast and he became aware he was hyperventilating. Glenn tried to slow his breathing and was aware of two shadowy figures bending over him.

"Why are you Carters so stubborn?" asked Andocia. "You seem to ignore good advice."

"My... my eyes... I can't see clearly," stammered Glenn shakily.

"Well I did warn you not to fight me, but you were lucky. You crumbled before I could do any permanent damage. Take it easy for today and by tomorrow, you will have regained your sight. I must contact Tanus now and tell her the good news. I do believe you'll all be re-united soon – if only for a short while. From now on, I expect you to behave. Deliah will take you back to your quarters."

Everything around him was blurred. He stood up and took a tentative step forward, but his foot kicked something. Deliah moved over and took his arm and his flesh crawled, but he had no choice, so he held onto her and allowed her to guide him back to the room. His breathing had slowed considerably, but he could still feel his heart beating too quickly. The door closed behind him and he held on to the wall for support. Dimly he saw the figures of Tarmin and April and he sat down heavily on the bed. Tarmin rushed to him.

"Oh Glenn, are you all right?"

"No, but I will be. That... that woman is everything Dad said she was, and more. Oh Tarmin, I tried to hold out, I really did, but she won in the end."

"You gave her the information?"

"Yes, I couldn't stop myself. My eyes hurt! I can't make out anything other than shadows. That devilish woman said I was lucky."

Tarmin placed a wing under his chin and looked into the dull eyes. "Has... has she...?"

"No my condition is only temporary she says. I can make out shadows at the moment, but not much more. I should be better by tomorrow. I have such a terrible headache too."

"Glenn, can you describe what happened?" asked April gently.

Her brother shuddered and hugged his legs. "No, I don't want to talk about it! Leave me alone April, please. I need to lie down and rest awhile. One thing

I can tell you for certain though; we have to get off this spaceship as soon as possible."

Glenn lay down and slept deeply for several hours. He woke up feeling weak but better.

The next morning, Deliah brought them their breakfast. She was very pleased with herself. "I just thought I would let you all know we got in touch with your father late yesterday evening. He was very distraught to hear the news and it looks as though he'll be here in two days. He would have come today, but my mother and I have a very important meeting with some friends of ours, so you get to live another two days anyway. I guess I'll see you about suppertime."

"Why, isn't your meeting on the ship? I just know how you love to gloat and you get a chance at every mealtime," replied April snidely.

"No, we're going out for the day, but I'll make up for it at suppertime," she promised.

Deliah closed and locked the door. When she was out of earshot, Glenn stood up. His sight had returned marginally. "If I have my way we won't be here at suppertime."

"Why, do you have a plan?" asked April excitedly.

"Yes I do, but it's risky. April, I wasn't shown around the ship at all. Do you happen to know where the docking area is?"

April smiled broadly. "I know the location of most places on this ship. When Andocia brought me here, I managed to look around the whole observation deck. Where is your ship?

"I am not sure, but I was brought up to the observation deck by Andocia and her cronies. The access hatch must be there somewhere."

"Can you remember how many floors you travelled in the escalator, Glenn?"

Glenn pondered for a while and then his face brightened. "Yes, actually I counted them subconsciously in my head. We went up three floors."

"Our cell is on the second floor." April calculated. "Therefore, we need to go down one floor from there. I saw a lift not far from our cell."

Glenn and Tarmin exchanged surprised looks.

"You are very observant, April," Tarmin replied.

April shrugged her shoulders.

"If Tarmin shrinks to the size of a small bird, my ship can accommodate all three of us. Before we implement this plan though, we must make sure Andocia and Deliah have left the ship." Glenn stated.

"All right, we'll do that, now what's the plan, Glenn?" asked Tarmin excitedly.

"April, you have to pretend to be sick. I'll call for help and when the guards come to check on us, I'll knock them out. You can help me if I get into difficulties, Tarmin. My sight is returning all the time, but it's still fuzzy. Once we have escaped, we can head for the White Planet. You know how to get us there Tarmin."

She nodded eagerly and they sat down to wait.

The group allowed an hour to pass, then they put the plan into action. April lay on the bed, writhing and screaming, while Glenn hammered on the door.

"Please help us! My sister is ill! She needs a doctor!"

A guard opened a small gap in the door and peered through. "What's going on here?"

"My sister is ill and I don't know what the problem is. Please, you have to do something!"

The guard saw April on the bed and Tarmin was standing over her, fanning her with her wings.

"All right, move away from the door; we're coming in."

Glenn obediently did so and two guards stepped inside. One hurried over to April, while the other covered them.

"What's wrong with you, Miss Carter?"

"I... I don't know!" she gasped. "My stomach hurts."

The guard turned to his companion. "Hurry, get the medic down here!"

The second guard shouldered his weapon and ran away to do as he was told. Glenn sneaked up on the one bending over his sister and hit him over the head with a metal basin they used to wash in and he crashed to the ground, unconscious. Glenn grabbed his weapon. "Come on, there's no time to waste. Which way must we go, April?"

"This way!" she indicated.

They ran down the passage, keeping close to the walls. Not wishing to confront any of the guards, they hid in various rooms on the way down. April led them to a lift, which took them silently down to the lower regions. As they got out, they came face to face with a guard. The surprised being had no time to react before Glenn's fist connected with his abdomen, which he followed with a strong uppercut to the man's chin. His eyes rolled in his head and he collapsed. Glenn grabbed the guard's weapon and thrust it into his sister's hands.

"Here, you know how to use these weapons. I've set the controls to 'stun'. Just aim and fire if anyone gets in the way."

This level was relatively quiet and only a few soldiers stood in their way. Finally, Glenn saw his ship standing in the docking bay and they rushed for it. Tarmin shrank to the size of a parrot and perched on April's shoulder, digging her claws firmly into the fabric of her friend's clothing. They climbed into the ship and soon they were speeding out of the landing bay. A few ships tried to follow them, but fine shooting on Glenn's part kept them on the run. When they had cleared the ship, Glenn put them into time lapse.

Tarmin jumped up and down excitedly. "Oh you were wonderful, just wonderful! Your father is going to be so proud of you."

"Speaking of my father, we have to contact him. He mustn't go to Andocia, otherwise all this will have been for nothing."

Tarmin showed him which frequency to use and soon they had imparted the good news to their father. Then the bird showed them how to get to Tanus's planet. Glenn landed where he was told and several of Tanus's followers came to meet them, holding weapons. Tarmin stepped out ahead of the children and spoke to the guards.

"These are Craig Carter's children. Tanus is expecting them."

They clicked their heels sharply and formed a guard of honour.

Glenn and April stared breathlessly at the wonderful sight. The palace was made out of crystal and sparkled brilliantly in the warm sunshine. By this time, Tarmin had returned to her normal size, thus dwarfing the children. She led them to a large room where Craig, Tanus and several of her followers were seated around a table. Spread out all around them were various holographic charts and sketches.

On seeing her father, April ran to him and he hugged her tenderly. "Daddy, oh Daddy, it's so good to see you again! I missed you so much!"

Glenn approached and his father shook his hand vigorously, then put his other arm around his son, holding them both. "Oh it's so good to be with you both again. Are you all right?"

The meeting adjourned for a while so the family could catch up with all the news.

Craig and his children sat near a stream, but Glenn was still worried. "Dad, what's going to happen now? Will Andocia come after us again?"

"Not as long as you are here on Tanus's planet. It's still school holidays for April, so we don't have to hurry back just yet. I need more time to plan the strategy with Tanus and I feel you have both earned the right to sit in on the discussion. I'm proud of you two!"

Glenn hung his head in shame. "I don't deserve such praise, Dad. I was the one who went foolishly into Andocia's clutches. I know you have told me repeatedly how wicked that woman is, but I still thought I could handle it on my own. Well, you were right and I was wrong. I'll never take your warnings lightly again. I was the one who told Andocia where you were."

"I thought so. She gave you a hard time didn't she?" asked Craig gently.

"Yes. She blinded me, but it was only temporary. She said something about my resistance having crumbled quickly, so the damage wasn't permanent. I don't know what she meant by that, but it felt as though she was torturing me for hours."

Craig put his hand on his son's shoulder. "It's over and done with now. No one can resist that evil woman – she's just too powerful. I don't blame you for it, but something good has come of this situation, for you learnt a valuable lesson. You won't ever take Andocia for granted again, I'm sure."

"No, I most definitely won't! I'll avoid her from now on. What's our next move going to be?"

"I have to discuss this with Tanus, but I feel very strongly that your mother must be brought here as well. Now that Andocia and Deliah have lost their bargaining tools, they might very well go after her and I can't allow that to happen."

"But Dad, you dare not go out into Space to get Mom. I'm pretty sure those two evil women have this planet under surveillance. If you venture out, they'll probably capture you," said April.

"More than likely April, but I won't go. Tanus will arrange something I'm sure."

They had a word with Tanus and she offered to send some of her own personal guards to fetch their mother. After a short break, Tanus and Craig asked the others to tell them what had happened on Andocia's ship.

"I suppose there is one question I need to ask you all; is Deliah as powerful as her mother?"

"I'll answer that one, Craig," volunteered Tarmin. "The answer is no, not yet, but she's getting there. She managed to paralyse Glenn in order to subdue him and that's how she got him to the mother ship, but I'll let Glenn fill you in on all the relevant details if you want. April had a fight with Deliah again and Deliah came off second best. She hasn't got the barrier that Andocia summons, so at the moment she can be harmed. I don't know if that comes with experience either, but be wary of it. Craig, where did April learn her defence moves?"

Craig grinned proudly. "Do you approve, Tarmin?"

"Well they were a little unorthodox, but effective nonetheless."

"Well as long as she got the job done, I don't mind. We'll have to jack up your karate, etc. though April. If and when Deliah does get stronger, you'll need a lot more experience than you have at present. At the moment you have lots of luck, but that won't hold out forever," he decided.

"Dad, Glenn underestimated Andocia and she gave him something to think about."

"I know, we went over this before. It's only natural to fear her, but that fear will keep you alive. Now you know what sort of a foe she is, you'll be a lot more wary."

Glenn nodded vigorously.

"I don't want you to feel ashamed, Glenn. I also fear her when I set eyes upon her and I have braved many things that were far more frightening."

"Is Mom afraid of her?" asked Glenn curiously.

"Yes of course she is. Glenn, would you and your sister accompany Tarmin on a walk so she can show you the planet? I just want to have a few words with Tanus."

The threesome moved off and Craig turned to his friend. "Tanus, we must find some way to defeat Andocia and Deliah once and for all. I love my family, but how can I do my job properly when they live under constant threat of capture? I can't protect them all the time, but I want reassurance they'll be safe."

"I understand, of course. I have no family, of my own, but Tarmin qualifies as such. You are right of course; your family deserve to live a peaceful life, but I don't think that will happen anytime soon. Just encourage them to be vigilant always and make sure April learns to defend herself properly. Glenn is a fine young man and I believe he'll go far in Space exploration. For now, let's just put our heads together and try to figure out a solution."

28

The group were locked in discussions for most of the day and when they finally reached a stalemate, Craig sighed and went to stretch his legs. One of the technicians came to look for him. "Mr Carter, I'm sorry to bother you, but Commander Perry wishes to speak with you."

Craig followed the man to the vidlink and spoke to his commander.

"Craig, I'm sorry to bother you right now, but I wondered if you could do me a favour. One of our spaceships passed that way not so long ago, but something went wrong with the cargo hatch. The valuable cargo was jettisoned and it contained important supplies for one of the Meltonian planets. Do you think you could retrieve it? It landed on Cobb, an uninhabited planet."

"I suppose I could do that Sir, but I've only got the craft Glenn was piloting. It's very small."

"It doesn't matter; the parcel was just a small one anyway. There's a Meltonian ship cruising around, but it can't land. All you have to do is retrieve the parcel and they'll collect it from you. It'll take a few hours."

"All right Sir, I'll do it."

Commander Perry signed off and Craig broke the news to Tanus and his family. April was aghast. "But Daddy, you can't do it! What if Andocia or Deliah are around?"

"I'll just have to take my chances then. Relax, I'll be fine. I have the ring Tanus gave me and it will get me out of a tight situation if the need arises."

Craig took the small ship and went on his errand. The planet was easy to find and so was the parcel. He contacted the Meltonians, who docked with him and took possession of their parcel. They thanked him gratefully and the two ships separated. Craig set the controls for the trip back to the White Planet and looked at his watch. He estimated he would be back in an hour.

A noise alerted him and his laser gun had cleared the holster by his side, even before he turned around.

"Well, well, if it isn't Deliah in the flesh! Your mother must really have faith in you to send you out after me."

"I thought Glenn and April were in this ship," she complained.

"No, I borrowed it. They are safe and sound on Tanus's planet."

Deliah knew she had no barrier to defend herself with and the laser gun was pointed unwaveringly at her heart. She had to be careful, but wanted to get rid of the gun first. Her eyes never wandered from Craig's face and she kept him talking. Deliah raised her hand in one quick movement and before Craig could follow it, a red beam hit him on the arm, numbing it. The gun clattered from his grip and she kicked it away.

"You little vixen!" he snapped angrily.

"I had hoped to capture your children, but you make a far better prize. I daresay my mother will be pleased to see you and find out what you and Tanus have been planning."

"Sorry if I don't tremble in fear, but you're still very inexperienced. You have taken on more than you can handle."

"You think so?" she gloated. "I can deal with you!"

Craig's movements were a blur and he picked up a heavy piece of metal and hurled it with all his might at Deliah. She saw it coming and stopped it in mid-air. While her attention was elsewhere, Craig dived for her legs, bringing her down heavily. He pinned her to the ground and she spat in rage.

"How dare you! My mother will teach you a lesson."

"I doubt it," he replied, "now it's your turn to be taken prisoner."

"You'll never hold me!"

"Think again, young lady," said Craig as he got up and pointed the ring Tanus had given him. A cage formed about her and Deliah was imprisoned within. She hurled abuse at him, but he ignored her.

He arrived back on Tanus's planet, where she greeted him anxiously.

"Did it go well? Was there any trouble?"

"A bit, but I brought you a visitor. Deliah tried her stunts on me, but lost the round. Take charge, won't you?"

Tanus went into the ship and chuckled when she saw the angry girl in her cage. She snapped a pair of powerful handcuffs on Deliah and marched her down the stairs. Tanus's guards escorted her to a cell.

Not long afterwards, the ship containing Constance arrived safely on the White Planet and the family were re-united. Tanus called a meeting and they all listened as she spoke.

"I'm so glad you made it without incident, Constance. However, I feel I must warn you all of impending trouble. When Andocia discovers we have her precious daughter, all hell is going to break loose. She'll try anything she can to get her back, so be prepared. Whenever you go for walks outside, go in pairs at least. No one is to go out alone. My guards will be everywhere."

However, Craig was forced to leave the safety of the planet to answer a distress call on Neptune. It was a toss-up between him and Glenn, but he was afraid to let his son venture out, knowing Andocia was lurking around. Glenn was happy to turn the job over to his father. The distress call was soon dealt with and Craig returned to the Golden Way once again. He knew, inevitably, that Andocia would seek him out. He was right. Even before she announced her presence, he knew she was inside the ship with him. Craig turned to face his adversary. "Hello Andocia, I've been expecting you."

"Then you know what I want. Where is my daughter?"

"She's with Tanus. How does it feel, Andocia, knowing someone you love is a prisoner and there's not a thing you can do about it? You put me through such hell a while ago, I'm glad you can experience some of what I felt."

"Carter, I suggest you contact Tanus immediately and tell her I'm with you. If she ever wants to see you alive again, she had better free Deliah."

"I can contact her if you want me to, but she won't bargain with you. My life isn't that important to her as I told you before. I knew you were watching us, but I had my orders."

"Look, I don't want to fight any more. I'm tired of these petty squabbles. It's time to make peace."

"Oh sure, and what would your answer be if Deliah wasn't Tanus's prisoner. You just want your daughter back and then you'll continue this vendetta."

Craig extended his hand and Andocia saw the ring. Instantly a red beam encircled his hand and placed a shield about it.

"Sorry, but I need to talk to you. I understand you don't trust me, but I'll prove it to you. Without the power of that ring, you are helpless against me. I could do anything I like with you, even force you to tell me what you and Tanus were scheming about, but I won't."

The woman removed the beam from Craig's hand.

"There you are, use it against me if you want to. Granted, I'll only be dazed for a second, but it could buy you valuable time. Well?"

Craig hesitated, wanting to believe her. "All right, I'll give you the benefit of the doubt. Do you want me to contact Tanus for you?"

"No, on second thoughts, don't."

Andocia walked over to the console and typed in a few digits.

"I see we should be landing on the White Planet in about 30 minutes. I'll speak to Tanus in person."

Craig stared at her. Are you crazy or something? You have never landed on the White Planet – you wouldn't dare!"

"Craig let me ask you something. If your children were in trouble, wouldn't you risk everything for them?"

"Of course I would, but there are limitations."

"Very few though. You were going to give yourself up to me when you realised I had captured both your children, weren't you?"

Craig nodded in the affirmative. "Yes I was, but they escaped before I left, thank goodness."

Andocia smiled. "Yes, they definitely take after you. Both show great promise."

The White Planet came into view and Craig moved to the console. "Andocia, I have to tell them I'm coming in. I need clearance."

"Very well, but don't mention my presence. I want it to be a surprise. Ask Tanus to meet you at the landing strip."

"All right, but I still think you've lost your mind."

She smiled coldly. "Not really – you see, I still have you. If Tanus makes one threatening move against me, I'll kill you in front of your family."

The explorer contacted the planet and he was given the relevant instructions. He knew it took about five minutes to settle down and cool his engines, so he risked a quick look at Andocia. She was deep in thought and he decided not to disturb her.

Unbeknown to Craig, she wasn't merely thoughtful, but had concentrated her efforts on finding the location of her daughter. She sensed her presence and frowned, but Craig was unaware of this, as he had his back to her. In her prison cell, the manacles snapped apart like twigs and Deliah concentrated all her efforts on the steel door, which flew open, thanks to their combined power. The alarm went off and Deliah despatched several of the guards. As the ship touched down and Craig heard the sirens wailing urgently, he gasped as the door of his craft opened and Deliah stepped inside.

"Hey! How do you both do that!" he complained.

"That's our secret," Deliah smirked.

Craig looked at both women and sighed.

"I guess the peace talks were a lie then."

Deliah frowned. "Mom, what is he talking about?"

Andocia grabbed Craig's hand when she saw him bring the ring up again.

"Don't be foolish, Craig! Deliah, listen to me, I want to declare a truce with Tanus and I intend to do so. You stay here, out of harm's way, while I go to meet her."

"But mother…"

"If Tanus tries to capture me, I'll kill Craig. Just wait a few moments – my ship will be here soon to get you. Come on Craig, let's go!" she said, still holding his hand firmly.

Both of them exited the craft and a humming noise claimed Craig's attention. He looked up and saw a trident ship hovering high above them. Tanus and his family were staring wide-eyed at him and Andocia. On cue, several of Tanus's guards pointed their weapons at the two figures. The woman in white glared at her adversary.

"Andocia, you are taking a considerable risk landing here like this. My guards could injure you. Even with the barrier around you, it will not survive a constant barrage."

"Listen to me Tanus, please. I come in peace. I wish to declare a truce."

Tanus signalled to her guards and they lowered their weapons, but held tightly onto them, just in case. Craig took a step towards his family, but Andocia held him back.

"A truce you say? Why the sudden change of heart?" she asked suspiciously.

"Look Tanus, all I ask is a few moments of your time. If you promise to hear me out, I'll let Craig go to his family."

The Carters exchanged looks and Constance nodded.

"Very well Andocia, you may have your few minutes." Tanus signalled to her guards and they lowered their weapons and moved some distance away.

Andocia released Craig's hand and he joined his family, placing his arm about his wife's shoulders.

"All right Andocia, we're all ears. What do you propose?"

"I no longer have any desire to rule both universes. It would take up too much of my valuable time and anyway, I want to spend it doing something more useful. Please understand why I freed Deliah – she's my daughter after all and she should be with her mother. I give you my word that she won't bother you either."

"How do we know you mean it Andocia?" asked Tanus suspiciously.

"If I didn't mean it, would I have willingly placed myself at your mercy? Well Tanus, do you accept my truce?"

Tanus was unsure and looked to her friends for the answer. Andocia came forward slowly and extended her hand. "I offer my hand in friendship Tanus. Take it and let there be peace between us!"

For a moment, Tanus stood, undecided, then extended her hand and the enemies clasped hands firmly. Tarmin was also watching the proceedings with interest and whispered in Craig's ear. "I would never have believed this if I hadn't seen it with my own eyes. Imagine, two sworn enemies actually shaking hands!"

"Yes, it's quite incredible! I didn't believe she was serious," remarked the explorer pensively.

Andocia waved goodbye and Deliah did the same. They were taken up in the trident ship, which soon disappeared from sight. The Carter family were baffled by the turn of events.

"Do you think she really meant it?" asked Constance.

"Well she seemed genuine enough, but I'll still be prepared for anything. Those two are crafty and may be trying to lull us into a false sense of security."

On the trident ship, Deliah confronted her mother. "Did you have to make such a fool of yourself! Why do you want a truce with her?"

"We need time to think and plan for the ultimate take-over." Andocia remarked patiently.

Deliah smiled wickedly. "Now I understand. We'll have a lot of planning to do though."

"Of course, but when the time is right, we can break the truce."

Back on the White Planet, Tanus and the rest talked about this strange new development.

"You know Tanus, I could have sworn she even looked kinder," decided Craig.

"Not Andocia! She only does things if they are going to work in her favour. That woman is up to something and I could tell Deliah wasn't at all happy about the new development. However, I'm grateful for this reprieve, because I also have things to plan. I'm sure that it is safe for all of you to return to Earth now."

Craig removed the ring from his finger and held it out to Tanus. "Here Tanus, I guess I won't need this now."

"No Craig, keep it. She won't just disappear forever and may return one day. Keep it for such an eventuality. Besides, it will be useful against your other enemies as well."

After thanking her, he placed the ring back on his finger.

"Thank you for giving us refuge on your planet as well, Tanus," replied April gratefully.

"Think nothing of it. Do come again anytime. Glenn, remember not to underestimate your enemies in future."

"I'll be careful, especially since Andocia showed me what a fool I was."

The Carters took their leave of the White Planet and as usual, Tarmin flew part of the way with them. They waved farewell as she turned to return to her mistress.

Life returned to normal for the Carters. The school holidays were over and April returned to her studies. Craig and Glenn continued to explore Space for their commander. Constance too, went on the occasional mission.

29

One fateful day, a year later, something went terribly wrong in Space. At that time, both Craig and Glenn were away on different missions. A violent tremor shook and buffeted the planets, changing their orbits slightly. This baffled the scientists in every country, but no explanation could be offered. There followed many anxious moments for Constance and April, because neither of the men could be contacted. A month dragged by before a battered craft landed in the Space Control Centre. The occupant was badly bruised and unconscious. Glenn Carter was rushed to hospital and treated for his injuries. Of his father, there was no sign. When Glenn finally regained consciousness, he woke to find his mother and sister at his bedside.

A week later, he was up and about and ready to resume work. Constance took him home and sat him down. "Glenn, I wanted to tell you this before, but the doctors advised against it. Your father never returned. You were lucky."

"Never returned, but…"

"I'm sorry to have to tell you this, but you had to know. Commander Perry has put every available person on the job, but so far we have heard nothing."

"Mom he isn't dead – he can't be!" wailed Glenn unhappily.

"Glenn, I want to believe that so much, but there's no trace of him anywhere. He must be dead. You came home barely alive from goodness knows where. Your ship is only suitable for scrap now."

Glenn's lip trembled and he mumbled something before leaving the room and shutting his bedroom door. Constance had told April the news earlier and she had cried herself to sleep.

Constance went into her bedroom and looked at a picture of her husband. Her tears flowed freely as well.

"Why did this have to happen to us now my darling? We have been married for twenty-one years. I love you just as much now as I did when we first married. You can't be dead; I refuse to believe it!"

Tanus appeared and comforted the distressed woman. "My dear, don't fret so! I wish I had better news, but I don't. I have personally searched everywhere for Craig, but he isn't in either universe. I'm so sorry!"

After Tanus offered her condolences and left, Constance became a changed woman. She no longer laughed, but kept her feelings to herself. She never neglected her duty of caring for her children, but they noticed the old spark had left her. Finally Glenn couldn't stand his mother's depression and confronted her. "Mom, we have no proof that Dad is dead. Maybe he landed on some planet and hit his head. He could have temporarily lost his memory."

"No I doubt it. Tanus would be able to find him if he was alive. We have to deal with the facts and move on.'

"Well I want proof of his death before I accept it. I'm going to search both universes until I find some trace of him."

"Glenn, the explosion probably shattered him like a glass when it is dropped. You would have to go around picking up the pieces."

"If that's what it takes, that's what I'll have to do, until I have his entire body. He deserves to be buried in the land he loved and served."

"The journey will be long, for the universes are enormous. You would probably be away for a year or more."

"I understand, but it's something I must do. Once I'm satisfied there is nothing else I can do, I'll return home and accept whatever my search brings to light."

Constance sighed. "Oh Glenn, April and I will miss you terribly, but if that's what you want to do, go ahead. I won't stand in your way. I guess I would also like to know the truth."

Glenn went to the Space Centre and filled a ship with enough supplies to last for six months. His mother and sister went to see him leave and watched until his craft was only a tiny speck in the sky. He started his search on the Moon and accepted the condolences of his colleagues. He stayed for a short while, then made for Mercury. The young Space explorer took the necessary precautions, but there was no sign of his father on that planet. He went on to Venus where he was welcomed in a friendly manner.

"Hello Glenn, it's wonderful to see you again."

"Thank you. I did promise to visit, but time always seems to get ahead of me. I wish I could stay awhile, but I'm looking for my father. Do you perhaps have any news for me?"

"No, he hasn't been here at all. I'm sorry."

"Well, thanks anyway."

"Glenn, our thoughts go with you. We wish you luck and hope your journey will not be in vain. Many people will be rooting for you."

Glenn nodded and returned to his ship.

His next destination was Sonambra. He had got used to the gravitational pull by now and landed like a true professional. Sonambro was waiting for him and treated him immediately against the extreme radiation. He too sympathised with the young man.

"Your father was a wonderful man and you can be proud of him. I hope you find him."

"So do I."

Glenn stayed for a short while before making his way to Pluto. He hovered as close as he dared and scanned the entire planet, but knew if his father had landed here, he would be dead. The Plutonians jeered at him and invited him to join them, but he declined of course. The inhabitants told him they hadn't seen Craig, so he moved to Neptune.

There he contacted Lolita, who came to the surface and commiserated with him. They spoke for a while, then Glenn thanked her and left, after finding out they hadn't seen him at all.

He went to Uranus and stared in disbelief when he found it no longer existed. He double-checked the map of the universes and established he was indeed in the right place. In confusion, he contacted Mission Control. "Commander Perry, I have disturbing news. Uranus is no longer in our solar system. I have tried to locate it, but it has just vanished without a trace."

"That's terrible! We get our Uranium from that planet, now we'll have to find an alternate source. Do you have any news about your father?"

"None yet, but I'm still hopeful. Sir, I'm going to Saturn now."

"Give my regards to the Saturnians," his boss said.

"Yes Sir, I'll do that."

Glenn switched off and set his controls for Saturn where friends once again welcomed him. "Oh Glenn it's good to see you alive and well. The news about your father isn't encouraging though, is it?"

"No, but I'll keep looking until there is nowhere else to go. Only then will I give up."

"He was a fine Space explorer and his memory will live on in our minds for ever."

The strain of the journey finally got to Glenn and he lost his temper.

"Damn it! Why does everyone talk about my father in the past tense? It hasn't been confirmed that he's dead yet!"

Karnd patted Glenn sympathetically on the shoulder. "I'm sorry, forgive me. I hope you will prove us all wrong."

Glenn sank to the floor in misery and his eyes shone with unshed tears. "No, I apologise. I so badly want him to be alive, but I'm beginning to give up hope now as well."

"It's very disheartening, I agree, but come and eat something and maybe you'll feel a little better. You look tired."

"I am, but I'll survive. I can sleep between planets anyway."

"Where have you travelled to so far?" he replied sympathetically.

"The Moon, Venus, Sonambra, Pluto, Neptune and Uranus, except that Uranus has now disappeared."

"Disappeared?" asked Karnd curiously, "how can a planet disappear?"

"I have no idea, but it's definitely no longer in its usual orbit."

Karnd paced the floor worriedly. "It must have been that Space quake then. Every planet has moved slightly off course and I don't know why. Perhaps the epicentre was somewhere near Uranus."

"It's possible I suppose. I guess I've had enough of a rest now. I would like to be on my way again."

"Of course, don't let me stop you. Where are you going now?"

"I'm going to Jupiter. Thank you for your hospitality once again. I hope I'll have better news when next we meet."

Glenn went to Jupiter, but found nothing there, so he moved on to Mars. Again he met with no success.

Glenn headed for the jump vortex that would take him to the Golden Way, when he received an unexpected visitor. Tyrus had heard of Glenn's quest and was curious about the young explorer, so decided to pay him a visit. He materialised in the ship and Glenn sensed rather than saw anything. He whirled around and looked at the strange creature.

"Hello youngster!" he replied pleasantly.

"Who or what are you?" asked the startled young man.

"My name is Tyrus. I'm an electrical being."

"That name seems familiar. Yes, I believe my father has spoken of you. He doesn't like you very much."

"The feeling is mutual, I assure you. I was just curious actually, because I wanted to meet the son of the legendary Craig Carter. I must say the resemblance is unmistakable. You are also, handsome. I believe that is the word you humans would use."

"Well now that your curiosity has been satisfied, I would like you to leave my ship. I'm on a mission."

"Yes, to look for your missing father. I would strongly advise against it though. He has been missing for quite some time now and he's probably dead. Actually, I hope he is, as he has caused me much grief over the last couple of years."

241

"You know Tyrus, I've been wondering the same thing these past few days, and I was almost about to give up on him, but thanks to you, I've had a change of heart. I'll comb every inch of the Golden Way until I get some clue as to my father's whereabouts, then I'll bring him home. Get lost now."

Tyrus glared at him. "You have inherited your father's cheek too I see. I could so easily cure you with a dose of electricity."

"You don't scare me one bit Tyrus, now go away," snapped Glenn angrily.

"Yes Tyrus, do as the man says."

Glenn and Tyrus were startled to see Deliah near the controls. Her arms were folded across her chest.

"Deliah, what are you doing here and when did you arrive?"

"I only arrived about a minute ago. I was listening to your conversation. Well Tyrus?"

"I was just leaving," he replied sullenly.

When he had gone, Glenn confronted Deliah. "Okay Deliah, why are you here?"

"Andocia wants to talk to you."

"Just talk, or is it something more sinister?" he wanted to know.

"We have a peace treaty remember. It's just a social visit."

Glenn shrugged. "Oh well, I was on my way to the Golden Way anyhow. I suppose I could start there. We're going to the Red Planet, aren't we?"

"Yes. I'll have to come with you, because you aren't familiar with the route."

He wasn't going to argue with that, so he let her accompany him. They entered the Golden Way and he landed the ship on her planet. When they disembarked, Glenn felt uneasy. Andocia's followers watched him intently.

Deliah led him to a room where Andocia was lounging on an overstuffed couch. Her shapely legs were stretched out in front of her and her red hair trailed behind her. One strand fell seductively over her left shoulder.

Glenn was thoughtful. "If only she represented good, but the evil shines out of her eyes. It seems to cling to her and that alone makes her unattractive." Glenn mused.

"Ah Glenn, do take a seat; you too Deliah."

Both complied and gave her their fullest attention.

"Glenn, I'm speaking to you as a friend. I know you're looking for your father, but you'll be wasting your time."

"Why?"

"Because you won't like what you find." she stated curtly.

"Do you know where he is, Andocia?"

"Yes, but it's difficult to explain. You won't find him in either universe."

"Is he alive?" asked Glenn hopefully.

"I don't know for sure. Your father is probably on a planet known as Saurus. The planet is uninhabited at the moment and is known as Darr on your maps."

"I don't understand! If they don't exist yet, how can he be on that planet?"

"As I said, it's difficult to explain. You may have noticed Uranus has vanished from your galaxy."

"Yes, I did notice, but what has that to do with the situation concerning my father?"

"Your father obviously crash landed on Uranus and it was knocked into the future by the Space tremor. I guess somehow Uranus landed up close to Saurus. Many years ago, your father and I went through a rift in Space, but it was closer to Tanus's planet at that time. We ended up on Saurus. It seems that somehow this anomaly opens up time vortexes in more than one place now. We were lucky that time, but I don't know if your father will have survived if he was injured. He could be dead."

Glenn paled visibly and sank down onto the couch. "No, I won't believe it until I see his body!"

"Glenn, he might have survived, but there's a very powerful being who lives on Saurus. She wanted to wipe your father's mind when we were on the planet, but I know her and because of my influence, I refused to let her do it. You see, I didn't know how to find my way back to my universe, but your father figured it out and I needed his help. It happened eighteen years ago, before you were born."

Glenn did a quick calculation in his head. "I'm eighteen years old now. Was my mother pregnant with me at the time?"

"Yes she was!"

"If what you say is true Andocia, I have to take a chance and try to go there. My father figured out how to get back to our universes, so it must be possible! Anyway I promised everyone back home I would return with his dead body if he has in fact died. He's still my father, no matter what may have happened. If the Saurians have somehow wiped his mind clean, then I can't leave him there! Maybe the Saturnians will be able to help him regain his memory."

"That's a lot of 'ifs' Glenn. Maybe Uranus was destroyed! Who really knows what happened. It's very risky."

"Then what do you suggest I do, Andocia? How can I go forward in time? No one has ever done it before – well not on Earth anyway. You obviously know how to do so, otherwise, how would you know so much?"

"I'm capable of many things, but our trip to the future was an accident. I can't help you any further, I'm sorry."

Glenn stood up straight and a determined light burned in his eyes. "All right, I'll go then. I'll find some way to rescue my father! I appreciate you telling me. At least I know there could be a chance of finding him, even though it's a very slim one."

The young explorer took his leave of the two women, who thoughtfully watched him go.

"Mom, do you suppose he'll figure out how to get to Saurus?"

"I don't know. Their spaceships do have the capacity to travel through time, but their scientists haven't managed to work it out yet. If he manages to rescue his father though, he still has Valdena to contend with. She won't take kindly to an intruder. Well I told him what I saw; now the rest is up to him. If he doesn't make it for some or other reason, I won't complain. It'll mean two less thorns in my side."

⚔ ⚔ ⚔

Glenn had an idea and contacted Mission Control where he spoke to Commander Perry. "Sir, I may have a lead regarding the whereabouts of my father and I want to pursue it. Andocia mentioned that she and my dad had accidentally landed on a planet that exists in the future. On our current maps of the universes, it's known as Darr, but in the future, it's called Saurus. They landed there by accident eighteen years ago. Can you have someone check the archives and email me that file please? I would like to know what I'll be dealing with. Meanwhile I'm going to return to the orbit where Uranus disappeared, because I think that's where the gateway is."

"I'll have someone send you that file Glenn, but you do realise it is very risky. You are going on the assumption your father really is there, but what if he isn't?"

"I understand the risk Sir, but what if he is?"

"Point taken! All right Glenn, I'll have that file sent to you as soon as possible. Just keep in touch with me so I know what's happening."

"I'll do that, Sir," Glenn promised.

Not long afterwards, he checked his mobile device and saw a new email had arrived. He expanded the display to activate the computer mode, and opened the email. Glenn was amazed at what he discovered. It read like some fantastic fantasy story. He studied the drawings of all the strange beings his father had come into contact with during his adventure. Craig had included every detail, no matter how trivial it seemed. There was also a drawing of Valdena and Glenn looked intently at the picture. He felt a small tremor of fear ripple through his body when he realised Valdena and Andocia were both immortal. His father had made notes about the two females and the young man realised just how tenuous his father's situation had been. Glenn also understood what Andocia had said about Craig's mind being wiped. If he had landed on Saurus again, Glenn wondered; would Valdena remember him? Perhaps, without Andocia's influence, she would take advantage of Craig and do what she had originally intended. Glenn shuddered at the danger his father could have faced, yet here he was, eighteen years later, doing the same thing. At least he knew what to expect, so that was an advantage. He read and re-read the file, committing it to memory and began planning what to do. His father had been very thorough and had helpfully included instructions on how to reprogram the computer on their ships to return its occupants back to their own universes. That would help him tremendously.

30

A few weeks earlier

Craig had been cruising near Uranus when the Space tremor began. His ship was buffeted about violently and he strapped himself into his chair and tried valiantly to control his ship, but the computer wasn't responding. Bolts of energy danced around his spaceship and although he tried to avoid them, one hit his ship, causing a power failure. He tried calling for help, but the computer had shorted out. Desperately he took out his mobile device and tried to contact Mission Control, but the electrical storm prevented it. Craig watched in dismay as the mobile device's screen began to change randomly and an error message popped up. The device became hot in his hand and he dropped it on the floor, where it exploded. The emergency lights flickered on and off and he watched horrified as the planet Uranus loomed closer and closer. Craig swore and pulled on the levers, but the ship went into a steep dive, and the last thing he remembered was an agonising pain as his head connected with something hard. Then everything went dark.

As he lay unconscious on the planet Uranus, amidst the debris that had previously been his ship, another violent tremor rocked the planet. It seemed to be enveloped in mist and then suddenly it disappeared from its orbit and vanished into a huge chasm.

Uranus reappeared in another universe, a short distance from Saurus. Craig had no way of knowing he had once again been catapulted into the future.

As he lay senseless in his wrecked ship, he was unaware of beings lifting him up gently and placing him in a ship, equipped with state of the art medical equipment. They scanned his body from head to toe and injected him with some medication to deepen his unconsciousness, so he could rest comfortably. The scan showed some broken bones and head trauma.

Craig woke a few days later and looked around. A doctor came into the room and pushed him gently down on the pillows.

"Where... where am I?" he asked groggily.

"Take it easy Craig. You had an accident and you're in hospital."

A wave of pain hit him and he groaned aloud. "What happened? I don't remember anything!"

"Your ship crashed and you hit your head. Don't worry, everything will be fine. You should remember what happened in a few days' time." The doctor replied as he rolled back the sleeve of Craig's hospital gown and injected him with a strange device. "I've given you something for the pain."

Carter wanted to question the doctor some more, but his eyes closed immediately and he drifted back into unconsciousness.

A few days later he was more alert and a nurse brought him something to eat. He questioned her, but she shook her head. "You are still very weak. Dr Brunswick will be here to answer your questions soon."

Craig was sitting up in bed when the doctor came to visit him. He smiled at the man. "You look much better Craig. How are you feeling?"

"Much better. Where am I? Am I on Earth?"

Dr Brunswick looked curiously at him. "No, you're on Saurus. You do look a lot better. Luckily your head injury was minor. There was a bit of swelling on your brain, but it's gone down now. I'm afraid you weren't so lucky with your leg. You broke it in three places. We had to operate on it and join the bones with a special resin. Don't worry though, you'll soon be back on your feet again. Do you remember what happened yet?"

Craig tried to remember, but his thoughts were fragmented. He remembered crashing on Uranus and hitting his head. The rest was still hazy. Dr Brunswick put a comforting hand on his patient's shoulder and squeezed it gently.

"Don't worry about it yet. The memories will return I promise you."

The doctor put a set of crutches next to the bed. "You had a very bad accident so take it easy. If you feel well enough to get up, use the crutches, but only stand up when someone can help you to get out of bed, okay."

A few days passed and Craig became stronger. He could get out of bed on his own and go to the bathroom unassisted. As Dr Brunswick had promised, his memory did return and he remembered what had happened. At the same time however, he realised he was in a very bad predicament. Carter's experiences on Saurus eighteen years ago came back to haunt him. He realised the doctor at the hospital had called him by his name, yet he didn't remember ever having told the man who he was. Carter wondered if sometime during his hospital stay, he had perhaps woken up and told the Doctor, but he doubted it. Then again, everything was hazy and he did have some lapses in his memory.

He was discharged from hospital the next day and taken to the guest rooms as before. As Craig sat on the bed and looked out of the window, he was concerned. The explorer missed his family and wondered if he would ever see them again. None of them had known about his visit to Saurus eighteen years earlier. The last time he had come here, he still had a ship to escape in, but this time his ship had been destroyed in the crash. He wondered if spaceships still got dumped in The Forbidden Valley, but he doubted he could make it there, even if he somehow managed to get some help. He had also been eighteen years younger then.

Carter only spent one day in the guest room before he was summoned to the 'inner sanctuary'. Valdena was waiting for him and the smile on her face told him she had known about him all along. He bowed from the waist, remembering Andocia had insisted he be polite all those years ago. In that moment he was transported back to the time when he stood before this woman once before.

Valdena smiled brightly at him. "This is an unexpected pleasure! I never thought I would see you again, but the gods have been kind to me. You always had a place in my thoughts. There has never been anyone quite as brave as you in all the years I have lived on this planet."

She pointed to a chair nearby and asked him to sit down. The man stared at her. She was just as beautiful as he remembered, but she wore her hair shorter now. Valdena's clothing was just as figure-hugging as he remembered. Today she wore a burgundy dress with a scooped neckline. Her sandals matched the fabric perfectly.

She sat opposite him and questioned him about Andocia and he informed her that as far as he knew, the woman was fine. She laughed and wanted to know if they were friends yet and Craig had shaken his head. "Not now, not ever!" he remarked.

Valdena had laughed as though it was the funniest joke she had ever heard. She questioned him about his family and he told her he was still married and had two children.

Valdena soon got tired of being polite and her expression hardened. "Craig, do you remember what I said to you all those years ago when I shared with you how I acquired my human labourers?"

"I remember clearly," he answered.

"Do you also remember I asked Andocia if I could keep you here with me and she refused?"

"Of course I do," he replied.

"You know of course why I asked you if the two of you were friends yet."

"Yes, I do but we never were friends and I doubt we ever will be. Look Valdena, let's get to the point, okay. I'm not a child so don't treat me like one. You are taking people away from their families and forcing them to do your work. To make matters worse, you are using them as guinea pigs and their DNA to make your creatures. I assume you're still conducting these experiments."

"I am indeed. I don't abuse anyone, I just make them better."

"I know, I know! Humans are violent and unpredictable and you are creating a better life for them. I wonder how many others have stood before you and given you the same answer."

Valdena stood up and walked over to him. "I admire you Craig! You aren't afraid to speak your mind and I wish I could just keep you here with me as my advisor. You are very intelligent and I see why Andocia has kept you alive all these years. You fascinate her and her life would be boring without you to bother her. Well, her loss is definitely my gain! I don't trust you, but I do need you! Your computer skills are almost as good as your fighting skills, so I'm going to wipe your mind, but you won't be a lowly farm worker! I need computer programmers I can trust. Lately we have had a number of people hacking into our systems, but we don't know who they are. Your job will be to enhance our security and create programs that cannot be tampered with."

Craig looked at the woman. "Before you make any decisions, may I ask you something?"

"Yes, of course! What do you want to know?"

"I crashed on Uranus during a Space quake, but I have never experienced anything like that before. Were you responsible for this?"

"Yes, I was actually," she replied proudly. "My system works wonderfully and everyone gets along with one another on Saurus. I wanted more opportunities to obtain even more humans, so I created another gateway."

Craig shook his head. "If I was your advisor, I would tell you that you have made a mistake! This 'gateway' or vortex, whatever you want to call it, is very unstable and it seems to be growing exponentially daily. Not only are you causing havoc in the Milky Way, your gateway has swallowed an entire planet. I'm not a scientist like you, but even I can see trouble brewing. That vortex caused me to crash on Uranus and then the planet was pulled through to your time period. If you don't close it soon, maybe other planets will also get sucked through. If they are big enough, they could slam into Saurus and destroy everything you have accomplished so far. Another possibility could be that you will be too successful, resulting in overpopulation on Saurus. You would be back to starting all over again."

"I never thought about that," she replied. "Maybe you have a point there."

"There could be another problem. I don't know why no one else has discovered this time vortex, but in the near future, maybe military people will decide to come through and visit Saurus. They would take it by force and that will be the end of your dreams. None of your human beings know how to fight, because you took away their memories. The androids you use won't be able to keep experienced fighters away."

Valdena sighed. "You are a very intelligent man Craig! I would be happy to have you at my side. Your input would be invaluable to me. If you agreed to help me willingly, I wouldn't have to wipe your mind and you would never want for anything ever again."

Craig shook his head regretfully. "I'm sorry Valdena, as tempting as your offer sounds, I just couldn't do it. I miss my family and friends. I could promise to obey you, but you are telepathic and you'll know I was lying."

"You're giving up an incredible opportunity! Your family probably think you're dead anyway."

"If you wipe my mind, I may as well be dead! I want to be around to hold my wife and raise my children, but you don't care about that, only what's best for you!"

Valdena pressed a buzzer and four guards came in, their weapons pointed unwaveringly at him. Craig glared at her. "If I wasn't handicapped, I would fight back! I could easily take out four puny guards. I'll promise you one thing though, I won't make it easy for you. I'll fight you mentally, as much as I possibly can. Maybe you'll win in the end, but at least I'll have tried! I can only hope one day someone will manage to stop you."

Two of the guards yanked him to his feet and held onto him so he wouldn't fall down. The third one pressed something against his neck and he felt a sharp, stinging sensation. The last thing Craig remembered was Valdena's smirk of satisfaction, before his eyes closed and darkness descended once more.

⚔ ⚔ ⚔

Craig woke screaming and threw the blankets off his bed. He tried to get up but his broken leg wouldn't support him. A woman hurried up to him and held him tightly.

"Craig, it's okay! You had that horrible dream again, didn't you?"

"I... I crashed. I couldn't stop myself from falling! I tried, but I failed!"

"Sweetheart, it's okay now! See, you're at home safe with me. It was only a dream."

He came to his senses and looked around. For a moment he didn't recognise his surroundings, but the woman took his hand.

"My darling, the doctor said you'll have nightmares, but it will pass in time."

"Where am I?" he asked.

"You're at home with me"

The man was still remembering his dream, when the woman sat down and stroked his hand.

"I'm Monica – your mate! You crashed your transport while on the way to work a few days ago. When you fell, you hit your head and that's why you forget things. You also broke your leg in three places. You were lucky it wasn't worse. I could have lost you! The vehicle is a write-off though but your firm will give you another one. You were given sick leave so you can recover from your head injury. I have to take you to see the doctor today and he'll tell us if you can return to work."

Craig looked stupidly at her. "I'm sorry honey, but what sort of job do I have?"

She looked strangely at him. "Craig you're a computer operator, don't you remember? This memory says you're one of Valdena's best employees! Maybe the doctor will have to book you off for your lapse is bothering me!"

The man smiled at her. "I'm okay, just a bit shaken from that dream I had. I'm sure I'll be fine tomorrow. I'm going to have a shower to clear my head. What time must we be at the doctor?"

"Not before midday so we have plenty of time. I'll fix us some breakfast in the meantime."

That afternoon they went to the hospital in Monica's transport. It was a two seater vehicle that ran on solar power. There was one lever with the letters LRFB arranged in a circle around it, as well as a small steering wheel. The brake pedal was mounted on the floorboard.

When they arrived at the hospital, Dr Brunswick greeted them. "Hello Craig, how are you feeling now? Does your leg still hurt?"

"Yes it does doctor," he replied.

"Okay, I'll prescribe some more painkillers for you then. Just stay off that leg as much as possible and when you sit down, raise it up slightly higher than your body. How's your head?"

"I still get headaches, but they aren't as severe as they were before."

Dr Brunswick watched Craig carefully as he examined him, but there was no recognition in his eyes. The man wasn't aware he had spoken to the same doctor before. He smiled at Craig. "I think I must send you for a quick scan so we can check on your head injury. Go with the nurse now and we'll see you soon."

When Craig had left, Dr Brunswick questioned Monica. "How's he doing, Monica?"

"He still has nightmares about crashing his spaceship. I told him he crashed his transport while going to work. He believes me, but sometime he has lapses of memory. When will he get better?"

"Just be patient a while longer. It is early days yet. Valdena wants him to start work tomorrow, but I don't think he's ready yet. I'm going to suggest he stay at home another day or two. Just be there for him and encourage him. I want you bring him back for another check-up in three days. By that time the nightmares should have stopped. Valdena won't be patient much longer if we can't get him to forget."

Craig came back and Dr Brunswick checked the scan. "Everything's looking good. I still see some inflammation on the brain, so I'll also give you some more antibiotics to take. Monica will bring you back here in three days. I'll see you then."

Craig thanked the doctor and the two humans returned home.

Dr Brunswick stared unhappily at the man's departing back, and shook his head. A nurse questioned him. "Is something wrong, doctor? Is he sicker than you're letting on?"

"No nurse, I'm just upset! I hate what Valdena does to these people. What right does she have to make them forget everything about their lives, just so she can make them work for her. Craig is a decent man, like so many others before him. He doesn't deserve this!"

The nurse looked nervously around. "Be careful what you say doctor! Someone might hear you and you could end up in the same predicament as so many of your patients."

31

Meanwhile, out in Space, Glenn was getting close to where Uranus had disappeared and hovered in the orbit where the planet had previously been. He sat down at the computer and began typing calculations. "I have to somehow reconstruct what happened to my dad, then try to duplicate it. The file my dad saved will help me tremendously, but his destination was different, so I'll have to adjust the calculations accordingly."

He worked at it for a while and finally came up with a reasonable idea. Glenn put it to the computer. "Well Jayne, is this possible?"

<It certainly is Glenn, but there is a great risk attached. You must allow for a safe return, or you will be lost in another time period for the rest of your human existence.>

Glenn agreed and did some more calculations. He programmed the results into the computer, so it would remember how to make the return journey.

He flew closer and closer to the spot and because he was aware of the rift, he saw it clearly. The computer confirmed his suspicions. <Warning! We are approaching the vortex.>

"I see it Jayne. Approach slowly!"

Glenn Carter took a deep breath and the ship crept slowly forward. He saw what looked like a mist approaching and he strapped himself into the seat. For a moment he could see nothing, then the ship whined and shook and the engines screamed desperately. He hung onto the steering tightly and his ship lunged forward violently. Glenn watched as the clock on his control panel whirled madly. The whining increased until he thought he would go mad, then suddenly all was quiet. Glenn stared at the clock, which now indicated he had travelled forward in time to the year 4700. He had calculated correctly and found himself hovering close to Uranus. The map on display showed the planet Darr as Saurus.

Glenn yelled in triumph. "I did it! I really did it!"

He checked the computer, which seemed to be functioning normally, and found Saurus was only a short distance away.

Glenn approached cautiously and switched on his scanners. He hoped they wouldn't be expecting him, but he shouldered a laser rifle anyway. He hid a smaller gun in his waistband and another small one in an inside pocket, which he zipped up. He placed a knife in each sock.

"No sense letting them get the better of me, otherwise I'll end up like my father. I must be prepared for every eventuality!"

The explorer took the ship down to the planet and climbed out. Then he returned it by remote control to the sky and put it into time lapse. Glenn took out binoculars and scanned the surrounding areas, but there was nothing nearby. He decided the inhabitants were most probably indoors.

He hid behind a tree when he heard movement and watched as a man and a woman walked down the road. They were wearing clothes Glenn had seen in his father's file. Glenn looked down at his uniform and realised he looked out of place, so he kept to the trees until he came to a house that looked deserted. He peered in the windows but saw nothing moving. The young explorer was so busy looking around him that he didn't look upwards, where a birdlike creature sat concealed in the high branches of a tree. It flew soundlessly away. Hidden cameras blinked and took his picture, relaying it back to some people sitting at computers. Glenn was unaware he had landed in Hillvale, just as his father had accidentally done eighteen years earlier.

He tried the only door of the house, but found it locked. Glenn pulled out a thin piece of wire and inserted it in the lock and the door opened. Carter went inside and began opening and closing drawers, looking for something to wear. A sound disturbed him and when he looked up, he was staring down the barrels of a few laser guns.

"Didn't your mother teach you not to steal!" One of the men snarled at him.

Glenn dropped the pair of pants he had been holding and put up his hands. "Please don't shoot me!" he begged. "I was trying to find something to put on over my Space suit. It's too conspicuous."

The man came a little closer and looked at the young man. He waved his gun in the direction of Glenn's shoulder. "Remove your weapon, slowly and kick it over to me."

Glenn took the rifle off his shoulder and did as he was ordered. The man picked it up and gave it to someone else to hold. Glenn kept his hands in plain view.

"Where are you from?" the stranger demanded.

"From Earth," he replied nervously.

"What are you doing here? Did you crash? We never heard anything!"

"Uh, no, I didn't crash. I came here purposely. I'm from the year 4022."

The man looked at his friends. "He comes from the past, on purpose! No one has ever come here willingly before. It's impossible!"

"Not anymore!" Glenn smirked. "I just did it."

Another man came closer. "If you came here on purpose as you say, you must have a reason for wanting to be here."

"I do have a very good reason! I think my father is on this planet."

"What gave you that idea?"

Glenn looked at the men. "Can I put my hands down please?"

The men nodded and he dropped them slowly to his sides.

"The planet Uranus has just ended up in your universe. It got knocked out of orbit by a Space quake, and I believe my father crashed on it just before the planet disappeared."

The men looked enquiringly at one another.

"We'll have to get Jonathon to check if he's telling the truth," one man replied.

They turned back to the young explorer. "What's your name, young man?"

"I'm known as Glenn Carter. My father is Craig Carter."

The men shook their heads. "Sorry, I can't say I recognise the name, but lots of spacemen have landed here over the years."

Suddenly Glenn had an idea. "What's the name of this city?'

"It's known as Hillvale, why?"

"My father was here with someone eighteen years ago. Does Galen still live here?"

Everyone stared at him. "How do you know of Galen? He's our leader."

"My father mentioned him in a report he made after he had returned safely to Earth. I studied his file."

The men shook their heads in disbelief. "No one has ever managed to leave this place and return home again. It's impossible!"

"My father did exactly that!" Glenn replied proudly.

The leader spoke to his friends and they lowered their weapons.

"We have to take this young man to see Galen. If anyone can clear this matter up, he can."

The men agreed.

"May I call you Glenn?"

"Yes, please do."

"Okay, Glenn. First you had better see if those clothes you were rifling through, will fit you. There are still spies loyal to the leaders of this planet and it won't do for them to become suspicious."

Glenn chose a pair of trousers and a top and put them on. One of the men was carrying a sack in which he placed Glenn's Space suit. Then they made their way to Galen's house.

The group reached Galen's house and knocked softly. The man opened his door and saw his friends standing there. He quickly looked around, but seeing no one in sight, beckoned the group inside and shut the door.

"What are you doing here! We agreed we would only meet when it gets dark!"

"It was important, Galen!" the leader of the small group replied. "We found this youngster sniffing around. Says his name is Glenn Carter. Apparently, his father was here some time ago, but he managed to leave Saurus and go home again."

"What was your father's name, son?" Galen asked curiously.

Glenn reached into his pocket and took out his mobile device. He showed the man a picture of his father. "His name is Craig Carter. He was here eighteen years ago, before I was even born."

Galen snatched the device from his hand and peered intently at the picture. He looked at Glenn. "I see the resemblance, but I don't believe it!" He looked at his friends in amazement. "I remember him! He was here with a woman who had green skin – that's why it stuck in my mind. Craig landed on Saurus by accident, like so many others, but he hid his ship and the 'higher powers' never found it until much later. I helped him and his friend by taking them into my home. Craig is the one who gave me the incentive to begin this rebel movement against Valdena and her cohorts. He's my hero!"

Galen shook Glenn's hand vigorously. "It's an honour to meet the son of the legendary Craig Carter! How is he by the way?"

Glenn looked miserably at Galen. "I don't know! We were both away on separate missions, when there was an explosion in Space. I made it back, but my father didn't return. I've been looking for him ever since, but I've had no luck so far. One of the planets in our solar system got sucked though a rift in Space and landed up near Saurus. I think my father was on Uranus when it got hurled through time, and he crashed. When I came through the vortex, I saw that Uranus is now situated near to Saurus. I'm hoping he was discovered on Uranus and brought here, but I don't know if he is here or not. I promised my mother and sister I would look for him and if he's dead, I want to take his body back home to be buried on Earth. I owe him that much at least. You are my last hope! If he isn't here, I'll have to return home empty handed, because I'm out of options!"

Galen put a comforting hand on the young man's shoulder. "Approximately how long ago was it that your father disappeared?"

"It was about five months ago."

"I promise you we'll do everything we can to help you. If he's here on Saurus, we'll find him and return him to you. Until we have answers for you, I would like to extend my hospitality to you, as I did with your father long ago. Daphne will be home shortly and I know she's going to be very pleased to meet you."

Galen turned to his friends. "Jonathon, you go to the computer bunker and get the guys to tap into the main computers. Check on all the new arrivals over the last five months. I've printed out some pictures of Craig, from Glenn's device. Scan them into the computers and see if you can find a match. Gary, you have a friend who works at the hospital. If Craig was injured, they'll have a record of it. Find out what you can and let me know."

"It will be our pleasure!" they replied.

Once they had left, Daphne arrived, together with the couple's two children. Galen introduced them to Glenn.

"Daphne, you won't believe who this young man is!" he explained excitedly. "This is Glenn Carter – Craig's son."

Daphne shook his hand. "It's a pleasure to meet you! I've never forgotten your father. What an amazing man he was!"

She indicated to her two children. "This is our son Zack. He's fifteen. My daughter Annabelle is thirteen."

Glenn shook their hands politely. "Glad to meet you! My sister April is fifteen as well."

After they had eaten their dinner, there was a knock at the door. Galen smiled as he went to open it. A blue cat with a peacock's tail came in. She didn't greet Galen's family, but went straight up to Glenn. She looked intently at him and spoke in a high voice. "Well hello! Word gets around quickly in this place. I believe you are Craig's son. This is a great honour for me!"

Glenn looked in amazement at the creature. "You must be Mia! My dad spoke fondly of you."

The cat was amazed. She looked adoringly up into Glenn's eyes and jumped on his lap. Immediately she began to purr. "Oh! He knows who I am!

I see Craig has passed his good genes onto his son. He is very handsome!" she sighed.

Glenn laughed. "Well thank you for that comment Mia. My father was here so long ago, I didn't expect to meet any of the beings who he knew."

Mia purred. "Well I was only a year old when I met Craig. I'm not as young as I was back then, but I still remember him. We went on quite an adventure together. He was an inspiration to us all!"

"Are any of the other beings who shared your adventure, still alive?" Glenn asked curiously.

Mia's expression turned sad. "Alas, the centaurs were warriors and they usually had a very short lifespan because of the work they did. Out of the four who accompanied us, only Lori is still with us. Valdena has created other centaurs, but none of those living now would know who your father was."

Galen interrupted them. "A lot has changed in the eighteen years since your father came to Saurus. Did he mention in his report to his superiors, what he did for me and my mate?"

"Briefly, but not in any great detail, why?"

"That kindness on his part is what spurred Daphne and I to begin making plans to topple Valdena and end her nasty experiments. Craig managed to tap into their computers without the so called 'higher powers' being aware of it. We now know Valdena is an immortal and cannot be killed, but we have plans to stop her and her experiments on humans. If we manage to destroy her work, maybe she'll move away to conquer other planets. Your father managed to break into the personal files and he brought me a device before he left. On this reading device he had copied mine and my mate's original history. This was before our minds were wiped clean and she gave us other duties to perform. I was a Nuclear Physicist, and Daphne was a Neurologist. Neither of us has any memory of our past lives. Now I farm for a living because that's what Valdena wanted."

Daphne sat down next to her mate and held his hand. "We were understandably surprised to hear our minds had been wiped, but the technology Valdena uses is very advanced, so we weren't even aware it had happened. That woman kept everything simple so we had no access to anything even resembling computers and other such devices. We also don't know how to go back to our time periods and our previous lives, so we decided to just make the best of the situation. Galen and I decided to stay together, because we understand one another. We have two precious children now and that was partly why we decided on this course of action. Neither of us wants to see our children grow up being used as guinea pigs in that horrible woman's experiments, so we plotted and planned."

Galen began to explain further. "Craig gave us the names of people and doctors whom he thought would be sympathetic to our situation, and we contacted them. Everyone we spoke to was horrified to find they had become a part of Valdena's experiments, and we made useful contacts. Some of the computer staff in the main structure also decided to help us and over the years they have stolen small parts from the computer room, and helped us to build our own computers. The computer staff have been invaluable in creating change. Valdena sits in her glass tower and plans her next lot of strange animals and never comes into the cities to see what is happening, so we work in secret to change things."

Mia was listening and nodding her head attentively. "The animals have always been in charge of the humans. They are the ones who have weapons and keep the peace and until now the human population has always respected them. Craig had learnt so much from Valdena because his companion Andocia was given a tour of the 'glass tower' as we like to call it. She chose to share much with your father and he learnt very interesting things about both the human population and the animals. All of this information he stored on the device he gave to Galen, and humans with whom he shared this knowledge, were very grateful as well. Now most of the animals are on our side. I was a watcher in my young days and as such we earned the admiration of the other animals."

Glenn was puzzled. "What is a 'watcher'?"

"Watchers are spies, for want of a better word. They are the ones who look out for strangers who accidentally come through the time vortex, and then report them to the higher authorities. The watchers report these strangers to Valdena and she arranges for their capture. There were those who crashed on Saurus though and were taken to hospital. When these poor beings recovered, they were taken to Valdena and 'interviewed'. It is common knowledge that those who entered through the 'inner sanctum' were mentally changed, so they never remembered entering in the first place."

"How did my dad make it out and manage to return home?" Glenn asked curiously.

"That was Andocia's doing," Galen remarked. "We heard a rumour she needed him for something, so Valdena let them go. Your father never explained what she meant and we didn't ask! We do know for a fact though, your father had figured out a way to return home and his companion was badly injured, so she couldn't fly her ship alone. If it wasn't for Andocia, things would have been different."

Glenn scowled. "I know Andocia, but not very well. She didn't do it out of kindness! As you said, she needed my father's help."

"I understand," Galen replied. "When we managed to hack into the main computers, we tried to access the personal files, and in some instances, we've been lucky. We have built up our own data base and everyone we could trace, we contacted and told them the truth about their past lives. It's a very delicate situation though and some people don't believe us, so we have to be careful who we approach. Many of the inhabitants in the various cities are fiercely loyal to the 'higher powers' and don't want to believe us. They could inform on us, so we have to be very choosy. Occasionally we manage to rescue someone before Valdena gets to them, but they don't know how to return to their various planets either, so they become troublesome. It isn't the ideal situation but under the circumstances, we've had to abandon the idea of helping them and allow the watchers to report their whereabouts, so they get their minds wiped. Even if we figure out a way to travel back to our own times, we have no ships to fly. Valdena removes the computers that control them, and then destroys these. Occasionally we've been lucky and managed to salvage some computers from the ships, and adapt them for our needs. Valdena is aware of rebels doing this and has increased the security. At the moment we are trying to get some of the security personnel to help us, but it's going to take time."

Glenn was amazed. "My father will be so happy to hear your people have advanced so much in the last eighteen years. I hope he's alive, so I can tell him about this someday soon."

Galen sighed. "I hope so Glenn. It's getting late, but I want to show you our computer bunker. We could use your expertise and advice on how to improve them. Maybe you could help us build a device like the one you carry."

Glenn pulled out his mobile device. "This is a very sophisticated piece of equipment, but I'll see what I can do. My father knows more about computers than I do. He used to be a spaceship technician when he first started at NASA."

The man kissed his children goodnight and Daphne closed the door behind them. Galen handed Glenn a solar torch. Together with his friends, they set out in the dark to see the computer bunker. Mia bounded along with them.

Jonathon walked beside Glenn. "We do our normal jobs during the day and at night we scout around. As Galen has already mentioned, the animals are our friends, so they don't bother us anymore. If we poke around during the day, some of the watchers who are still on Valdena's side will report us and we can't afford to have that happen. I'm just going to show you the computer area now, but I'll go back early in the morning before it gets light and start my search for your father. If I try to hack the main database now, an alarm will go off in the glass tower, because no one will be working. It's just how Valdena has set up her system. During the day, so much activity takes place in the main computer area that no one will notice anything amiss."

As the humans walked, several animals greeted them and the party responded. Glenn said nothing, but smiled at the strange creatures. It was very dark and he could only make out shapes.

Gary explained. "We have purposely not installed lights here because we want to travel in secret. The animals don't bother us when it's dark, but if we happen to come across one that doesn't belong to our circle, we simply stun them. Our weapons are not lethal, but we have someone working on a more effective weapon."

The group stopped at a blank wall and Glenn watched in amazement as a door opened and closed silently behind them. Inside the well-lit complex, they descended a flight of stairs and entered a huge cave. The lights from the stairway blinked out and a door closed quietly behind them. More lights came on and Glenn saw the rows of computers against the walls. They looked nothing like the modern computers that Glenn knew, but were impressive anyway. Jonathon explained proudly what each computer could do and they spent a while discussing what they would do to find Craig. By the time they left, it was quite late. The rebels dispersed when they were close to Galen's house and vanished into the night. On the journey back, Mia complained her feet hurt and Glenn scooped her into his arms where she lay contentedly snuggled against his chest.

Galen went inside and Daphne made them something warm to drink. Afterwards, Galen excused himself and got ready for bed. Daphne followed soon afterwards, leaving Glenn alone with the peacat.

"Shouldn't you be getting home now?" he asked her curiously.

Mia yawned. "My friend knows I sometimes wander and she doesn't question me, but I'm too tired to walk another step. Can I sleep with you on your bed? I'll be very quiet."

Glenn had a quick wash and brushed his teeth. He climbed into bed and Mia joined him, snuggling beside him and soon both were fast asleep.

The next morning Glenn woke late. He had slept peacefully, even though he was worried about his father. The house was quiet and everyone had left. Carter assumed the children attended school, and Galen had told him he was a farmer, so he was probably out tending to the fields.

Daphne returned a while later and asked Glenn if she could get him anything, but he declined. He had found some fruit on the dining room table and snacked on that. Mia returned about midday and invited him to go for a walk with her. She took him to a cool stream and stretched out on the soft grass.

"This is my favourite spot to come and visit. It's very isolated and we are safe from prying eyes. It won't help if one of the watchers discovers you and reports your whereabouts to the 'higher powers'. I know you're worried about your father, but if there is any news, Jonathon will tell us tonight."

Mia and Glenn spent the afternoon telling their stories. The blue cat questioned him about his mother and sister and he showed the cat some pictures of them stored on his mobile device. Mia told him about life on Saurus. The time passed quickly and they made their way back to Galen's house in the late afternoon.

After supper, Jonathon and Gary came to visit. They got comfortable on the chairs in the small living room.

"Did you find anything on Craig?" Galen asked.

Jonathon looked very unhappy. "Yes I did. The good news is he is alive and well here on Saurus, but the bad news is he's living in Computerville."

"Why is that bad news?" Glenn asked. "He's alive, thank the stars!"

"Oh no!" Galen exclaimed. "Computerville is hostile territory! None of the animals or humans who live there are friends of ours. That area is so heavily guarded, even a mouse won't get through undetected. The animals there have orders and they shoot to kill! They don't ask questions. Craig must be working on the computers in the inner sanctuary. It's where all the elite and talented people work. Computerville means exactly what its name suggests! Everyone there is a computer operator. Some work in the laboratories where Valdena creates her unusual animals, while others operate the mind wipe machines. The computer staff have their own transport and live in bigger houses than the ones you have seen so far."

"Yes, and there are high gates patrolled by their most vicious animals," Jonathon replied mournfully. "Unless you have a special pass, you cannot enter. I'm unable to duplicate these passes."

Glenn stared stubbornly at the men. "We have to find a way to get inside! I'm not leaving without my father!"

"It's hopeless!" Gary complained. "We have to assume if he has access to their computers, his mind has been wiped! Even if we find a way to get inside and his memory has been erased, he won't come willingly. Craig could give us up to the authorities!"

The group discussed every possibility and couldn't find a solution. Daphne overheard and sat with the men. "Gary, you have friends in the hospital wing. The security there is much more relaxed than anywhere else. Every citizen of Saurus has to go to the hospital for a monthly check-up. Couldn't you rescue him then?"

Galen laughed and hugged his mate. "I knew there was a reason I kept you around! That's perfect! Gary can you find out when he's due for a hospital visit?"

"I can do that. I'm going to visit my girlfriend tonight anyway. She's a nurse at the hospital, so I'll ask her to check the patient's files. I'll come by the farm tomorrow sometime and let you know."

Jonathon nodded. "I'll also hack into the hospital records and see if I can get an answer, just in case your girlfriend doesn't get a chance to look for us. There's another problem though. I checked the address where Craig stays, but he's been given a partner. You know how Valdena is! She wants them to be fruitful and multiply!"

Glenn covered his mouth. "Ugh, don't tell me that! My mother will kill him herself if she finds out."

"Then don't tell her! Anyway, the reason I mentioned it is because I did some snooping on his mate. Monica lost her previous husband a few months ago. He had a tragic accident! According to the records, he went to drink some water at a river that flows near his house, but he tripped over a rock and hit his head on a bigger one nearby. He fell into the river and drowned! Monica works closely with Valdena. She might even be one of the beings who help that witch create the animals that are supposed to guard us! Valdena knew exactly who Craig was the moment her security forces found him! There's no other explanation for his present location, although his computer skills probably did help! She tried to keep Craig here the last time he arrived, but Andocia put a spanner in the works. That woman wants your father close by! Anyway, if Craig disappears suddenly, Monica will run to the authorities immediately."

Galen thought about it for a moment. "We have to arrange Craig's rescue at a time when Monica won't miss him for a while. The hospital can be accessed from the inner sanctuary, so it would be more convenient if he could go for his check up after work. The hospital isn't very busy at night so we stand a better chance of getting him away at that time. Obviously the later, the better. Then with a bit of luck, Monica will only miss him the next morning and you should be well on your way."

Gary agreed. "I'll speak to my friend and see what she can organise."

"I'll still check when he's due for his next hospital visit," Jonathon replied.

His visitors left and Galen spoke to Glenn. "It's a good plan and I have every confidence we'll succeed in rescuing your father. Once Jonathon and Gary report back to me tomorrow, we'll plan our strategy. I know you're anxious to have your father safely in your ship, but just be patient a little longer. If all goes well, we can implement the plan within the next two days."

The man got up and smiled. "Glenn you have no idea just how amazing your father is! He had such foresight about the possibility of this happening to him. Just wait a moment – I have something to show you!"

Galen went to his wardrobe and brought out an electronic reading device. He sat down next to Glenn and switched it on.

"This isn't the original device your father gave me; it's a more modern one we managed to obtain from one of our contacts who work with Valdena. I transferred the data onto it because the other one was very old. Every time

I feel downhearted, I open this file and read what your father wrote all those years ago, but there's something on it I would like you to read."

Galen scrolled down until he found the place he wanted and handed it to Glenn. The young man began to read.

Dear Galen,

It has been a great privilege to meet you. I cannot thank you enough for risking your life to help Andocia and I. As I mentioned before, she and I aren't friends, but I had no choice in the matter. She has kidnapped my wife and unborn child. This is my problem and I'll sort it out once we return to our universes. I have downloaded this information because you deserve to know what yours and Daphne's origins were.

I don't know what you plan to do with this knowledge, but I'll leave that up to both of you to decide. I have spoken to a number of people who might be able to help you, and their names are written at the end of this letter. I wish I could have found out more information, but Valdena was becoming suspicious and I didn't want to risk it. My dear friend, I never revealed to anyone that you were helping me because I didn't want to get you in trouble. If Andocia hadn't needed me, I would have been one of Valdena's subjects by now.

I do have one request though; if I should find myself back on Saurus, for whatever reason and Valdena succeeds in erasing my memory, I hope fervently that someone will come looking for me. Please Galen, if this happens and you find out about it, I would be very grateful if you would do everything you can to help them find me. There are very intelligent beings living in the Milky Way who could perhaps help me regain my memory. Even if they don't succeed, I know my family will take care of me.

Your friend,
Craig.

Glenn finished reading and wiped his wet eyes. He was touched by his father's heartfelt words. Galen nodded in agreement. "Your father is an amazing man and a good one too. Do you understand why I would risk my life to save him?"

"Yes, I do! He's an inspiration to my family as well and we need to have him back in our lives, so let's do this thing and rescue my dad!"

"Yes, we will! Now we just have to be patient and let my friends do their research. It won't be long before you and your father are reunited again."

The next afternoon, Jonathon and Gary arrived to see Galen. He was busy planting seeds and they followed him into the corn field, where the crop grew higher than their heads, shielding them from possible watchers who could be flying around.

Gary was the first one to report.

"I spoke to my girlfriend and she checked the hospital records. Craig is due for an examination in two days. His appointment is scheduled for 15H00. He sees Dr Brunswick and our sources tell us that although he is loyal to Valdena, he has doubts about her methods. I'm sure he will help us. My girlfriend has assisted him in some of his operations and they have a good working relationship. She says she can persuade him to come up with some way to help us and Craig."

Galen thought about it. "Two days gives us plenty of time to implement this. We have a lot to organise so we had better get started! Firstly though, we need to change the time of his appointment. Check Dr Brunswick's diary and see what time he finishes work, then schedule Craig's examination for the last appointment of the day. That should give us plenty of time to whisk him away. Gary, can you ask your girlfriend to speak to Dr Brunswick and find out how we can attract the least amount of attention? We'll need his help on this quest."

"I'll get right on it!" he promised.

"Jonathon, you hack into the hospital computer and change Craig's appointment. We had better meet at someone else's house tonight. The watchers might get suspicious if they see I have the same visitors three days in a row."

Jonathon grinned. "Well Isabel has been nagging me to invite you over for dinner, so let's do that tonight. Maybe Gary can bring his girlfriend if he wants to. That way we can fill her in without wasting any more time. Glenn has to come along of course, but if we are questioned, I'll say he is my nephew from Meadowbrooke. That way the watchers won't be suspicious because different beings are responsible for each city."

Galen nodded enthusiastically. "That's a good idea! Okay, we'll see you tonight!"

The men left and that evening Galen explained what they had found out.

Galen, Daphne and Glenn went over to Jonathon's house and the other conspirators joined them. After introductions all around, the group of rebels sat down to discuss their plans. Jonathon reported he had changed the time of Craig's appointment to 19H00. Dr Brunswick would be on duty for the whole evening though and this suited them nicely. Diane, Gary's girlfriend promised she would speak to the doctor and report back to Gary the next day. She confirmed the time had been changed and Craig would now come in later. They spent most of the evening making plans and parted company late that night. The next day, Galen complained to his farmhands he wasn't feeling well, and stayed home to make final plans for Craig's rescue.

32

Meanwhile, in Computerville, Craig woke at the usual time and sat down to have his breakfast. Monica fussed over him and made sure he had everything he needed. When he was ready to leave, he kissed his mate goodbye.

"I'll be home late tonight Monica. I have to go for my monthly check at the hospital. I'll probably put in a bit of overtime because there's no point in coming home and then leaving soon afterwards anyway. Don't worry about supper for me. I'll eat something at the hospital's cafeteria after my examination."

"I understand, my love. See you much later tonight!"

Craig climbed into his transport and waved goodbye to Monica.

That evening, "operation rescue" began. Craig finished work and went through the doors that led to the hospital. He was met by Dr Brunswick, who shook his hand vigorously.

"Good evening Craig! How are you feeling?"

"I'm fine, thanks."

"I'm glad to hear that. Are you sleeping better now?"

"Yes I am."

"Have you had any more nightmares?"

"No, thank the stars! I used to feel so agitated, but now everything is fine."

"I know your leg was bothering you a while ago. Has that improved?"

"Definitely! I still get twinges when it rains though."

The doctor chuckled. "That's perfectly normal I assure you. Is anything bothering you? No headaches or other pains?"

"No, everything's good."

Dr Brunswick asked him to lie down while he checked Craig's blood pressure and reflexes. He was glad to find Craig in excellent health.

"Okay now we have one more thing to do! You need to have a full body X-ray done so I can check everything's working the way it should. Diane will wheel you to the X-ray department and I'll see you later, okay."

Craig grinned. "I know the routine! I can find my own way there."

Dr Brunswick patted him on the shoulder. "I know you can, but it's a new hospital policy that has recently been implemented, so bear with us, okay."

Craig nodded and climbed into a wheelchair. He waved to the doctor. "See you soon!"

Dr Brunswick nodded. "Goodbye Craig!"

Diane pushed him into the X-ray department. It was already late so he was the only patient present. Diane waited while he had the scan done and climbed back into the wheelchair. The X-ray department closed for the night and handed his scan to Diane. They made their way back to Dr Brunswick, who barely glanced at it. Craig sat with his back to the nurse so he didn't see the nod that passed between the doctor and nurse. Diane removed an instrument from her pocket and leaned over Craig.

"It's almost over now and then you can go home."

Dr Brunswick distracted him and the nurse placed the device against their patient's neck and pulled the trigger. Carter's eyes opened wide in surprise and he tried to speak, but before he could utter a sound, his head fell forward and he was fast asleep.

Diane hurried to the door and beckoned to someone dressed as an orderly. Together they pushed a bed closer to the entrance and both men laid Craig on top of it. Diane threw a sheet over his body, covering him completely. The "orderly" wheeled the bed down the passageway towards a building marked MORTUARY. Another nurse passed by and stared at the bed. The orderly shook his head and sighed. "Poor guy didn't make it! He had a heart attack."

The nurse nodded and continued on her way.

Galen allowed himself a smile of satisfaction and wheeled the bed through the mortuary and out a side door where a delivery truck waited, engine idling.

The driver got out and quickly helped his friend to unload the sedated man. He was placed on a mattress and covered with clean linen. Dirty linen was randomly placed over the body of the sleeping man, but they left a space to allow him to breathe. Glenn Carter watched as his father was placed in the van and then jumped inside the truck. Galen climbed in the back of the truck with Craig.

They drove for a while, then stopped the truck in some dense bushes. Galen whistled and a man and woman came out of the bushes. They embraced one another and introduced the newcomers to Glenn. The men took Craig and placed him in another vehicle piled high with vegetables. Glenn climbed in the back of the farm truck and covered himself with the produce as well. The newcomers wore the uniforms of the linen company to which the truck belonged and drove it away. The rest of them drove to Galen's house, but Daphne came hurrying out and whispered urgently to her mate. Galen ran to the driver of the farm vehicle.

"There's been a change of plan! Take Glenn and his father to the computer bunker and hide them there!"

"What happened?" Glenn asked nervously.

"I'm not sure, but somehow the 'higher powers' found out that Craig was missing. They have issued a warning that every house in every city is to be searched! There's a reward for the capture of the perpetrators. If they are caught, they will be executed immediately! I'm sorry, but you'll have to stay in hiding until the furore dies down, No one knows about the computer bunker, so you'll be safe there."

"What if my father wakes up in the meantime! I was counting on him remaining unconscious until we were safely away from here!"

"There's nothing I can do about it! You're a smart kid, so think of something to keep him quiet. I have to go inside and pretend that everything is normal. No one is going to get any sleep tonight."

"My ship isn't far from here. I'm sure I'll make it." Glenn replied desperately.

Galen squeezed his shoulder. "It's not safe! Valdena has extremely sophisticated spaceships unlike anything you have ever seen before. You won't even get out into Space and she'll have you in her clutches. I don't know her very well, but if she's anything like Andocia, you won't stand a chance, now get going! There's supplies in the bunker so you should be okay for a while. Someone will check up on you when it's safe. I'll let you know when everything is back to normal."

Glenn climbed reluctantly back into the truck and the driver sped off. He stayed only to help the young explorer carry his father down into the bunker, then left. He drove the truck out into the field and parked it under a make-shift shelter, before melting quietly into the undergrowth.

The young man checked on his father, but he was still fast asleep. He found some supplies in a cupboard, but was too nervous to eat anything. Glenn looked at the computers and saw a screen mounted on a wall. He switched it on and the cameras Galen and his friends had placed around the trees, came to life. The explorer sat on one of the chairs and watched as the forest suddenly filled with humans and strange animals carrying nasty weapons. They fanned out, but it was obvious the strange creatures were in charge, because they ordered the humans around. He looked at his father and wondered why they made such a fuss about one individual. As he looked at his father's face, so peaceful in sleep, he began to realise just how amazing he must be. He was a "legend" in Space, earning the title because of his incredible success in capturing criminals. However, when anyone asked for details, he would smile and reply it was his job. Everyone treated him with great respect and Glenn vowed if the Saturnians could help his father, he would question him extensively about his life. It had come as a shock to Glenn when he realised why Craig had helped Andocia all those years ago, instead of leaving her on Saurus. His mother had never told him she was being held captive, nor that she was pregnant with him at the time. Glenn watched the monitors for a while, then lay down on the narrow bed, next to the one his father was sleeping in.

Glenn woke suddenly and realised he had managed to fall asleep despite his fears. He jumped up suddenly when his father's face came into view.

"Who are you and where am I?" he asked angrily.

Glenn sat up and rubbed his eyes. "Oh, you're awake! Please don't freak out on me!" he pleaded, "I can explain."

Craig folded his arms across his chest. "Well, I'm waiting for an explanation! The last thing I remember was being at the hospital for my monthly check up. Why have you brought me here?"

"I know it sounds ridiculous, but some of us rescued you last night. Do you recognise me at all?"

His father stared curiously at him. "No, I can't say I do. Have we met before?"

"Yes, we have! My name is Glenn and I am your son."

Craig stared at his offspring as though he had grown another head. "I don't have any children! Is this some kind of a joke?"

"No I swear it's the truth. You aren't a citizen of Saurus. You live on Earth with my mother, Constance, myself and your daughter April. Don't you remember anything at all? Try your best to remember them please. It's very important!"

Craig shook his head. "I'm sorry young man, but I don't remember any of you. I have a mate who I live with here on Saurus. Her name is Monica and she's going to be very worried about me. I have to get back to her."

Glenn put his hand on his father's arm. "Dad, I know this is hard for you to understand, but we'll think of a way to get your memory back."

Craig shook his head. "I'm not going insane! I have a mate here and a job in the administration block. You have to take me back to her before you get into trouble."

Glenn walked over to the computer screen and pointed outside. "I'm already in trouble! They are looking for you. In any case, the door to this bunker has been locked from the outside, so even if I wanted to set you free – which I certainly don't, we are stuck here until our friends come and fetch us."

His father pointed to the weapon in a holster by Glenn's side. "If you are trying to help me, why do you have a gun?"

"It's not to scare you, but I need it for protection in case we are discovered. Don't try and grab it please, I'm begging you. I don't want to hurt you."

Craig looked at the gun in disgust. "Why would I do that? I don't even know how to use one of those things! I'm just a computer operator."

Glenn stood up and sighed. "All right, can we just call a truce for now? I'm hungry and I could use something to eat and drink. You must be starving as well."

Craig nodded. "Now that you mention it, I could use something. What do you have?"

"I don't know what's here. Let's go and check."

The young man scratched in the cupboard and fridge and found some butter, jam and eggs. His search yielded a loaf of bread as well. There was a small cupboard containing some supplies, as well as a kettle and toaster. Canisters containing tea, coffee and creamer stood in a row nearby.

Glenn got busy and cooked breakfast and they ate silently, each occupied with their own thoughts. Afterwards he made them some coffee. His search the previous evening had uncovered a small bathroom containing a shower, toilet and washbasin. The young man allowed his father to freshen up first and then sat down with him.

"Dad, I know you don't believe me, but please keep an open mind for now. I have to know I can trust you, otherwise I'll be forced to restrain you. I don't know when we'll be able to leave this place, but just bear with me for a while. I mean you no harm, I swear it on my mother and sister's lives."

Craig looked kindly at his son. "I can't explain it, but I'm starting to feel some sort of a connection between us. I'm prepared to trust you and hopefully we can resolve this problem. I still have no recollection of you and the rest of your family though. I just have one request. Please call me Craig. It feels strange to be referred to as 'dad'."

"I can do that… Craig. Do you mind if I go and freshen up now? Afterwards you can ask me any questions that are bothering you and I'll try to answer them, okay."

"Okay Glenn."

Glenn went to freshen up and returned to find his father staring at the computers.

"These are nothing like the ones in the administration block. Those are more modern."

"I guess the rebels had to make do with whatever they could find. I'm not all that interested in computers."

"What do you do for a living Glenn?"

"I explore Space."

His father was surprised. "That's a dangerous profession! I hear there are many perils out in the universes. What made you decide to explore Space?"

"You did," he replied. "You are… were a Space explorer too. I decided to follow in your footsteps. Mom also explores Space, but April is still young so she doesn't like to leave her alone for long periods of time."

"What can you tell me about your sister?"

"She still attends school. She's only fifteen. I'm eighteen."

They spoke for a while. Glenn kept checking the monitor, hoping things would quieten down and they could leave. It did seem quieter, but they still saw some security forces wandering around. Glenn wasn't expecting anyone to come and visit because of the increased security. He was very surprised therefore when they did receive an unexpected visitor.

Glenn heard a scratching noise coming from the bathroom and went to investigate. Mia was outside the small window and he let her in.

"Mia, what are you doing here? Did anyone see you?"

The peacat looked haughtily at him. "Huh, I wasn't a watcher for nothing you know. I have mastered the art of sneaking around without being seen."

Glenn laughed. "I apologise! I'm forgetting who I'm talking to!"

"Is Craig awake?"

"Yes, he woke up earlier on. Come and say hello."

Mia looked at him enquiringly and tapped her head with her paw. He shook his head mournfully.

Mia walked slowly in the room and Craig stared at her. "Who is this?"

"Dad... uh Craig, this is Mia. Don't you remember her?"

Craig stared at her for a long time. "No, I'm sorry, I don't! I've seen pictures of her somewhere though."

"Probably on the computers in the admin block," Mia suggested.

"Yes, that's probably where I saw your picture. You're a watcher aren't you?" Craig enquired.

"I was, but I'm retired now."

"What are you doing here?" he asked curiously.

"I guess you don't remember me," she sighed. "We had a great adventure together, long ago."

Craig shook his head. "No, sorry, I don't."

Mia looked kindly at him. "Well I still admire you! I've never met anyone like you before, but it doesn't matter. You will always be in my thoughts."

She turned to Glenn. "Galen sent me to update you on the situation. It's been very hectic outside. I have never seen so many guards in one place at the same time. They desperately want to find your father, but I think they will be giving up soon. According to some of my contacts, they believe he has been taken into Space and has left the planet. When it gets dark, they'll give up their search and you can take your father and leave. Galen will come here after the sun sets and he's bringing Jonathon and Gary with to make the final arrangements. Until then he has asked you to stay here. Meanwhile I've brought you some fresh fruit to eat. Oh, Galen also wanted to know how far away your ship is."

"It should take me half an hour to reach it, heading in a northerly direction."

"Okay that's fine. We only have one problem and that is, we cannot give you any supplies. The rebels want to travel light so you can all cover as much ground as possible in a short time. It's too dangerous for the two of you to stay here any longer. It would only endanger yourselves, as well as the rebels."

"It's not a problem Mia. Once we reach our own universe, I'll stop at a Space station and get some if I need anything."

"Good, it's settled then."

The blue cat looked sadly up at Craig. "I'm sorry you don't remember what happened last time, but I want to wish you and Glenn well. I'm going to leave soon and I doubt if we shall ever see one another again. I'm old now and my lifespan will be ending soon. I won't go and see you off either, because my steps have become slower now and I'll just hold you back."

She jumped on Craig's lap and kneaded him with her paws. "I wish you well and a safe journey! I hope your friends will be able to give you back your memories. Goodbye dear friend!"

She went to Glenn and he cuddled her. "You take good care of your father, no matter what happens understand! I'm glad I got the opportunity to meet you. If you are anything like your father, you might become the next legend in Space. It has truly been an honour and I'll cherish these memories until the day I leave this place forever and cease to exist."

The cat went back to the bathroom window and they heard her meowing softly and sadly before she climbed out of the window and left them alone.

Craig wiped his eyes. "I wish I remembered her! She seems very special."

Glenn also had a lump on his throat. "I only met her a few days ago and she has charmed me too."

That evening Galen and his friends came to visit. They each brought something to share for supper, but the women weren't with them. It was felt they would be safer at home as the situation was still tense. Galen shook Craig's hand and explained how he came to be helping Glenn and didn't seem to mind that his friend didn't remember him. Jonathon however was very curious and recognised a computer expert when he met him. The subject turned to the computers they used in the bunker and Craig told them about the ones in the inner sanctuary. Jonathon sighed and explained their situation about the limited access they had because of security protocols. Craig sensed these men were truly honourable and decided to help them. He asked for permission to use their computers which they granted. He then proceeded to write down all the security codes which would allow them unlimited access to the computers in the administration building and showed them what to do. Galen and his friends were speechless with joy and Craig explained his actions.

"I don't remember any of you, but according to Glenn, you are the ones who require this knowledge. Valdena cannot continue to experiment on animals and people the way she has been doing. Whether or not I regain my memories isn't important, but your future is. If what Glenn tells me is true, my life will be in great danger if I ever set foot on this planet again. Next time Valdena won't just wipe my mind, she'll probably kill me."

Jonathon's expression was grim. "You can bet on that, Craig! By giving us the security codes, you are committing treason against her and her cohorts. It was an honour to meet the legend Galen was always bragging about, and now we understand exactly why he sang your praises. Your story will be used as an inspiration to our children and grandchildren."

They all stood up and clapped.

"Now let's get you home!" Galen replied.

The small party left the safety of the bunker and walked quickly to the spot where Glenn had sent his ship into Space. He pressed an icon on his mobile device and the ship appeared, landing quietly on the grass. The door opened silently and the two Earthlings went aboard. Galen suppressed an urge to ask for a tour and they waved goodbye. A few minutes later, the ship rose into the sky and disappeared from sight.

33

Craig looked around the spaceship as though seeing it for the first time. He couldn't remember ever having flown one before. The man sat in the co-pilot's seat and watched as Glenn did all his checks, but nothing came back to him.

"Where are we going now, Glenn?"

"I'm taking you to the Saturnians. Maybe they can help you regain your memory, but first we have to get back to our own universe."

Glenn put in the codes he had learnt from his father's notes and soon they had passed through the thin veil of fog that separated the future from the past. He breathed a sigh of relief when the digital clock on his computer began counting backwards and stopped at their time period once more. Glenn re-entered the time vortex where he had initially gone through to rescue his father. The ship appeared near where Uranus had disappeared and he saw the planet had still not returned to its original orbit, but at least he was closer to Saturn and had not gone through the blue universe, thus avoiding Andocia's territory.

Craig had been silent for a while, but now he voiced his concern.

"I still don't remember very much and it disturbs me. What if I never get those memories back? My career will be over!"

"Don't be so pessimistic. The Saturnians are the cleverest race in the universe and they will do everything in their power to help you."

They landed on Saturn and Craig smiled politely at those he had known before, but he was very formal. Once they had sat down in one of the laboratories, Glenn explained what had happened. He was shooed outside and told to amuse himself, while they did tests on Craig so they could assess the damage. Glenn wandered around aimlessly, hoping desperately for some good news. Finally he was called into a private room, where Lara spoke to him. Her face was grave.

"Glenn I don't know how to tell you this, but we can't help your father. I have no idea how they did it, but there's nothing to work with. Your father is still the same person he was before, but he's like a child. The Saurians didn't damage his brain tissue, thank goodness, but your father will have to re-learn everything from the beginning. It's like when your people program a robot, or computer. You start with the bare essentials and feed it knowledge until it knows everything you want it to. That's what your colleagues will have to do."

"Lara, that's all very well, but he had a lifetime of experiences. If it's impossible for him to get all that knowledge back, what will become of his career?"

"I can't answer that, I'm afraid. At the moment he doesn't know who his friends or enemies are. Think of the danger he'll be in! He could allow someone like Tyrus for example, to get close to him, and then the silver creature would kill him. At best I would say that Space Control Centre would have to grant your father an early retirement. I'm sorry the news isn't encouraging. Take him home now and just be supportive."

Glenn nodded and smiled, but his lip trembled. Lara knew he was fighting for self-control and tactfully took her leave of the handsome explorer. The young man stayed alone in the room for a while until he had composed himself, then went to meet his father. Craig was depressed, but tried to put on a brave front. They left soon afterwards and began the journey back to Earth.

They hadn't gone far before problems developed in the ship. Glenn set the controls for Earth, but they wouldn't respond. His father came to look. "What's wrong, Glenn?"

"I don't know! I'm trying to set a course for Earth, but the computer has shut me out."

Craig was worried. "Oh dear, do you suppose you damaged it by going so far ahead in time?"

"It's possible I suppose, but I doubt it."

Craig leaned over his son. "Let me take a look and see if I can isolate the problem."

Glenn let his father sit in the pilot seat and watched him carefully. His father typed in a few commands, but everything was working perfectly and he could find no fault with it at all. Craig consulted with the onboard computer and a sulky female answered. <I am undamaged and there is nothing wrong with my system!>

"I am shut out of your operating system. Can you return control to me?" Craig asked politely.

<Negative! I am not in control. Unknown forces are controlling me.>

Father and son stared bewildered at one another. "What now?" Craig enquired.

"I guess we will just have to wait and see," Glenn sighed.

"What if Valdena has found us!" Carter asked wild-eyed.

"Ohhh, I hope not."

Glenn stared stupefied as the computer came on line once again and showed a course correction for the Golden Way. Both men sighed and decided to let the ship take them wherever it had been programmed to go.

They cleared the nearest jump vortex and emerged in the blue universe. It was obvious that the computer was communicating with something, but they weren't sure what. The craft sailed on until a Space station came into view.

"What Space station is this, Glenn?" asked his father interestedly.

"I don't know! I've never entered this part of the universe before."

Their ship sailed into the docking area and came to rest on a landing pad, of its own accord. The door swung open and Glenn peered nervously outside. He stared in awe at the Sofagins and Craig was just behind him. He too saw the beings, but he had no memory that they even existed.

"Welcome to you both. Please step down. Rest assured, we mean you no harm."

Glenn's hand still hovered close to his laser gun though, but he never took it out.

"Who are you?"

"We are known as the Sofagins and have come to hear of your plight. Your mother, Constance Carter knows of our existence. She requested our help a while ago when Tyrus and Andocia were terrorising the Saturnians in your universe."

"She has never mentioned you before," replied Glenn suspiciously.

"Ah yes, of course, but you were very young at the time. We swore her to secrecy. She knew of our existence, but was unable to share that information with others. She probably told your father about us, but now of course he has little or no memory to speak of, so he won't remember anyway."

"How do you know that?" queried Glenn.

"Very little of what happens in this universe escapes us. We have been following your brief career with interest, Glenn Carter, and you show great promise. Perhaps you will be the next legend of Space."

"Why have you brought us here against our will? You obviously controlled our computer."

"Yes indeed! Your equipment is so antiquated and it was easy to hack into your system. Please follow me and I'll explain why we brought you here."

Both men followed the Sofagin to a comfortable room, where they were invited to sit down. The being came straight to the point.

"Your father has gone through a traumatic time at the hands of the Saurians. Valdena seems to think she has a right to play with humans as though they were toys. We have the means to help your father regain his memory, but we need permission to go ahead."

Glenn turned to his father. "Dad, it's your life and therefore your decision. Do you want to risk it?"

Craig was hesitant. "I don't know about this. What guarantee can you give me that you won't destroy my mind completely, leaving me insane?"

"I understand your reluctance, but we helped your wife once as I mentioned before. In fact, you and I are also acquainted. You obviously don't remember because of what the Saurians did to you. I know you went to the Saturnians and they couldn't help you. What have you really got to lose?"

Craig hesitated and the being continued.

"Mr Carter, what waits for you back on Earth? Your memory is gone and with it all the skills you learnt. I'm willing to bet that if someone engaged you in hand to hand combat, you wouldn't know what to do. We have followed your illustrious career right from the beginning and know you have very powerful enemies. If Andocia arrived unexpectedly, what would you do?"

"Andocia?" queried Craig. "Who's that?"

The being turned to Glenn. "See what I mean? You know what she can do, even if your father has forgotten. She is his most powerful enemy. Need I say more?"

Glenn sighed. "I don't know if we can trust you. It looks as though we don't have a choice, but the final decision is still up to my father."

Both of them turned to Craig.

"All right, I'm desperate enough to try anything. I agree to place myself in your care, but how long will I have to stay?"

"I can't be sure just yet. We need to subject you to various tests. I know you resent that, but it can't be helped. When we have done what we can, we'll contact your son. Do you agree?"

"All right, it's settled then," replied Craig.

Glenn left soon afterwards and they returned him to his own universe. Once he had cleared the jump vortex, they relinquished control of the craft and gave it back to him. Glenn knew he had cut several days off his travelling time, but he didn't want to question the Sofagins too closely. He had been warned not to speak about them and he agreed.

On returning to Earth, Glenn went straight home. His mother and sister embraced him joyfully.

"Oh Glenn it's so good to see you again!" exclaimed Constance happily. "Did you have any luck?"

"Yes, but it's a long story. Mom, Dad is alive, but he isn't well. I left him with some beings who promised to help him. Dad sent his love and said you mustn't worry about him."

"But when will Dad be back with us?" asked April curiously.

"I don't know yet. These beings said they would contact me, so we just have to wait and see."

↓ ↓ ↓

One day, a message flashed on the computer screen at the Carter home and Glenn read it. In his excitement, he forgot to switch off the computer and ran to his mother.

"Mom, Dad is much better! I have to go and get him."

"That's wonderful news. Hurry up, because I long to hold your father in my arms again."

Later, when Constance walked past the computer, she saw it was switched on, but there was no message. It had been deleted.

Glenn returned to deep Space and the computer developed a mind of its own again. This time he sat back and enjoyed the ride. Once back in the Space station, he was taken to see his father. He approached with trepidation, not sure what he would find. Several Sofagins were fussing over him, but they moved aside when Glenn approached. Craig stood up and despite the onlookers; he grabbed his son in a bear hug.

"Glenn, it's wonderful to see you again! I've missed everyone so much. Thanks to the Sofagins, I've regained my memory. I remember how I came to be captured by the Saurians, but not what they actually did to me. I don't think I want to know though. The Sofagins blotted that experience out of my mind."

"That was probably a wise decision on their part. Do you remember everything else?"

"Yes, I do and it's a wonderful feeling! Not only do I remember everyone and everything about my life, I still have the knowledge Valdena gave me. I knew a lot about computers before, but now I know so much more! I want to go home and hold your mother in my arms. It has been much too long! How is she holding up?"

"She has been wonderful throughout this whole nasty experience."

Glenn turned to the Sofagins. "Thank you for helping us, but could you perhaps explain how you managed to give my father back all his memories, without any side effects?"

The leader smiled at the two explorers. "It was actually a very simple procedure. When we did a scan of your father's brain, we found some of his neurological pathways had been altered. Both of you work on computers, in your ships and at home. When you want to save something for future reference, you open a new document, or file for that information to be stored in. The human brain is very similar. For many years it has become common knowledge that human beings only use a small section of their brains. Therefore the brain has many unused files, for want of a better word. Do you understand what I mean?"

"I think so," Craig replied.

"Yes, well in simple terms, that's what Valdena did. She relocated your existing memories to one of the unused files where they were stored. Then she enhanced your computer knowledge to the level that suited her, and made that your dominant memories. So, she didn't erase anything, she just stored it in the back of your mind, which you weren't using anyway. We redirected the information back to the correct pathway and that's why you remember everything. Nothing has been lost."

Craig and Glenn thanked the Sofagins for their help and set off back to Earth. When they arrived, Constance and April were waiting for them at the Control Centre. Brother and sister winked at one another and excused themselves, so their parents could have some time alone.

34

However, the Carter family were destined for more trouble in the very near future. The peace treaty between Tanus and Andocia was broken and they were once again at loggerheads with one another. The first inkling of this reached the Carters when Deliah contacted them via the linkup.

"Well Deliah, to what do we owe the honour?" asked Craig curiously.

"I have news for you and your family. The peace treaty has been dissolved and Andocia asked me to tell you about it. We have planned everything down to the last detail, so now we are going to take over your universe. The delay was simply to allow us time to plan everything. You don't seem very surprised, Mr Carter."

"Should I be? I knew your mother was stalling for time. Thanks for the warning; I'll be on my guard from now on. Was that all?" he asked dismissively.

"No, that's not all. You had better settle your affairs quickly."

"Why, does Andoica want to kill me?" asked Craig snidely.

"Not at the moment, but things change. She plans to capture all of you and exile you on another planet for the rest of your lives. You'll be helpless to stop us taking control of your world and the others in your solar system."

"First you have to catch us!" challenged Craig.

Deliah glared at him and the screen went blank.

Craig then contacted Tanus and a few hours later, Tarmin appeared. She too wasn't surprised. "We expected this, Craig. Andocia isn't one to let the grass grow under her feet. She has plenty of ambition and your family are the only real obstacles that stand in her way, apart from Tanus of course. It just worries me she actually warned you. They must feel very confident that success is within their grasp; otherwise they would just have taken you by surprise. Where are Glenn and April?"

"Glenn is out in Space. He and April were invited to spend a few days on Neptune."

"They should enjoy it there. Neptune is a beautiful place. Craig, I would love to stay and chat, but I have to get back to Tanus. Are you going to contact Neptune and tell them about this threat?"

"Yes, I'll contact them when you leave," replied Craig.

"Craig, remember you still have the ring. If things get too hot for you and you find yourself in difficulties, prise the stone loose and it will return to Tanus. She'll send help."

Tarmin perched on an open windowsill and then flew away. Craig contacted the Neptunians and the message was relayed to his children. They were anxious to return home, but he put their minds at ease.

A few days later, Andocia attacked, but she had been clever. Husband and wife were seated in their lounge, their arms about one another. Craig sniffed the air curiously.

"What is it, darling?"

"Don't you smell that? It smells almost like an antiseptic."

Constance sat up straighter and inhaled. "Yes, you're right. What is it?"

"I don't know."

Before long, they began to feel stiff and Craig groaned unhappily.

"Damn that crafty witch! The stuff is paralysing gas! No wonder she was so confident; the effects last a few hours and should give her enough time to take over our planet without anyone being able to raise a hand to stop her. Constance, help me! I have to get this stone free and warn Tanus!"

There was no answer from his wife and Craig stared miserably at her shocked face. She was frozen, like a statue. He summoned all his strength and his left hand hovered close to the stone, but the gas took effect before he could dislodge it. He swore at Andocia under his breath, but it was too late.

He watched helplessly as Andocia and Deliah approached in triumph. The paralysed couple were picked up effortlessly and floated out of the apartment, towards the waiting ship. Craig cursed Andocia and everything she stood for, but she shrugged his insults off. He could only communicate telepathically and Andocia grinned triumphantly. When they were nearing the entrance to the ship, the hatch opened up, reminding the explorer of a deadly beast of prey, ready to swallow them whole.

Suddenly a blue/green beam shot out and engulfed both Andocia and Deliah. Both simultaneously let out a cry of pain and fell unconscious to the ground. Their followers hurried outside and grabbed their mistress and her daughter, casting a frightened glance at the heavens above, then the ship blasted off, leaving Craig and Constance lying, still paralysed, on the ground.

Constance watched in trepidation as an unfamiliar ship landed next to them and the Sofagins got out. Craig recognised them. The beings approached and greeted Craig like an old friend.

"Relax, Mr Carter and we'll soon have you back to normal again."

They were carrying portable oxygen masks and placed them over the noses and mouths of the Carters.

"Breathe slowly and deeply and you'll start to regain control of your muscles," they advised.

It wasn't long before both husband and wife felt better. They wanted to remove the oxygen, but the Sofagins stopped them.

"No, don't do that! If you do, you'll be paralysed once again. Your control centre is nearby, so I suggest you get a ship ready and leave this planet.

Andocia has paralysed the entire world, but we took care of her. When she recovers from our attack, the Earthlings will have woken up again. There is sufficient air in those containers to last you for six hours. Leave it for a few days, then come back here. Perhaps you should join your children on Neptune. When you have left Earth's atmosphere, you may remove those masks, for the gas will have been contained on your planet alone."

They thanked the Sofagins, who rose up and vanished in the blink of an eye. The couple ran to the Space Control Centre and readied a ship for departure. All their colleagues were frozen into various positions. When the craft had cleared Earth's atmosphere, they removed their masks. Constance was bursting with curiosity.

"All right, what do you think this all about? Why were they helping us?"

"I don't know what their plans are, but somehow I don't feel very reassured." Craig remarked. "The Sofagins are very powerful; you saw what they did to Andocia and Deliah."

"Yes I saw, but they did lend me a weapon to help the Saturnians when they were being threatened, so we know they are a threat to Andocia and Deliah," his wife replied.

"I was wondering if Andocia really knows of their existence," Craig remarked. "In all my dealings with her, she has never mentioned them."

"Well up until now, very few did. We knew, as did Glenn. They did mention that the two immortals knew of them, but I believe they were lying to us."

"So Andocia and Tanus have no real idea of their strength?" Craig surmised.

"Obviously not, or they would have taken steps to destroy them long ago. Where do we go from here, Craig?"

"I don't know, but something tells me we shouldn't bother Neptune at the moment. I think we must stay well away from Glenn and April for now. No one told the Sofagins that our children were on Neptune, so they have been spying on us for some reason. Did you notice they seemed keen for us to go to Neptune to be with Glenn and April?"

"Now you mention it…" stated Constance thoughtfully. "Should we warn the children?"

Craig shook his head emphatically." No, it wouldn't be a good idea. For all we know they could be monitoring our calls. Let's wait and see what happens in the next few days. I think it might be wise just to cruise around the universe for a while and not land on any planet."

"What about Andocia and Deliah? Won't they come after us with a vengeance now?"

"Maybe they'll try to track us down in a few days, but not just yet. They should be sick for a while at least, so we have time to spare. Afterwards, who knows! I think it would be wise for us to cruise around for about four days, then we can contact Glenn and April and warn them of a possible attack."

Three days later, Craig had a feeling of impending doom, so he broke the silence and contacted his children. They wanted to meet with their parents right away, but Craig stopped them. He told them to leave as soon as possible and cruise around, just as they were doing, and promised to keep in touch.

"Why didn't you let them come to us, Craig? Surely there is safety in numbers?"

"Not in this case, dearest. If Andocia launches an attack against us, she'll have us all in one tidy little parcel. Why should we make life easier for her?"

Constance nodded sagely. "That makes sense of course, but we can't stay up here for ever."

"I don't intend to. I'm not cruising around longer than a week. Things should have settled down on Earth by that time."

A few days later, Glenn contacted his parents and told them that he and April had left Neptune and would be cruising around. When he wanted to give his location, Craig stopped him.

"No, don't do that! If one of our spacecrafts falls into unfriendly hands, the other will have a better chance to escape detection. We'll stay here for another day, and then we'll be returning to Earth."

PART THREE

35

THE SOFAGINS

The next day, Craig pointed his ship towards Earth and began the journey back. He was running a routine diagnostic check, while Constance watched something on the built in video.

Suddenly the ship lurched and she jumped up.

"Craig what's happening?" she asked curiously.

He was staring morosely at the controls and muttering. The computer had gone into override mode once again and Constance tried desperately to regain control of the ship, which turned around of its own accord and headed elsewhere.

"Craig, what's wrong with you? Help me get the ship under control!"

Her husband placed his hand on her arm and sighed. "You have a short memory my love. Remember when you went to the Sofagins for help? They took control of the ship then as well."

Constance scowled and put her hands on her hips. "We really need to do something about this. I'm tired of being treated like a fish being reeled in on a line!"

"Why do you think they have made contact with us again?" Craig wondered.

"I don't know. Perhaps they want to tell us that Earth's atmosphere is liveable again."

"Maybe, but that doesn't make sense!" he reasoned, "why not just contact us on the comlink? Surely we don't need to go there."

Craig's jaw was set in a taut line as he removed his laser gun and checked the charge. It was almost full.

"Constance, I think we've been barking up the wrong tree, to quote an old saying. I have a feeling we are in trouble."

A Sofagin ship docked with them 15 minutes later and several of the beings entered their spacecraft. They were smiling, but there was nothing friendly about the Candy guns in their hands. The beings were equally surprised to find that husband and wife also had their weapons drawn. The leader stepped one pace in front of his colleagues and surveyed the couple.

"Oh Mr and Mrs Carter I'm disappointed! I thought we were friends."

"So did I!" retorted Craig furiously. "What are you up to?"

"I've been ordered to take you to our planet for safekeeping. Our leader wishes to meet with you."

"What if we aren't feeling sociable?" replied the explorer.

"This isn't a request, it's an order. You have to comply."

"No I don't! Why has he expressed an interest in us after all this time?"

"He will explain everything to you when we land. Mr Carter, be reasonable. You aren't a foolish man and you know the odds are against you." He looked at Constance. "You saw what this weapon did to Andocia; imagine what it can do to you."

Constance glanced at her husband and put out her hand to stop him, but he pushed it aside angrily.

The explorer aimed his laser gun at the creature's stomach and his finger tightened on the trigger. One of the guards took aim and the weapon spun out of Craig's grasp. He tensed to attack and a Candy gun was pointed at him. When the Sofagin pulled the trigger however, Craig found himself encased in a greenish/blue bubble. He pushed with all his might, but he remained trapped. Constance stared wide-eyed at the spectacle and was unsure what to do.

"Mrs Carter, put your weapon down and kick it towards me, otherwise we will kill you!"

Constance looked at her husband, and did as she was told. The Sofagin picked it up and handed it to someone else. Constance stood rooted to the spot and kept her hands in plain sight.

"What's going on?" demanded Craig angrily.

"I told you our leader wants you safely tucked away, so you can't jeopardise our mission."

Craig went cold. "What do you mean?"

"Our mission to take over Earth of course, but this is just the beginning. We lied to you about your planet. Your people are now comatose and no one can stop us taking over. Of course we have Andocia to thank for that, but she isn't being very gracious about it at all. Don't worry though; we will rule your planet fairly and wisely."

Craig and Constance exchanged worried looks.

"You won't succeed!" exclaimed Constance furiously. "When Andocia recovers, she won't take kindly to this, nor in fact will Tanus!"

The Sofagin grinned triumphantly. "You are mistaken, Mrs Carter, because all opposition has been suitably dealt with. At present, Tanus, Andocia and Deliah are our guests. Soon your husband shall join them!"

Craig caught the menace in the Sofagin's voice.

"What do you mean, I'll join them? What about Constance?"

The Sofagin sighed. "Alas, we have no use for her," said he as he raised his hand. A Candy gun was aimed at Constance and she sank slowly to the floor of the craft.

"No!" screamed the man, beating ineffectually at the barrier around him.

"Relax, Mr Carter, your wife is just unconscious. She will be taken to another destination far from you. When the others see you, they will realise we mean business."

"What do you want from me?" he asked curiously.

"Your job will be to convince Tanus and Andocia to stop fighting us. With your wife far away, you'll have every incentive to get that point across. Should you give us any reason to distrust you, your wife will die."

Carter watched helplessly as his wife was picked up and taken away to the ship docked alongside. He watched as the ship separated from his and vanished into Space. Another Sofagin piloted Craig's craft. He remained encased in the bubble, but he was curious.

"I don't understand why you went to all this trouble. Why didn't you just refuse to help me when the Saurians tampered with my brain?" he asked the leader, who sat down nearby.

The Sofagin smiled knowingly. "Why should we have done that? The circumstances could not have been more favourable. We were fascinated by your species and recognised you could be a danger to us in the future. Your species are very intelligent, just not as technologically advanced as us. We wished to study a human and you were available. Thanks to you, we have learnt a great deal which will be beneficial to us in the future. We healed your brain, not because we wanted to, but because we wanted to see if we could."

"I knew you weren't to be trusted," spat Craig viciously. "Anyway, Andocia hates me, so she won't listen to anything I have to say. I'm not sure I even want to convince her to give up. How do I know the universes will be a better place under your people's rule anyway?"

The Sofagin walked away and went to speak to his colleague. Craig lapsed into sullen silence.

When Sofania finally appeared on the screen, Craig stood up. They landed and the bubble disintegrated. He was urged forward and followed the spokesperson to a large building. The door to a room opened and he was ordered inside. At the far corner stood a gigantic cage and Craig could only gape at the incredible sight. Staring balefully back at him were three very angry occupants, namely Tanus, Andocia and Deliah. His arms were held firmly and he shrugged free.

"I can manage on my own," said the explorer as he made his way to the cage. A Sofagin opened it for him and he went inside. They sealed the door and left the group alone. Tanus hurried to him.

"Are you all right?" she asked kindly

"The only thing injured is my pride," he replied morosely.

Andocia and Deliah pointedly ignored him.

"Where is Constance?" asked Tanus curiously.

"They took her to another planet, but wouldn't tell me where she is. They said something about ensuring my good behaviour if we were separated."

"Craig, you don't seem surprised in any way. Have you met the Sofagins before?" asked Tanus curiously.

"Yes, a few times. I never really liked them though, but I just couldn't figure out why I distrusted them so much."

"Why didn't you tell us, Carter?" grumbled Andocia, who had finally found her voice.

"What was I supposed to tell you? They said you knew of their existence."

"Well they lied! I have to know something. That time on Saturn when I tried to take over that planet – your wife shot me with a strange weapon. Was it their creation?"

"Yes it was. I guess they have the last laugh after all! They have been using me as a guinea pig and I let them do it. The Sofagins obviously wanted to test their weapon on you and that's why they gave it to Constance. I owe you an apology Andocia; in fact I apologise to all of you. Tanus, I believed them when they told me you knew about them, so I never bothered to question you. If I had, you would have known what to do. Both Constance and I had a bad feeling about those beings and we were suspicious of them, but we never mentioned our suspicions to anyone. Now it's too late for all of us. All the time we kept quiet, they have become stronger. Both you and Andocia know everything about both universes, so how come you never knew about the Sofagins?"

Tanus shrugged her shoulders in confusion. "I don't really know how they have kept their presence from all of us, but I'll certainly look into it," she promised.

"Well it seems we owe this mess to you indirectly," remarked Andocia snidely. "Do you have any suggestions as to how we can get out of this situation? Apparently Tanus has none!"

"Don't be sarcastic, Andocia," he snapped, "It won't do any good to fight amongst ourselves. If we are ever to get out of this situation, we'll all have to work together!"

Tanus backed him up. "He's right you know; fighting amongst ourselves won't solve our present predicament."

"Well fine, seeing as you seem to have the answers Carter, what do you suggest?" asked Andocia crossly.

"You and Tanus have been fighting for centuries and I would say you are both evenly matched. I'm very aware of your powers Andocia and those of Tanus's too. Deliah is still a mystery to me though," said he, looking at the girl. "The Sofagins are very advanced in their own way, but I don't know the real extent of their powers. Couldn't you and Tanus team up and combine your powers in some way. Surely you could somehow blast your way out of this cage. I daresay Deliah can contribute whatever powers she has."

Andocia paced the cell and rubbed her chin thoughtfully. "It's possible of course. What do you think, Tanus?"

"We'll have to try it out then, but we need a plan. Craig, did they say where Constance was being held?" asked Tanus.

"No. Before we try anything out though, we must learn of her whereabouts. I don't want my wife to be killed. The Sofagins warned me they were holding her to ensure my continued good behaviour. Do you know what they wanted me to do?" he asked pointedly.

"What?" asked Andocia.

"They wanted me to persuade all of you to give up struggling against them. They intend to take over Earth and use it as a base of operations which will span both galaxies."

"If that's the case, why are you doing the opposite?" asked Deliah curiously.

"Because my dear girl, I don't like being taken for a fool. Besides, none of you would just take that lying down, would you?"

All three women nodded in unison.

"All right, so let's start planning our escape."

↓   ↓   ↓

Out in Space, Glenn and April were cruising around. Glenn had tried several times to contact his parents, but received no reply.

"Glenn what should we do? Should we return to Earth and see if they landed perhaps?"

Glenn shook his head. "No, I'll contact the Space Control Centre. I tried to contact Mom and Dad at home too, but there was no answer."

The young explorer contacted his base, but received only static in return. After trying unsuccessfully for a while, he got as close as he dared to Earth and switched on the long-range scanners. He and his sister stared in total amazement at the sight that greeted them.

Everywhere they looked, people were lying down. Nothing moved, not even an insect.

"Glenn, do you suppose they are all dead?" asked April nervously.

"I don't know – I hope not. I'm going to launch a probe and see what it records."

The probe came back and registered the atmosphere was breathable and indicated the people were merely asleep. April looked at her brother. "Well it's safe, so are we going to land?"

"No, I don't think so. If everyone is asleep, what's the point? Mom and Dad must be in trouble. If they are on Earth we can do nothing for them, but if they are prisoners of Andocia, we'll be contacted, I'm positive."

They hadn't gone much further, when their screen beeped. Glenn gave his sister an "I told you so" look and switched on the screen. Imagine his amazement when a Sofagin confronted him. April stared curiously at the creature, because she had never seen them face-to-face before.

"Ah, it's the young Mr Carter. Good day to you Glenn – and that must be your sister," said the being cheerfully.

"Yes it is. Can I help you?" he asked guardedly.

"Not really, but I have news for you about your parents…"

Glenn interrupted him. "Andocia has them – I knew they were in trouble!"

The Sofagin raised one hand to stop the young man. "Your parents are in trouble, but Andocia is not the cause. My people have them."

Glenn was stunned. "But why are they with your people? I thought you were our allies."

The creature smiled cynically. "You were supposed to think that, but sadly you are mistaken. Your father is our guest, along with Tanus, Andocia and Deliah. Your mother is on another planet where she is being taken care of by some loyal friends of ours. Earth will soon belong to us, and no one can stand in our way."

The Sofagin laughed at his own joke.

April stared disbelievingly at the creature. "You have to be joking of course. It's impossible to capture all of them."

"I speak the truth, young lady."

April turned to her brother. "Surely that's impossible? Not both Tanus and Andocia!"

"Oh, we have Deliah as well," the being smiled fiendishly.

Glenn gave the Sofagin a withering stare. "If this is true, why are you telling us?"

"I saw no reason not to. What can a mere boy and girl do against the mighty Sofagins? Even a man of your father's calibre was unable to prevent this happening. You are welcome to join him if you wish, but I don't care either way. If for some reason you become troublesome, your mother will suffer the consequences. Do I make myself clear?"

"Like crystal," agreed Glenn, then the transmission ended.

April stared disbelievingly at her brother. "I can't believe this is happening! He's right you know, what can you and I do against them? You have only been exploring Space for a few years and I'm still in school. If they caught Dad and Mom, we don't stand a ghost of a chance."

Glenn was thoughtful for a while, then brightened. "We still have a chance April. I think we should go to the White Planet and team up with Tarmin. If they think we are so helpless, they won't bother trying to intercept us, leaving us free to look for mom."

"It sounds like a good plan, but how can one spaceship explore both universes – it's impossible!"

"Not really. Tarmin will get Tanus's people to help us; I'm convinced of that. They can send out unmanned probes to every planet in the galaxies simultaneously. Mom would have activated her distress signal by now and we can program the probes to latch onto her signal. If the Sofagins have confiscated her mobile device, we can include a picture of her in their collective data banks. One of them is sure to find Mom, then we can rescue her. Once that has been dealt with, we'll somehow have to get word to Dad and the others that the coast is clear. I'm sure once they realise Mom is safe, they'll think of something. We are going to need a bigger spaceship, because we need a ship with at least one escape craft on board. The Moon always has a supply in readiness."

Brother and sister exchanged their craft for a bigger one and brought their people on the Moon up to date with the situation. They then set off for the Golden Way and were soon talking to Tarmin.

"Oh thank the stars you are both okay! I've been going mad here trying to figure the situation out. Tanus is missing!"

"We know. She's fine I'm sure, but the Sofagins have her."

"Who?" asked Tarmin stupidly.

Glenn remembered she didn't know of their existence, so he enlightened her. The pair brought Tarmin up to date on the situation and she whistled in amazement.

"Well I never! They have Tanus, Andocia, and Deliah too! We will have our job cut out for us, so let's get to it immediately!"

The three got into a huddle and began to plan. Tarmin had her mistress' people launch the probes and they watched as hundreds took to the sky.

Each of the probes sent back their messages and Constance was found on a planet named Gybor, which was inhabited by various exiled creatures of different planets. Glenn, April and Tarmin studied the map of the universes and found it very quickly.

"All right, now to rescue Mom," decided Glenn.

April put her hand on her brother's arm. "No wait! Let me go and get her. Our big ship is sure to attract the wrong kind of attention. We have to use the rescue ship. There doesn't seem to be any sentry robots in place, so I should be fine. You and Tarmin stand by in case of an emergency."

"April, I can't let you do this! You have no training!" exclaimed Glenn unhappily.

"No, I don't but I won't be able to manage the bigger ship. I'll take a laser gun with me. At least I can shoot my way out of trouble. My karate isn't that bad either. Stay close though, just in case."

"All right, I'll let you do it, but at the first sign of trouble, get out of there. I'll go in and get Mom later, if I have to."

Reluctantly he let her go and followed a safe distance behind her. April found Gybor easily and hovered above, looking for a suitable hiding place. She found one in a grove of trees and set the small craft down. Touching her laser gun, for security, she began the search. A group of buildings stood not far from her and she recalled seeing them in the shot from the probe, so she made for it. Her luck was in, and she saw her mother sitting on a bench, angrily crushing the head of a flower in her hands. A quick search revealed she was alone. April crept up to her mother and put her hand on her shoulder.

"Mom, it's me; I've come to rescue you. Hurry, we don't have much time!"

"April! You took a chance landing here. There are guards all around."

"I never spotted any. Let's get out of here!"

Mother and daughter sprinted for the ship, but both were brought to a halt by a commanding voice.

"What do you think you are doing, Miss Carter?"

"What... oh no!" she groaned.

"I tried to tell you darling, the sentries were well hidden."

The guard came closer. "I don't know how you managed to find this place my dear, but I can't allow you to leave. I'm afraid you will have to become a resident. Hand me your gun!"

April slowly removed the gun from its holster and held it by the barrel. In one quick movement, she flung it at the Sofagin and it hit him on the side of his face, stunning him temporarily. As he struggled to his feet, Constance kicked him under the chin and he fell backwards with a barely audible groan.

"Wow, well done Mom!" replied April admiringly.

"Their powers lie in the weapons they have created. They can't fight on a one to one basis," her mother deduced. "Now let's get out of here. More could turn up any minute!"

"I came in a rescue craft, Mom, so it's going to be quite a squeeze, seeing as they are really built for one."

"I don't care! I'll just be glad to get off this wretched planet."

They climbed into the craft, with Constance taking the controls. She steered to the bigger ship and docked inside it. Glenn and Tarmin hugged her happily.

"Right, now we have to find some way to tell your father I'm safe. I'm sure he and the others will make their move when they know the Sofagins have no real hold on them."

"How can you be sure they have a plan?" asked Glenn curiously.

"Your father always has a plan," she remarked decisively.

They all returned to the White Planet and Tarmin led them to a laboratory.

"I can make a small transmitter for each of you. It's very tiny and should escape detection by the Sofagins. It doubles as a homing beacon, so you can all remain in contact with one another if you like."

"Thank you Tarmin, that will be very useful for us. At least we can warn one another if the Sofagins grab one of us. They may have confiscated everyone's mobile devices so we can't risk contacting anyone that way. What's our plan though?" asked Constance curiously.

"Well, my mistress's people would gladly storm the planet, but they probably have a very effective defence system in place. They could get shot down," replied the bird.

"No, we can't risk that Tarmin," replied Glenn thoughtfully. "We have to go in by ourselves, but we only have two ships, so someone has to double up, or stay behind."

This brought a cry of protest from April. "No way are you leaving me behind! I want to see this through to the end!"

"April, it's too dangerous!" complained her mother.

"No, I want to help," she demanded stubbornly.

Tarmin intervened. "Let's do it this way; once we have made the transmitters, we'll all go. I would like to help where I can as well. Glenn can take the small ship, while the rest of us ride with you, Constance. He can scout around, after which we'll plan our attack."

"That sounds wonderful, Tarmin, but there's one small problem…"

"What is it, Glenn?"

"I have no idea where Sofania is. When the Sofagins agreed to help Dad, they took us to their Space station, not their planet."

A collective groan escaped each one of them.

"Then this whole idea is useless! Unless we know where Sofania is, we can't help your father."

"There is a way, but it's dangerous," replied Glenn.

"Let's hear it anyway," decided their mother.

"Well I know where their Space station is – roughly anyway. If I cruise around that area, the Sofagins might confront me. I could have them take me prisoner as well."

"Out of the question!" exclaimed his mother. "The object is to free the others, not give the Sofagins another prisoner. I can't allow you to do that!"

Tarmin interjected. "Wait, I see what he's getting at! With the transmitters our people will manufacture, you can keep tabs on Glenn. When they capture him, he'll lead us right to the planet Sofania."

"Exactly!" remarked Glenn. "Then you can follow at a safe distance and I'll tell you when to strike. Maybe some of Tanus's security forces can give us some back-up firepower."

"They would be glad to do so, I assure you."

Constance wasn't happy, but she realised the sense of the argument, so she agreed reluctantly. They waited while three transmitters were constructed. Glenn hid his in a compartment in his belt, while April concealed hers in a locket she was wearing. Constance put hers in a hidden pocket and zipped it up. All that remained was to go over the final details of the rescue mission. They were ready.

Glenn took the small ship and headed for the Space station. Some distance away, Constance piloted the big ship. April was studying the instrument that Tarmin had given her.

"See, that blip over there is Glenn's transmitter. All we have to do is follow it and stay hidden until he can tell us what the next move will be. If all goes according to plan, they'll lead us to Sofania."

36

Glenn cruised around for a while and tried to find evidence of the planet by himself, but the scanners in the little craft were weak and didn't have much of a range. Suddenly, above his head, an alarm went off and he realised he was caught in a tractor beam. The computer went into override, and Glenn allowed himself a smile of satisfaction. As his ship was so tiny, he was drawn into the bowels of the big Sofagin ship, where he sat and waited for instructions. His screen clicked on by itself.

"Identify yourself!" the Sofagins demanded.

"Glenn Carter of Earth," he replied.

The Sofagin smiled as he recognised the name. "Ah Mr Carter; this is a pleasant surprise! Someone here is just dying to meet you again. Please leave your ship and join us outside."

The explorer opened the door and climbed out. As he alighted, several Sofagins slammed him none too gently against the hull of his ship. His laser gun was confiscated and they conducted a thorough search of his clothing, finding a few little surprises tucked away, but they never thought to check his belt. Another Sofagin came forward and Glenn recognised him as the one who had taken charge of his father when he had gone to them for help.

"So we meet again. I for one am delighted."

"Sorry, I can't say the same," declared Glenn snidely.

He indicated to a chair and Glenn sat down. The Sofagin produced a set of greenish blue handcuffs and dropped them in his lap.

"Kindly place one of the bracelets on your wrist and attach the other to the arm of that chair."

Glenn glared at him, but obeyed. The Sofagin sat down opposite him and waved the guards away.

"Why have you come to this sector, Carter?"

"I wanted to find my father. I came to rescue him."

The Sofagin smiled amusingly. "You must be a very stupid or very brave, young man. Did you really expect to get past us without being noticed?"

Glenn shrugged indifferently. "I hoped to remain undetected and that's why I used this tiny ship. I guess I was wrong. So what happens now?"

The being spoke smugly. "Well, I don't want to disappoint you, so we'll take you to him immediately. Is stubbornness part of being human?"

"For some of us, yes."

"Where is your lovely sister then?"

"She is elsewhere," he replied vaguely.

"And where is your mother?"

Glenn smiled. "She's also somewhere else."

The being stood up and clasped his hands behind his back. He walked behind Glenn and grabbed him by his hair, tilting his head so his throat was exposed. He withdrew an instrument from his garment and held it against Glenn's neck.

"Why do you Carters persist in angering me? I was prepared to let you live in peace, but now that won't happen. I'm taking you to join your father and his companions, but I will also put the word out in Space that your mother and sister are to be apprehended and brought to me. Your world will soon belong to us, but no Carter shall remain alive to see it. I'm so tempted to use this on you. It's a very lethal form of poison. Once injected into a vein, you will take a week to die and every moment will be agony."

He applied pressure and Glenn remained very still. For a moment, the young man regretted his decision and tensed for the prick that would signal something horrible, when the Sofagin's hand paused, as someone entered the room.

"Forgive the interruption, but we are nearing Sofania."

The Sofagin straightened up and put the syringe away. Glenn realised he had been holding his breath and he released it in a grateful sigh. For the moment he was ignored while the Sofagins prepared to land on their planet.

He was taken to the room where his father was imprisoned, along with everyone else. Craig jumped up and hurried to the front of the cage as Glenn was unceremoniously thrown inside. He stretched out his hand to help his son up. "Glenn, how did they manage to catch you? Didn't I ask you to stay far away from the Sofagins. I told you they were not to be trusted!"

However, he said nothing until the door had closed behind the Sofagins.

"Dad, believe it or not, I did it deliberately!"

"What possessed you to do something so crazy?" asked his father angrily.

"Dad, listen to me, Mom is safe. We found her and she's with April right now. Tarmin is also with them. I offered to get caught on purpose, for none of us knew where Sofania was." Glenn turned apologetically to Tanus. "I hope you don't mind, Tanus, but Tarmin took it upon herself to make us some pretty neat transmitters. Your people are close by, just waiting for the order to attack. This transmitter is like a homing beacon and soon all your security people will know where this wretched planet is."

Tanus was delighted. "Oh how wonderful! As it happens, we had thought about a plan too, but we first wanted confirmation of Constance's rescue. Your father persuaded all of us to work together. Now we can put that plan into action."

Glenn held up his hand and glanced at each one in turn. "No, don't do anything just yet. Mom discovered the Sofagins are useless without their weapons. They can't even fight to protect themselves, unless they have weapons handy. It'll take at least a day or two for your forces to gather, Tanus. Let's give them time to get into position. It might not be that hard to escape from here if we have the element of surprise on our side, but the Sofagins know what all your weak points are. Unless we hurt them really badly, they'll return and exact vengeance. Earth may escape their tyranny now, but what about next year, when they improve on their weapons?"

Andocia smiled and turned to Craig. "Your son has a good head on his shoulders. I agree with him; we should wait two days. It will be worth it if we can smash the Sofagins forever and I know just how we can do it. What do you say, Tanus?"

"I agree. Obviously you have another scheme though, Glenn. I can sense your excitement."

"Yes I do. I want to play on the Sofagins' vanity and try to persuade them to let me go on a tour of their planet. I'll scout around and try to find their weapons arsenal. Once that's done, we can make the first shot from your fighters really cause an impact."

Even Deliah, who had been sitting morosely in the background had to agree it was a good idea. Glenn took out the transmitter and contacted Constance, telling her what they planned to do. She offered to pass the word along.

Much later, the leader returned and smiled gleefully at his prisoners.

"I just thought I would let you know, our robots are in position around

Earth and should be going down soon. When we have put everything in place, we will show you the results of the takeover. In the meantime, all of you will remain imprisoned for as long as it takes, so get used to it. When the Earthlings awaken, they will be governed by a new regime. When we are satisfied that everything is going as planned, you three mortals will die."

He turned away and Glenn hurried forward. "Wait, please!"

The Sofagin turned around. "What do you want?"

"On Earth we have a custom. You said my father, me and Deliah will die, well it's considered good to allow people a final request."

"What does this 'final request' mean?"

"Well we get to ask you a favour and you grant it. For some this might mean a sumptuous meal; others might like something good to read."

"Ah, so you would like this 'final request'?"

"If it is at all possible," Glenn remarked diffidently.

"What would you like, assuming I'm prepared to grant this?"

"Well your technology far exceeds ours, we admit it. Everyone agrees you Sofagins are the supreme ones. Why, Andocia was just saying how brilliant you were in capturing her, weren't you Andocia?"

She took her cue and nodded her head vigorously. "Oh yes, absolutely! In all the years I have roamed this universe, no one has ever managed to do what you did. I'm sure when Earth becomes aware of your powers, they'll be glad to submit to your rule."

The Sofagin beamed proudly. "Do you really think so?"

"Oh yes," agreed Tanus. "No one can stand in your way."

The Sofagin smiled at everyone, pleased by their acquiescence. He turned his attention to the young man. "Very well, Glenn Carter, what is your final request?"

"Could you show me around your planet? If I'm to die soon, I would like to see your technology in operation. Earth may take years to reach this advanced state, but I won't be around to see it."

The Sofagin considered it, then shook his head. "Forget it! The moment I let you out of your cage, you'll try to escape. I won't fall for that. Think of something else."

"Please, that's all I want. I give you my solemn word I won't attempt to escape. If I do, you can kill my father immediately."

The being hesitated and Glenn continued. "Look, you of all people know how much my father means to me. I risked my life trying to save him from the Saurians. Would I have done that if I didn't care deeply for him?"

"Very well, I'll grant your request, but there's a condition involved. I want to put an electronic tracer on you. You may roam around freely, under light guard of course, but I want to know where you are every minute of the day."

"That's fine with me," agreed the young man.

The Sofagin pressed a buzzer and some guards came into the room. He spoke to them for a moment and they moved to the cage. The Sofagin opened it and urged Glenn out. As he was marched out of the room, he turned and winked surreptitiously at the group behind him.

Glenn was taken to a laboratory where he looked at the equipment in awe. A device was put on his left arm and strapped into place.

"All right Glenn Carter, I'll show you out, and then I have to leave you in the company of my subordinates. By the way, that device is booby-trapped. If you try to unbuckle it, you'll blow yourself up and no one will be able to pick up the pieces."

Glenn spent the day looking at the spaceships and weaponry, but he toured some of the planet as well, just to mislead them. Everything of interest that he saw, he noted mentally. This included the armoury and their control centre. Some places were out of bounds to him though, and he made a special note of their position on the planet. By the time he was returned to his cellmates, he had gathered a wealth of important information. Glenn contacted his mother and she recorded the conversation, transmitting it simultaneously to Tanus's fleet of ships that were waiting patiently.

The next morning, Glenn was allowed to look around some more and he spent his time confirming his information. By the afternoon, he was ordered back to his cell and told that the Sofagins were too busy to indulge him further, for they were about to put the final touches to their plan. Glenn went willingly and told everyone about the news.

"Glenn, you were incredible!" Tanus enthused. "But now we are running out of time. Once those robots land, Earth will be lost forever. The time is now! Give the signal to attack!"

Glenn spoke into the transmitter and uttered one word. "Attack!"

37

They waited in anticipation, their senses heightened. Craig, Glenn and Deliah moved to the back and Andocia and Tanus concentrated all their power on the cage surrounding them. The room was filled with an eerie glow as their powers combined and the cage began to rattle. The bars vibrated faster and faster until the mortals thought their eardrums would burst. Some Sofagins were alerted by the noise and came to investigate. Deliah elbowed her way forward and concentrated on their jailers. A red bolt shot from her hand, killing them instantly. There was a loud grinding noise and the cage shattered, freeing its occupants. Deliah noticed the electronic surveillance unit was still firmly attached to Glenn's arm. She aimed at it and sliced through the strap. Glenn smiled his thanks and pitched it forward towards the door as more Sofagnis blocked their path. It fell in the midst of them and exploded, leaving the door clear. They tumbled out and Glenn raced to the front, the others following close behind. Confusion reigned as the Sofagins reeled from the surprise attack.

Out of the corner of his eye, Craig could see Tanus's ships land and spill out their own heavily armed warriors. From their vantage point in Space, Constance and April watched the planet being torn apart by well-aimed blows. They were told not to join the fighting and were glad to stay and observe. Tarmin had left them though and headed for Sofania to see if she could help.

Below, Craig had gone to the control centre and was sabotaging their equipment. He fired indiscriminately at the levers and dials and soon everything began to short out. The robots stationed around Earth, exploded, instantly becoming Space junk. Several well-organised teams went into the hangars and disabled as many craft as they could. Glenn went to the armoury and placed dynamite everywhere. He hid behind some bushes and pressed the switch. Immediately the place became an inferno. The fighting raged for most of the day and by evening, it was all over. Both sides suffered losses and the medical ship was taking care of as many as possible. Glenn was tired and dirty and his clothes were torn. He had tied a piece of material carelessly around one leg, which had caught the edge of a blast from a Candy gun and blood seeped through. Craig had several small lacerations on his face and neck, but neither was seriously injured.

Now the Sofagins stood in a pathetic group, surrounded by Tanus's warriors. Tanus and Andocia stood before them to pronounce judgement.

"You Sofagins have been deceitful from the beginning. Everything that you have done was for yourselves," Tanus began. "You had all the technology that could have saved many worlds from destruction, yet you kept these to yourself. We could all have worked well together."

"Yes," stated Andocia, "I agree with Tanus. You have no morals and we cannot trust you. Neither Tanus nor I have any desire to keep you around here, so this is your punishment. We, the immortals, are speaking on behalf of both Galaxies and we sentence you to complete exile. Your planet will be flung to the most distant reaches of Space where you will remain forever. All your weapons have been destroyed and your ships disabled."

Andocia raised her hand as though giving a final salute and everyone present began to climb into his or her spacecrafts. The Sofagins stared helplessly at those who had bettered them, but their leader was angry. He pointed his finger accusingly at Andocia, Tanus and Deliah.

"You may have gained victory this day, but we shall return some other time when you least expect it, and exact our revenge. We will emerge victorious, this I promise you. As for the Carter name, I spit on it. Even if it takes hundreds of years, our descendants will exterminate anyone who bears that surname, for they will be your cursed descendants!"

Deliah took aim, but Andocia stopped her. "No, leave him be! This punishment is enough."

By this time, everyone had climbed into their respective ships. Craig and Glenn were in Tanus's mother ship and were watching via the scanners. The entire company watched with bated breath as Tanus rose into the sky, flanked by Deliah on her left and Andocia on her right. On a pre-arranged signal, their powers combined once again and three beams emerged.

There was a sound like a sonic boom and the planet began to move, slowly picking up speed. It went faster and faster, until it had vanished from the naked eye. A resounding cheer went up and several guns were fired in salute of the mighty immortals and Deliah. When the deed had been done, Deliah went to her mother's side and held her hand. Both stared at Tanus, then left without another word. Everyone knew the temporary partnership was over and the immortals would fight again someday.

The two immortals went in different directions, Andocia to her planet and Tanus to hers.

They were tired from their efforts and the Carters knew they would want to rest for a while. Without being asked, the Carters accompanied Tanus to her planet. They were content to amuse themselves quietly until Tanus was ready to receive them. Craig knew, as did the rest of his family, that this was not the end of the saga.

By the next day, Tanus was feeling stronger and she called the family in. They all sat down in comfortable chairs and waited for their friend to begin. By this time, Craig had told her everything he knew about the Sofagins, including the number of times they had made contact with his family. The woman in white smiled gratefully at all of them in turn. Her eyes were sparkling with happiness.

"Craig, I owe you and your family a great deal. If it hadn't been for the team effort on your family's part, goodness knows what would have happened. Thanks to your children, Earth is safe again. I had a look on my scanners and your people are beginning to wake up. By tomorrow, things should go back to normal. Naturally Commander Perry will welcome your input, for he will be very confused. The Sofagins turned out to be very dangerous, but we dealt with them, so they shouldn't bother any of us for a while."

"Tanus, it's obvious you feel the same way as we do about them. We also came to the conclusion that you have just slowed them down, not conquered them forever," remarked Craig.

"Yes, a race as sophisticated as them will be back. I hope we destroyed the plans for their weapons, but I can't be sure. Everything happened at once. Well no matter what, I'm going to make my own plans to repel them next time they do battle with me. I'm sure Andocia and Deliah will do the same. Craig, it's important your technicians start working on a way to improve the computers in your spaceships. If the Sofagins can gain control of them every time, your people will be in serious trouble."

"I know and that's one of the first things I'll speak to Commander Perry about," he promised.

Tanus turned her attention to Glenn, who reddened in embarrassment.

"Glenn you were wonderful out there. It was very brave of you to do what you did. They could have killed you."

Glenn had an immediate flashback to the needle pressed against his neck and shuddered.

Tanus continued. "You have the makings of a very good Space explorer and Commander Perry is lucky to have you working for him. I applaud your courage and tenacity, but a word of warning; no matter how easy the situation appears to be, don't ever underestimate your enemies. Space exploration is a risky business!"

Everyone nodded in agreement and Tarmin squawked approvingly.

"April, you are still young and inexperienced, but you too show great promise. Constance told me how you kept your cool when the Sofagin confronted you. You were very brave to go alone and rescue your mother. I don't know what you plan to do with your life when you graduate, but I'm sure that whatever you set your mind to you'll make a success of it. I have words of caution for you too though; because of whose daughter you are, your life will always have an element of danger to it. You all, in your own way, have made some powerful enemies. April, keep up your self-defence classes. Learn everything you can about self-preservation."

"I will," she promised.

They spoke for a while longer, then split into little groups. Tarmin offered to walk in the gardens with April, and she accepted. Glenn and Craig wandered off to discuss putting together a report for Commander Perry, while Constance and Tanus retired to the castle.

⌁ ⌁ ⌁

Meanwhile, on the now exiled Sofania, their leader was angrier than ever.

"How dare they treat us this way!! I swear if it's the last thing I do in the time left to me, I'll pay every single one of those beings back for what they have done. Everything was going so well until the Carter children showed up! Children! Mere children beat us!! I made a very big mistake by allowing them their freedom. They should have been taken care of, along with their parents."

His subordinates kept clear of him, but they knew his rage was justified. The leader went to a pile of metal that had once been Candy guns, but was now only good for scrap. He picked up some of the broken weapons and threw them down contemptuously once again.

"Damn them all! There must be at least one that made it unscathed!" he snapped, sifting through the pile.

One of his junior officers stepped hesitantly forward. "Our technology outstrips anyone else's, Sir. We can build them again, but this time we will make them better than before. Our time of glory will come again."

"Maybe it will later, but not yet! We are in some strange part of the blue universe and don't even have instruments that can tell us where we are, much less direct us back to the immortals and the others."

The leader stormed off to the hangar where he stared at the mass of tangled metal that had once been fighting ships. He beckoned to some technicians who hurried forward.

"All right, there's work to be done! I want all of you to go over these ships with great care. Even if we only make one or two serviceable again, we'll have a chance. Our tools are still intact fortunately. Get to work!"

The Sofagin left them and stormed outside. He stared up into the skies and smiled sardonically.

"You have defeated us for now, but we will recover from this. When we do, look out! Now that we know who or what we are dealing with, we'll take that into account. We will definitely be seeing all of you again."

He turned on his heel and went inside to supervise the repairs.

⚓ ⚓ ⚓

On the White Planet, Craig and his family were preparing to leave. Tanus hugged each of them in turn.

"I wish you all a safe journey back to Earth. I hope there will be a time of peace now."

"Thank you Tanus and we wish the same for you," Constance replied.

The woman in white smiled. "Alas, my situation will never change. Andocia and Deliah will always be waiting patiently to plan my defeat. I'll see you all again sometime. When you're in the neighbourhood, come and look me up."

"We definitely will!" promised Glenn.

They climbed aboard their spacecraft and blasted off. As usual, Tarmin flew with them until they had left the White Planet's atmosphere, then with a final chirp, she said goodbye.

Craig was in control of the ship and they cruised for a while. Constance came and stood nearby and he put his arm around her waist. "What are you thinking about my darling?" she asked gently.

"I was just thinking about our future. Every time I think we have solved the most difficult problems, even bigger ones come and take their place. I wonder what's in store for us in the future."

"Only good things, I hope," she replied earnestly.

"So do I, but I often wonder, what does the future hold? At any given moment, we may have a crisis on our hands."

"It's possible Craig, but for now let's just be concerned about today and let tomorrow take care of itself."

He smiled at his wife and kissed her tenderly. Glenn called out to them. "Come and look over here!" he exclaimed excitedly.

They went over to their son and stared outside. Uranus had reappeared in the Solar System.

"Wonderful! Now everything is truly back to normal!" declared April cheerfully.

"Yes and when we return to Earth, you have some catching up to do! You missed some schooldays!" admonished Constance gently.

April pulled a face and the others laughed ruefully.

April became serious and turned to her family. "I have something to tell you," she said as she looked to each one in turn.

"What is it, honey?" her mother asked.

"Mom, Dad, I know you aren't going to like what I have to say, but I'll tell you anyway. I want to explore Space with the rest of you when I have finished school."

Craig stared unhappily at his daughter. "Why do you want to do that April? You have already realised first-hand how dangerous Space travel is!"

"Yes, I know, but I still want to make it my career later."

Constance looked at her daughter. "You know, there is no limit to what you can do with your life in the future. You are a smart girl and can study for any degree that takes your fancy. You are only fifteen and the rest of your life lies before you. Why do you want to risk your life doing something so dangerous?"

April shrugged her shoulders. "I enjoy Space travel and meeting new beings. I know it's a thankless profession and also a dangerous one. I'm not looking to get medals pinned on my chest – I just want to make a difference to others. Let's face the facts though; no matter what I decide to do in the future, my life will always be in danger because of who I am. Each one of you have made enemies and every one of them will use me as a lever to get back at all of you! There is no such thing as a 'safe' job for me, even if I decide to stay on Earth and do something else, I can be captured and used as a lever against you all. I may as well do what I can to help others. I know I have a lot to learn, but I'm prepared to take whatever courses I need to better myself. I refuse to be the weak link in the family chain. When we have settled down at home once more, I want to enrol in self-defence classes!"

Craig looked at his wife and son and shrugged his shoulders. "I don't know about you, but I understand why April has chosen this path. I'm not happy about the situation but it's April's decision."

Constance was unhappy but she had to agree that April did have a valid point. "April, you might still change your mind later. You have two years of school left before you graduate. If you still want to explore Space at that time, then you have my blessing."

All eyes turned to Glenn. He smiled at his sister. "Sis, you have a good head on your shoulders and you don't panic quickly and that's important in our profession. I also have some reservations, but if you want to explore Space, then you should do it."

April smiled and hugged each member of her family in turn. "Thank you all for having such faith in me! I love you guys!"

Craig grinned. "Okay then, when we have been debriefed, I'll have a word with the good commander and see if he can arrange a suitable tutor for you regarding self-defence classes."

"I would really appreciate it," April replied. "This was a tense time but seriously, I'm glad to be going home."

The family watched as the planets scooted by. Finally Earth appeared on their scanners and they informed the Control Centre they were coming in to land. Everyone was back to normal and Commander Perry welcomed them gladly.

"It's wonderful to hear from you all. I'm glad everyone is home safely. Craig, Glenn, you may go home and rest for a while, but I want to see you both in my office promptly at 08H00 hours tomorrow. I believe you have plenty to tell me."

"Yes Sir," they chorused in unison.

Craig disconnected and turned to his son with a sigh. "Oh well, no rest for the wicked. It's back to the grindstone, as usual."

They left the control centre and walked to their vehicles. As they headed home, Craig looked up at the sky. It was a full Moon and even the stars seemed brighter.

"Well another adventure has ended! I wonder what's in store for us tomorrow?" he thought. "I'm proud of my family – they are all special in their own way."

He picked up speed and his thoughts turned to relaxing at home with his precious family.

www.ingramcontent.com/pod-product-compliance
Lightning Source LLC
Chambersburg PA
CBHW070215030726
47505CB00006B/1695